THE DRAGON'S MARBLE

Seeker's Precept

CLINTON CAMPBELL

To the reader who sought out this book, I hope you enjoy yourself.

THE DRAGON'S MARBLE

Content Warning

Strong violence. Crude language. Mature Themes. Sex Scenes.

One

Sora did a self-check on his internal mana stores and found that he was dipping below the halfway mark. He'd have to pack it in soon, but he was more than happy with the day's earnings. The market itself was buzzing with activity, far more than he was used to, and the same rumour seemed to be on everyone's lips—Princess Eri had been attacked during her gifting ceremony. That the Princess was injured but still alive seemed to be the only part of the rumour that was consistent. Some spoke of an unstoppable Ogre who had slaughtered everyone in the palace, while others said it was a singular assassin with long red hair. Sora had no way of authenticating any of the stories, but the overall situation was fascinating to think about. How anyone expected an Ogre to have broken through the walls of the city, passed by thousands of gate guards in the process, stormed into the palace, and *then* fought off the Kingsguard was simply ludicrous. But where there was smoke, there was usually fire. A break in the pattern of foot traffic caught his eye as a woman limped out into view, an assortment of tools, restraints, and weapons hooked into the harness she wore around her chest. The woman's left leg seemed to be the issue, and given the tracks of blood she left in her wake, it seemed to be a pretty serious injury. Sora removed his own booted foot from the seat beside him as she continued her approach towards him.

"I don't remember doing anything to warrant a bounty hunter being sent after me." Sora said in greeting, "I hope you're just here to get healed."

"Funny," The woman said, a pained edge to her voice. "Fix me up, and I'll give you a headstart."

Sora waved her towards the recently vacated spot, and she followed the gesture, stepping around the stall. She took the proferred seat and then set about trying to pull her own pant leg up. Sora caught her hand before she could mess with it any further than that.

"I've got it," Sora said, carefully lifting her foot up to rest against the top of his thigh. "Try not to move it, please."

The woman grunted in agreement, and he set about rolling up her pant leg, making sure it avoided pressing against anything important. Her leg was practically coated in blood, most of which had started to dry up and cling to her skin. Once he had a clear view of it all, he took a moment to investigate the injury. A three-inch wide-cut ran across the very bottom of her calf, deep enough that he could see flashes of white amongst the mess.

"Names Sora," Sora said. "What did you say your name was?"

"Malko," Malko said, wincing as he turned her leg to the side.

"Damn," Sora said with a low whistle. "This is a rough one. What happened?"

Sora didn't particularly care *how* she'd been injured because he'd long since burned away most of the curiosity he'd had about the myriad of ways people had injured themselves. He was far more interested in how the spell would interact with the wound.

"Bastard set a trap by his door," Malko muttered, "He made a run for it while I was busy trying to get my damn leg out of it. What a complete waste of a day."

"Knew you were coming, huh?" Sora offered, carefully laying his hand against the wound. "You still going to track him down? *Scour.*"

The spell's command phrase fell from his mouth, and the same familiar pattern twisted into existence. Mana sparked across his hand, coating it in milky white light, before slipping down into the wound on her leg. The spell found four contaminants inside the wound, and he directed it to wrap up three of them in a thin film of mana. They were a series of rusty metal flakes that had clearly been left behind by the trap. He carefully directed the spell, pulling the flakes out until they sat on his palm before going back in for the last one. Once he'd gotten all of them out, he turned his hand over and tipped the mess onto the ground at their feet.

"You better believe I'm going to track him down," Malko said, finding her voice again. "Then I'm going to snap that trap closed right around his dirty cock."

"Yikes," Sora winced, "Now the image is stuck in my mind—*Meldflesh*."

"Sorry," Malko offered, sounding anything but.

The pattern he'd practised half a million times twisted beneath his fingers, seeping into her skin and out of sight. He could feel it, touching muscles, tendons, nerves, and flesh, finding the severed parts and bringing them back together. The mana blended the tips of each broken connection into one another, slowly rebuilding the cut from the inside out. So many moving parts, but all of it was familiar, the process entirely automatic at this point.

"That feels good," Malko murmured, "The pain is kind of bleeding away."

Sora had heard *that* half a million times as well; it was a common reaction to the feeling of so much concentrated Mana passing through your body, and he'd healed his own wounds enough times to know that it helped mask the pain. Sora took his time with it, more out of a desire to prolong his own observation of the spell than anything else; he probably could have fixed something like this in a few seconds if he'd really pushed himself. But casting spells on real people with variant injuries was an invaluable resource for seeing just how the spell interacted with the differences on a minute scale. Once he'd exhausted what he could learn from it, he sealed the wound completely, drawing his hand back and revealing the smooth expanse of unbroken skin.

"How's that?" Sora asked, massaging her calf to see if he could elicit anything. "No more pain? Discomfort? Pressure? Odd sensations?"

"Nothing like that," Malko said, "You do massages as well, do you?"

Sora patted her leg a final time before rolling the pant leg back down to her ankle.

"Only for the clients I really like," Sora said, placing her foot back on the ground. "Should be no complications; everything's back to perfect condition."

"Thanks," Malko said, pulling her coin pouch out. "How much is this going to cost me?"

"One silver should do it," Sora said, straightening up in his chair.

"One silver?" Malko said, taken aback. "I wasn't serious about coming after you, you know?"

"And that's not a discount," Sora said, amused. "It's my going rate."

"The last time I paid someone to fix me up, it cost me *twenty* silver, and the damage wasn't *half* as bad as what you just healed," Malko said, holding a single silver in her fingers. "How are you able to charge so little?"

"This costs me a little bit of time and some mana," Sora said, accepting the coin from her. "I'm not really concerned with the former, and the latter regenerates."

"You could be charging the prince's handmaid a gold coin for her scraped knees," Malko said, bemused. "You really like the work this much?"

That would mean working topside with the frilly skirts, and the more distance between him and those old bastards, the better—he'd seen more than enough of them already.

"I like *magic*," Sora said, tilting his head at her. "Healing people is just a way for me to use it every day."

"If I had the chance to bring in money like that?" Malko said, shaking her head. "I'd be eating up there in the Palace with the Ogre."

"Then I'm glad I'm only charging a silver," Sora said, laughing. "Any idea what actually happened up there?"

"Just rumours and speculation for now," Malko admitted, tapping her foot on the ground to test her leg out. "But you can bet I'll be waiting by the boards for the bounty to get posted."

"You and everyone else in Satu," Sora nodded, "Stay out of trouble, Malko."

"I'll try," Malko said in parting. "Thanks again."

Sora waved her off before kicking his foot back up onto the chair. Malko had been correct, though, healers were well respected, and payment always came *after* you fixed something, so it filtered out the ones who weren't able to actually perform—he *could* have been up there with the nobles, fixing scraped knees. It wasn't the first time someone had commented on his rates, and he'd had to deal with some of the more established healers getting on his case about it as well. As if there weren't enough injured or sick in a city this big for them to fill their own pouches. If his own master was still around, Sora was sure she would have set up shop directly opposite them just to teach them a lesson. Still, renting a stall in the market and pulling in a few hundred silvers whenever he was running low was a decent enough way to keep himself afloat. As far as healing went, there was never a real shortage of clients. Satu was massive and easily one of the ten largest cities in the world. Most of that population had been drawn to the city by the presence of the Great Satu Library. The largest magical repository in the world and the one with the most rules and restrictions present. Without Salas, he'd found his access to learning immediately blocked by a hundred obstacles, but that had only lasted long enough for him to find his master's key and, with it, the complete freedom to borrow pretty much whatever tome, scroll, tablet, or book that he wanted— provided nobody realised that the owner had died over three years ago. There *had* been a few close calls in attempting to use it, though, enough that he'd taken to borrowing more books at once to decrease the frequency of his visits. Sora hadn't really done much to build himself a reputation, and without his master, he was pretty much a non-entity within the city. While he could have taken his own paperwork up to the library and got it officialised by the Archmage, he'd be forced to deal with all kinds of troublesome things—like answering the calls of the old bastards whenever they wanted something done or being taken to task about undercutting the others. It made him feel like a ghost at times, somehow avoiding all of the politics that Salas had ranted about. But it certainly left him plenty of time to do what actually interested him—practising magic. Sora glanced up as what was unmistakably a palace guard stepped into the market, looking pale and tense. The man scanned the area, stopping people with cloaks or head coverings, checking each before letting them go. Sora caught sight of the man's back for the first time when he was only a few metres away—five thin grooves had been cut into his chainmail, blood soaking down into the back of his clothes. The guard turned again, spotted him, and then stepped forward, jaw tight.

"I need to ask you some questions." The man said.

"Sit down first," Sora said, patting the stool beside him. "I'll take care of your back while you ask."

The man hesitated for a moment before clearing his throat.

"Very well," The man said, stepping around the stall. "I may need some assistance."

Sora helped the man uncouple his armour and then placed it down beside the stool before he sat, back facing him. The five rents had gone through his chainmail, the cloth beneath it, and into his back from his right shoulder to his left hip.

"Have you healed a Meld with horns today?" The man said, tensing as Sora pulled the back of his shirt up to bunch at his shoulders.

"*Scour*," Sora said before answering. "I healed a Meld this morning. Beetle, single horn in the middle of her head."

There were no contaminates, but he noted that the cuts themselves were exceedingly shallow considering the damage done to the armour like the attacker had pulled back once they'd broken through the armour—aiming to wound but not to kill.

"Two thin horns emerging from the top of her forehead, pale white skin, long black hair, yellow eyes." The man said, "It had wounds all over its chest and arms, although we believe it may have had the ability to regenerate."

"*Meldflesh*—I haven't seen anyone like that," Sora admitted before hesitating. "The description you just gave doesn't sound like a Meld; it sounds like an Oni."

He took his time again, content to drag out the interaction and learn more about what had happened. The man sagged slightly as the mana began masking the pain, and some of the tension in his voice vanished.

"I don't know what that is," The man admitted, "A monster of some kind?"

"They're *technically* classed as a monster, but they've been extinct for almost a thousand years," Sora corrected, "Human-level intelligence, enhanced hearing and vision. They are much, much faster than any human and strong enough to tear through metal with their bare hands."

"If they've been extinct for that long," The man said, "Then it can't be one of them, can it?"

"All of the Oni were bound to objects by mages and then forced into servitude," Sora said, "I've heard rumours that a couple of those objects still exist—none in Satu, though."

"A golden coin was being presented to Princess Eri by the assassin," The man said, turning his head enough to look back at him. "A monster appeared from within the coin, and she took it with her when she fled."

"Sounds like an Oni to me," Sora said, "Who's the assassin that gave her the coin?"

"Chiyo Himura," The man said, the name like ash on his tongue. "We have every guard in the city searching for her as we speak—she was injured as well; perhaps you've seen her?"

"I think I've heard the last name before," Sora admitted, frowning. "What does she look like?"

"Red hair, shoulder-length, bright red eyes, five-foot-five," The man said, the feature list sounding rehearsed, "Her father, Mashirao Himura, was the Master of Commerce before his death."

"I haven't seen her," Sora said, frowning as the cuts were almost healed. "Any idea why she would try to kill the Princess?"

"The king's advisor suspects it was some sort of twisted revenge for her father's death," The man said, shaking his head again. "Chiyo was previously very close to the Princess; we are *extraordinarily* lucky she never took a chance while they were alone together."

"Is the Princess alright?" Sora asked, tilting his head. "I imagine she's got a bunch of mages up there clamouring to heal her."

"Princess Eri was healed within a minute of the event," The man admitted, "The monster only managed to land a single scratch on her before the kingsguard forced it to retreat—it injured at least a dozen guards on the way out, including myself, but thankfully nobody was killed."

"Your back is looking good as new," Sora said, studying the man for a moment. "How does it feel? Discomfort? Pain? An odd sensation?"

The man stood and rolled his shoulders around in an attempt to stretch his back out, but it was pretty clear that he was suffering no aftereffect.

"It might even be better than before," The man said, cracking his neck. "Thank you for your assistance—what do I owe you?"

"The Princess is safe, and you were a part of making that happen," Sora said, waving him off, "Good work today."

"That's kind of you," The man smiled, clapping him on the shoulder.

"No problem," Sora said, handing the man his chainmail. "I'll keep an eye out for Chiyo and the Oni—what's going to happen to them?"

"Thank you," The man said, "The king's already made his decree. Chiyo Himura will be publically executed as soon as we can find her, and if the monster is still around, I'm sure it will find a similar fate."

Sora listened to the man's words, watching as he slipped back into his armour. He nodded to the man as he left, vanishing back into the market to continue his search. He sat back on his stool, wondering about the situation. It was a strange outcome, considering the events that must have led up to that moment. Oni were bound by their word and to fulfil the orders of the one who held their object. If Chiyo Himura had ordered it to kill the Princess, it wouldn't have retreated after a single scratch; it would have died trying to fulfil its task. It sounded like the order had been something subvertible—something like, 'strike the princess,' 'make the princess bleed,' or 'try and kill the princess.' If the Oni was doing the absolute minimum to accomplish the order without actually killing the Princess or any of the guards along the way, then it was a far sight less violent than the one who had given it the order. Depending on who the last person to hold the coin was, the Oni would return to them—likely Chiyo Himura. Most of the literature regarding Oni painted them as extremely violent and nigh unstoppable for the unprepared. Mages could deal with them, but trying to actually target such a fast-moving creature could be outright impossible without knowing you needed to be on guard first. Given that Oni were traditionally used in exactly the way that Chiyo Himura had just done, there was rarely any warning to be had. Sora mulled over the information before he found himself eyeing a woman wearing a full-body cloak with a far-eastern scarf wrapped around her face. The figure was short, and they kept their eyes narrowed down to thin slits as they moved through the market. Sora noticed the attention she was giving his stall, and when she got closer, he knew, without a shadow of a doubt, who he was looking at. The woman stepped around the stall and sat on the seat without a word, taking a moment to place an ornate gold coin with a small hole in it on the counter.

"I have a cut on my back." The woman murmured. "One gold coin."

Sora took a moment to go over his options and how to best deal with the situation. He couldn't do anything to her considering the coin was sitting right there. If there were any standing orders given to the Oni to protect her, then he'd be dead within seconds of any violent action. Which left him with one real choice he reached out and touched the coin. Sora felt the thread of mana tethering it to Chiyo Himura as he made contact, and a second weaker tether stretched off towards the east of the city, already fading away. Whoever owned the coin before her had no current standing orders, and the ownership was in the process of transferring completely to Chiyo. He twisted his mana into the correct pattern for *Dispel*, snapping both of the connections without a word, and felt as a new connection was built, tethering him to the Oni. He lifted the coin up off the table, feeling the hardened crystalline mana—of what could only be a *permanent* contract spell—etched into the metal, and beneath it all, in a dark place within the confines of the coin, he felt the Oni.

"How very generous," Sora said, frowning. "Let's have a look at you, shall we?"

Sora reached out and carefully lifted the back of her cloak all the way up to her shoulders. The expensive shirt she wore underneath would have given her away to anybody that had seen it, completely at odds with the scarf and the beaten-up old cloak. He slipped a hand up the back of her shirt to rest against her back, a new pattern twisting into existence.

"*Still*," Sora murrmured.

The spell snapped into being, yellow light sinking into her skin and freezing her in place—immediately, he felt her struggling against the spell, muscles straining to move against the paralysis. He could feel her jaw trying to open, her throat, tongue and lips trying to form words. He twisted the pattern, weakening the points in a specific way that would allow her the ability to speak.

"Let me go." Chiyo managed, terror in her voice. "*Please*."

The Oni shivered inside of the coin, its presence sharpening in response to what was happening around it. Sora lifted the torn shirt up to join the cloak and studied the long bloody cut that bisected the woman's back from shoulder blade to hip. It was deeper at the top, tapering off as it went down—a glancing hit from one of the guards as she attempted to flee.

"Chiyo Himura," Sora said, stretching out the name. "Why did you attack the Princess?"

"I didn't attack her, I swear it," Chiyo said, voice desperate. "I was tricked into doing it. Eri is my friend, and I would *never* hurt her on purpose."

He lifted his hand up to rest above the cut, and Chiyo started to struggle again.

"*Meldflesh*," Sora said, "Who set you up?"

Chiyo breathed out at the feeling of the spell washing away the pain of the cut and then seemed to realize what he'd actually said.

"You believe me?" Chiyo swallowed.

"I asked you a question," Sora said, "Don't make me repeat myself."

"Koshiro Konishi," Chiyo said, speaking quickly. "He gave me the coin as a gift for Eri, told me the word that would activate it—it was supposed to be illusionary magic, a *flower*—"

That wasn't how you interacted with a bound Oni; you simply spoke to it like a person. Even now, it could hear what was going on around it, he could give it an order, and it would be forced to fulfil it.

"Who is Koshiro?" Sora wondered.

"He is one of the advisors to the king," Chiyo said, voice quiet. "Koshiro is—*was* a friend of my father, he—he—I didn't do this, *please*."

"What did he tell you to say to activate it?" Sora asked.

"*I'm not saying it again*," Chiyo said, anguished. "Last time, it turned into a monster and tried to kill Eri."

"I already told you that I'm not going to repeat myself," Sora said.

"You—he told me to say the word *flower*," Chiyo said, waiting a long moment in an attempt to avoid saying it. "With the word *moon* before it."

"Moonflower?" Sora said, frowning. "That's not a spell—"

"Don't *say* it," Chiyo said, horrified.

The mana signature inside the coin that he was associating with the Oni shivered at the word, but the creature took no action—and then everything clicked together. Koshiro had set a series of commands in place before handing the coin over to Chiyo. Including a command phrase that, when spoken, would activate a specific set of orders for the Oni to follow. Namely, attacking the Princess. Now that the orders had played out, ownership of the coin had reverted to the last person that had touched it, and the command phrase no longer applied. Chiyo's reactions were genuine, as far as he could tell, and it was obvious that she was working from the position of someone who had no idea how the binding worked.

"What did the monster look like?" Sora asked, just to see if she'd lie.

"It had yellow eyes, with skin the colour of chalk dust. It had two horns coming out of its forehead and long black hair all the way to its feet," Chiyo said, listing it all off. "It *looked* like a woman if not for the horns—and it was completely naked."

The story matched everything the guard had said, and the fact that she hadn't deviated from it at all told him that she was at least trying to be honest about what she had seen. The cut was gone from her back, and he left the spell active for long enough to ask his final question.

"Anything else that seemed strange about it?" Sora asked.

Sora pulled his hand back, and Chiyo must have felt the finality in his words because she started struggling against the spell again. He waited patiently for her to realise that she wasn't going to be able to break it.

"It was crying," Chiyo managed, sounding like she was about to start crying herself. "Please don't do this."

"The king has already given the order for your execution, and every guard in the city is looking for you," Sora said, leaning forward to speak more quietly. "Wearing a scarf like this is only going to draw their attention to you."

He unwound the scarf until only the cowl of the cloak was covering her hair from view.

"This spell will change your hair colour, but it's only going to last for about ten minutes, and if anyone else touches it, it's going to break," Sora said, reaching up and placing his hand on top of her head. "The south gate is closest. *Dispel. Colourant.*"

Chiyo fled his stall without another word, the cowl falling to lay against her shoulder blades, her red hair now a bright blonde. Sora stared at the place she had vanished for a long moment, wondering if he was going to regret helping her. Technically, he still had an hour or so left before he'd need to vacate the rented stall, but with the Oni's coin burning a hole in his coin pouch, he had something much more important to do. He left the stall behind, leaving the market the same way he'd come, and headed south. There really were guards everywhere, stopping people in the streets, knocking on doors, and entering homes. Sora would bet his new, ornate coin that this sight was repeated across the entire city. The city wall grew taller as he approached his master's old home. Wagons, caravans, and horse-drawn carts were already lining up in an attempt to set out from the city, but the gates were locked down tighter than the Princesses' bed chambers. Dozens of guards stood between the traders leaving the city and the gate. It was pretty clear already that Chiyo wouldn't be finding a way out within ten minutes. Sora turned off the main road and spotted the tails of a cloak vanishing down an alleyway. He unlocked the door to his master's home and then locked it behind him. Sora removed the ornate coin from his pouch and placed it down on the table in the middle of the room.

"You know, if someone had told me I'd be meeting an Oni today," Sora said, moving to sit on the comfiest seat in the room. "I would have called them a liar."

The coin remained where it was, content to pretend it was nothing other than what it looked like. An Oni could only receive orders directly, and hiding its presence was a good way of preventing any unaware owners from even knowing it was something out of the ordinary.

"Please come out," Sora said, "I like to see the person I'm talking to, and I would rather not order you to do anything."

A horned woman sat on the counter beside the coin, with chalk white skin and black hair that pooled around her legs on the table—two bright yellow eyes, slitted, locked onto his own, and for a moment, the two of them stared at each other. The being turned sideways, raising its knee up and hiding its uncovered body from him. He found himself studying the small, unadorned fingers and wondered how something that looked so soft could rend through metal.

"My name is Sora," Sora said, "I'd like to make a deal with you."

The Oni was quiet in the face of his question, but she curled forward slightly into her knee, hair dragging against the tabletop until it fell in front of her hip.

"You answer all of my questions for the next hour," Sora said, meeting her gaze. "In return, I'll free you from the coin."

The Oni, already statuesque, stilled entirely as the words washed over it. Even with simple terms and a positive outcome, the being didn't immediately move to accept the deal. Given that a deal was responsible for her current status—bound in servitude for what could have been thousands of years—he couldn't exactly blame her.

"Humans are not bound to their word," The Oni murmured.

"I suppose I could order you to talk to me for one hour and *then* free you anyway," Sora said, speaking his thoughts out loud for her benefit. "But like I said, I'd rather not order you to do anything—do you accept?"

The Oni watched him, yellow eyes searching him for signs of deceit. Sora waited patiently for her to come to a decision and then almost missed it when she gave a tiny, fractional nod—Sora smiled.

"What is your name?" Sora asked.

"Fubuki," Fubuki murrmured.

"Fu-bu-ki—that's a pretty name," Sora said, sounding out the syllables. "The eastern word for snow, named for your pale skin?"

Fubuki hesitated at the question.

"If you don't know the answer, you can just say that," Sora said, guessing at the cause. "I'm not going to get upset."

"I don't know," Fubuki said.

"Chiyo Himura was telling the truth, wasn't she?" Sora asked.

"Yes," Fubuki said.

A single word, no elaboration, either a preference to avoid talking or as a precaution against making a mistake and destabilising the deal he'd offered.

"What was the exact order that Koshiro Konishi gave you in regard to the princess?" Sora asked.

"When you hear the word Moonflower, strike at the princess," Fubuki said, speaking slowly. "Hurt anyone between you and the target."

"I thought it would be something like that," Sora said, closing his eyes. "You struck at her once, a shallow hit, and then returned to the coin—you're pretty clever, aren't you?"

Fubuki curled further into her knee, hair slipping further forward until she was watching him from behind a curtain of hair.

"Do you enjoy hurting people?" Sora asked.

"No," Fubuki murmured.

"Do you intend on killing or hurting anyone in the future?" Sora asked.

"No," Fubuki said again.

Sora lifted a hand up into the air, and Fubuki tensed at the motion, the change in dynamic enough to set her on edge.

"Toss me the coin, please," Sora said.

Fubuki reached down between her legs and took hold of the coin. She hesitated for a moment before flicking the coin across the room. Sora snatched it out of the air without effort, and Fubuki twitched as the magical connection reacted to his touch.

"Nice throw," Sora mumbled.

A permanent magical artifact—the only one he'd ever seen in person was the water well they had topside, although in that case, it was a water purifying spell. This, on the other hand, was nothing more than a *Subspace* and a *Permanence* tied to a *Siphon* to keep it charged at the expense of the Oni's internal mana store. The binding itself was a result of the Oni's own nature—unable to lie and compelled to adhere to any deal they agreed to—while he didn't know the exact wording, it was almost certainly something along the lines of;

"So long as this coin remains, you will follow the commands of the one who holds it." Sora said, "That's what the deal was—or something like it."

"Yes," Fubuki murrmured.

Sora ran the coin between his thumb and forefinger, feeling out the entirety of the pattern—but each of the spells was primitive, with nothing to be learned from them. A permanent magical artifact was something that was crystalised over hundreds of years, and no human could start a project like that and still be alive when it was completed. With or without the Oni being present, this coin was worth more money than he could make in a dozen lifetimes.

"Fubuki, I'm putting my trust in you to avoid hurting anyone if you can manage it—that's not a request or a deal that you need to adhere to—I'm just *hoping* that you'll keep your good nature even when you're free," Sora said, watching her. "I'd hate to have to kill something as unique as you, *Dispel*."

The crystalline mana resisted the spell in a way nothing else he'd felt ever had, but he just leant into it, sharpening the pattern, building it up until the teeth of the spell could shred even something as dense as this—the pattern began to erode, and then the entire thing dissolved. The coin couldn't withstand the loss, and it turned to gold dust in his hand. Fubuki shivered for a moment, curling forward onto her own knee as the thing that had kept her bound for what might have been millennia shattered.

"You heard what I said to Chiyo earlier about the guards and everything else," Sora said, scattering the gold dust onto the floor between them. "They are going to check here eventually, especially this close to the wall, so you'll need to find somewhere to hide."

Fubuki said nothing, unable to take her eyes off the gold flecks littering the floor.

"You could try and climb the wall, but they'd see you," Sora wondered. "Your horns and eyes would give you away without a disguise—do you know any magic?"

Fubuki lifted her gaze from the floor to stare at him again, and he wondered if she'd even heard what he said.

"If you don't already know any spells, then I probably couldn't teach you anything that would be useful," Sora said, humming. "Not without a few weeks of work, at least."

"Why?" Fubuki said.

"It takes a lot of practice to learn how to control your mana," Sora admitted before folding his arms behind his head. "Not me, though; I'm built different. You're looking at a certified *genius* of magic—"

"No," Fubuki said, still staring. "Why are you helping me?"

Sora winced at the question and how his own attempt at levity had gone completely missed.

"Why wouldn't I?" Sora said, "You're a sentient creature with thoughts, feelings, goals, and desires."

The rickety table creaked slightly as Fubuki shifted in place.

"You aren't violent, or you would have attacked me the moment I freed you, and you went out of your way to avoid doing unnecessary harm to the Princess," Sora said, "You deserve better than to be trapped in a coin and forced to kill people for the rest of your existence."

They fell into silence after that, and Sora was fine with it, content to watch her. If he was being honest, staring at naked women was already something of a hobby of his anyway. Fubuki had turned her head to face him more fully during the discussion, watching him as well, although he doubted she was having the same naughty thoughts.

"I don't know what to do," Fubuki said.

Sora dragged his eyes up from her thigh long enough to respond.

"Do whatever you want," Sora said before trying to give her some direction. "What do Oni like? Or rather, what does *Fubuki* like?"

Fubuki twitched at the sound of her name, and he was left wondering if any of her previous owners had ever bothered to learn it. He turned his mind towards the literature on Oni, but he couldn't recall hearing about anything on a personal level; most of the information was regarding ways to avoid being immediately slaughtered.

"Music," Fubuki said, biting down on her thumb. "Stories."

Sora laughed at the mundane things she'd chosen, almost exactly what he'd expect if he'd pulled someone off the street and asked them the same question. Fubuki turned her head the rest of the way until she was staring at him directly.

"Sorry, sorry, I was surprised by how normal your answers were," Sora said, smiling. "I like stories as well; it's actually something of a hobby of mine."

"Hobby?" Fubuki murrmured.

"Something you do for fun or because it interests you," Sora said, tilting his head. "Music? Hm. You could buy an instrument and learn how to play it—can you sing?"

"I don't know," Fubuki said.

"You'd need to figure out how to earn some money, pay for some lessons, or a book on how to play." Sora said, "That means wearing some clothes and covering your horns to avoid people running away from you."

Fubuki turned away at the words, retreating back behind her curtain of hair.

"Don't get me wrong, you're beautiful, but people will try and capture you again," Sora said, in case he'd hurt the creature's feelings. "That means you're going to need a disguise—probably something like what Chiyo was wearing, although you'd need to leave Satu first as well."

Sora drummed his fingers against the chair beneath him, a staccato of taps that drew Fubuki's eye.

"As for stories, you could find some wandering storytellers and listen to them." Sora said, "I like messing around with that when I'm on my own; illusion magic makes a good accompaniment for stories, you know?"

"I don't know," Fubuki said.

"Trust me, magic makes *everything* better," Sora said, going out of his way to ignore all the things it hadn't. "Still, we're pretty off track here—Fubuki, no matter what you intend to do with your freedom, you need to get out of the city first."

"How?" Fubuki asked.

Sora turned his mind to the task, closing his eyes for a moment. If it was him trying to flee, he'd be able to pull on a whole host of different spells to accomplish it. Casting spells on yourself was far more effective than casting them on someone else; if the person you were casting on couldn't recharge the spell, then it would be constrained entirely to the original duration. Even something simple like using *Colourant* on Chiyo would only last until the mana was used up. A *Blink* spell, tuned for distance, would be able to clear the thickness of the walls, but he'd have to be right next to it, and that would get *him* spotted as well.

"Most of my spells won't last long on you if you're not maintaining them yourself, or they would require me to literally walk you out of the front gate, which won't work after they get around to having a Mage check for spells," Sora admitted, "The spells I have that would get you outside of the wall without using the gates would need us both to be out in plain view of the guards, and then my head would be on the chopping block as well—think you can climb up the wall?"

"Yes," Fubuki murrmured. "Not quickly."

"I could cast *Haste* on you, speed up your body by about two times," Sora said, resting his cheek on his palm, "It would only last about a minute, though—but with your natural speed, you should be able to get up there pretty quickly."

Fubuki turned to face him, dropping her raised knee down until she was sitting cross-legged on the table—because he was a man, his eyes immediately dropped to look between her legs. By nature of just how long her hair was, some of the black mass had fallen over her legs and tragically obscured everything from sight.

"Alternatively, I could cast *Shrink* on you, and you could try and sneak through the holes in the gate," Sora said, wondering if he should suggest a haircut. "But that is where most of the guards are, so it would be pretty dangerous—it would probably only last about two minutes, as well."

Fubuki turned to follow his line of sight before looking back up again; not at all ashamed of his wandering gaze, he kept on looking—because he wasn't the hero of his own story, he was the villain.

"*Shrink* would make me small?" Fubuki asked.

"Correct," Sora said, "I could probably tune it and drop you down to about three inches tall? That might shave some time off the duration, though."

Sora watched as she reached down to play with some of the hair pooling against the inside of her thigh.

"Both?" Fubuki said.

Shrink, combined with *Haste*, was possible, but the conflict would increase the cost of both spells, thereby reducing the duration of each by almost half.

"It's possible," Sora said, "But you'd only have about thirty seconds before both spells unravelled—"

A short scream rang out, coming from the alleyway several buildings away, and despite only having a single conversation with her, he knew exactly who the voice belonged to. Sora pushed himself to his feet, and Fubuki *moved*—blurring across the room and leaving the table rocking under the force before she landed on top of the wardrobe in the corner. Sora ignored her entirely, moving towards the door. He stepped outside, catching sight of a guard turning down the alleyway and then started forward. Sora made it halfway there before he realised he didn't have a plan or any real idea of what he was going to do. Chiyo pleaded with the guard, begging him to stop, and he heard a dull crack as something broke—she screamed again, long and loud. Sora stepped around into the alleyway with his hand raised.

"*Shockwreath*," Sora murmured.

A burst of crackling white energy emerged from his hand, crashing into the guard's back, and the man seized up. He toppled sideways, writhing under the effects of the spell as his nervous system tore itself out of his control. Chiyo gasped as the man crashed down on top of her legs, struggling to pull herself out from under him. Sora lowered his hand, and the guard stared up at him, wide-eyed and unable to move.

"This—is exactly what it looks like, I'm afraid," Sora started before sighing. "Fuck."

It was the same guard from earlier, the man whose back he'd healed. Which meant that the moment the man was free, his description would be proliferated as some kind of accomplice. Chiyo grabbed onto his ankle, dragging herself forward, her broken, smashed legs trailing behind her and leaving smears of blood as she went.

"*Help me*," Chiyo cried.

"You probably aren't going to believe me when I say this," Sora said, staring at the guard's face. "But Koshiro Konishi is the one who gave the coin to Chiyo, and the Oni was forced to follow through on his orders. Maybe keep that to yourself, though, because it sounds like the kind of thing that would get you killed—*Sleep*."

Sora broke apart the *Shockwreath* spell as the new one settled in, watching as the man attempted to keep his eyes open before he succumbed to it entirely. He bent down, prying the hand off his leg and forcing her onto her back in the alleyway.

"*Still*," Sora murmured, "*Meldbone*."

Killing the guard was off the table because he wasn't a bad man, and he was only doing his job. Which meant that he couldn't stay in Satu, not when the guard knew his face. The man had seen him working in the market, and it wouldn't take them long to find someone who knew the name of the man who'd spent so many days healing people at that stall. The fact that he was a Mage would narrow the pool of suspects down immensely and a healer even more than that. As soon as that information got back to anyone up at the Library, they would start asking about him until they stumbled on someone who remembered that Salas had once had an apprentice by that name. The sound of chainmail reached his ears, and Sora spun to his feet as another guard stepped into the alleyway, sword already out of its sheath. A pale hand caught hold of the man's arm as he swung his sword down, and they came to an immediate halt.

"Let—" The man snarled.

"*Sleep,*" Sora said, overcharging the spell.

The man collapsed and then fell sideways, held up only by Fubuki's hand that remained wrapped around his wrist.

"Thank you, Fubuki," Sora said, breathing out.

Chiyo's muscles surged in response to seeing the Oni, and she began fighting hard to break the spell. Sora twisted the pattern for *Still,* adjusting it to allow her to speak.

"Why did you bring that *monster* here?" Chiyo managed, crying from the pain.

Fubuki flinched back from the vitriol and turned sideways, using her hair as a shield between them. Sora dropped back down beside Chiyo, hand returning to her shattered shin, and she gasped as the spell masked the pain once more.

"Don't call her that, or I'll leave you here for the guards to find," Sora said, voice flat. "Oni are bound to fulfil the orders of those who hold the coin; your hatred is better aimed upwards."

"Koshiro," Chiyo managed, anger destabilised. "It—it's still danger-ous."

"*It's* a person, and her name is Fubuki," Sora muttered, "You just had to get caught near my house, didn't you? Fuck, now I'm going to have to leave Satu."

Fubuki shifted, moving further into the alleyway to stand beside him.

"I—I'm sorry," Chiyo swallowed, eyes on the Oni standing above her. "But it's not like I wanted any of this."

"I think that goes for all three of us," Sora said with an explosive sigh. "Fubuki? Could you get something for me?"

"Something?" Fubuki murmured.

"A book sitting on the table beside my bed and the cloak hanging by the door?" Sora asked. "Please."

Fubuki *moved* again, vanishing around the corner in a blurring motion and a rapid staccato of footfalls. Sora fixed the second break and then switched spells to start mending the flesh around them—a rush job, but they didn't have time to do it properly.

"The spell ran out before I made it to the front of the line," Chiyo said, "Can you—can you get me out?"

"You don't ask for much, do you?" Sora muttered. "Just my entire life here—and some extra help on top."

Fubuki returned, coming to a complete stop beside the two of them, the cloak whipping out from the remaining momentum. His coveted book remained safely within the grip of her other hand, and he offered her a look of gratitude.

"Thank you, Fubuki," Sora said before doing an internal check to judge his remaining mana. "I have enough mana to get you both to the other side of the wall, and then maybe enough for a *Haste* each—after that, you're on your own."

"*Thank you,*" Chiya managed, "I'll repay you one day, I swear it."

Sora doubted he'd ever see her again, given that the entire kingdom was going to be looking for the three of them. He finished up on her legs and then broke the *Still* spell. Chiyo scrambled to her feet, stumbling on the sleeping guard's leg as she rose. Fubuki reached out with the arm that held the cloak and caught her before she could overbalance. Chiyo drew back from the touch, shock and fear colouring her face. Fubuki dropped her gaze to the floor, unable to look at her.

"Fubuki," Sora said, drawing her attention. "May I?"

He held his hand out towards the cloak, and she carefully placed it in his hand. Sora took it, wrapping his fingers around the opening at the front and stepped towards her. Fubuki took a step back, eyeing him with startled eyes.

"Stay still," Sora said, impatience leaking into his voice. "We don't have time for you to be scared of me."

Fubuki stilled at the tone or the words, and he stepped forward, swinging the cloak up over her head until it fell around her back and settled down onto her shoulders. He pulled it shut around the front, tying it closed with the cord.

"Keep that book safe for me, please," Sora said, "Follow me and stay close, I'll need to touch you both to move you across, and we are definitely going to get seen."

He stepped over the guard, moving to check the street, and then when he thought it was clear, he dashed across to the other side. The three of them crossed past the garden that had been planted beneath the wall, out into the open, and then towards the wall. Sora could already see the line of traders and how some of the guards turned to look in their direction. He stopped beside the wall, reaching out to place his hand on both of them. Four patterns twisted into existence, *Haste* and *Blink* in duplicate—he tuned the first two for increased duration and the latter for increased distance until he was certain they would clear the wall.

"Good luck," Sora said, "*Haste, Blink.*"

They vanished, one after another, and the guards started running, realising that their targets were disappearing. He built two more of the patterns faster than before and then spoke the command phrases, the mana drain dropping him below a quarter. An open field of grass appeared ahead of him as he was shunted onto the other side, and they stood in the shade of the wall. Chiyo had already started running, but Fubuki remained, watching him from beneath the cloak, book in her hand like a painting of some demonic mage from a myth. Sora leant down, planted his foot and then burst forward into a sprint—grass washed up into the air around him as he cut a path through it, each step faster than the last. The wall drew away from him in an instant, and Fubuki appeared beside him a moment later, matching his pace without any kind of effort. Even with *Haste* in effect, Chiyo wasn't a runner by any stretch of the imagination; her noble lifestyle left her slow and clumsy at these speeds. The three of them reached the treeline at almost the same time; the lead Chiyo had built vanished quickly. The trees towered above them, and he felt the spells he'd placed on both of them break, leaving Chiyo to attempt to deal with the furious speeds without any of the reaction time to manage it. Fubuki surged forward, blurring even to his enhanced reflexes and caught her around the waist before she could slam into a tree. Fubuki spun, swerving around it with a feat of footwork that Sora wouldn't have believed if he hadn't been watching it. Chiyo cried out at the sudden loss of contact with the ground, and then Fubuki weaved through the trees slowing down gradually to avoid the whiplash from a sudden stop. Chiyo scrambled to get her feet under her and then continued running at a fraction of the speed she'd been moving before. Sora broke the spell still draining his mana as he fell in step beside the two of them.

"Nice save," Sora managed, breathing heavy.

Fubuki turned to watch him as the three of them slowed to a jog, aiming for distance now that they were out of sight of the walls. Chiyo panted for breath, no sense of control or evenness left to her, just trying to drag in as much air as she could manage. Minutes passed, the light beginning to fade as the greenery grew thick, swallowing the sky above and leaving them to the dark. Sora turned his mind towards the future, using the run as a tool to focus his mind. Satu and the central mass of Fabah were lost to him, there would be bounties sent out, and the patrols would learn their descriptions as soon as the news of the failed assassination had time to proliferate. He'd have to aim to leave the country, which meant northeast towards the river cities and to Bilaar. From there, he could cross the border into Malnia. He turned to check and found the book sitting comfortably inside Fubuki's careful grip. Sora found his mind seeking out the destinations listed there, all the myths and locations he'd meticulously researched over the last decade, and a journey he'd never found the courage to set out on. With Salas gone, there wouldn't ever come a better time for him to begin his search—it was just a shame that he'd lost his ability to go home in the process.

"I can't," Chiyo gasped, falling to all fours amongst the detritus. "I need—to rest."

Sora came to a stop a few meters away, in a state that was almost as bad as the noblewoman. Fubuki, damn her, looked as fresh as she had when they'd first started running—she wasn't even *sweating*.

"Ten minutes," Sora managed, hands linked behind his head. "We were spotted leaving, but they weren't ready to pursue. Closest pursuit is thirty minutes by horse, half that if they have mages *and* horses on hand."

"God," Chiyo gasped. "We're going—to die."

"Sora," Fubuki murrmured.

The sound of his name sent a shiver down his back, and he turned to look at her, managing a smile.

"Where will you go now?" Fubuki asked.

"I was just working that out," Sora said, taking a deep breath and then letting it out slowly. "I've been meaning to set out on a quest for a while, and if I can't go home anymore, then I may as well start searching now."

"Searching," Chiyo said, making it back up to her knees, "For what?"

Sora eyed her for a moment before nodding his head at the book in Fubuki's hand.

"Nothing I'd tell to a frilly skirt that I only just met, that's for sure," Sora said, managing a laugh. "What do you two plan to do?"

"I don't know," Chiyo said, swallowing. "Do you have a suggestion?"

"Might want to avoid Satu," Sora offered in jest. "I hear there's been a bit of a stir there lately—something about a red-haired assassin."

"Thanks for the advice," Chiyo strangled out.

"Fubuki?" Sora asked.

"I don't know this place," Fubuki said, "The world is different now."

Sora tilted his head at the words; she spoke pretty good common tongue for someone who was at least a few hundred years old. Considering the origin of her name, she might have originally come from a country on the eastern continent—Jelan or Aqia, perhaps. If that was the case, then she had a long, long way to get home.

"We are on the western continent, in the country of Fabah, central west," Sora said, "Your name comes from Jelan or Aqia, countries of the eastern continent."

"I don't recognize those names," Fubuki mumbled.

"How long were you in the coin?" Sora asked, almost recovered.

"I don't know," Fubuki murmured. "I could not see the sun or the moon."

It hadn't really occurred to him before, but given the simplicity of the spells involved, the folded space she'd have existed within would have been an empty, lightless place. To be trapped in a place like that, for years at a time, would have driven him mad; the fact that she'd retained so much of herself spoke well of the strength of her mind.

"You can follow me for as long as you feel like it," Sora said, making the offer. "I have a bunch of stops to make first, but if we live long enough, eventually, we will end up crossing the sea."

There was a moment of silence where she stared at him, an indecipherable expression on her face before she carefully nodded her head.

"I will follow you," Fubuki said, clearly hesitant.

"I'm coming with you," Chiyo said, climbing to her feet. "Angon, Larta or Lyston?"

Sora eyed her for a moment; she'd picked out the three best options for leaving the continent without even needing to consult a map—her geography was good.

"All three," Sora said, rolling his shoulder. "We've rested long enough; time to move."

"God," Chiyo managed. "Not again."

#

The sun vanished, leaving the three of them stumbling through the dark as they headed south, and he kept track of his slowly regenerating mana throughout the journey, tempted to use magic for convenience, but knowing that he would need to conserve it. They'd slowed to a walking speed, unable to run in the dark, the leaves crunching under their feet as they moved. Fubuki seemed to lack any of the struggles he and Chiyo shared, able to navigate the darkness without any issues.

"Where are we going?" Chiyo said, breaking the silence. "Are we still moving south?"

Fubuki's yellow eyes turned to stare unerringly in his direction, awaiting an answer to the other girl's question.

"We are still moving south," Sora said, "We're aiming to get deep enough in that they can't follow us on mounts, and then we're heading directly west, then north again from there."

"West?" Chiyo frowned. "Asdar, Alhat, Shal—The Third Talon. North from there would be; Judra, Akh, Maar, then Bilaar, and then from there to Lyston?"

Sora tossed another glance in her direction, wondering again why a noble who'd probably never wanted for anything was so well-versed in geography.

"That is actually the exact route I was thinking about," Sora admitted, humming. "Were you born in a map room?"

Chiyo huffed at the comment and then squawked as she almost tripped over a fallen tree, half buried in the leaf litter.

"I spent most of my childhood learning about every village, town, city and trading post in the world and which roads linked them all together," Chiyo muttered, sounding a bit bitter. "Fat lot of good that will do me now—I'm penniless, without connections, and with a price on my head."

"Rough childhood, huh?" Sora said, rolling his eyes. "What was it like having servants kissing your ass all the time? Did they use tongue?"

"*What*?" Chiyo said, alarmed.

"Tongue?" Fubuki murmured.

"Of course, they didn't—I would never ask someone to do that," Chiyo said, aghast. "That's *disgusting*."

"If you say so," Sora said, amused.

"What did *you* spend your childhood doing?" Chiyo demanded. "I'm sure it's something really important—*not*."

"My childhood?" Sora wondered. "Stealing whatever else I could get my hands on to sell for food money. I was a street kid—until I got caught, anyway."

"What?" Chiyo said, hesitant now. "How could an urchin become an Adept?"

"I'm not an Adept," Sora said, bemused. "I'm a Master—and I have a title."

"But you're so young," Chiyo said, surprised. "I thought most Masters were in their forties?"

"For one thing, I'm *nineteen*, which isn't even that young," Sora said, annoyed. "For another, the average age for a Master is *thirty* years old, but there's a bunch of younger ones running around—maybe stick to learning about roads, map-for-brains."

"I'm not—that doesn't defeat my point," Chiyo said, frustrated. "You're ten years younger than the average master and claiming to be one."

"I'm not *claiming* to be one, girl; I *am* one," Sora said, genuinely pissed off, "I earned my mastership when I was fifteen years old, and *Salas the Scholar* gave me my title personally—think carefully before you drag her name and mine through the mud."

"I wasn't trying to—" Chiyo managed, sounding far less sure of herself. "I'm a year older than you are; you can't call me a *girl*."

The fact that she was older than him only served to annoy him more.

"*Fifteen?*" Chiyo said belatedly. "I still haven't mastered my first spell, and I've been training for an entire year."

That destabilised his anger by a significant degree as he tried to figure out if he'd just heard her correctly.

"What?" Sora said, squinting at her in the darkness. "A whole *year*? Who was responsible for your training?"

"Wartol," Chiyo said, sounding defensive. "He's an Adept from the Great Satu Library."

"How often did you take lessons?" Sora said, frowning.

"Two hours, once a month," Chiyo said, "Five gold coins per lesson."

"*What?*" Sora managed.

Here he'd thought that the old bastards running the Healer's guild were overcharging people— *five gold* for two hours of instruction?

"Why didn't—you could have signed up at the Library for *one* gold a month and then spent as long as you wanted inside teaching yourself," Sora said, shaking his head. "Tell me—when you piss the bed, do you wake up in a puddle of gold coins?"

"You're *disgusting*," Chiyo squeaked, "I'm just—I'm not good at self-directed study; those lessons did way more for me than anything I could have learned on my own. It was *worth* the cost."

"No, it wasn't," Sora said, "What spell did Wartol *pretend* to teach you?"

"He wasn't *pretending*," Chiyo said, flustered. "It was *Gleam*—It's a difficult spell, okay?"

Sora was starting to feel a bit bad for her at this point.

"Didn't you ever compare what you were learning to someone else?" Sora said, coming to a stop in the dark. "You must have asked someone why it was taking so long?"

Fubuki's glowing yellow eyes came to a stop a few feet away, flicking between the two of them as their furious exchange continued.

"Of course not," Chiyo said, affronted. "You *never* speak of lessons without your instructor present."

"This is actually sad," Sora said, wondering if he was speaking about Chiyo or himself. "I spent *years* stealing food just to survive, and I could have just scammed a frilly skirt out of *five gold a month*?"

"It wasn't a scam," Chiyo said, but her conviction was shaken. "Magic is expensive."

"Chiyo," Sora said, "I learnt *Gleam* in two days, from a book, when I was seven years old."

"Seven?" Chiyo managed.

"Who introduced you to Wartol?" Sora asked.

"Koshiro," Chiyo swallowed, "He—he was always close with our family, and after my father died, he said I should learn magic to better protect myself."

"A history of learning magic, at which point you hand over a 'magic coin' to the Princess and cast a spell in front of the entire palace," Sora said at length. "Wartol wasn't teaching you magic, and Koshiro wasn't looking out for you, Chiyo—they were bleeding your coin pouch dry."

Chiyo said nothing in response, but he heard the way her breathing grew shaky and how her words caught in her throat. Whatever satisfaction he'd hoped to derive from teasing her had long since fled in the wake of how much of her life had been twisted by the King's advisor. How long had he been planning this? What was the point of it? To isolate the Royal family from the other nobles? To sow distrust? Had he been coaching the King about the eventual betrayal and was now reaping the rewards of his ignored insight? What had his plan really been?

#

Two

Sora rubbed at his eyes, trying to ignore just how tired he really felt. This far south, the trees had grown tall, thick and closer together, the tangle of roots making each step more difficult than the last. Their pursuers wouldn't be able to match their pace, not when they had to scour every inch of the forest to see if they'd tried to hide amongst the mess. Their own path, on the other hand, was a straight shot, without any need to slow down other than to recover their breath. It would cost them, eventually, when the exhaustion crept to a level they could no longer ignore, but they weren't there yet. At least with the early morning light peeking through the few gaps in the trees, there was something to see by.

"My feet hurt," Chiyo managed, "I think I'm bleeding, as well—something scratched my leg."

Sora came to a stop at the comment, wishing she'd mentioned it earlier. Chiyo looked up, realising he'd stopped and then used a tree to help her slip down over a particularly large root. Fubuki followed directly behind her, walking down the root like a set of stairs, her balance perfect and her pace almost languid.

"Come, sit down here," Sora said, waving her towards a root. "We can't leave too many traces behind, or they're going to follow us the entire way."

Chiyo used her hand to keep her balance as she lowered herself down onto the root. Sora knelt down in front of her, catching her boot and tugging it off her foot. He rolled her pants up to her knee, catching sight of the red line running up her shin. Shallow, something that would heal in a day or two on its own and had already stopped bleeding. Chiyo winced as he checked the sole of her foot—red, with white patches of skin that had pulled up slightly and would soon begin to blister.

"*Meldflesh*," Sora murmured.

"Oh god," Chiyo groaned. "Why does it feel so good?"

"Not the first time a girl has said that to me," Sora said, "Usually costs me a few silvers first, though."

"Don't *say* things like that," Chiyo said, swatting at his head. "You're *disgusting*."

Sora laughed at the attack, ducking his head down to avoid her getting at his face. He pulled her other foot up onto his knee as well, almost tipping her over backwards in the process, and moved onto her other foot.

"I don't understand," Fubuki murmured. "What is disgusting?"

"He's—he was talking about paying for sex," Chiyo said, sounding flustered. "With a streetwalker or a whore at a brothel."

"There's nothing wrong with that," Sora said, glancing up at Fubuki. "Not every woman has a silver spoon to put in her mouth like Chiyo. Some prefer a nice big—"

Chiyo smacked him over the back of the head again, and he lifted an arm to hold her off.

"You're the *filthiest* mage I've ever spoken to," Chiyo said, red-faced.

"Every single of those old bastards at the Library has spent more time buried in between a girl's thighs than in the pages of any book," Sora said, defending himself. "They just put up a façade for the frilly skirts because you pay the best."

Sora let the spell fade away as he finished repairing the damage and then dropped her feet into the mess on the ground.

"Maybe *you* should put a façade as well," Chiyo said, dragging her boots back on. "God, I'm thirsty."

"We're still hours out from any kind of water," Sora admitted, nodding his head in the direction they'd been travelling. "Think you can hold out for a while longer?"

"Do I have a choice?" Chiyo muttered.

His careful conservation of mana throughout the night had given him plenty of time to regenerate his internal stores, and he was in a much better position to start using magic again.

"Come here and open your mouth," Sora said, turning back to face her. "I'll make it worth your while."

"You are *disgusting*," Chiyo strangled out.

"Fubuki, come here," Sora said, smiling.

Fubuki stepped forward until she was looking up at him, and not for the first time that morning, he found himself peeking through the gap in the cloak she was wearing. He lifted his hands up, cupping them in front of her face. Chiyo moved to watch the two of them, looking suspicious. The pattern twisted into existence, and he focused on the point that dictated the rate at which the conversion from mana to water would occur, weakening it.

"*Flow*," Sora murmured.

The spell snapped into existence, a tiny trickle of water rising up between his cupped hands. Fubuki ducked her head forward at his beckoning, lips pressed against his fingers as he tilted his hands to direct it into her mouth. Sora tried to ignore the way her throat rose and fell with each mouthful—all this talk about brothels and whores was getting to him. Fubuki pulled back once she was done, the back of her hand swiping across her mouth as she slipped to the side.

"Well?" Sora said, wriggling his eyebrows. "Are you going to open your mouth for me, Chiyo?"

"Stop *saying* it like that," Chiyo managed, stepping forward. "Just —ugh."

Chiyo pressed her hand under his own and then lowered her head, drinking from his hand. He ignored the frustrated noise she made when he spilled some of it down the front of her shirt and waited for her to finish drinking. Once she'd pulled back, he lifted his hands up to his mouth to sate his own thirst. He let the spell fall apart once he was finished and wiped his own mouth clean—he eyed Fubuki's uncovered feet for a moment.

"Fubuki, we'll need to pick up some boots for you soon," Sora said, frowning. "Travelling barefoot is going to destroy your feet."

"I heal quickly," Fubuki murmured.

"That doesn't stop it from hurting you," Sora said, shaking his head. "Let's keep going."

"I don't suppose you can magic us up some food?" Chiyo asked, sounding hopeful.

"Can't make food the same way," Sora said, "There are rabbits in this forest, so if we catch a few of them, we can eat them—"

Fubuki dashed forward, speeds leaving the details indistinct as she cut a line through the forest, pressed a foot against a tree and then dove past a fallen log.

"What are you doing—" Chiyo said, startled.

A squeak rang out before there was a crack and then silence. Fubuki rose to her feet behind the tree, a dead rabbit hanging from her hand, before crossing back into their path. Fubuki lifted the rabbit up, holding it out towards him, and he blinked.

"Oh," Chiyo managed.

"You really do have good eyesight, huh?" Sora said, taking it from her. "It was that close, and I didn't even see it."

He took one of the leather straps from his belt and tied the animal to it, leaving it to hang there.

"I'll set a campfire when we finally stop to rest and prepare it," Sora said, "If you find any more, feel free to grab them too—good job, Fubuki."

Fubuki just watched him silently, the book she was still holding onto pressed flat against her uncovered belly.

"We're going to *eat* that?" Chiyo asked.

"There is no way you've never eaten rabbit meat before," Sora said, bemused. "I don't believe that for a second."

"Of course I have," Chiyo said, flustered, "It's just—I don't know."

"Never seen a rabbit before it hit your plate?" Sora guessed, "Surprise—rabbit meat comes from rabbits."

"I know that," Chiyo said, looking away. "Forget it."

#

The weariness grew stronger as the day passed him by, and eventually, Chiyo's pace had dropped to a slow, stumbling walk. To her credit, she didn't stop moving forward until it was almost dark again, and then she fell to her knees, unable to take another step.

"I can't keep going," Chiyo said, legs splayed around her. "Can we stop? Please?"

"Now is as good a spot as any," Sora said, "I'm surprised you lasted as long as you did—well done, really."

"Thanks," Chiyo mumbled.

"Whoever they sent after us won't move through the forest at night. Too much chance of missing us in the dark," Sora said, "They'll count on catching us on the roads nearby, so we should be able to get a few hours of rest."

Sora eyed the area, picking out the best anchors for an exclusionary zone—there were enough trees that he had his pick of them. He snagged a rough-looking stone up off the ground before stepping forward to the first tree. Sora built up the pattern for *Etch* before activating the spell—his index finger became enshrouded in smoky black mist. He took his time scribbling out the pattern on the trunk of the tree, looking for flaws in his own casting to correct. *Sanctum* wasn't a spell he'd used more than a few times, and while he could probably burn it into the bark in a few short seconds if he pushed himself, he'd rather use it as a learning experience.

"What are you doing?" Chiyo asked.

"Along with the guards, soldiers and bounty hunters that are looking for us, there are also monsters and animals in this forest that will gladly take any opportunity to eat us; Redcaps, Tanglebears, wolves, potentially the odd goblin—if they somehow managed to come this far south," Sora said, running his hand across the tree, "Sleeping out in the open is a death sentence, so instead I'm going to create a barrier around us."

"There are *monsters* in here?" Chiyo managed. "Don't people go hunting in these woods—why haven't they cleared all of the monsters out?"

He finished the first pattern before moving on to the second tree. Fubuki trailed along after him studying his spell-infused finger as he set about completing the task.

"Who is *they*?" Sora wondered.

"Satu," Chiyo said like it was self-evident. "They should have paid someone to keep it clear."

"Commoners don't have the money for something like that, and nobles aren't going anywhere near the forest, to begin with, so why would they bother?" Sora said, shaking his head. "The only time you frilly skirts would get involved in something like that is when the situation starts directly affecting your coin pouch."

He kept on moving and finished off the next tree while he spoke.

"That's not true at all," Chiyo said, a bit startled.

"Sure it is—if the monsters in the forest started attacking people on the roads, say a Caravan from a nearby city that was owned by a noble in Satu," Sora said, working as he spoke. "How quickly do you think they'd fund an extermination mission? There would be posters up on the town board asking for Redcap caps, wolf pelts and goblin ears within a day, a silver piece for each."

The fourth tree finished, he brought the rock up and scribbled a *Permanence* spell out before adding the *Sanctum* control component within it. Sora pressed his finger against it and then dumped a tenth of his mana into it. The mana inside the *Permanence* began to bleed into the *Sanctum*—he felt the invisible lines of mana snap into existence, linking the four trees together.

"That doesn't mean we don't help in other ways," Chiyo said before glancing up as Sora tossed the rock onto the ground. "Was that supposed to do something? Nothing changed."

"Those four trees with the symbol on them are the edges of the barrier; there is an invisible line stretching between each," Sora said, "Cross over the barrier and then turn around; you'll see what it does."

Chiyo fought her way back to her feet, and then she stepped across the now invisible border. Fubuki followed after her a moment later, and the two of them turned to look back before blinking in surprise.

"You—vanished?" Chiyo said.

Fubuki slipped her hand across the border and then pulled it back again. While he couldn't see it from his side, he knew that from her perspective, her hand would have just vanished from sight. The two of them messed with it for a few moments longer before crossing back over again.

"So it makes us invisible?" Chiyo said, "You really *are* a master."

"It's *incredibly* annoying to hear you say it like that," Sora said, aggrieved. "*Sanctum* is a one-way perception alteration. Anyone on the outside of the barrier cannot hear, see or smell anyone on the inside."

Sora moved to sit down against a fallen log, content to rest for a bit now that they were safely hidden from sight. Fubuki sank down onto the ground a few feet away, watching him. Chiyo studied the mess of leaves coating the ground and then sighed before moving to sit with the two of them beside the log.

"We're about three or four hours out from the Twin Satu Rivers, the first one, anyway," Sora said, letting his head rest back against the dried-out wood. "We should leave early, say, six hours from now."

"More walking," Chiyo said. "I can't wait."

"Your finger was glowing," Fubuki murmured.

"That is a spell called *Etch*; it's used for marking out spells in written form. Unless it's tied into a *Permanence* spell, the ink will fade away after about an hour," Sora said, rubbing at his eyes again. "It's a pretty useful spell, but the pattern is a bit hard for most beginners, so it's usually taught to Novices after they complete the exam."

"What is a pattern?" Chiyo asked, sounding hesitant. "I've never heard of that before."

Sora closed his eyes for a moment.

"Chiyo, I'm sorry to say it, but you need to forget everything Wartol taught you," Sora said, sighing. "If he never mentioned mana patterns to you, then *nothing* you know is real."

Chiyo pulled her legs up to her chest and tucked her face into her arms. Sora took a moment to really consider the situation and the two who were now fleeing Satu alongside him. Fubuki wouldn't be able to enter any kind of human city looking the way she did—chalk-white skin, horns, glowing slitted eyes. Chiyo could go just about anywhere, except for the fact that she would get snatched up by bounty hunters the very second someone spotted her hair. If they really were intent on following him, then they were potentially going to be together for a significant amount of time—or at least until they were found and killed. Without access to the library, he wouldn't be able to keep working on his own education—these two, however, would greatly benefit from even a little bit of instruction and a few choice spells.

"My name is Sora the Seeker, apprentice of Salas the Scholar," Sora said, repeating the words that Salas had once spoken to him. "Master of magic, finder of things—the two who stand before me, do you seek my guidance?"

"What exactly are you offering us?" Chiyo said, hesitant.

"I'm offering an apprenticeship to both of you," Sora said, shifting against the log until the branch was no longer stabbing him in the back. "So long as you choose to follow me, I will teach you magic—*real magic*, not the crap that Wartol was teaching you."

"What is the cost?" Fubuki murmured.

"Cost?" Chiyo said, shaking her head. "I'm carrying everything that I own—I no longer have any money, standing or resources."

"One silver," Sora said, "Payable the day you decide you no longer want my guidance."

"That can't be a serious offer," Chiyo said, staring at him.

Sora wondered if this was how Salas had felt after dealing with him.

"Don't interrupt someone when they're being too generous, idiot," Sora sighed, "Listen, do you want to learn magic or not? Yes, or no, I'm not going to ask again."

"*Yes*," Chiyo said, "Of course I do."

Sora turned to look at Fubuki and found her watching him, yellow eyes searching his face for something.

"Yes," Fubuki murmured.

"Then from this moment, until *I* die, until *you* demonstrate your mastery, or when either of you pays me the one silver severance fee,"

Sora said, listing off the conditions. "I accept you as my apprentice, Chiyo Himura and Fubuki."

"Thank you," Chiyo said, swallowing. "I—what are the duties of an apprentice?"

"Exactly the same as wifely duties," Sora said, in jest, "Only more often and with twice the enthusiasm."

"That's—you are *disgusting*," Chiyo said, flustered. "I swear—"

"What are wifely duties?" Fubuki murmured.

"He's—" Chiyo managed. "This *beast* is talking about—about *sex*."

Sora laughed at her hesitation to say the word.

"I was only joking, Fubuki. Apprentice duties are simple," Sora said, amused. "When magical instruction is taking place, you listen to everything I say without argument, and you must apply yourself to the best of your ability."

"Is that all?" Chiyo said, frowning.

"That's all I'm asking for," Sora said, "My own master had a whole bunch of other things I had to agree to, but I don't really care about any of that."

"Are there Master duties?" Fubuki murmured.

"Yes—your safety is my responsibility during magical instruction, and should you come to any harm through the process of learning, I am required to facilitate or pay for your healing," Sora said, listing them off. "I must also make my best effort to instruct you in an accurate, effective and timely manner."

Fubuki watched him for a long moment, taking in the words before giving one of her tiny fractional nods to show that she understood.

"I'm the reason you can never go home again," Chiyo said, "Why would you offer this when you get nothing out of it?"

"I've been trying to work up the courage to leave Satu since my Master died, and now here I am, finally outside of its walls," Sora said, folding his arms behind his head. "Besides, I made a choice to save you on my own; you don't get to take responsibility for my actions."

"You didn't answer my question," Chiyo said, not letting him get away with the evasion.

"I figure if you hang around long enough, I'll eventually catch you with your shirt off," Sora said, peeking at her with one eye open. "The tits of nobility—I hear they're something special."

Chiyo made a strangled noise in the back of her throat.

#

Morning came quickly, and despite the danger present in staying in one place for too long, Sora had a difficult time dragging himself back to the waking world. When he finally managed to talk himself into sitting up, he took in the area—the *Flamestay* spell had long since faded away, and the uneaten remains of the poorly butchered rabbit remained in the space they'd cleared of leaf litter. Fubuki remained curled up in the same place he'd last seen her, hair tangled in the mess of leaves and sticks that coated the ground. The unnatural stillness that she carried with her while awake was gone, her chest rising and falling with each breath. The borrowed cloak was pulled tight against her skin, and the cover of his book barely peeked out of the gap, clutched in her hands. Chiyo had fallen sideways to sleep against the log, red hair carefully tucked into the cowl of her own cloak to protect it from the mess. Sora turned to get his knee under him and used the log to push himself up to his feet. The ache that came with sleeping on the ground hadn't changed at all over the years, except maybe to get a few shades worse. Still, it was quickly subsumed by the ache in his legs from all the running they'd done. He moved to the nearest tree, leaves crunching beneath his feet and then fished out his cock; he turned slightly when he heard the sound of movement behind him—Fubuki was already on her feet, and Chiyo was sitting up now, watching him. Chiyo muttered something under her breath and turned away, rubbing at her eyes. Sora finished up his business, tucked himself away and then turned back around.

"We overslept, so we need to get going," Sora said, cracking his neck. "If you need to take a piss, now is the time."

Chiyo looked entirely uncomfortable at the comment or the idea of doing something like that in front of two strangers. Sora turned away, aiming for the rock he'd left in the middle of the clearing, unwilling to leave the *Sanctum* up for their pursuers to discover. Dissolving the

Permanence on the rock was enough to ruin the integrity of the spell, and the ink on the bark would fade away without any more mana to keep it there. Chiyo stepped behind a tree, checking once to make sure nobody was coming to peek before vanishing again. Sora kicked the leaf litter over the top of the remains of their dinner, burying it beneath the mess. The wildlife would probably find it before their pursuers.

"Fubuki," Sora said, "Are you sick of carrying my book yet?"

"No," Fubuki said.

"What's so special about it?" Chiyo asked, stepping back into the clearing. "Is it a magic book?"

"There are a few active spells on it if that's what you think constitutes a *magic* book, but it's really just filled with my personal research," Sora said, bemused. "Come on, let's not waste any more time."

He slipped out of the clearing, and the two of them followed along behind him. Moving helped lessen the pain in his legs, the increased blood flow washing away some of the aches.

"Personal research?" Chiyo asked. "What kind?"

"Myths," Sora admitted, "Stories, fables, legends, fairy tales—that kind of thing."

Fubuki lifted the book up to her face, eyeing the cover with renewed interest—he recalled their first conversation back in his home. The Oni had admitted to having an interest in stories and music, hadn't she?

"Why?" Chiyo asked.

"I like to find things," Sora said, shrugging. "The best things to find are ones that are hidden, locked away, or that people don't even think exist."

"*Sora the Seeker*," Chiyo said.

Sora nodded at her use of his title.

"A Master bestows the title upon the apprentice when they demonstrate mastery," Sora said, "Salas chose something fundamental about me, my desire for things outside of my grasp—our very first meeting involved me breaking into her home to find something expensive to steal."

"You broke into a Master's home?" Chiyo said, aghast.

"I broke into a lot more than that; trust me. I had something of a talent for finding unlocked doors," Sora said, shaking his head. "That's what I thought anyway; it turns out I was actually using magic to unlock them, and after I broke through a spell-locked door, Salas realised I had some talent."

They'd had a rocky start, and it hadn't been until almost a month later that he'd gone to the woman's home to demand knowledge, but that was where his lifelong obsession with magic had begun.

"The quest you wouldn't tell me about," Chiyo said, "You're going to look for these myths?"

"Figured me out, did you?" Sora said, "Every myth in that book follows a certain theme or contains a specific line that speaks towards a singular subject—I intend to find out if any of the objects spoken of in those stories are real."

"What is the subject?" Fubuki said, still looking at the cover of the book.

"Immortality, rebirth, and cheating death," Sora said, "There are quite a few stories in that category."

"I bet there is," Chiyo said, amused. "Can't imagine why that would be popular."

"What stories are in here?" Fubuki murmured.

"There are probably about a hundred or so in there," Sora said, eyes searching the trees ahead. "The most promising ones were; *The Dragon's Marble. The Bone Needle. The Eternal Mandate. The Trickster Beads. The World Tree.*"

"I've heard of *The Eternal Mandate* and *The World Tree*," Chiyo said, hesitating. "*The Eternal Mandate* takes place in the Dread Forest of Sagia. You're not actually planning on *going* there, are you?"

"Eventually, but it's not at the top of my list," Sora admitted, "Either of you heard of *The Dragon's Marble*?"

"No," Fubuki murmured.

"It's not a Fabah myth," Chiyo frowned.

"It's a *really* old one from Malnia, inscribed on an ancient stone tablet," Sora said, "It takes place north of Bilaar, where the Three Talon Rivers meet before the ocean—map-for-brains?"

"Dragon's Claw?" Chiyo asked, blowing a breath out of her nose at the name. "Isn't that entire place overrun by goblins?"

"Yes," Sora admitted, "That's the first stop on my quest, although there's a half-dozen set of stops between here and there. If you plan on jumping ship at any point, Bilaar might be a good place to find that silver coin."

"Right," Chiyo said, biting her lip.

"What is the dragon's marble?" Fubuki asked.

"It would be a waste to just tell it to you now," Sora said, smiling. "Ask me again when we stop to rest, and I'll show you something special."

Fubuki looked caught between caution, impatience, and an intense sort of curiosity that was hard to weather. Chiyo, on the other hand, held an expression that was far more suspicious than he thought was warranted.

#

The sound of water reached his ears long before he spotted the river, the noise carrying far through the otherwise silent forest. For the first time in hours, Sora could see the sky again, completely unobstructed, the trees not willing to put themselves at the mercy of the first of the Twin Satu Rivers. The area opened up on either side of it, stretching away from them and vanishing as it curved into the distance. Twenty meters wide and deep enough that crossing it would require the ability to swim, or for the less courageous challenger, to seek out some kind of bridge.

"So much water," Fubuki said, wide-eyed.

"Have you never seen a river?" Chiyo asked, frowning.

Fubuki shook her head, the movement sending her leaf-tangled hair swaying about her legs.

"Despite their great strength, the life of an Oni is fraught with dangers—forever hunted by mages who would seek to bind them into servitude," Sora said, considering the water. "The life of a bound Oni is bleaker, trapped in an unmoving object for centuries, and taken out only at the whim of their owner, used as a weapon to harm their enemies before being returned to the dark."

It would be a day before their pursuers had finished searching the forest, and at that point, they'd reach the river. To avoid being followed west, they would need to mislead them, and that meant leaving tracks in a direction away from their own.

"I didn't realise—that's—that's horrible," Chiyo managed, sounding disturbed. "Fubuki? How long have you been trapped for?"

"I do not know," Fubuki said, tilting her head. "There was no sun or moon."

"Can we—is it *possible* to free her?" Chiyo said. "Sora?"

"I already did that," Sora said, frowning at the embankment. "About ten minutes before you got caught—Chiyo, I'm going to need your underwear."

"*What?*" Chiyo said, alarmed.

"I need a piece of your clothing, and you need to keep your cloak on to cover your hair," Sora said before tilting his head at her. "Unless you want to take your shirt off—"

"*Why* do you need my underwear?" Chiyo demanded. "What's it for?"

"Our pursuers are going to be tracking us through several methods," Sora said, turning to face them. "One of those is scent—"

"You're going to make a diversion?" Chiyo said, eyes sharp. "Make them think we went in a different direction? How?"

"Take off your underwear, and I'll show you," Sora said, wriggling his eyebrows. "Trust me, I'm ready to start whenever you are."

"Don't *say* it like that," Chiyo strangled out. "*Ugh.*"

Chiyo stomped towards the treeline; before stepping out of sight, the sound of leaves crunching and cloth rustling flowed out to them.

"Fubuki," Sora said, trying not to smile. "You should go ask if she needs some help."

Fubuki moved to the treeline without pause and stepped out of sight—a moment later, Chiyo squeaked out something that might have originally been intended to be a word.

"*Fubuki*," Chiyo managed, voice pitched high. "I don't need help—stop *staring*—"

Sora moved towards the river and knelt down beside it, scooping up a handful of water to bring to his mouth. It wasn't anywhere near as pure as the magically cleaned well-water from Satu, but he didn't mind the more natural taste of it. He cleared a space amongst the leaves until he could see the ground below and then placed his hand flat against it. Chiyo stormed out from behind the tree, red-faced. Sora covered himself as she tried to smack him over the back of the head again, laughing at her anger. Fubuki came to a stop beside them, looking hesitant at the ongoing attempt to slap him to death.

"No more, I yield, I yield," Sora laughed.

Chiyo breathed out of her nose like some kind of great dragon of old and then finally stopped her assault. Sora snatched the underwear out of her hand, ignoring the way she tried to hold onto it, and then weathered a final slap as best as he could manage.

"Why does it have to be mine?" Chiyo muttered.

"Because it's going to take them a few days to actually find out where I live and get something with my scent on it," Sora said, stretching the silky piece of clothing out a few times. "Your blood was all over that alleyway, and they already know where you live, so they'll probably have something of yours already."

"Then how is leaving them here going to help us?" Chiyo frowned, "We're leaving a marker behind for them to follow."

"The plan is a *little* bit more complicated than leaving your panties behind for some lucky guard to find," Sora said, hand back on the soil. "Have a little faith, please—*Golem*."

Sora drew his hand up off the soil, moving slowly as the earth rose up with him. It shifted, filling out into a humanoid shape. The construct was unnaturally smooth, without features, but with all the limbs needed for movement and balance.

"I see," Chiyo said, "You're going to send it in another direction, and it will carry my scent with it."

He took his time with it, making it as durable as he could manage, and then stopped when it reached the same height as Chiyo.

"*Etch*," Sora said.

He added a *Permanence* spell, nothing more than basic mana storage to keep it running without him present to refuel it, and then dumped half of his mana into it—the loss of so much at once had him sagging under the strain for a moment.

"Is it alive?" Fubuki murrmured.

"*Golem* is simply a hardened shell of mana that is filled with compacted soil—it has no soul, if that makes more sense to you," Sora admitted, managing to straighten up. "It contains a series of autonomous functions and will follow simple instructions until its mana source runs out."

"How long will it last?" Chiyo asked.

"The spell has surprisingly low consumption for what it does, and I put way more mana into it than we really needed," Sora said, reaching out and hooking the pair of panties over its face like a mask. "It should have enough to last about twelve hours—if nothing destroys it before then."

Sora sent the mental command, and the Golem turned away from them, stomping forward parallel to the river, heading east. They watched it walk away until it started to grow murky in the distance.

"Won't they be able to follow our scent west?" Chiyo asked, "They could just split into two groups."

"Correct, which is why we aren't going to leave a scent for them to follow," Sora said, nodding. "I hope you both know how to swim."

"I do not," Fubuki murrmured.

"I'll teach you," Sora offered. "It's not that hard."

"Sora," Chiyo said, looking at the water warily. "There are *monsters* in the river."

"Absolutely," Sora said, stepping into the shallows. "Not quite as cold as I imagined, but it's definitely terrible."

He waded out, grunting as the water grew higher, and then almost cancelled the entire idea when the icy water washed up past his groin.

Sora scrunched his face up in agony before carefully moving deeper until he was up to his waist. He built up the pattern for *Sense*, tuning it for range and duration at the expense of just about everything else.

"*Sense*," Sora murmured before raising his voice. "Hurry up, will you?"

Chiyo and Fubuki both lit up in a bright white outline, and when he turned his gaze back to the water, he found a trio of white-wreathed fish passing by. Fubuki stepped into the water but stopped as it reached her knees, moving to hold the book directly above her head. It warped the cloak, opening the gap at the front and revealing her naked form in all its pale glory. His cock remained entirely inert, strangled to death by the river god's icy grip. Chiyo gave a horrified gasp as she stepped into the shallows, the water filling her boots within seconds.

"The book is waterproof, Fubuki," Sora said as she made it up to her waist. "You can hold it underwater; just don't drop it, okay?"

"Okay," Fubuki murmured.

Sora watched as she carefully lowered the book beneath the water level and then brought it back up again, staring with interest as the book remained completely dry. Chiyo stumbled in up to her waist with a noise of distress, clearly having trouble dealing with the temperature. Sora moved further out into the river until no part of his body was touching the riverbed and then sunk beneath the water for a moment. He could see the fish, waterbugs, and tiny monsters moving through the dark, more scared of the humans that had suddenly invaded their domain than the other way around. Provided nothing larger or more intelligent was lurking ahead of them, they'd be fine. Fubuki tilted her chin upwards as the water reached her mouth and then came to a stop, hesitant to go any further. Chiyo fought her way free of her cloak, throwing it over her shoulder as she reached the two of them.

"Fubuki, you can push yourself upwards by sweeping your legs beneath you," Sora said, reaching forward to the latch at the front of her cloak. "Drawing your hands down will accomplish the same thing. The resistance of the water against your skin will propel you up to the surface—move slowly at first until you know how much you need to keep yourself near the top."

Sora unlatched the cloak to free up her arms and then tossed it over his shoulder as Chiyo had done before reaching out to take hold of Fubuki's bicep. He pulled her further into the water and helped to hold her up as she attempted to do just that.

"Breathe evenly; there's no need to rush," Sora said, taking the book from her. "Cup your hands so the water doesn't slip between your fingers—I'm going to let you go for a moment, ready?"

"Yes," Fubuki breathed.

He let go of her arm, and Fubuki kept herself afloat without any kind of issue, the ability to swim coming to her as naturally as breathing. Chiyo was clearly a strong swimmer as well, given the ease by which she was managing it—he'd heard tales of some frilly skirts having their own indoor pools, although he'd never seen it. Given her previous status, she was probably one of them.

"Perfect," Sora said, swimming forward a bit. "Avoid going too close to either side, so we don't leave any traces that we went this way, and make sure you go underwater a few times as well."

Fubuki sunk beneath the water almost before he'd finished the sentence, and Chiyo followed, a pool of black and red hair following them. They resurfaced a moment later, Chiyo fighting to clear her face of the hair, but Fubuki remained unbothered by it clinging to her skin.

"We've got a fair way to go," Sora said, "Stay near me, and I'll warn you of any monsters coming to nibble on your toes."

"Don't *say* that," Chiyo said, horrified.

The two of them surged forward to follow him, splitting the water with each movement of their hands. He'd probably gone swimming a few hundred times in his life, in *this* river, in fact, but miles away, where the Twins met at the top of Satu. Like now, it was usually far too cold to be willing to go inside, except for the hottest parts of the year, but there hadn't been much choice for getting clean as a child; it wasn't like filthy street kids were allowed into the public baths. Within minutes, it became more than clear that he was actually the worst swimmer of the three. Chiyo was far more practised than either of them, but

Fubuki seemed to have an innate ability for movement regardless of the medium, and her physicality far surpassed either of them.

"How far are we going to swim?" Chiyo asked.

"At least an hour, but more would be better," Sora admitted, "The more distance we put between us and our tracks, the more likely they are to follow the golem."

"How do you know what they will do?" Fubuki wondered. "Is it magic?"

"It's strategy. You model the behaviour of others, considering what resources and skills they have at their disposal." Chiyo said, turning to get eyes on her. "Once you determine what their goal is, you figure out what actions they are most likely going to take."

"That's a good explanation," Sora said, impressed.

"Of course it is," Chiyo said, frowning. "I'm a member of the nobility; I am well educated, and strategy is one of the many topics that was covered."

"I wasn't making fun of you; I was just surprised," Sora said, "Fubuki?"

"Yes?" Fubuki said.

"A man has been tasked with cutting down two trees every day, and at the end of every second day, he must send a magical message to the King, a report of what he has accomplished," Sora said, constructing it on the fly. "He has three tools at his disposal to complete this task; an axe, a knife, and a spell that will instantly cut down a single tree but will leave him without mana until the next day. How will he accomplish his task?"

Fubuki stared at him, yellow eyes peeking out above the waterline as she swam beside him without effort. Chiyo hummed at the hypothetical he'd designed, looking like she wanted to answer.

"You can ask Chiyo questions about the puzzle, but she's not allowed to tell you the answer." Sora said, "Take your time."

"Chiyo?" Fubuki murmured, "Which tool did the king tell the man to use?"

It was telling that she expected the man to receive explicit orders on what to do rather than the fact that he might possess some autonomy to act outside of the king's desires—a learned behaviour from her own life in servitude.

"Sora didn't say," Chiyo admitted, "But it's implied that he can use whichever method he wants to accomplish the task."

"Can a human cut down a tree with a knife?" Fubuki murmured.

Another odd angle, but one that made sense given that she had no real idea about what the man in the puzzle was capable of.

"It would take weeks to cut down a tree with a knife," Chiyo said, swimming sideways for a moment to answer. "It's the worst tool of the three for cutting down trees."

"Is the man strong?" Fubuki asked, hesitant.

"At *least* as strong as me," Sora said, clapping a hand on his bicep and splashing water everywhere in the process. "That mean's he's super strong."

Chiyo rolled her eyes.

"He should use the axe," Fubuki said, watching them. "Its purpose is to cut trees, and if he is like Sora, he can cut many."

Sora grinned at the comment.

"He *will* use the axe," Chiyo said, drawing her attention. "But there is something more that he can do to make the task easier."

Fubuki was quiet for a long moment, clearly thinking about the question with Chiyo's added context.

"The spell will make him tired, but he can use it on the first day," Fubuki said, clearly hesitant. "The second day, he can't because of the message."

"Perfect marks," Sora said, watching a white-wreathed fish swim beneath them. "You want another one to solve?"

"Yes," Fubuki murmured.

#

The three fish he'd tied off on his belt flopped around at his hip as he turned to watch the others. Fubuki stepped out of the river like a naked spirit, pale, languid and dripping with water. Chiyo stumbled out like a drunk that had fallen off a bridge, dragging herself forward with each step, water sloshing about in her boots. Her expensive shirt clung to her breasts, hiding nothing from sight, and Sora nodded at the sight—even hidden by wet cloth, the tits of nobility were powerful indeed. He tossed the cloak back around Fubuki's shoulders, latching it up at the front again, even as Chiyo attempted to do the same to her own.

"You did a good job of keeping it safe," Sora asked, holding the book out. "You want to look after it for me again?"

"Yes," Fubuki said.

Fubuki took it from him, moving to hide it beneath the cloak once more, and he patted her on the shoulder in thanks before turning away. He started up the embankment, moving into the treeline on the opposite side to which they'd started. It was best to stay away from the river now to avoid anyone picking up their scent if they did send people scouting east along it. Moving with wet gear was even more annoying than trying to fight through the brush normally. An hour of walking put them deep in the forest again, and then after that, he turned to direct west, aiming to break out of the forest somewhere within the next day's journey. Chiyo spoke up after they'd spent another miserable hour trudging along through the mess.

"Are we going to Asdar?" Chiyo asked before pausing. "Are we that far south? Or are we closer to Shal?"

"We're closer to Asdar, but we're going to neither," Sora admitted, and Chiyo frowned at the news. "We're cutting straight through the plains; the closest city we will be passing by is actually Alhat. Once we reach the Third Talon, we'll turn north to Judra."

"What's your reasoning?" Chiyo frowned.

"We don't want to be seen in any of the towns or on any of the roads directly surrounding Satu because both of you are distinctive, and when the rumours get out, they'll have a direction to start looking," Sora said, eyes on the trees. "Riders will reach Asdar, Shal and Alhat before *we* do, and they'll have people searching the roads as well. We're going to slip past the cage they will be attempting to build around us, and then we'll be free to breathe."

"Why Judra?" Chiyo asked.

"Because the normal route to get there is by coming south from

Bilaar and then taking a boat from Maar to Akh and then to Judra." Sora said, "It's secluded because of how far down the Third Talon it is and the fact that it's surrounded by forest on all sides—news about us isn't going to reach Judra for weeks."

"So we're going through the forest and then heading north to Judra along the river?" Chiyo said, biting her lip. "Do you have some kind of obsession with forests that are filled with monsters?"

"It puts the rhythm in my hand every night," Sora said, shaking his fist up and down. "Just thinking about those Redcaps, with their cute little—"

"You're *disgusting*," Chiyo squeaked. "Those are monsters—*and it's illegal.*"

Sora couldn't help but laugh at her priorities.

"Your red hair and Fubuki's yellow eyes are going to give us away to anyone that's seen or heard the story," Sora said, "So we can't really go any further than Judra until the two of you can cast—and hopefully maintain—the *Colourant* spell."

"That's the one you used on me in Satu," Chiyo said, hesitating. "Can we even learn something like that in a few weeks?"

Sora blew a breath out of his nose—if he ever ended up back in Satu, he was going to find Wartol and kick the man's ass. They were far enough from the river now that nobody was going to pick up on their scent and far enough west that there shouldn't have been anyone for miles. He came to a stop next in the grassy clearing ahead of them.

"Hang your clothes up somewhere, and then come sit down," Sora said, struggling to peel his wet, clinging shirt off. "This is going to be your first lesson."

"I can't take them off," Chiyo said, flustered.

"Then you'll be walking in wet clothes for the rest of the day and sleeping in them at night," Sora said, unbothered. "I'll leave that choice up to you."

He started working on his boots, shaking them out as best he could before dropping his pants to his ankles. Chiyo spun around to face the other way, red-faced and stuttering. Fubuki watched him undress without even pretending that she wasn't looking. Sora squeezed out his clothing before hanging them up on a low-hanging branch. Once he was unburdened, he moved to sit in the middle of the clearing, crossing his legs beneath him. Fubuki unlatched the cloak, placed it carefully beside Sora's clothing before moving to join him. Chiyo added her own cloak to the branch and kicked off her shoes, but she couldn't bring herself to do any more than that.

"This is embarrassing," Chiyo mumbled, sitting across from them both. "Can't you cover yourself?"

Sora had spent half of his life bathing in the river and in front of everyone who walked by, so any shame he may have once had about being naked was long since eroded. He said nothing to her request, waiting for them both to settle down, and then cleared his throat.

"Mana exists everywhere, in trees, rocks, blades of grass, rivers, insects, fish, people, monsters, goblins," Sora said, prefacing the lesson with the fundamental truth of magic. "The air around you, the breath in your lungs, the blood in your veins, even your hair, mana lives inside of everything."

Sora held his hand out between them, palm facing downwards, fingers splayed.

"It's surrounding my hand right now," Sora said, "Can either of you feel it? See it? Hear it?"

"No," Fubuki murmured.

"I can't either," Chiyo admitted.

"Most can't sense ambient mana without direction, so let's start with that," Sora said, "Hold your hand out like this, and then close your eyes."

Sora reached out and pressed the tip of his index finger against the back of their hands. Chiyo peeked for a moment before quickly closing her eyes again. He concentrated enough unshaped mana into his fingers that it began to glow with diffuse blue light.

"Mana without shape is magic without purpose; to cast a spell, you shape the mana into a pattern," Sora said, closing his eyes. "Patterns direct the mana towards an effect, and there can be multiple layers to a pattern, each of which adds a new level of complexity to it. The more complicated the pattern, the more difficult the spell is to master."

Sora sent the mana in his finger down through the back of their hands, and both of them shifted slightly. He spun the mana into a tight circle, the size of a coin in the centre of their palms; their own internal mana began to accumulate around the edges of it.

"There are more patterns possible than stars in the sky, and only a fraction of them have been written or studied," Sora said, adding a line through the middle of each circle. "Memorisation, willpower and practice. Learn the pattern, bend your mana into the correct shape, and then repeat it until you can't sleep without dreaming about it—can you feel it?"

"Yes," Chiyo said, swallowing.

"Warmth," Fubuki murmured.

Sora twisted his mana into the pattern he'd spent so much time practising.

"Mana has no intent, it had no form, it's not alive, nor sentient, nor does it possess any will. In large enough quantities, and with unclear direction, it will begin to cause odd occurrences, change things, warping them in strange ways." Sora said, feeling as their mana slowly sealed his own away within a hardened shell. "Every species has variances in how they interact with it, and every individual has a different shade of mana, but from an outside perspective, they are entirely indistinguishable unless you know what to look for."

Sora began to withdraw, letting his mana fade away within the shells, their focus and expectation keeping the pattern firmly in place without even realising that he was no longer the one sustaining it.

"A source of foreign mana injected into your body will excite the mana within you. It acts as a force that draws the two together. Like moss growing on a rock, the moss accumulates, slowly surrounding it," Sora said, settling his hands in his lap. "The pattern is the structure of the spell and where the effect is trapped. The command phrase is an association for your mind to lock onto and a way for the spell to find release."

Sora could feel it now, the spell growing brighter as more of their mana began filling in the gaps in the shell.

"There are many classifications of spells, but they are all categories thousands of mages have constructed to make sense of something we don't fully understand; they don't map onto the world in any physical way," Sora said, leaning back onto his hands. "A *healing* spell is no different from an *elemental* spell, or a *teleportation* spell, or a *binding* spell, or an *exclusionary* spell. The patterns themselves *do* map onto the world, and once you learn enough of them, you'll begin to understand what that really means."

Sora waited a few moments longer, gently touching their hands again to help bring the pattern to completion and making sure each of them had reached the threshold needed to full cast the spell.

"This spell is an *illusionary* spell if you are one for categories. It creates sparks by converting mana into light, but there is no heat or physical pressure attached to it," Sora said, "The pattern, as you've clearly noticed, is shaped oddly like a diamond. The command phrase is *Gleam*—speak it, and then open your eyes."

A shower of white sparks fell from their hands as they spoke the word, falling to the grass and vanishing on contact with it. Sora tracked the mana as the spell ate away at it and felt as the fragile shells they had built shattered. Fubuki looked completely entranced as the last of the sparks fell away—but when he turned back to Chiyo, he found that she was actually crying.

"Congratulations," Sora said, hesitating for a moment. "I'm surprised you both managed to keep it going for so long; most people shock themselves out of it during the middle of their first cast."

"I did this?" Fubuki murrmured.

"You did, and now that you know what it feels like, you'll be able to do it again—eventually," Sora said, "It *will* take a few days for you to develop the necessary focus and control to manage it without a guide, but that's normal too."

"I feel like such a fool," Chiyo managed.

"A fool is someone who doesn't learn from their mistakes, and even a king can be a fool," Sora said, stealing one of Salas' idioms. "You *may* be a fool, but then the question becomes—are you going to *remain* a fool?"

Chiyo shook her head and blew out a frustrated breath when her hair stuck to her still-wet cheeks.

"You're too young to say things like that," Chiyo mumbled. "You need a beard first."

"I *have* a beard," Sora said, offended. "I just—I shaved two days ago."

Chiyo breathed out a laugh at his tone while she did her best to wipe her face clean and then attempted to straighten up a bit.

"Sora," Fubuki murrmured. "How do I practice?"

Sora eyed Chiyo for a moment longer, not quite happy to just let the slight on his facial hair go. He held his hand out again, this time palm up, and both of them copied him immediately until three hands filled the space between them.

"Every movement of your body can be felt within your mind. You know where your arms are when you're not looking." Sora said, glancing between them, "You can feel all of your toes, the movements of your eyes, lips and tongue. This phenomenon is known as—"

"Kinaesthesia," Chiyo said.

"That is correct," Sora admitted, "Now, what happens to that sensation when you're not focusing on those movements?"

Chiyo frowned at the question, turning to stare at her palm for a moment. Fubuki wiggled her fingers about, the goofy motion at odds with the look of intense scrutiny on her face.

"It's still there," Fubuki murmured. "But ignored?"

"Correct," Sora said, nodding. "The same thing happens with your internal mana pool. You are born with it, it lives inside you every moment of your life, but you've spent years, decades, or even centuries without interacting with it at all."

"It's fallen out of focus?" Chiyo asked.

"Yes, so now, the very first thing you need to do is learn how to actively feel your own source of mana—you've already done it once already," Sora said, telling a bald-faced lie. "Close your eyes, sink your *kinaesthesia* down into the centre of your palm, a single patch of skin."

Sora watched as the two of them closed their eyes, faces scrunched up in concentration. Once again, he touched a finger to their palms; this time, he made no attempt to bring his own mana forth.

"You know what my mana feels like," Sora said, speaking quietly to avoid disrupting their focus. "Warmth, gathering in the centre of your palm and pooling against the skin."

He dragged his fingertip into a circle against their skin. They had entirely different reactions; Chiyo shifted slightly, a series of tiny bumps dimpling the skin of her arm as the sensation raced up towards her neck. Fubuki stilled entirely, even as his finger continued drawing the circle without slowing.

"Can you feel it?" Sora asked.

The trick worked immediately—the expectation of finding that same warmth inside their hands clashing against the reality that there was nothing there. The realisation that they weren't able to feel anything triggered some heuristic in the back of their minds. The panic, built from a perceived failure to perform, sharpened their focus to a razor's edge as they strained to discover his energy when it had never been present in the first place. Sora smiled as, within seconds of one another, their own mana started to react to the sudden force of will and direction. Both of them shifted as the warmth bled into their palm, condensing into rough, amorphous blobs of diffused mana.

"Well done," Sora said, sitting back again. "Now, without opening your eyes, move it towards your fingertips."

Chiyo turned her head to the side, her focus dragging her body along for the ride as she tried to wrestle the newly found energy in the direction of her fingertips. Fubuki carefully tilted her hand to one side as if the mana would be drawn downwards by gravity.

"It's a part of you, but mana holds no intrinsic weight. It doesn't act as a liquid either," Sora murmured, "Link it to your kinaesthesia, to your willpower. It's yours to control, to move, to form. *Your* intent is the only desire mana has to fulfil."

He watched them for a few minutes as they slowly figured out how to actually direct the mana, binding it to that sense of kinetic understanding that came so naturally to living beings. Building up a certain level of expectation was what made it work, and eventually, that expectation would simply become a reality in which they willed it, and the mana would bend. It was a small step in the journey of a mage, but they'd taken it, and their education had begun.

#

Sora drew the skewered fish out of the roiling orange orb of the *Flamestay* spell. He checked it for a moment before sighing and holding it back over the flame. Chiyo checked her own fish a moment later, looking a bit queasy at the still *fish-shaped* meal. She'd had the same re-action to the rabbits they'd cooked. Sora was willing to guess that most of the Noble class had probably never seen what most of the things looked like before they'd eaten. Or if they had, hadn't managed to link the image of a living creature with the finely butchered, seasoned, and prepared piece of meat on their plates. Fubuki's own fish hadn't been checked a single time; instead, her attention was still focused on her palm as she practised condensing mana there.

"Fubuki," Sora said, holding out his hand. "Pass me your food. It's going to burn like that."

Fubuki glanced up and then pulled the skewered fish out of the fire before carefully handing it over. Sora took it, checking how unevenly she had cooked it, before turning it over to address the mistake.

"Sora?" Chiyo asked. "How close are we to the plains?"

"Shouldn't you be the one telling me that, map-for-brains?" Sora wondered.

"I can't tell anything about where we are while we're stuck in this stupid forest," Chiyo said, breathing out in frustration at the nickname. "How long did we even travel today? Six hours?"

"Eight, although that includes the hour of swimming," Sora said, checking the skewers again. "We should be two or three hours away from the plains; we're leaving early again, three in the morning."

"How do people even travel between the towns by foot?" Chiyo murmured, rubbing at her feet. "I'm covered in blisters again."

"They wear *actual* boots, for one thing, and they don't roll out of bed every morning to have their asses powdered by the maids," Sora said, nodding towards the pair of cloth boots. "Spend enough time walking around, and you'll develop tougher feet."

"Nobody has ever *powdered* my ass," Chiyo said, flustered. "That's not a thing *anybody* does."

"If you say so," Sora said, tilting his head to make his disbelief known to her. "Come over here, and I'll fix them up for you."

Chiyo, unwilling to actually stand up, crawled over to sit beside him. Sora took a moment to make sure the fish was cooked before clearing his throat. Fubuki looked up at the noise, and he held the skewer out to her.

"Eat now, practice after," Sora said, handing it off to her. "Watch out for the bones, okay?"

"Okay," Fubuki said.

He took a bite of his own fish and bullied Chiyo into holding onto it for him. Then he pulled her feet up onto his legs.

"*Meldflesh*," Sora murmured.

"Gosh, it feels so nice," Chiyo murmured, shifting a bit at the feeling of his spell. "How did you get so good at healing?"

"Are you really in a position to evaluate how good a mage is after you dribbled out a few sparks with that limp wrist of yours?" Sora said, amused. "What makes you think I'm particularly good at it?"

"That's not what I meant, and you know it," Chiyo said, flushing at the words. "I broke my arm when I was nine, and my father hired a healer to fix it; it took him almost an hour to deal with it, and he used half a dozen different spells to do it."

Chiyo eyed her fish skewer for a moment like it was some kind of dangerous beast.

"You fixed both of my legs in that alleyway in just a few minutes, and you only used *two* spells." Chiyo said, "You *were* better than that man was, right?"

Fubuki took a bite out of her fish with far less care than either of them, enough that he could hear several of the bones snap under the force of her teeth—maybe he should have warned the bones about *her*.

Sora hummed at the question, taking his time with her foot, content to look for the variations in how the spell performed.

"That depends on a lot of things," Sora said, "Do you know if he was one of the old guys from the Healers guild?"

"I think so, but it was over a decade ago," Chiyo admitted.

"The old bastards have a very strict system they follow, and it involves using very specific spells for very specific ailments," Sora said, digging his thumbs into the sole of her foot. "They do it that way because when they write up their itemized list at the end, they get to charge you for a dozen different spells instead of one or two."

Chiyo drew in a breath as he started massaging her foot.

"They probably know a dozen spells for each type of problem, even though most of the healing spells have massive amounts of overlap in function," Sora said, "They probably have me beat for variety, but I'm willing to bet that I'm vastly more proficient with the spells I do know then they will ever be."

"Why is that?" Chiyo said, making no attempt to retrieve her foot from his lap. "If they've had decades to learn—you're only young."

Sora scrunched his face up at the words.

"The cost of healing magic is prohibitive for most people, and they share clients amongst the guild, so individually they only heal about three or four people a week," Sora said, annoyed. "I've been sitting in the marketplace for almost a decade at this point, healing people every single day for a price that just about anyone can afford."

"How much do you usually charge?" Chiyo murmured.

"One silver per client," Sora said, "Although, I've gotten to know most of the streetwalkers pretty well over the years, and *they* liked to pay me by—"

Chiyo gave a startled cry at the sudden, dangerous direction of the conversation and attempted to tear her foot out of his grasp—he let her go without a fight, the job long since finished.

"I've got a *lot* more practice doing it than anyone at the guild," Sora said, waiting for a beat. "I'm pretty practised at healing too."

Chiyo glared at him from her place on the ground, red-faced and the foot he'd been massaging cradled in her hand.

"You're *disgusting*," Chiyo managed.

Sora laughed again, and then to avoid sending her into another embarrassing rage that would only end with him fending off a flurry of smacks, he left it well enough alone.

"Sora," Fubuki murmured.

The fish on her skewer was more or less gone now; an inch of the spine still remained below the head, the rest devoured entirely—she was far more game than he was, or hungry, he supposed. He lifted his gaze to her face and found her watching him. Sora waited for a moment to see if she would follow his name up with anything, but she didn't.

"Yes?" Sora asked.

"What is the dragon's marble?" Fubuki asked.

Sora took another bite of his fish, judging it for a moment to see if there was anything substantial left of it to eat, and then tossed it into the ball of fire. He wiped his mouth clean with the back of his hand.

"I was wondering when you were going to ask," Sora admitted. "The Dragon's Marble is an object spoken of in a nameless myth from Malnia. The only version of it that has been discovered was carved into a stone tablet and written in a language nobody speaks anymore. It was purchased from a trader in *Hondan*, of all places, and then brought back here to be stashed away in the Great Satu Library."

"Traders carrying it around the continent," Chiyo said, hesitantly rejoining the conversation after she'd recovered. "How did you read it if nobody speaks the language?"

"The written language shows up piecemeal quite a bit in old Malnia books," Sora offered, "We have a partially completed dictionary in the library, so I used a copy of that to decode the tablet."

"Nobody has done that before?" Chiyo asked.

"If they did, they didn't leave a translation behind for the library," Sora admitted, "Either way, it took me a few months to do, which leaves me to believe that I am the only person alive today who knows what it says—Fubuki, do you want to hear a story?"

Fubuki had been listening patiently as they discussed the origins of the tablet, legs curled up beneath her, but the question brought some real interest to her expression.

"Yes," Fubuki said.

"You're supposed to say *please* when you want something and *thank you* after they deliver it to you," Chiyo said, the lack of manners apparently getting to her. "Yes, please. That would be nice, thank you, or some combination of the two."

"Yes, please," Fubuki murmured. "That would be nice, thank you."

"Perfect," Chiyo said, pleased.

Fubuki eyed her for a moment, a strange expression on her face at the word. Sora pushed himself to his feet and took a few steps back from the fire so he wasn't in direct firelight. He ran his hands together for a moment, mana moving beneath his skin as he prepared himself.

"I'm going to embellish a little bit, but nothing that changes the core components of the story," Sora prefaced, even though they couldn't possibly have known. "This is the story of the Dragon's Marble."

Sora clapped his hands once, twisting together a series of patterns, layering them on top of one another and tuning each of them towards his own ends. He slowed the rate at which they would move, brightened the lumination, and shifted the colours, pushing the pattern into something far beyond what the spell had been designed for. After years of constant practice, the patterns were almost automatic, a natural extension of one another that he barely had to think about, too ingrained to need any kind of preparation. He drew his hands apart, and light burst into existence between them. A full-scale man made of sparks rose to stand in front of him, a monk with stacks of thick bangles surrounding his arms. He wore a necklace of beads, and his eyes burned bright white in the low light.

"*What?*" Chiyo said, startled. "How are you *doing* that?"

Sora made no response to her interruption. Instead, he kept his focus on the dozens of overlapping patterns, making adjustments to animate the man.

"A nameless monk once wandered the land. A man who existed in a time filled with evils but who had *chosen* to be good. He was described by all those he encountered as a saint," Sora said as the monk lifted his hands up into a prayer. "Using his vast magical talents, the monk built homes for the poor, he healed the sick, fed the hungry, uplifted the weak, and disparaged the cruel."

Sora added more patterns to the weave, a flat plane of sparks behind the monk that showed distant scenes. An injured man standing up to walk again, a child receiving bread from the monk, a crowd standing behind the monk as he stood in front of a king whose eyes glowed a sickly orange.

"Eventually, the monk grew old, as all men do, but he did not despair of his fate because he had lived a life of *good*, unmatched by even the most altruistic," Sora said, and the monk moved to kneel on the ground. "He had never committed violence against the weak or taken actions unjust against the strong. He had never once taken a life, but he had saved thousands in turn."

The backdrop changed as he twisted the patterns together until it showed a man with a glowing red hand approaching from the distance. The monk's hair and beard grew long, turning white even as time whittled away at his once-strong frame. The cowled figure eventually reached him, placing the glowing hand on his shoulder just once before it vanished into red sparks. The monk turned to look back, but the figure was already gone, so he returned to his kneeling prayer.

"The monk knew his destination after death because he'd lived a life no man could hope to live, and so at his deathbed, he bowed his head, passing on without regrets," Sora said, and the monk of sparks bowed his head. "In balance, this nameless monk had set an unattainable standard for all others who came after him, but one that all men sought to reach and uphold. Statues, temples, and scriptures were constructed in his honour, by lakes, rivers, and countless villages—a lasting testament to the man who'd sacrificed everything in his life for others."

The backdrop behind the monk slowly changed from whites and yellows, darkening to reds, oranges and rust-browns. Fire surrounded the unaware monk; countless eyes, horns and vicious grins appeared behind him, a repeated pattern of sparks to showcase a place that was as far from paradise as one could imagine.

"So why then—when the nameless monk who had lived a life so deserving of praise lifted his head—did he find himself in hell?" Sora said as the monk lifted his head, an expression of horror on his face. "Tormented by the mockery of its denizens and by the question burning away in his chest, the nameless monk felt something he'd never known in life—he grew to know hate."

The monk of white sparks now held a single red patch where his heart should have sat. The man twisted to his feet in a spin that sent his robes spiralling around him as he turned to face the demons. He stepped into the backdrop and became a part of it, striking a path straight for the fire without fear.

"The nameless monk's capacity for good was only exceeded by his capacity for hate—hate for the demons, hate for how he'd wasted his life, hate for the humans he'd given so much for," Sora murmured, letting the backdrop fall away entirely. "In time, that hate had grown so strong that his body could no longer contain it."

The monk spun back into existence on all fours, the sparks in his chest glowing bright red. The man's body warped, hands turning into claws, wings surging out of his back. The monk was gone now, replaced by a dragon with burning red eyes.

"The hatred for humanity twisted his body into something as far from human as you could imagine. It continued to coalesce in the monster's great chest, growing stronger until an orb of untold power was born—a marble," Sora said, lifting his hands up into the air. "Now untouched by death, the dragon broke free of the trappings of hell, its great wings carrying it back to the human world. It tore the world apart, reshaped the land, and burned the continent with its rage."

The dragon of red sparks flapped its wings and then lunged upwards, bursting into a shower of red that rained down on the three of them.

"Humans fled the destruction, fleeing by way of the rivers, a bastion untouched by the dragon's flame. They passed countless villages, turned to ash, each of them survived only by the stone gaze of soot-covered statues. Eventually, they found safety where three rivers met beneath a great statue of a nameless monk," Sora said, lowering his voice again. "Even then, the dragon's hate proved insurmountable; the great statue sunk into the river, shattered by its claws. The daughter of a butcher stood amidst the ruins of the statue, the last of her family and her village. As punishment for her humanity and her perseverance, the dragon consumed her whole, condemning her to waste away in its belly."

The sparks were drawn back towards his hand, spreading across the ground until a woman stood with a knife in her hand. The dragon grew back slowly, mouth opened above her, a moment of frozen time before the jaws snapped shut around her, consuming her whole. The dragon sat back on its legs, a group of white sparks sliding down its throat before it closed its eyes, content to rest amongst the river of sparks washing past its body.

"She slid down the beast's throat and settled below, in some dark, unknowable place without light, without warmth, without other," Sora said, "In that place, she thought about all she had done, and everywhere she had been—and in those memories, she found a spark of something bright, in a face that had been with her throughout all her life."

The dragon vanished, and a small, sad face appeared in its place, wrought in blue light, surrounded by the dark.

"The statue in her village that she had left behind to burn, the shrine they had taken shelter at after they had fled," Sora said, raising his hand. "The countless ashen villages and the implacable stone gaze that had watched their passing, and even now, in a place that was somewhere further below even *this* dark place, the nameless monk remained, a constant unwavering companion—and a source of hope."

The glowing blue girl stood in the dark and turned her gaze upwards before she vanished. The dragon took her place, the blue sparks sitting in its belly growing bright, ascending somehow, moving towards the glowing red of its core. The dragon spread its wings in outrage as the two conflicting orbs collided, and then the monster exploded. A girl remained with a knife in one hand and a glowing red marble in the other.

"The butcher's daughter found her strength, and with it, she took from the beast its boiling hate," Sora said, "The river carried the nameless dragon away, and the girl, unwilling to carry the creatures suffering with her—tossed the marble into the water, to be watched over by the shattered remains of the unwavering monk."

Sora let the patterns of mana go, the woman vanishing in a few short moments.

"The end," Sora said, clapping his hands together. "Well? What did you think?"

Fubuki just stared at the space where the woman had been, yellow eyes sparkling in the firelight.

"I've been to stage plays with *dozens* of mages working together, and those illusions weren't half as detailed as what you just did with *sparks*," Chiyo said, shaking her head. "How are you this good?"

"There's a *reason* I became a master before I was twenty, you know?" Sora said, dropping back down to sit by the fire. "The connection I have with my mana is far stronger than a normal mage, and my control is a dozen times better because of it."

"Can I do this?" Fubuki murmured.

"Absolutely," Sora said, leaning back on his hands. "Practice every day, focus on how the pattern affects the spell and then experiment to see what kind of shapes you can twist the output into."

"I want to practice," Fubuki said before glancing over at Chiyo. "Please."

#

Three

The morning came quickly, and this time when Sora woke, the aches of the previous day had grown strong enough to warrant trading some mana to return himself back to full capacity. His clothes had been mostly dry before night had even come, and by the time he'd actually gone to retrieve them from the branch, he found them in good shape. When he knelt down beside Chiyo and laid a hand on her shoulder to shake her awake, he found that her shirt was still damp to the touch.

"Chiyo, it's time to go," Sora said, "Are you awake—"

"I'm awake," Chiyo mumbled, sitting up. "Gods, what time is it?"

"Yes," Sora said in answer.

He moved to kneel beside Fubuki and found her watching him, a single eye barely cracked and visible even in the dark. Sora waited for a moment to see if she would say anything, and when she didn't, he completed the motion, gently touching her on the shoulder.

"Fubuki," Sora said, amused. "Your eyes glow in the dark, so I can tell you're awake."

"Oh," Fubuki murmured.

"How long has it been since you've seen your reflection?" Sora wondered.

"One day," Fubuki said.

"I mean in the dark, in a mirror, not the river," Sora managed, scratching his cheek.

"I don't know," Fubuki said.

"Well, you better put that on the list," Sora said, pushing himself to his feet. "Come on, it's time we go."

"What list is that?" Chiyo asked.

Sora stretched his arm down behind his back, pulling at his elbow to try and earn himself a satisfying crack, but instead, all he was left with was a vast disappointment.

"We've got a sheltered noblewoman who's never left Satu before and an Oni who was trapped in a coin for so long that she couldn't even remember that her eyes glowed in the dark," Sora said, summarising it for them. "I'm making a list of things that either of you might want to do before we all die; Fubuki said she liked music, so we should teach her some songs. You want to kill Koshiro, so we'll have to figure out a strategy to make that happen—"

"Sora," Chiyo managed.

"—you both wanted to learn magic. I want to find out if the myths in my book are real. Fubuki needs to see herself in a mirror," Sora said, continuing to list off everything he could think of. "Anything else you two want to do? Kiss a boy? Kiss a *girl*? Bang an ogre? Walk through the Dread Forest of Sagia? I think I'll buy out the entire brothel in Maar and request that all the ladies treat me like King Elric—"

"For *one second*," Chiyo said, blowing a breath out of her nose, "I was tricked into thinking you *weren't* a complete degenerate."

"Hey, it's not like I'm hiding it at all," Sora said, shrugging. "You're just not very observant, map-for-brains."

"Don't call me that," Chiyo said, visibly annoyed.

"Denied," Sora said, "Fubuki, don't forget your cloak."

"*My* cloak?" Fubuki mumbled.

"It's a gift from me to you—congratulations on your first real possession," Sora clarified, "Now, can we go? We've spent *way* too long in this forest, and now that I know what awaits me in Maar—"

"If you finish that sentence," Chiyo warned, "You'll *never* make it to Maar."

"Is this how apprentices act these days?" Sora said, feigning outrage.

"Threatening to kill their masters? Back in my day, noble *girls* had a bit more in the way of manners."

Sora stepped out of the clearing, angling west and settling himself in for what was probably going to be another long, tiring day of walking.

"I'm older than you," Chiyo said, following behind him. "Back in *your* day doesn't even exist."

"What would a sheltered, frilly skirt know about *my* day?" Sora wondered. "You didn't even know where rabbit meat came from."

"I *did* so," Chiyo said, flustered. "I just—"

"I mean, it's right there in the name, isn't it?" Sora interrupted, trying not to smile. "*Rabbit meat.*"

"I'm going to hit you," Chiyo warned.

"Makes me wonder if you've got *anything* going on upstairs other than maps and roads and routes and strategy?" Sora continued, digging the hole as deep as he could manage. "Fubuki, have you ever seen anything like a *Chiyo* before?"

"I have not seen a Chiyo before," Fubuki confessed.

Sure enough, Chiyo took a whack at him in the dark, but he managed to block the better part of it. Sora scrambled ahead, crunching the leaves to death beneath him in his rush.

"It's not *a* Chiyo—and *I'm* not *a* Chiyo." Chiyo managed, giving up on trying to get him. "I'm not an object or some strange species. Gods. It's my *name.*"

"Hey, Fubuki, you ever heard of a *Himura* before?" Sora said, pronouncing the name queerly. "Strangest thing I've ever seen, red-furred, with round powdery cheeks, and it's always running around forests without any knickers on."

"I have not," Fubuki admitted.

Sora had to dive forward again as she tried to kick him between the legs, the near-fatal attack glancing off his thigh.

"It's a joke, a *joke*, damn it—" Sora cried, startled by his close brush with death. "Stop trying to beat me up all the time."

"I don't have round powdery—*anything*," Chiyo strangled out. "Nor do I have *fur.*"

"Himura's keep things tidy downstairs, do they?" Sora said, unable to help himself. "*Unhand* me, you furless beast—I am your *master*."

#

The trees started to thin out around the same time as the sun first rose, which made it a hell of a lot easier to see where they were going. The thick roots that had made it such slow work started to recede back beneath the earth, the distance between each trunk grew larger, filled with healthy green grass, and the trees themselves grew thinner, newer, younger. Then almost before he was ready for it, they stepped out into the sun, the grassy, empty plains stretching ahead of them, with only the rolling hills to block their view.

"*Finally*," Chiyo said, "If I ever see another spiderweb, it's going to be too soon."

"Yeah, won't find *any* of them out here in the grass," Sora said, rolling his eyes. "Snakes, lizards and tanglebears, on the other hand, are going to be everywhere."

"*Snakes?*" Chiyo managed.

"What is a *tanglebear*?" Fubuki murmured.

"A plant warped by mana that looks like a ball of vines, with claws and a big mouth," Sora said, stepping into the long grass. "They breed quickly, but they're generally scared of people, so they shouldn't come near us."

"The snakes?" Chiyo said. "What about them?"

"Snakes are assholes in my experience," Sora admitted, "If you accidentally stand on one, it's absolutely going to bite you—I wouldn't worry about it, though; I can deal with venom."

Chiyo didn't seem nearly as reassured by that as he'd expected. It was kind of amusing to see both of them practically vanish into the grass. Chiyo, as reported by the guard he'd spoken to back in Satu, stood at a respectable five and a half feet, and Fubuki probably topped out at about five-two on her best day. Everything below Fubuki's chin was hidden by the grass, with dark hair and a pair of yellow eyes peeking out. Chiyo's prodigal height had earned her a bit of neck to go with her head. Sora himself was doing a little bit better than both of them, with the grass coming up to just below his shoulders.

"We should be passing by Asdar right now, right?" Chiyo murmured, turning her head to face north. "I can't see it, though."

"You ever been there?" Sora wondered. "Or was I right about you having never left Satu?"

"You were right; I've never really had a reason to leave," Chiyo admitted, closing her eyes for a moment. "Asdar—population of twenty-five-thousand people, built on a bend of the West Twin, they trade mostly with livestock and by-products, sheep, cows, chickens, rabbits. Wool, milk, cheese, eggs—that kind of thing."

"Is that right?" Sora said, tilting his head. "I'd heard they had a lot of cows, but the rest is new to me."

"They do fish as well, but Satu has two sources of its own, so they don't really buy any of it." Chiyo added, "I believe they trade most of the fish to Shal and Alhat, although Satu does as well."

"What about Shal?" Sora wondered. "They're out in the plains; they do livestock as well?"

"They have enough livestock to sustain their own population, and it's been growing larger in recent years, but they aren't in a position to trade it yet." Chiyo said, "Woodwork is their main export; they have some of the best carpenters in Fabah. Most of their resource imports are from Satu."

"How many people?" Sora said, curious if she'd memorized that as well.

"Fourteen thousand," Chiyo said, "Expected to hit twenty in the next ten years."

"That is a lot of humans," Fubuki murmured.

"Technically, it's not *all* humans," Chiyo corrected, "Fifteen per cent of Fabah's overall population is made up of Meld."

"Fabah is eighty-five percent human?" Sora said, having never heard the breakdown before. "What about Hondan?"

"Ninety-three percent human, seven percent Meld," Chiyo rattled off, "That seven percent is almost entirely on the border of Pegia."

"What's the breakdown for Malnia?" Sora challenged.

"Do you actually care, or are you just trying to see if I know the answer?" Chiyo said, eyeing him with suspicion.

"So you *don't* know," Sora said as if he'd caught her in the middle of some foul act. "I knew it—so much for becoming a mapmancer."

"I absolutely do not believe that's a real thing, but for your information, *Sora*," Chiyo said, scrunching her face up. "Malnia is sixty percent human, thirty percent Meld, nine percent Marmaros, and one percent other."

Malnia was a great deal more tolerant than most human-dominated countries; that was certain enough—Chiyo went mad, ripping her cloak off and just about causing his heart to explode from the suddenness. Fubuki vanished into the grass, moving so quickly that he'd only managed to catch the edge of her cloak disappearing into the mess of green as he turned around. Chiyo ripped the hem of her shirt upwards, over the back of her head and then flung it away from her with another shrill cry, attempting to slap at her now naked back. Sora watched, stunned, as she threw herself in the other direction, grabbing him by the arm and attempting to push him towards the shirt.

"*Do something,*" Chiyo squealed, "*Don't just stand there staring at me—*"

Sora managed to tear his eyes away from her tits through a monumental effort of will and then turned to pick up the shirt in an attempt to find out exactly what the hell was going on. A long-limbed spider scuttled out of the bottom of the shirt and up onto his hand. He caught it with his left hand before it could make it further than his forearm. Chiyo squealed again, slipping behind him in an attempt to get away from it—he tossed the writhing insect out into the grass.

"Fuck me," Sora said, heart beating in his chest. "You almost gave me a heart attack."

Sora turned around to face her, lifting the shirt up for her to take, but she swung an arm out at him in her panic, stepping backwards in an attempt to get away from it.

"You didn't even *check* it," Chiyo accused before finally remembering to cover herself. "*Stop staring at my—my—*"

Sora sighed before turning the shirt inside out a few times, making sure nothing else had managed to make its way into the cloth. He made a big show of it to clear whatever threshold she was setting for the check before announcing that it was spider free. Chiyo practically wrenched it out of his hands and rushed to try and get it back on. Fubuki retrieved the discarded cloak and reappeared, staying out of direct sight of Chiyo, like she might start losing it again at any second.

"Sora," Fubuki said, holding the cloak out. "Check."

Sora wondered when he'd been reduced from a master of magic into some kind of spider-detecting wizard. Once he was done with the chore that was *totally* beneath him, he handed it off to Chiyo.

"Listen, we're trying to keep a low profile, you know," Sora said, scratching his cheek. "Screaming girls in fields are going to attract attention, half-naked ones even more so."

"I *know* that," Chiyo managed, wrenching the cloak back over her shoulders. "I was—frightened, that's all."

"Come on then," Sora said, jerking his head. "Let's get moving before that spider comes back for another nibble."

"You're *not* funny," Chiyo insisted.

#

The further they walked, and the more the forest faded into the distance behind them, the further his thoughts spiralled. Without the heart-pounding fear of someone stumbling on them in the forest, his mind felt free enough to wander, and his thoughts continued to come back to the same realisation—he was never going back to Satu. He'd never again drag himself out of the house every day and trudge his way into the market. He'd never slip into the Great Satu Library through brilliance, skill, and by his mastery of avoiding talking to anyone who might stop him. He'd never even find himself tangled up in the silky sheets of a Satu brothel, buried between some girl's legs. The place where he'd spent his entire life was gone now, locked away as a memory he'd never again make real. He'd made some rash decisions in his life, breaking into a master mage's home being one of them, but nothing so big as this—or so many in quick succession. Healing Chiyo instead of turning her in. Taking Fubuki's coin and snapping the bond. Attacking an elite guard in the process of apprehending a criminal. Even after all of that, he'd attached himself to them, offering an apprenticeship to both. An ill-framed assassin with a bounty on her head and an eldretch, ageless creature like Fubuki—to whom teaching magic would have been outright forbidden if anyone had ever bothered to codify such a thing into law. Now here he was, trudging through the itching grass in the quickly fading light, with bugs and snakes, and tanglebears, and oni and frilly skirts—instead of reading through a new tome in his dead Master's bedroom.

"Can we stop?" Chiyo muttered. "I'm sick of walking, and I can barely see anything anymore."

Sora felt his jaw tighten a bit, his deteriorating mood serving to turn the otherwise expected words into knives in his ears.

"We've been at this all day," Chiyo said, taking her frustration out on the grass around her. "My feet are burning, and we haven't stopped to drink anything in hours—"

"*Fine,*" Sora snapped, trying and failing to keep his voice level. "We'll stop here for the night."

Chiyo said nothing in response, and he realised that it was his tone that had robbed her of the desire to speak—unwilling to draw his ire, now that she was aware of it, and that just made him feel worse. Sora planted his hand down on the ground, using it to drop all the way onto his ass with a grunt of effort. He laid down in the grass, bending the tall stalks in the process, which gave him something of a soft surface to lay on. Chiyo laid her cloak down, her movements stilted, wary of his anger and probably wondering how to best deal with it. Fubuki followed her example, laying her own cloak down between the two of them and then sitting down on it right in the middle. Sora kicked his shoes off, the soles pulling painfully at the blisters on his own feet.

"*Meldflesh,*" Sora muttered.

He took his time with it, dealing with his own injuries allowing him a far greater insight into the minor changes going on. There was something about using your own mana to heal yourself that was different than healing others, but he'd never quite managed to map out completely—there was a lack of *resistance*, maybe, the usual magnetic effect on the patient's internal mana non-existent when it was just *him*. It didn't make it easier, not really, just different, and he wasn't sure if he liked it or hated it. Chiyo's unfortunate choice of footwear was soon deposited on the grass beside her cloak with far more care than he'd attempted with his own feet. Even with the relative dark and the distance, he could almost see how bad a state they were in, even compared to his own. Sora bit down on the flash of something that raced up his neck, the realisation that he'd kept them walking for far too long, channelling his bad mood into physical effort worked as a release for him—but he should have been more considerate of the others. Fubuki might have been far more resilient than either of them, but her lack of shoes was still a problem as well. Sora pushed himself up, ignoring the way Fubuki turned her entire body to follow his movements, rotating in place on her cloak until he'd dropped down between her and Chiyo on the grass.

"Feet," Sora said, not quite willing to apologize yet.

Chiyo turned, bending her leg at the knee as she lifted her leg up off the cloak, and he shuffled forwards in the grass, palm catching her calf muscle. He carefully drew the other leg up as well and then placed his hand against the bottom of her feet.

"*Meldflesh*," Sora murmured.

"Oh," Chiyo said, voice shaky. "Thank you."

Sora said nothing, burying his attention in the way his mana interacted with his own, feeling the resistance his own injuries had lacked. Resistance might not have been the right word for it, though, because it was a pull, not a barrier—the attraction between two different sources of mana. He sunk into that same meditative state he often found while working, thumbs pressing into the soles of her foot as he did another unnecessary check for damage. Chiyo dropped back onto her cloak with a sigh, enjoying the process that had already left healing behind, and was now just a foot massage with extra steps. It was far easier to do something like *this* than apologize—partially because he didn't want to say the words, but mostly because she was still the cause of his current suffering. He gave her another minute of the treatment before displacing her legs back onto the cloak and then turning to Fubuki.

"Feet," Sora repeated.

Fubuki watched him for a long time before slipping from her half-curled-up position and carefully placing one of her feet in his lap. Sora lifted her leg up into a better position and then caught her other leg by the calf, adding it to the pile. Fubuki fell back onto her elbows as he pulled her towards him a few more inches, eyes narrowing as she watched him.

"*Meldflesh*," Sora said before stilling. "What?"

The spell lasted all of three seconds before he let it unravel, and he turned to look down at her feet for a moment, unable to understand what he'd just felt. Sora turned his head to the side in an aborted motion, the hundreds of dots intersecting the already faded pattern like an image burned into his mind. Chiyo sat back up, trying to figure out what was going on through the still-fading light.

"Fubuki," Sora said, carefully returning his hands to her feet. "When was the last time you were actually healed?"

"I heal by myself," Fubuki murmured.

"That's not what I asked," Sora said, frowning now. "Another person actually *treating* your wounds, not your natural regeneration pulling you back together."

"That has never happened," Fubuki said.

"*Scour*," Sora said and then flinched as it gave him a much more detailed accounting. "This is—"

His mana began spreading through her skin, searching through the mass and reporting back information about every contaminate present —there were *hundreds* of them in her right leg alone, splinters, chips of ceramic, glass, metal, and foreign bone matter. He shifted his hand up her ankle, shin, and thigh, finding the mess of contaminants pervasive through the entirety of her limb.

"You have fragments of—*everything* inside of you," Sora said, leaning forward and shifting his hand up her chest. "Glass, metal, wood, bone, dirt, sand, thread—every time you get injured and something gets into your body, your regeneration is just sealing it all away inside of you."

Fubuki tilted her head back, chin rising as his hand passed over her throat—her eyes stayed locked on his face the entire time, and he felt her swallow against his palm.

"It's literally everywhere I look," Sora said, feeling a chill run down his spine. "How are you even *moving* right now?"

"I don't understand," Fubuki mumbled.

"Fubuki," Chiyo said, speaking up. "Does it hurt to move?"

"Yes," Fubuki said.

Sora stared at her with incomprehension, unable to understand the nonchalant attitude in regard to something that must have been excruciatingly painful. With every movement she made, her muscles, nerves and tendons were pulling at the debris throughout her body, creating new internal wounds before they'd immediately find themselves sealed back up by the strength of her regeneration.

"Why didn't you *say* something?" Sora managed. "No—the answer is obvious; nobody would have cared if you'd said anything before, so you never *understood* you were supposed to say something now."

Sora placed her feet back down on the cloak and then crawled forward, placing his hand on her shoulder. He pushed her backwards, and without even seeing her move, he found her hand wrapped around his wrist before he'd managed to get her halfway down. Sora pushed her the rest of the way down, ignoring the dangerously tight grip that was more than capable of tearing through metal—Fubuki held on for a moment longer before letting him press her down against the cloak, and he turned until his knees were settled against her hip. He organised her left arm until it was propped up against his thigh and then took hold of her hand.

"This is going to take a long time," Sora said, "So don't move around—*Scour*."

#

For someone who didn't have the supernatural constitution of an oni, this many contaminates would have killed them a hundred times over—infection, internal bleeding and even poisoning, depending on the metal—those were all outcomes that could occur with prolonged exposure to foreign bodies. But the only possible way someone could even find themselves in this position required some kind of in-built regeneration, the mechanism of which *ignored* these kinds of problems entirely. As a kid, before he'd learned to heal anything, he'd gotten a single splinter buried in the heel of his foot after accidentally putting it through someone's roof. It had made walking a painful affair, but it had been buried too far in for him to remove with his fingers. It had ended up getting infected, and what must have been a week later, he'd finally managed to muster up the will to cut it out with a stolen knife. The entire process had been a horrible experience, and he'd never, ever gone roof hopping without shoes again. The fact that Fubuki had been in such a severe state, one that completely eclipsed his singular splinter —for what must have been *hundreds* of years left him feeling almost physically sick.

"Sora," Fubuki said. "I want to use magic."

"So long as you don't move around, you can practice your spell," Sora said, "Just keep it away from where I'm working."

"Okay," Fubuki said.

Chiyo reached over and picked up the fleck of metal that had just emerged from below Fubuki's collarbone, moving it out of the way. Fubuki murmured the command phrase before the pattern had a chance to even reach the threshold for a full cast, and a singular spark of light struck out from her palm. It collided with his thigh and vanished before it could accomplish anything. He pushed it out of his mind, focusing on maintaining the same spell he'd been using for the past hour. The strain was building, and while it wasn't a requirement to keep it running, it helped fight off the monotony of systematically encasing the foreign particles in mana and then bringing them up to the surface. The fact that her natural regeneration was cutting out what was usually the most engaging part of the process just caused it all to feel thoughtless and very unmagiclike. He did find it interesting to see how her regeneration worked, fueled by her internal mana stores in an unconscious, automated process. There were enough similarities present to the *Meldflesh* spell that he was left to wonder if mages hadn't discovered the pattern after studying it.

"*Gleam*," Fubuki said.

Another below-threshold cast and another spark struck upwards, passing under his elbow and fading away on contact with Chiyo's shirt. Chiyo took it as a challenge, aiming her palm at Fubuki, and firing off a spark of her own, but it vanished before it could make it halfway there. Sora focused his attention on the angular scale that was lodged almost directly over her heart, at least two inches tall. It emerged from the top of her left breast, the light of the spell glinting off the surface. Chiyo reached out and took the scale, lifting it up into the air, the battle of the sparks becoming entirely one-sided.

"Is this a Pangolem scale?" Chiyo asked. "Fubuki, why were you fighting something like that?"

"I wasn't," Fubuki murmured.

Sora grunted as the spell finally shattered, the mana vanishing outwards in a pulse of fading light; he shook his hand out at the backlash, vaguely annoyed that he'd been unable to sustain it any longer. He ignored the attention it had generated, taking a moment to stretch his back before bringing his hands back around and recasting the spell. Sora reorientated himself, moving to encase a series of glass fragments lodged in her left breast. He found himself stretching out more threads of mana, now able to attack more contaminates at once than he'd been able to handle before—considering he'd received more practice with the spell in the last hour than the last two years combined, it wasn't exactly surprising. Most people who required this specific spell were like Malko, with a few small contaminants. This, on the other hand, was a wealth of experience that allowed him to discover how the spell functioned with a variety of shapes, sizes, materials and locations—feeling a bit happy about the chance to see all the interactions wasn't appropriate, but he couldn't help his nature.

"How did this get inside you then?" Chiyo said, holding the scale above her face.

"There was a man with green eyes," Fubuki said, shifting down against the cloak. "He was trying to leave. I stopped him."

"You were sent after the rider," Chiyo said, hesitating at the topic now. "What happened to the Pangolem?"

"It fell on me," Fubuki murrmured. "I had to hurt it."

Sora watched as a thin piece of jewellery chain was drawn out of her skin, a tiny latch at one end, the other end sheered off by some unknown force. Fubuki shifted against the cloak again, a common response brought on by mana seeping into areas of the body with large clusters of nerves. *Scour* wasn't anywhere near as bad as *Meldflesh* was—or as *good* if he was bringing it out at the brothel in an attempt to make someone fall in love with him—but it was still an annoyance when it came to getting patients to sit still.

"I know it's uncomfortable, but please try to keep still," Sora said, shifting down to the top of her rib cage. "I don't want to cause more damage pulling this stuff out, even if it does heal afterwards."

Fubuki settled down, either adhering to his request or the location no longer worthy of disturbance. Chiyo lured Fubuki into another war of sparks, the two of them slowly discovering how best to twist the pattern to adjust the firing angle. It was interesting seeing the improvements they were making, the sparks growing more opaque as they became accustomed to recreating the pattern and with less mana bleeding off with each attempt. They still hadn't figured out that they were supposed to wait for the pattern to contain enough mana to clear the threshold. *Gleam* might have been a better starting spell than he'd originally given it credit for. The simple pattern, low cost and lack of cooldown made it easy to practice, while the visible progress worked as motivation for them both to succeed. It had a lot in common with *Colourant,* and anything they learned from it should help them transition. *Colourant* was a far more complicated pattern in every respect, and it wasn't something he'd have expected most Novices to even bother learning, but their current situation made it a priority. As much of a charlatan as Wartol must have been, he chose a good spell at least.

#

Sora watched as the inch-long piece of ceramic passed through the heel of her foot, falling to land on his palm. He let the spell fade away for the last time, the glow vanishing and leaving him in complete darkness—the light of the moon not quite able to find them amongst the too-tall grass. He breathed a quiet sigh of relief, not able to recall a single patient that had taken half as long to treat as this. His hand was shaking, a combination of the stiff position and the hours of continuous channelling. A check of his internal mana told him that he was just under half, his immense familiarity with the spell the largest contributor to his reserves remaining as high as they were. A partially-formed word broke the steady pattern of Chiyo's breathing, too muffled for him to decipher. Fubuki's eyes had vanished hours ago, her ability to sleep at all in her previous state something he'd never be able to understand. Sora winced as he pushed up off his knees, the position leaving him in an oxymoronic combination of numbness and hypersensitivity as the feeling came rushing back. He stumbled a step before he got his leg completely under him and then straightened, head above the grass for the first time in what had to be six or seven hours. The moon was bright in the sky, the field of grass illuminated in a cool blue-green beneath its light. A diffuse orange glow lay to the north, a distant series of specks that could only be the city of Shal; he'd missed it entirely during the day, his eyesight not good enough to pick it up. The proximity of it meant that they were actually pretty well in line with where he'd hoped to be; it also gave him a pretty good idea of how much further they'd need to walk to pass through the grasslands entirely. If they spent about seven hours travelling tomorrow, it would put them in sight of Alhat, and then one more day would get them all the way to the Third Talon River. Sora took one last look at Shal before ducking back down into the grass—he noted that Fubuki was awake now, the two glowing eyes a dead giveaway. Sora dropped down onto the ground, twisting over until he was lying flat on his back, arms spread out around him, the back of his hand sinking into the grass. As lumpy as it was, being able to finally lay down was blissful.

"You know, I just realised we skipped dinner," Sora said, groaning in relief. "Explains why I'm so hungry."

The grass shifted a bit as Fubuki twisted around on her cloak, but he couldn't bring himself to open his eyes.

"We'll have to hunt something down in the morning," Sora said, rocking his head to the side in an attempt to get comfortable. "Snakes, maybe—so we can see the look on Chiyo's face when she has to eat it."

"Sora," Fubuki said.

Sora kind of flapped his arm against the edge of her cloak in an attempt to show that he was listening. Fubuki said nothing to his primitive attempt at communication, apparently not fluent in the language of I-can't-even.

"Fubuki?" Sora prompted.

"It doesn't hurt anymore," Fubuki murmured.

"Good," Sora said, "Next time you get hurt, make sure you tell me—yes?"

"Yes," Fubuki said.

Sora shifted again, and he felt himself sinking lower into the grass in an attempt to reach a slightly higher level of comfort, but he was not really succeeding.

"Sora," Fubuki murrmured. "I want to run."

"Then go run around in the grass or something," Sora managed, fighting his way through a yawn. "Just stay away from the city, and make sure you get *some* sleep tonight—okay?"

"Okay," Fubuki said.

He cracked an eye open as the whisper of grass shifting about passed over him, but Fubuki was already gone.

#

"I've been thinking about what's going to happen when we finally get anywhere with people," Chiyo said, hand up in front of her face to keep something between her and the grass. "Even if you do manage to teach us that hair-changing spell by then, it's not going to be enough."

"You don't think it will work?" Sora wondered.

"They know we are a group of three, two women and a man. They know you can do magic, so they might even be expecting a hair colour change," Chiyo said, frowning. "Besides, my hair colour isn't the only distinctive thing about me."

"As long as you keep your shirt on, they shouldn't catch on," Sora said, amused.

"*That's not what I was talking about*," Chiyo strangled out. "Forget you *ever* saw that."

"I'll never forget for as long as I live," Sora denied before sighing wistfully, "The tits of nobility."

Sora ducked forward into the grass as she tried to kick him up the ass, laughing all the while.

"*Idiot*," Chiyo managed, blowing a burst of air out of her nose. "Fubuki's eye colour, skin colour and horns make it impossible to mistake her for a human."

"Colourant works on things other than hair, but keeping up multiple spells at once is probably asking a bit much from a pair of beginners," Sora admitted, starting up the incline. "The other stuff, though—we're going to need a few extra layers of deception."

"You've already thought about this?" Chiyo asked, watching him.

"Yes—anyone looking for us will be searching for a dishevelled group of three who are trying to lay low," Sora said, "We should flip that around and present ourselves as a group who's not trying to hide."

"Drawing attention to ourselves sounds like a *terrible* idea," Chiyo said, disturbed. "Are you trying to get caught?"

"No, think about it for a minute," Sora said, shaking his head. "They're looking for three fugitives, not a travelling group of—*entertainers*. We dress ourselves up in flamboyant costumes, lean into the role and use it to cover up some of our notable features in the process."

"Entertainers who don't know how to entertain," Chiyo said.

"I'll play the role of a mage who tells stories," Sora said in answer. "You said you could play an instrument, so you're our musician, and Fubuki can be our dancer-slash-acrobat."

"I don't know how to dance," Fubuki murmured.

"I could teach you," Chiyo said, biting the tip of her thumb. "Sora, won't they be suspicious if they know you're a mage?"

"We're in Fabah; there are more mages *here* than anywhere else on the continent."" Sora said, shrugging. "Actually, maybe we should lean into that as well—a travelling band of magic entertainers; they won't be looking for a group of *three* mages."

"It would give us a way to make money as well," Chiyo said, sounding like she was almost on board with it, "Maybe if—I don't have an instrument."

"We can try to pick one up in one of the river cities," Sora said, "Maar is a pretty big place, so they'll probably have something."

"Okay, fine," Chiyo said, "It's a decent plan."

"Sora," Fubuki murrmured. "They will be scared of me."

"You're not scary at all, Fubuki," Sora said, reaching out and tugging on one of her horns. "I'll figure out a way to cover your horns, and they won't even know the difference."

Fubuki stared at him with narrow eyes, and he grinned at the look. The people of Judra, Akh and Maar, would remember a pale girl with glowing yellow eyes and horns—he'd have to come up with something to deal with that. Her skin colour wasn't inhuman on its own; he'd seen plenty of people in the Great Satu Library with a similar complexion. A floppy wizard's hat would work to cover the horns. Sora came to a stop, leaning down to get at the legs of his pants; he took the knife from his belt, cutting through the material until he'd reached just below his knee.

"Why are you destroying your pants?" Chiyo said, almost running into him. "You aren't about to get undressed again, are you?"

"You wish, map-for-brains," Sora said, "I'm making something."

Sora cut the pants leg off under his knee, leaving him entirely lopsided but with a rectangle of cloth to use. He hooked the knife back on his belt before starting forward again; he spread the cloth out in front of him as he walked, trying to figure out the best way to go about it. Those hats had a wide brim, and he'd probably need to use something more rigid to provide some structure to it.

"*Shapecloth*," Sora muttered.

His mana seeped into the fabric, growing thick as it filled every thread and stitch. He dragged his fingers over the edge of the cloth, blurring it together and rounding it off to stop any additional fraying. This was a spell he'd mostly used to fix tears, holes and loose threads, but it was capable of far more than that if you really worked at it. He started bending the edge, drawing it between his thumb and forefinger as he messed with the pattern. The straight edge of the rectangle began to curve, the outer edge growing thicker as he continued pulling it through his pinched fingers. He ran off the edge and then moved back to the starting point, giving it another run-over, increasing the curvature as he went. It took four more runs until he the natural curve of the material was almost a complete circle, and the width of the strip had thinned out considerably. He blended the edges of the cloth together until it was a single piece and then moved his fingers to the inner track of the circle. He rounded the edge off, leaving himself with a thin but decently sized brim.

"We should have kept those rabbit skins." Sora sighed, reaching down to cut off his other pant leg. "Sacrifices must be made."

"You're making a hat?" Chiyo guessed, moving up beside him so she could see better "What are you doing to make the cloth change like that?"

"*Shapecloth*," Sora said, as a command, and in answer. "It's not too far removed from the *Meldflesh* spell you've seen me use, although the pattern is about a thousand times less complicated."

Sora held the inner edge of the brim and the new piece of cloth together with his fingers, blending them together into a single piece. He was left with a long rectangular strip hanging from the centre of the circle, which allowed him to start building the base of the conical portion. The strip of cloth grew steadily shorter as he moved the majority of the mass horizontally. It took about three minutes of effort to complete the circuit, rejoining the cloth into a short conical shape and sealing the edge shut. It was about half the size of what he wanted, as well as being far too thin, so he went ahead and cut off his sleeve at the elbow.

"I'm running out of material to use here." Sora muttered, "Maybe I *am* going to end up naked by the end of this."

The sleeve was enough to build an impressively floppy cone, but the proportions were off, and he ended up having to shift a bunch of the mass downwards, widening the brim and shorting the cone. He stuck the brim in his mouth and cut off his right sleeve. Sora cut it in half, giving himself a longer, thinner strip, and then made an attempt to tie it into a bow shape; when it failed, he threw it in Chiyo's direction before pulling the hat out of his mouth.

"You know how to make one of those bows?" Sora asked, "The big ones—if you get it close enough, I'll be able to fake it."

Chiyo, with access to two hands, and the knowledge of a frilly skirt, managed to twist it into the shape he'd been trying to manage.

"A *master* wizard," Chiyo said, voice dry. "But you don't know how to make a bow?"

"Whatever," Sora muttered.

Sora handed off the wizard's hat to her for a moment, taking the bow out of her hand using his thumb and forefinger to keep it from unravelling. He blended the edges into one another, forcing it to keep its shape, and then moved to widen the width of the bow to better match the floppy nature of the hat. He passed her the ribbon and the bow to hold and then took the hat back. He turned it over, frowned and then set about widening the base of the cone again, realising it would have to clear both of her horns. Once he was pretty happy with the overall shape of it, he changed spells.

"*Stain,*" Sora muttered.

A patch of faded black seeped out across the patchy brown, trailing his thumb as he rubbed it against the material. It took almost fifteen minutes to completely blacken the cloth and then another ten minutes of going over the previous areas to make the entire thing pitch black. He planted the hat on his head, retrieving the bow and ribbon from Chiyo. He blended the ribbon into the back of the bow, ensuring it was a singular piece, and then set about colouring them both. The *Stain* spell turned the accessory a vibrant yellow as his thumb dragged across the material. Once he was finished, he took the hat back off and slipped the circular ribbon over the top, working it down over the conical protrusion. He spoke the command phrase—

"Not *there*," Chiyo said, reaching out and snagging his wrist. "Down, *down*—"

"What?" Sora squawked. "It looks fine."

"It's *not* fine," Chiyo fussed. "Turn it to the side as well; it looks silly right in the middle—"

"Just—" Sora tried, "Just put it in the correct place then, you damn frilly skirt."

"Don't *call* me that," Chiyo muttered.

Sora almost lost his footing, too distracted by her attempts to re-orientate the bow that he'd misjudged his next step. He came to a stop, face scrunched up in duress as she fussed with the ribbon until it was exactly the way she thought it should sit.

"Are you done?" Sora said, squinting at her.

"Yes," Chiyo said, folding her arms across her chest. "I'm done."

Sora blew a breath out of his nose and then finished blending the ribbon onto the hat, leaving it as a singular piece. He gave it another once over, making sure he hadn't missed anything and then gave it a test flap in the air—impressively floppy. Sora turned around and then dropped his gaze in an attempt to find the third member of their group, but she was entirely missing.

"Fubuki," Sora said, "Come back here for a minute."

Fubuki's head emerged from the grass ahead of them quickly enough that she must have been standing there the entire time. Sora twisted the hat around and plopped it down onto her head, the slightly off-centre ribbon causing him to squint—but it worked as intended, the brim of the hat low enough on her forehead to keep her horns entirely out of sight.

"Now we just need to figure out something for your eyes," Sora said, "At least until you can handle that part yourself."

Fubuki reached up to touch the thing on her head before lifting it up to look at it.

"Fubuki could pretend to be blind?" Chiyo said.

"A fugitive oni, masquerading as a blind apprentice?" Sora said, impressed. "That's almost worthy of being a story itself—a blindfold is easy enough to make."

Fubuki seemed far more enraptured by the floppy hat than by the current discussion, now in the process of turning the object around in her hands.

"One of us would have to guide her around, but that takes care of most of her features." Chiyo said, "Black hair is pretty common, and the pale skin could be explained away as not getting the chance to go out very often?"

"That leaves you, but two blind apprentices might be pushing it," Sora said, turning his attention back to Chiyo. "Red eyes are pretty uncommon, but your hair stands out far more, especially at a distance—if a bounty hunter is close enough to see your eyes, we've probably got a bigger issue."

"Right," Chiyo said, brushing a lock of hair over her ear. "Can you teach me that spell?"

"The pattern for *Colourant* is an order of magnitude more complicated than the one for *Gleam*," Sora said, shaking his head. "I'll get you started on it when we reach the Third Talon; until then, I suggest you both figure out how to cast and walk—you'll need the practice."

#

Alhat was bigger than he'd imagined, although that might have been some inborn bias after living in a place as large as Satu. He'd heard the disparaging remarks and condescending tone from people when they spoke about the *rural* folk, with their small villages and their simple ways—clearly, most of that had been bullshit. Under cover of the *Falsity* spell and inside the guise of a frail of old man, he'd all but strolled into Alhat without any of the scrutiny he'd expected from the guards manning the gate. Just like he'd expected, there was a trio of terrible sketches pinned up on the board beside the gate. Only one of which actually had a name beneath it—Chiyo Himura, *Attempted Murder of the Royal Family*. Apparently, they hadn't discovered his name when these posters had been first sent out, although he could imagine the second wave would account for that. Instead, it was just a rough picture of his face and a line—Unknown Man, *Aiding Chiyo Himura*. Fubuki's picture was even rougher than his was, with scratchy black lined eyes with slitted pupils and a demonic smile that he'd never seen her wear. In place of her name, the word 'Monster' was written, and beside it, *Attempted Murder of the Royal Family*. Considering he'd revealed Fubuki's species as an Oni to the guard, that would be bound to make an appearance on the second wave. Sora eyed the buildings as he moved down the main stretch, plastering a kind smile on his face as he made eye contact with some of the residents. He spotted the general store and the tailors squashed close enough together that they might well have been the same building. The door opened with a squeaky hinge as he pushed his way inside, and a woman whose hair was only halfway greying slipped up off her stool behind the counter.

"Hello dear," Sora said, giving a trembling attempt at a wave. "Sorry to get you up and about at this hour."

"Business at any hour is good business," The woman said with a smile, "If you're in here now, you must be in something of a hurry."

"I'm afraid so," Sora admitted, "My adult daughter's somehow gone and lost one of her shoes during the trip—absentminded doesn't speak the half of it. Have you got a pair I can browbeat her with?"

"That's a new one, I'll give you that," The woman said, laughing. "I've got plenty, though; my husbands got something of a talent for them."

Sora made his way over to a table in the corner, a selection of travel boots arrayed on top. He picked through them before finding one of the smaller pairs, almost certain he'd have to take them in a bit to fit Fubuki's feet. The woman worked to upsell him to a travel pack and a set of women's clothes—including a travelling cloak that he intended on using himself—in case his daughter managed to lose those as well, and he let her talk him into it because it saved him the effort of coming up with another excuse.

"You wouldn't have a couple of waterskins, would you?" Sora asked, fishing some coins out of his coin pouch. "Probably best to stock up before we leave."

The woman fetched a pair of them for him, and he slipped her a generous tip because it was better she remembered him positively, as a sweet old man rather than anything more—people tended to forget the good experiences far quicker than the bad ones.

"You wouldn't know anyone of the musical inclination?" Sora asked as he packed it all into the new pack. "I've been thinking about trying my hand at something—never too late, you know?"

"That's a harder order to fill, I'd wager," The woman said, humming. "There's a little house right at the end of the street—a young man lives there, and his grandfather used to play this little lute on occasion—not sure if he's one to sell, but can't hurt to ask."

Sora got a better description of the place, thanked the woman, and then made his leave. It wasn't exactly a long walk, but maintaining the slow, plodding pace he'd started with stretched it out a bit. He caught the man as he was coming around the corner and flagged him down before he could completely vanish into his house.

"What's the matter, old timer?" The man said, "You need something?"

"I've been sent here by the lovely woman in the tailor's shop," Sora said, dabbing his hand against his forehead, miming at dealing with the sweat there. "I'm on the lookout for an instrument, and she tells me you once had a grandfather who played."

"That's right," The man said with a grimace. "It's upstairs, taking up space in my closet; the old man would never get rid of it. Suppose I don't have to worry about that anymore—you're going to take it off my hands?"

"I'd very much like to," Sora said, "What'll you take for it, lad?"

#

Sora kept the illusion up until Alhat was far behind him, and the light had rendered him unseeable from the city. Then he turned off the road, and no longer trapped by the expectant pace of a frail old man, he hit himself with a *Haste*. Sora sprinted across the field, covered his face with his hand, and then cut into the grass. He added a *Sense* a moment later, not willing to risk an immediate collision if they'd disregarded his instructions to stay far away from the road. Two hours was a pretty long time for a headstart, but nothing ate up the distance quite like a mana-enhanced run. Fubuki had been stoic in the face of the conversation, but there'd been something about her eyes that had seemed off. Chiyo had been outright suspicious of him and the idea of splitting up. Which had kind of pissed him off at first. She hadn't said it outright, but it was almost like she was expecting him to use this chance to ditch them—like he hadn't just uprooted his entire life to save hers. Either way, he hadn't been willing to let them wait for him right outside of the city—by the road—and for potentially hours at a time. There was enough risk in just his own attempt to enter the city without factoring in the chance of something going wrong. His sprint slowed to a jog; while the *Haste* spell was draining, it was still sustainable—the initial pace he'd set, however, burned through his stamina at a rate he had no chance of maintaining. Having an actual travel pack was a boon and something he should have thought to have Fubuki grab from his home along with his cloak and book. As funny as it had been to splash the chilly water down the front of Chiyo's shirt, the waterskins would allow the other two to access water without him having to feed it to them like little babies. The lute had been a stroke of good fortune, and although it didn't exactly look like it was kept in the best condition, that was something well within his ability to fix. His forearm was starting to sting, the concentrated attack of the grass stalks against his skin a constant annoyance. A white glow caught his eye in the distance, separating into two distinct signatures the closer he got, and when he was perhaps a hundred meters out, the shorter one came to a sudden stop. Sora slowed down on his approach, trying to fight the burn in his lungs with a steady descent, and by the time he was within a dozen meters of them, he was moving at little more than a clumsy walk, the run having left him at odds with his own balance.

"Imagine," Sora managed, planting his hands on his knees. "Leaving your master, behind. No respect."

"You *told* us to leave," Chiyo accused, but she sounded a bit relieved. "I literally argued with you about it."

"Don't correct me," Sora breathed, "When I'm making fun of you."

Sora made an attempt to straighten up and then decided there was no point in bothering. Instead, he dropped down onto the ground and unshouldered the pack, bringing it around to sit on the ground in front of him. Sora undid the strap and pulled the beaten-up Lute out of the pack, holding it up for her.

"You found one?" Chiyo said, a bit taken aback. "I—thank you."

Sora dug out the pair of boots, the set of clothing, and the two waterskins.

"It's not in the best condition, but it makes noise when you smack it," Sora said, waving her off. "Fubuki, these are yours—they might be a bit big, but I'll deal with that later."

Sora dumped the clothing and the boots into Fubuki's arms and then turned his attention to the waterskins.

"You're not supposed to *smack* it," Chiyo said, indignant.

Sora wedged one of the waterskins between his feet, standing it upright before uncorking the cap and angling his hands above it.

"*Flow,*" Sora murmured.

He grimaced as some of the water splashed into his left boot, adjusting his hands until the water was trickling into the opening.

"Let me help you," Chiyo said, moving to assist Fubuki with the bundle of cloth in her hand. "Take your cloak off—the hat too, please."

It was a bit annoying to get the thing completely full, but he managed to make it work, corking it again and then moving on to the next one. He glanced up during the process, watching as Chiyo pulled the shirt down over Fubuki's body and trapped her arms against her side in the process. The cloth caught on her horns, leaving her glowing yellow eyes staring out from the neck hole like some kind of misshapen, supernatural tortoise. Sora corked the second waterskin, dropped it beside the other one, and then drank some of the water from his own hands, the cool liquid passing down his dry throat.

"That's better," Sora sighed, "The waterskins are for you two; if you run out, just tell me, and I'll fill them up again."

"Thank you," Chiyo said, squinting down in an attempt to see it in the fading light. "Are we going to keep walking tonight? We're still pretty close to Alhat."

"Two more hours, just to be safe," Sora said, leaning back on his hands. "That puts us in a good position to make it to the Third Talon by midday tomorrow—as long as we start moving pretty early."

"Right," Chiyo said, trying to thread Fubuki's arms through the sleeves. "Did you see any bounties?"

The sleeves were too long, by about two inches, leaving her to roll them up to her wrists to allow her hands to settle all the way through—Fubuki stood there, hands kind of limp and without much of an idea on what to do as Chiyo had her way with her.

"All three of us have them," Sora groaned, "They aren't the best, but they were clearly set out as a rush job—the next ones will probably get sent out within a few days."

"How much did they put on us?" Chiyo asked.

"Five hundred gold each for you two if alive, three hundred if dead," Sora said, finally starting to feel like his heart wasn't pushing its way out of his chest. "Mine was only two hundred gold, dead or alive—that will probably go up after they figure out I'm the one who knocked out that guard."

"That is *not* good," Chiyo said, a bit shaky. "Finding even *one* of us is enough to raise an entire family into nobility—the moment anyone has the slightest idea of who we are, they'll turn us in."

"People would have turned us in even if the bounty was one gold, Chiyo," Sora said, "Nothing has changed, and there is no point in tying yourself up in knots over it—unless you're one of *those* girls, in which case I better go back to Alhat and pick up some rope."

"That's—you're *disgusting*," Chiyo managed, turning on him. "Can't you be serious for *one* minute?"

Sora covered his face as she tried to whack him with Fubuki's pants and found himself smiling—better she was angry at him than on the verge of breaking down again. Fubuki's left sleeve dangled in the air, and she looked like she was struggling to come to terms with the entire situation.

#

Four

The distant treeline continued to steadily grow as he approached, rising up into the air, and in turn, the towering grass started to thin out, the two forces in a constant battle for nutrients. They were well and truly in the wild now, the nearest city was Alhat, and that was at least a day's travel back in the other direction.

"No mother in the picture?" Sora asked.

"My mother died when I was very young, and I have no real memories of her," Chiyo admitted, hand held out at her side, bending the grass as they walked. "My father never really talked about her either—we had a painting in the dining room, and if it was in any way accurate, she was very beautiful."

"Who'd the red hair come from?" Sora wondered.

"My father," Chiyo said, "Have you really never heard of him?"

"I don't know what to tell you," Sora admitted, "Your type rarely ever came down to interact with us common folk, and I didn't have a habit of seeking them out either."

"By your own depiction, you spent a lot of time at the library," Chiyo said, turning to look at him, "That's certainly in my *types* territory."

"Your dad wasn't a mage, though, or you wouldn't have fallen for Wartol's bullshit," Sora said, rolling his eyes. "So he wouldn't have been in the library, would he, genius? Other than the odd painting, I've never even seen what the royal family looks like."

"That can't be the norm," Chiyo said, baffled. "What about during the assemblies and the speeches?"

"Why the hell would I go to something like that?" Sora said, just as confused. "Some old guy telling us we're going to be paying more just to eat? I'll find out when I buy something."

"The King—it's far more than just *that*," Chiyo spluttered, "It's about morale and keeping good relations with his constituents."

"From up on a balcony, where half of us can't even see the guy?" Sora said, frowning. "If he wanted good relations with anyone, he should be coming down from his castle and actually talking with us like we're people."

"That's absurd," Chiyo said, "He'd be putting himself in grave danger; *anyone* could make an attempt on his life."

"He's got dozens of elite guards following him around, and even *one* of the *kingsguards* is enough to destroy just about anyone that approached him," Sora said, hands folded behind his head as he walked. "I don't know what you frilly skirts have convinced yourselves of up there, but the royal family is just too distant for anyone bottom side to care about."

"I refuse to believe that," Chiyo said, crossing her arms under her breasts. "*Did you just—*"

"I've seen a great treasure, but it is protected by a powerful barrier," Sora said, peeling his gaze away from her shirt. "If I wish to catch another peek, I must keep vigilant."

Chiyo turned her nose up with a huff and returned to facing forward.

"Sora," Fubuki murmured, emerging from the grass beside them. "What lies beyond the barrier?"

"Fubuki," Chiyo said, scrunching her face up, "Don't encourage him."

"Goodbye, grasslands," Sora said, reaching out to run his hand across the tree. "I hope you're both ready to deal with spiderwebs again because it's forestry from here on out."

"Fantastic," Chiyo muttered, "Listen, can we take a break?"

"That's the plan," Sora agreed, unshouldering his pack. "I wanted to stop and give you both some more formal instruction, preferably before we get any closer to Judra."

Sora sat down against the tree, the rough bark poking at him, even through his shirt. Chiyo moved to sit against the exposed root of the same tree, a few feet away, giving her something to lean back against. Fubuki sank down to the ground directly in front of him, legs curled up beside her—the clothing was still hanging off her frame, something he'd have to get around to handling soon.

"Alright," Sora said, shifting against the tree in an attempt to get comfortable, "I want to see how far you've gotten—Chiyo, you go first."

"Right now?" Chiyo said, tucking some of her hair behind her ear. "Should I just—okay, here."

This close, he could feel the pattern forming across her palm, far larger than the one he'd first taught them. Like before, she didn't wait for it to reach the threshold, and when Chiyo spoke the command phrase, a large, bright spark emerged from her palm, moving slowly up into the air; it hovered for a moment before her furrowed brow and then destabilised, vanishing in a burst of light. Chiyo flinched back a bit as it broke apart, startled by the feeling before she glanced up to check his reaction.

"You've made it larger, slowed down its movement, and you almost managed to hold it still for a while there," Sora said, nodding. "That's pretty good for just unstructured practice—spot test; what, specifically, is responsible for making the spark larger?"

Chiyo's bright smile turned to concentration, her lip caught between her teeth as she considered the question.

"Is it the size of the pattern?" Chiyo said, sounding a bit hesitant. "The bigger it is, the brighter it becomes?"

"That's a common answer, but it's not correct; the size of the pattern actually has nothing to do with how a spell functions," Sora said, leaning forward a bit. "You could technically form a pattern the size of a pinhead, and it would function just the same as one the size of a lake."

"Oh," Chiyo said, staring down at her palm. "I kept making it bigger, and it kept getting brighter."

"That's a result of the density of the mana in specific locations of the pattern, and the larger you made the pattern, the more mana you were using to keep it stable," Sora said, "You can generate an increase in density without making it bigger; it's simply a matter of focus—give me your hand for a minute."

Chiyo held her hand out, and he placed his hand underneath her own, palm upwards.

"Form the pattern, but don't cast the spell," Sora directed, "Smaller, by half. Now, direct more mana into the pattern without increasing its size."

Chiyo's lip continued to receive its unjust punishment as she sucked it further into the grasp of her teeth. Sora glanced up for a moment as Fubuki leaned forward, eyes locked on their hands like she might be able to see what was happening if only she got close enough.

"I can't," Chiyo swallowed, brushing her hair back behind her ear as it fell in front of her eyes. "I don't know how to do what you want me to—"

"Chiyo, it's alright if you don't have everything worked out right away," Sora said, smiling at the edge of worry in her voice. "Relax, and close your eyes."

Chiyo met his gaze for a moment before glancing away and then finally closing her eyes. Sora lifted his other hand up, moving to place both of his thumbs against her palm as he held her hand between them.

"I told you once before that mana is directionless, and the only will it has, is what you give it," Sora said, brushing his right thumb from her wrist to the middle of the palm where the pattern remained. "A lot of mages use focusing or visualisation exercises at first, in the same way, that the command phrase works."

Sora continued drawing his thumb in the same line, wrist to palm, over and over.

"I want you to imagine a well, that big fancy one built up in the frilly-skirts layer of Satu," Sora said, feeling her hand begin to shift slightly with each short stroke. "There's always water in the well, even if it's usually too far down to see it—whenever you want a drink, you draw the bucket up, and there it is, pure, cool and clean."

Chiyo's thumb and index finger curled around his thumb as he drew it across her palm, probably unaware of what she was doing. The pattern remained in place, the task not yet thoughtless, and the larger portion of her attention spent holding it together.

"The well is your internal mana, and the bucket is your willpower, pulling out small portions of it when you need it," Sora said, eyeing the smattering of small bumps that were rolling up her wrist and disappearing beneath her sleeve. "Right now, the bucket only has a few inches of water in the bottom, but that's not enough to clench your thirst, Chiyo—you need more."

The repetition of the movement and the symbolism had already connected in her mind, a tiny stream of mana rolling down her arm, following the motions of his thumb. The pattern grew brighter to his senses, barely a shade at a time, as more of the Mana she was pulling on condensed within the structure of the spell. Her lip stretched, skin pulled over the teeth that were hidden inside, and her grip on his thumb grew tight.

"There are specific points in a pattern that affects the output, but right now, you're hitting everything at once at the same general level," Sora said, carefully untangling her hand from his own until her palm was facing up again. "It's a balancing act, a maintaining of split focus, and you'll eventually reach the point where you can hold a pattern and moderate how the mana is distributed, but you're not quite there yet."

Sora pulled his hands back and lifted his leg to rest his arm against his knee—he glanced over at Fubuki as she shifted, apparently startled by the movement.

"What both you and Fubuki have been doing during the last few days is a partial cast, which is casting the spell without reaching the minimum threshold of mana. That's why you're only getting singular sparks and why the spell sometimes hits you with some backlash," Sora said, voice quiet to avoid disturbing her. "The first time when I was assisting you both, you generated enough mana for the spell to function as intended. The technical term for this is a full cast, and you've just reached the threshold for that—open your eyes."

Chiyo slowly opened her eyes, eyelids heavy as she studied the palm of her hand.

"*Gleam,*" Chiyo murmured.

A shower of sparks erupted from her hand, rising up into the air and falling around them, the mana within the spell keeping it running for almost five seconds before it finally faded away. Chiyo stared at her hand for a long time until Sora spoke up, breaking the spell of silence that had taken over.

"A full cast doesn't mean you've mastered a spell, despite what some masters will tell you—and it's why I didn't stop you from partial casting," Sora said, clearing his throat. "Those little changes, the size of individual sparks, the rate at which they move, the shape of them, the amount, the opacity—there's a hundred different things you'll never figure out unless you experiment."

"I think I understand," Chiyo said, "What should I do now?"

"The biggest issue for anyone starting out is how much attention you have. If eighty percent of your attention is going towards holding the pattern, you've barely got anything left to direct mana into it and absolutely nothing left to experiment with," Sora said, "Practice directing mana into the pattern until you reach the threshold, and then let it dissipate without casting—you've probably only got a dozen or so full casts in you right now, and then you'll put yourself to sleep when you waste all your Mana."

"Okay, that makes sense," Chiyo said, carefully massaging her palm with her thumb. "Thank you, Sora."

"Sure," Sora said before turning to where Fubuki sitting. "Your turn, Fubuki—show me what you've got."

Fubuki shifted forward until she was directly in front of him and then lifted her hand up into the air. The pattern traced itself into existence in the centre of her palm, a few sizes smaller than the last time he'd felt it—it was clear that she'd been listening closely to the prior instruction. Fubuki attempted to send an unsteady mass of mana towards the pattern, doing her best to recreate the lesson, but it kept on diffusing before it got past her wrist. Sora reached forward to cradle her hand and then placed two fingers against her wrist where the mana was the most unsteady. He drew his fingers down her wrist, across her palm and to the pattern, and as Fubuki's attention was drawn to the sensation, her mana reacted. It tightened, attaching itself to the sensation and using it to refine the channel.

"Close your eyes," Sora said.

Fubuki closed her eyes, this time without any of the hesitance he'd seen in her before—he took that as a good sign. He kept up the contact, fingers drawing a pathway for her to build up her focus, and he felt the mana pooling around the pattern, loose, unformed.

"What are you thinking about right now?" Sora asked.

"Water," Fubuki murmured. "Swimming."

"Imagine you're back in the river, standing right in the middle as the water sweeps past you," Sora said, speaking quietly. "Sink your hand below the water, just enough for it to pool in the palm of your hand."

He watched as Fubuki's fingers curled, spreading out ever so slightly.

"The water in your palm is still part of the river, without form, a mass of potential but no direction," Sora said, drawing his fingers towards the centre of her palm and following the lines of the pattern. "The water in your hand is moving now, coiling into a familiar shape; you lift your hand from the river—what do you see?"

"A diamond made of water," Fubuki murmured.

"It's small, but it wants to be more than it is," Sora said, tracing the pattern. "Take more water from the river."

The fingers of her hand shifted again, her knuckles sinking down into his palm, and he could almost imagine her hand dipping below the waterline. A moment later, the pattern began to brighten, the unformed Mana pooling in her palm drawn into the pattern, crystalising into the form she was envisioning. Sora carefully withdrew his hand, leaving her fingers grasping at something he couldn't see.

"You're over the threshold, Fubuki," Sora said, "Open your eyes."

Fubuki followed his direction, eyes bright as she stared at her hand with a startling intensity.

"*Gleam*," Fubuki murmured.

The shower of sparks cascaded down around them, filling the air with dazzling lights—but even that couldn't quite mask the wonder in her eyes.

#

"Wouldn't the people of Judra have hunted them all down by now?" Chiyo asked. "I can't imagine why they'd leave goblins or ogres to run free."

"We're too far south for Judra to bother with," Sora admitted. "There's also no way a village that small has someone capable of fighting an ogre."

"Can't we start heading north *now*?" Chiyo argued, "Do we have to reach the river at all?"

"You've seen what the Third Talon looks like, right?" Sora said, glancing back at her. "We start going north now; we might miss Judra entirely."

"Show me that map again," Chiyo demanded, holding her hand out to Fubuki. "There's no way we'd miss it."

"Careful, Fubuki," Sora said, "Map-for-brains is getting hungry, and she might try to eat the book to replenish her fading powers."

Fubuki pulled her cloak shut, concealing the book she was carrying beneath it. Chiyo gave her a *look* to express just how betrayed she felt and then folded her arms across her chest.

"I don't *eat* maps, Fubuki," Chiyo mumbled. "You're both being so mean."

Fubuki seemed to have a moment of crisis, stuck between protecting the book from becoming the next meal in Chiyo's ever-growing hunger for maps and the red-haired woman's affected pout. Fubuki eventually gave in and carefully handed the book over.

"Thank you," Chiyo said, "Let's see—we entered the forest here about four hours ago."

Fubuki moved to see the map, visibly curious about seeing how Chiyo interacted with it. Sora slowed down to allow for Chiyo's distracted pace to keep them within a dozen meters of him.

"We're right at a bend, aren't we? That's why we haven't reached the river yet," Chiyo frowned. "It's probably another hour at most, then we'll be following the curve of the river—Judra is on the outer curve."

Sora nodded along with her interpretation.

"That gives us two days of walking along the river before we reach it," Chiyo said. "We could head directly north right now and be there in one day."

"You think the people of Judra are going to let a *Himura* walk into town, just like that?" Sora said, pronouncing her name like it belonged to some kind of strange creature. "Furless or not, you haven't even learned *Colourant* yet."

"I don't have—my red *hair* won't matter to them," Chiyo said, scrunching her face up at the teasing. "They won't have the bounties yet; you said it yourself."

"It will end with us leaving a trail for the bounty hunters to follow," Sora said, shaking his head. "The moment one of them steps into Judra, weeks or a month from now, they'll know which way we came from and where we went."

"Is two days even enough to teach it to me?" Chiyo said.

"Probably not, but you'll have a good foundation to build on by the time we get there, and I'll be able to keep it up for you so long as you stay in close contact with me." Sora admitted. "I'll pay for a room for us to stay in, and you can practice inside, out of view of the people who live there."

"Two more days in the wilderness," Chiyo muttered, kicking at the ground. "God, I hate this—

It's unbearable."

"Yeah, well, I'm not too fond of it either," Sora said, doing his best to bury his annoyance. "But this is our reality now."

"That's not—" Chiyo managed before cutting herself off. "I didn't mean it like that."

The group dropped into an uncomfortable silence after that, with only the sound of leaves crunching underfoot to mark their passing. Fubuki looked between them, not immune or unaware of the tension that now gripped them.

"Sora," Fubuki murmured some time later. "Is the dragon's marble real?"

The question knocked him out of his spiralling thoughts, and he glanced back for a moment, the book now sitting in her hands once more. Chiyo trudged along behind her, eyes on the detritus covering the ground.

"Define *real*," Sora said rhetorically. "The tale is certainly written on a real stone tablet, and it references several real places that actually exist in the physical world."

Sora snapped another branch off, clearing their path forward.

"There's no real evidence to suggest that dragons have ever existed, or heaven and hell, for that matter." Sora added, "It's entirely possible that the entire thing is made up, I suppose."

"If none of it is real, why are we going to look for it?" Chiyo mumbled.

"There's always an element of truth in stories like this, even if it isn't what you first thought," Sora said, eyes ahead of him. "Did either of you ever hear about the Chained City?"

"No," Fubuki murrmured.

"It's an old story about a city of ancient people who lived in the ocean," Chiyo said, lifting her gaze. "They all chained themselves to rocks to stop themselves from floating away with the current."

"You've really read a lot, haven't you?" Sora said as an olive branch. "Not many people know that one."

"It was a story my father used to tell me when I was a child," Chiyo said, rising out of the ashes of their most recent clash. "A hero set out from the Chained City by order of the king to find and slay a monstrous beast that was prophesied to swallow the city. He managed the task, but his chain was broken during the battle, and he was washed away, never to return."

"A monster?" Fubuki murrmured.

"A gigantic turtle, covered in spires of coral and dripping in broken chains," Chiyo said, smiling at the interest. "It was twice as big as Hondan—at least."

"The country from the map?" Fubuki said, a bit startled. "It's too big."

"That's the one," Sora said, amused. "Chiyo—what did you think about it the first time you heard it?"

"I was scared," Chiyo admitted, brushing a lock of hair over her ear. "It gave me nightmares for a while."

"Bedwetter," Sora accused.

"*Shut up*," Chiyo said, flushing. "I was *six* years old."

Sora smirked as she fanned at her face, an attempt to defeat her embarrassment.

"What did you think about the *setting* of the story?" Sora said, redirecting her. "A city at the bottom of the ocean, people chaining themselves down to avoid floating away, a king sending a hero out on a journey, a monstrous turtle—well?"

"I suppose I didn't really question it at the time," Chiyo said, "It was all internally consistent with the story, I guess."

"What if I told you there *was* a Chained City?" Sora said, turning his head enough to get an eye on her. "That it was a real place."

"What?" Chiyo asked, tilting her head. "How do you know it's real?"

"Because my Master found it a long time ago, when she was about our age," Sora admitted, "I've seen her research on it."

"How did they survive under the water?" Chiyo said, taken aback. "How were they breathing down there? Or dealing with the pressure or the fact that there wouldn't have been any *light*?"

"Sora," Fubuki murmured, adding to the list of questions, "What about the turtle?"

"Those are all good questions if you were to take *The Story of the Chained City* as unbroken truth," Sora said in answer. "Unfortunately, it isn't really a story about a hero rising to defeat a monster; it's the story of twenty-thousand slaves being left to drown."

There was a terrible silence that followed the words, and Sora nodded to himself.

"South of the Pegia-Hondan border," Sora said, "There is a bay—you know what it's called?"

"Sunken Spire," Chiyo said, thinking about it. "It's entirely impassable by boat, there are too many crags and stone spires reaching up out of the water—the trade route cuts around the entire thing, slows everything down."

"A long, long time ago, before Hondan ever had an Emporer, there was a landmass there. Some horrible shift in the earth caused it to break off from the mainland, and it sunk into the sea, taking an entire civilisation with it." Sora said, hands held out by his sides. "According to Salas, some of the buildings were still intact, although most of it was gone."

Neither of the two said anything in response, so he kept on going.

"The point of this is that although *The Story of the Chained City* had some elements of truth in it; a city at the bottom of the ocean, filled with people who were shackled to the ground," Sora said, "The majority of it was twisted to present a heroic narrative that almost certainly didn't exist—that very much may be the case with *The Dragon's Marble*, and every other story in that book."

"That's horrible," Chiyo managed, still stuck on the tragedy that had befallen them. "They just let all those people drown?"

"I'd wager that most everybody drowned eventually," Sora offered in answer, "The slaves just didn't have the benefit of being able to swim."

#

The trees were thinner here and spread further apart, letting far more light down to the forest floor. There was a slow transition of colour the closer he came to the river, the grass, leaves and bushes deepening to a lush spread of green. The water itself was dark, clean and moving north, past the river cities all the way to Dragon's Claw and then further still to the ocean. As far as maps go, they didn't technically need one anymore, although attempting the trip entirely on the water would be both foolhardy and dangerous—Maar was as far as they could go before land travel would be required.

"It's safe?" Chiyo asked, still searching the tree line like an Ogre was just waiting for her to let down her guard. "Nothing can see us?"

Sanctum was up, etched into the trees, and as far as anything on the outside was concerned, the three of them had mysteriously vanished.

"It's about as safe as we're going to get out here," Sora said, dropping his pack on the ground. "If you decide to bathe in the river, make it known—because the biggest danger here has just become the water."

"You keep saying these *awful* things without any explanation," Chiyo muttered, moving further away from the water and finding a tree to sit against. "What *exactly* should I be on the lookout for—besides your wandering gaze?"

"My gaze doesn't wander, it's *precise*, and it goes exactly where I direct it," Sora said, brushing his hair back out of his eyes to peek at her. "That just happens to be the ample mounds of treasure hiding nearby."

Chiyo huffed out a burst of air, somehow tilting her head back to look down at him from her seated position.

"There is treasure here?" Fubuki murmured.

"He's being perverse, Fubuki," Chiyo said, bunching her cloak up behind her back to cushion her placement against the tree. "He doesn't mean actual treasure; he's talking about my—about what's under my shirt."

"You can't just say the word?" Sora said, rolling his eyes. "I'm talking about her great, *heaving* tits, Fubuki."

"Don't just—" Chiyo managed, "You're *so* rude, gosh."

Fubuki looked between them for a moment, clearly trying to unpack the situation in her own special way.

"You're the one who brought them up this time," Sora said, shrugging.

"What about the river?" Chiyo said, wrapping her arms around her knees. "You still haven't said."

"Riverblights are common here from what I've heard," Sora said, dropping down to lay on his back, hands folded under his head. "There's probably a few Nymphs as well; I wouldn't let one of them get close to you, although I doubt they'll bother—most of them have learned not to mess with humans by now; it always ends badly for them."

"Riverblights?" Chiyo said, eyeing the water now. "Those are the hairy things that pull you underwater and drown you?"

"More or less," Sora said.

"Sora," Fubuki murrmured. "I want to swim."

"How can you want to swim after hearing that?" Chiyo said, alarmed. "Fubuki, what would you do if something *attacked* you?"

Fubuki looked more startled at Chiyo's reaction than the idea that something might attack her.

"I would get out," Fubuki said, hesitant.

"That's—" Chiyo started.

"Go ahead, Fubuki; as long as you stay within about fifty meters, I'll be able to help you if you get into any trouble," Sora said, waving her off. "Maybe leave your clothing behind so you have something dry to wear when you get out."

"Sora," Chiyo said, lips tight. "Isn't this too dangerous?"

"She's strong enough to tear through metal plate with her claws and fast enough that I can't follow her movements at close range," Sora said, "It would take dozens of Riverblights to keep her from moving, even in the water, and I don't think I've ever heard of an attack of that magnitude before."

"That doesn't mean it's *safe*," Chiyo managed.

"Very true," Sora agreed, "But I'm also here, and I wouldn't let anything happen to either of you—have some faith in your dear old master, would you?"

"I'm *older* than you," Chiyo muttered, tightening her hold on her knees. "How can she just—gosh."

Fubuki waded into the river, entirely without clothes, and then vanished beneath the water, her disturbance leaving a ripple across the surface. Sora searched the treetops from his place on the ground before closing his eyes, content to listen to the sound of Fubuki splashing about in the water.

"Do you think this is going to work?" Chiyo said.

"Which part?" Sora asked.

"Any of it," Chiyo said, "How long until someone finds us and figures out who we are?"

"Could be an hour from now, or just about never," Sora offered, "I suppose that depends on how quickly you two can learn enough to disguise yourselves without my assistance—you could go just about anywhere then."

"What if I'm never good enough?" Chiyo murmured, "What if *Gleam* is the only thing I can do?"

"It's not," Sora said, crossing one leg over the other at the ankle, "Given time to grow, you'll become something amazing, trust me."

"You can't *know* that," Chiyo said, voice muffled by her knees.

"I know what I know," Sora said in disagreement. "You're carrying a lot more self-doubt around than I'd have expected from a noblewoman."

"You keep—we aren't some kind of *monolith*. There are *dozens* of nobles who I disagree with or simply cannot stand to be around," Chiyo said, searching for a way to explain what she was feeling. "I'm my own person, and we *aren't* all the same."

"That's probably true," Sora admitted, "I guess it's hard to empathise with a group of people who, *on the whole*, would step on a commoner rather than help him up."

"I've *never* done something like that," Chiyo muttered. "Cruelty for the sake of cruelty is never acceptable."

"I'd say that makes you *exceptional*, Chiyo," Sora offered, "But my personal experience tells me that most nobles aren't."

#

"*Gleam*," Fubuki murmured.

A perfect full cast, a sliver above the threshold, and the spell took the mana, transforming the formless energy into an expected effect—they were both capable of it now, on their own and without his guidance.

"Perfect," Sora said, nodding. "Your attention is still dominated by holding the pattern together, but that's a skill that will come in time— your ability to visualise is definitely your strength here; the flow of mana was steady the entire time."

Sora weathered Fubuki's quiet intensity, once again feeling as if she was attempting to see through him, to read his internal state—the undivided attention was unnerving and flattering both.

"So she's the opposite of me?" Chiyo asked, speaking up. "Visualising this stuff is *hard*—how are you so good at it?"

"I don't know," Fubuki said.

"I imagine you've had a lot of time to think," Sora said, "Did you dream when you were in the coin?"

"Sometimes," Fubuki said, looking down at her palm for a moment. "About the outside."

Sora nodded at the answer and watched as Chiyo bit down on her lip—something he was beginning to recognize as a nervous habit.

"You understand the basics of manipulating mana, building patterns, and you can both full-cast without my direct assistance—so we're going to start preparation for *Colourant*," Sora said, "But first, I'm going to ask you a question; why do we cast spells from our hands?"

Fubuki remained entirely still, her eyes slowly sliding from his face down to his hand and then to her own. Chiyo clenched her own hand into a fist and then wiggled her fingers for a moment, almost like she was trying to get the blood flowing in them.

"Because we have way more feeling in our hands?" Chiyo tried, "It's easier to notice the presence of mana and to tie it to our kinaesthesia?"

Fubuki glanced over at Chiyo for a moment, eyes wide at the almost immediate answer to what was obviously a difficult question.

"It's standard practice for an apprentice to use their hands for that *exact* reason," Sora said, impressed. "You really are sharp—but it was actually a trick question."

Chiyo's building smile turned into a suspicious, heavy-lidded look as she realised he wasn't playing by the rules.

"A trick?" Fubuki murmured. "What is the answer?"

"The real answer is that for the vast majority of magic, we don't *have* to use our hands at all—it's just more convenient to do so," Sora said, smiling. "For certain self-cast spells, the location of the pattern is actually part of the targeting mechanism—Fubuki, if I were to attempt to change the colour of my hair with *Colourant*, where do you think I would create the pattern?"

"I don't know," Fubuki said.

"You're not going to be in trouble if you get something wrong," Sora said, amused. "Treat it like one of the word puzzles we were playing."

Fubuki hesitated for a moment longer, then reached forward, taking hold of her too-long hair and pinching it between her fingers. Fubuki glanced over at him, then back to her hand, and then closed her eyes. Sora could feel her channelling mana, trying and failing to build a pattern amongst all the fine, shifting threads—she settled for attempting to create a pattern on the top of her scalp, but while she was having far more success than before, she couldn't quite manage it. Fubuki let the pattern vanish and then reached up to put her hand on her head.

"Well done, you got it right. But keep in mind that not all spells work the same way, and even ones that have similar effects sometimes need to be placed in different areas to function," Sora said, smiling. "The basic in-built target areas for *Colourant* are; scalp, forehead, chest, hand, and feet—hair, eyes, skin, fingernails, and toenails, respectively."

"So I'll need to make the pattern on my scalp?" Chiyo said, reaching up to touch the top of her own head. "Is that difficult?"

"Order of difficulty from hardest to easiest is; feet, scalp, forehead, chest, hands," Sora said, nodding. "Fubuki, your target area is the forehead, which will change your eye colour."

"Okay," Fubuki murrmured.

Sora beckoned them closer before holding his hands out in expectation. Both of them held out a hand towards him, and she took hold of their respective hands, fingers resting against their palms.

"The process here is this—learn the pattern with your hands, and practice it until you can hold it in place at least temporarily," Sora said, "Once you've got it memorised, you'll be building and releasing the *Colourant* pattern in the areas I just told you."

"This doesn't sound that hard," Chiyo said.

"That's because you haven't seen the pattern yet," Sora said, amused. "If you manage to figure this out, we'll move onto actively maintaining a spell, which is a process that *Gleam* doesn't naturally require—close your eyes."

#

"Aren't you going to check it first?" Chiyo squawked.

"You just told me to go away," Sora said, outraged. "Make up your damn mind already."

"Check for monsters *first*, and *then* turn around," Chiyo demanded, hands fisted in the bottom of her shirt. "I'm not going in the river unless I *know* for sure I'm not about to be attacked by some disgusting—*why are you getting undressed?*"

"Because you're making this take ten times as long as it has to," Sora said, dragging his shirt up over his head and dumping it on the ground. "It's a bath, not a war council—hurry up, or you can wait until Fubuki gets back."

Sora kicked his pants off, tossing them into the pile, before stepping past her and heading towards the river.

"Don't turn around no matter what," Chiyo said, flustered. "I'm coming."

Sora sighed at the temperature of the water—here, he'd thought river bathing had become a thing of the past for him. It made him wonder just what other horrors from his childhood he'd be forced to endure from this point on. Submerged up to the hips now, he turned around, and Chiyo glared at him from the shallows, face bright red as she covered her chest with her hands.

"So much for being furless," Sora observed, "*Hi-mu-ra.*"

Chiyo squeaked out something that might have been a curse word and stumbled into the river as fast as she could manage. She let out another cry of protest at the temperature before she mustered the courage to sink below the waterline. Sora laughed at her embarrassment and turned away again, pushing out further until he was almost unable to touch the bottom. He glanced back at the camp but found nothing to indicate they'd been there, *Sanctum* rendering the entire area as untouched as the rest of the forest. Chiyo moved towards him—something he put down to her being more worried about the depths of the water than him getting a glimpse of her.

"Have you managed to make the pattern yet?" Sora asked.

"No," Chiyo muttered, face as red as her hair. "It's hard enough when I'm holding it in my hands—you're *disgusting*."

"I didn't even say anything," Sora said, holding his arm up to defend himself from the vicious splash of water. "Come on, be serious, please."

"Don't tell *me* to be serious when *you* were the one smirking," Chiyo managed, "It's harder to feel the pattern on my scalp—I tried it on my forehead, like Fubuki, and it was quite a bit easier."

"That's because we have a tendency to focus on the area right between our eyes," Sora said before lifting his hand and touching a finger against his sternum. "We do the same thing in the middle of our chests, like a constant self-check for some kind of internal danger—it helps when channelling."

"That makes sense," Chiyo mumbled, touching a hand against her own chest. "I don't think I'm going to figure it out before tomorrow."

"Come here," Sora said, beckoning her closer.

Chiyo glanced away from him at the request, waited a long moment, and then carefully crept closer. Sora lifted his hand up out of the water, and she closed her eyes as he reached forward, touching his palm against the top of her head. Chiyo sunk slightly from the contact before she caught hold of his shoulder to keep herself afloat. He felt her knee brush against his thigh, and somehow, her flush deepened.

"I can't touch," Chiyo managed.

"I'm trying not to," Sora admitted, "But it's certainly a test of my willpower."

"*Sora,*" Chiyo squeaked.

"*Colourant,*" Sora said.

Chiyo's hair turned black, taking both her eyebrows and eyelashes along with it—she sunk another inch under the water as the spell took effect before tightening her hold on his arm. The change in hair colour looked bizarre to him, but he knew that was a twist of his perception rather than some intrinsic fact of the world.

"Can you feel the pattern?" Sora prompted, "It might be a bit difficult to actually trace the edges of it, but it should help you get acquainted with it."

"I can feel it," Chiyo said.

"Good," Sora said, "Try channelling some mana towards the area."

Sora reached out with his free hand and took hold of her arm at the elbow, holding her steady in the water. Chiyo shivered at the touch, the spell or the chill of the water, he wasn't sure, but he could feel her pushing mana up her throat, neck and towards the pattern. It was mostly formless, but it was attracted to the existing pattern, adhering itself to the outside.

"It's easier like this," Chiyo said, her concentration stealing away her embarrassment. "It usually feels like I'm groping around in the dark."

"That sounds a lot more fun to me," Sora said, "You sure you don't want to try that?"

Chiyo's attempt to take control over the pattern building was shaken as the comment fully registered.

"You're *not* funny," Chiyo managed, tightening her hold on his shoulder. "This might be as much as I can do?"

"That's fine; you're not supposed to learn something like this in a day," Sora said, squeezing her elbow. "I'm going to let you go now, so try and keep everything where it is."

"Wait," Chiyo squeaked, "I'm not ready."

Sora gave her a little while longer to brace herself and then stepped back away from her. Chiyo's chin turned upwards as she sunk, the tip of her toes just keeping her above the water. He broke the spell as he moved. Chiyo's brittle, hollow shell of a pattern remained in place as she strained to keep the sudden lack of feeling from disturbing it.

"It's so hard," Chiyo said, strained.

Sora was impressed she'd managed to hold onto it at all, considering how complicated it was and how new she was to everything. The delicate balancing act wouldn't last, though; he could already feel pieces of the shell flaking away—may as well go out with a bang.

"Of *course* it's hard," Sora said in agreement. "Now imagine what it would be like if you actually touched it."

The pattern collapsed, the half-solidified mana falling back into formlessness, and he was forced to defend himself as she did her best to smack him across the face. Sora fled, twisting in the water and working hard to make some distance between them.

\#

The buttons were fake, the tailcoat *wasn't* actually separate from the waistcoat, and there was no real pattern to any of it yet, but it was starting to actually look like a tailcoat jacket rather than a travelling cloak stitched onto a shirt.

"What next?" Sora asked, drawing Chiyo's attention. "Can you see properly?"

Chiyo squinted at his clothing in the light of the *Flamestay* spell, reaching out and pulling the overcoat layer open before drawing a hand down the edge of it.

"You need to bring the edge out at the top and taper it outwards; it's just a straight line down, so it looks weird," Chiyo said, frowning. "You also need to thicken the edge of the waistcoat so it looks like it actually has a seam at all."

"This one?" Sora pressed, running his finger down the edge of it. "Out like this?"

"Yes," Chiyo said, nodding.

Sora let it fall back down onto his lap and continued his efforts to make something that would distinguish him from a down-on-his-luck guy who'd been wearing the same clothes for a week now. If he was going to play the part of a well off, travelling entertainer, then he couldn't walk around in street clothes forever. It only had to last until they reached somewhere where they could buy *actual* clothing rather than rely on his poor attempts to mimic the skill of tailors who'd probably mastered their craft before he'd even been born.

"Sora," Fubuki murrmured. "There's a hole."

"A hole?" Sora said, startled. "Where?"

Sora held it up in the light and followed her direction to the collar near the back left side. He flipped the collar up and spotted it, scrunching his face up in annoyance.

"Thank you, Fubuki," Sora said, moving to fix it. "You've been quieter than normal—is something on your mind?"

Fubuki shifted, curling her feet up beneath her, and turned her head back towards the *Flamestay* spell, letting the curtain of hair hide her face from view. Sora eyed her out of the corner of his vision, catching a sliver of yellow peeking out from behind her hair, still watching him. The strip of thick cloth she would be using as a blindfold remained, stretched across her thighs with one end of it caught in her hand.

"There will be humans soon," Fubuki said.

"That's true," Sora said, lifting his head for a moment. "Are you worried about how they will react to you?"

"They will run," Fubuki said.

"They don't have any idea who you are, Fubuki," Sora disagreed, "They won't have any reason to be scared of you."

"If they knew," Fubuki murmured, "They would run."

"If they knew that Chiyo attempted to kill the Princess, they would probably run from her as well," Sora said, ignoring the muttered denial from Chiyo. "If they knew that I helped you both escape, they might run from me as well."

"It's not the same," Fubuki said.

"You're right; it's not," Sora admitted. "But we can't change who or what we are—all we can do is look for a place where we *are* accepted."

"There is nowhere like that," Fubuki said.

"It's not a very big place, but there is *here*, with us," Sora said, offering a smile. "Sorry if that's not enough."

Fubuki hunched down slightly, the once meticulously neat-kept blindfold crumpled in the tight grip of her hand, but whatever she thought about his statement, it remained tucked away behind her curtain of hair, and she said nothing more. Chiyo mumbled something about trying to tune the lute, sounding a bit nervous at the direction the conversation had turned. Sora sighed, accepting that whatever value his offered companionship held, it wasn't enough to offset the unfair state of the world. He turned his gaze back down to his task, working at the false layer until it was flared in the correct manner. Once he was done, he moved on to tightening the sleeves and making sure the length was right for him. He added a third false layer at the neck, underneath the waistcoat, hinting at a buttoned shirt that certainly wouldn't exist. He stood and hung it from a nearby branch, temporarily adding the already finished pants to the bottom to see what it looked like. There was an obvious gap where the waistcoat met the pants, in which the skin of his belly would show through—Sora sighed again and pulled it back down, resigning himself to another attempt.

#

"We're three hours away from Judra, at my best estimate," Sora said, eyeing the map. "We can either keep on moving and arrive there in the afternoon, or we can spend the rest of the night here and arrive in the morning—what do the two of you want to do?"

Fubuki stood with her cloak pulled tight around her arms, tangled in her fists, and her hat was pulled down to hide her eyes, not yet covered by the blindfold. Even without offering an answer, it was clear enough to him that she wanted to prolong the time spent away from a human settlement, her history informing her of the danger it would bring. Chiyo, on the other hand, seemed to have had enough of the forest, and she wasn't shy about it.

"I still can't use the spell, and that's not going to change with one more night of practice," Chiyo said, clearly frustrated. "*You* can hide my hair until we can book a room in Judra, and no matter how long it takes for me to figure it out, I'll stay inside, and I won't complain, not even *once* that's a hundred times better than spending *one* more day out here."

"Glad to see your spending my coin before I get a chance," Sora said, eyeing her.

Chiyo flushed at the words, but she didn't back down; instead, she matched his gaze, apparently trying to conjure her choice into reality through sheer force of will—something that probably would have been better spent on figuring out how to cast *Colourant*.

"Fubuki?" Sora said, but the oni just tilted her head forward, further shadowing her eyes beneath the hat. "Today or tomorrow, the result is going to be the same; better we find out now, I suppose—the *first* time you complain, I'm going to make you do something embarrassing."

"I don't care," Chiyo said, sticking her chin up in the air. "*Nothing* could be more embarrassing than—I want a *proper* toilet and a *proper* bath."

"*Nothing?* Your imagination needs some work, Chiyo," Sora said, "Listen, don't get your hopes up to much; a place this small might not even have hot water."

Sora offered the book to Fubuki and was surprised that she was willing to come out of hiding long enough to take it. He started forward again, trudging along the embankment, running over everything he needed to keep in his mind.

"Word won't have reached here yet, but we're trying to avoid leaving a trail; that means we need to be ironclad about what information we're leaking," Sora said, cracking the knuckles on his right hand. "We also need a cover story to bridge the gap between our arrival at Judra and our trip to Akh."

"What does that mean?" Chiyo said, sounding a bit relieved that they were actually pressing on. "We're going to be entertainers, aren't we?"

"Except we're arriving in Judra by foot, from the *south*, and I'm the only one that looks anything like an entertainer right now," Sora said, "Fubuki has to pretend to be blind until she can change her eye colour, and *you* look like someone rolled a noblewoman through a cattle-pen."

"Two women and a man arriving in rough shape." Chiyo muttered, "If anyone comes to Judra and asks questions, they'll think that's suspicious."

"That means we need a reason for our current state, but it needs to be boring enough to not draw too much scrutiny," Sora said, "Thus, we are a travelling group of entertainers who got lost in this forest on the way to—"

Sora hesitated, closing his eyes and trying to figure out something that would make sense.

"We visited Karas and then decided to cut north through the forest to get to Judra, only we got lost on the way," Chiyo said, speaking up. "I wanted to travel by boat, but we were worried about Fubuki getting motion-sick."

"Karas," Sora said, nodding. "We were forced to leave most of our stuff behind when we ran into an Ogre near the start of our trip, and what we have on us is all we managed to save."

"That explains why we don't have any spare clothing, supplies, or other things with us," Chiyo said, "Karas does have a connection through the Third Talon River, although it's basically never used because they get most of their trade by caravan, from Satu."

"That leaves the three of us as individuals," Sora said, "I'm a mage, you're both my apprentices, and Fubuki is blind."

"If a young man who isn't even *twenty* goes around calling himself a master, won't that link us to your identity in Satu?" Chiyo said, hesitating. "They'll have found out who you are, right?"

"Shit," Sora said, frowning. "I didn't think of that."

The moment that they discovered where he lived, they would realise *Salas the Scholar* was his master. They would find all of the books he'd been taking out of the library for years under her name, along with the documentation that revealed him as *Sora the Seeker*, a master in his own right who'd never had everything officialised. If information got out about a young man in Judra who was claiming to be a master, it would immediately draw the attention of everyone who was looking for them. He would either have to keep up an illusion to make himself look older or rework the group so that all three of them were Adepts—only two of them wouldn't be able to use magic on that level, and if there were ever in a situation that would require proof, it would all fall apart.

"New story, the three of us are travelling entertainers, but I'm only an Adept, and neither of you are my Apprentice," Sora said, "Fubuki is a blind novice to explain away the hat, and that's about it—any holes?"

"If we aren't in some kind of obligated apprenticeship, then a young man and two young women who aren't related shouldn't be travelling around together like this," Chiyo said, biting her lip. "Fubuki and I are both at the perfect age for marriage, and we are both highly desirable—it's going to draw some attention."

Sora took note of the brag she'd managed to sneak in there at the end.

"New, new story—the three of us are *still* travelling entertainers; I'm an Adept, and neither of you are my Apprentice," Sora said, restating it again. "Fubuki is my nubile but unfortunately blind wife, while Chiyo is her big sister."

"*Nubile?*" Fubuki repeated.

"That doesn't work; I should be at home seeking a family of my own," Chiyo said, scrunching up her face. "I'll be your wife, and Fubuki is my blind sister, so we can use that as justification for her being with us—she needs someone to look after her."

"Then Chiyo will be my curiously *curvaceous* wife, and Fubuki can be her youthful younger sister," Sora said, nodding. "That should work —we'll have to use different names, though, something to think about on the way."

"*Curvaceous?*" Fubuki wondered.

"Stop adding in *unnecessary* descriptive words when you don't need to," Chiyo said, flustered. "Fubuki—ignore him; he's being perverse again."

"My beautiful, beddable, and *bouncy* wife is making a particularly pointed pontification," Sora said to himself, "But what does her sleek, sensuous, and *sultry* sister have to say about this stimulating but star-tlingly salacious scenario?"

"*Sultry?*" Fubuki murmured.

"*Stop alliterating,*" Chiyo said in outrage. "Fubuki, *ignore* him—"

#

Five

Judra was visible now, a single worn but well-made wooden bridge striking out across the width of the river, arching a large arc beneath it to allow boats to pass beneath. A wooden dock ran horizontally along the river on both sides, with a rope railing and two tall posts, a pair of unlit lanterns on each. Three old men and a short blonde boy sat on the opposite side, each dressed in worn, stained clothing. Fubuki stumbled again, the blindfold stopping her from being able to properly judge where she was going, and Chiyo paused for a moment to steady her.

"There are people watching us now, Fubuki," Chiyo murmured, voice low enough that Sora could barely hear it. "Make sure you don't do anything strange, okay?"

"What is strange?" Fubuki managed, clutching at her forearm. "What shouldn't I do?"

Chiyo leaned into her ear, the hat pressing against her now jet-black hair, and Sora couldn't hear the response. Sora let his hands trail across the small of Chiyo's back, using the brief connection to recharge the *Colourant* spell—she shifted slightly at the touch and sent a warning glance back up at him that he ignored entirely.

"Hello, friends," Sora said, coming to a stop on the opposite dock. "I do hope this is Judra—it is, isn't it?"

"It is," The oldest man said, bemused. "Where exactly did you just come from?"

"Karas," Sora said, making a show of relief at the confirmation. "I almost thought we'd ended up turned around again."

"*Karas?*" The man said, startled, before tossing a look back in the direction they'd come from. "That's a week's travel by flatboat—don't tell me you came by *foot?*"

"I'm afraid we made a regretful decision to do just that, but that was just the start of our troubles," Sora said, wiping at his brow. "Sorry to bother you all while you're working, but there wouldn't happen to be an Inn or a tavern for us to hide from this awful forest for a small while? It's been a long time since we've had more than river water and fish."

"We've got a tavern over there on your side of the bank, but if you hope to get away from fish, you're going to have even more troubles," The man said, gesturing across the bridge. "Judra is called a river city for a reason, you know? Fish is kind of a staple."

"I suppose I should have expected that," Sora sighed, "Thank you, gents; perhaps we will talk again when I no longer smell like a fish myself—just over the bridge?"

"Just over the bridge," The man nodded before glancing over at the blonde boy. "Sara, if you're not going to fish, make yourself useful and take them there, will you?"

"What am I, your servant?" Sara said, scrunching her face up. "Why should I?"

"Because if you don't, I'm going to toss you in the river, you little wretch—" The man said, making as if to do just that. "That's what I thought."

Sara scampered away further up the dock as the old man pretended to give chase, but she jumped the stack of boxes and made her getaway up to the bridge before he could get close enough to grab her. Sora touched Chiyo's back again, directing her to start moving. Fubuki murmured something under her breath, and Chiyo ducked low to console her. They met the blonde—*girl*, actually, not a boy like he'd first thought —on their side of the bridge, following the elevated path up onto the road. Her skin was a complete mess of dirt and grime, enough so that she looked almost as if she'd come in from the forest with them. The girl's hair was cut into a short, scraggly mop, and she was thin enough that he could see the bones of her forearm standing out against her skin

—he lifted his estimate of her age, her emaciated state and unfitting clothes hiding that she must have been a girl of at least sixteen.

"Thank you for your assistance, young miss," Sora said, keeping to his affected role. "Your name was Sara?"

"You're covered in shit, did you know?" Sara said, planting her hands on her hips and tilting her head back to look up at him. "You ever heard of a bath?"

The absolute hypocrisy of the statement was almost enough for him to break character, and his mouth pulled up to one side as he fought not to laugh.

"A bath?" Sora said, giving up and laughing. "Given the look of you, I don't think you could describe one to me if you tried."

"Fuck off," Sara said, scrunching her face up. "How'd you end up like this?"

Sora glanced down as Chiyo drew in a sharp breath at the language, but she somehow managed to keep her silence.

"If you'll direct us towards this tavern your friend told us about," Sora said, "I'd be happy to explain it to you."

"Whatever," Sara said, turning away. "He's not my friend."

Sora directed Chiyo forward again, and Fubuki did a hell of a lot better on the flat and relatively unmarked road than in the tangled roots of the embankment. Judra was about what he'd expected—a series of short, squat timber buildings stretching out on both sides of the river. There was a few larger building, one of which was right at the end of the street, in far better condition than just about everything else and had a man standing in front of the door, a sheathed sword at his hip. The presence of a guard marked it as either the home of the Mayor or some kind of abnormally wealthy resident.

"Why is she wearing all that on her face?" Sara asked. "The hat, too? Are you a mage or something, lady?"

Fubuki turned her head towards the sound of the girl's voice and then up to look at where she thought Sora was standing, clearly hesitant to speak.

"She's a novice mage, but I'm afraid she was recently blinded," Sora said, bemused at the sheer lack of tact. "Magically, or else I would have managed to fix it already—it's something of a mess to deal with."

Sara turned around at the words, walking backwards in order to watch him. Even without her guidance, the Tavern stuck out from the rest of the buildings, taller, with two stories and much longer than anything else nearby. There was a large horizontal window cut out of the wall of the building, almost ringing the entire thing, allowing a clear view into the room beyond—tables, chairs, an internal staircase that led up to the top floor, and a bar sat beneath the window on the inside, allowing the patrons to sit there, with a good look out at the street.

"You can fix something like that?" Sara said, narrowing her eyes.

A mage who earned his or her mastery through a non-healing focus probably wouldn't know how to fix something like that, but any Adept with even a *vague* knowledge of healing spells could pull it off— probably. He'd never really considered what he should or shouldn't be capable of doing; his hunger for learning magic had left him with an eclectic spread of spells overall.

"Normal blindness? Certainly," Sora said, "It's not so difficult."

"What about other things?" Sara said, planting herself in front of the door to the tavern and crossing her arms. "You can fix other stuff too, or just that?"

It was clear enough that she wasn't going to let them inside without getting her questions answered—he actually found her irreverence a bit endearing, but Chiyo didn't seem to appreciate it.

"We've been stuck in that forest for days," Chiyo said, speaking up. "If you're going to pester us with questions, you can at least let us sit down first."

Sara's frown deepened, and she glanced back into the building once before shaking her head.

"Just tell me," Sara insisted.

Sora reached down and curled his fingers around Chiyo's waist before pulling her against his hip—a warning and a point of contact for him to once again refresh the spell. Chiyo squirmed a bit against him, turning her head into his shoulder to hide her face. Fubuki remained, standing off to Chiyo's right, their joined hands pulled up into the air from the angle.

"I am an Adept; I can fix all sorts of things," Sora said, adding a bit of impatience to his voice. "If you desire to know about something more particular, perhaps you could ask me after—"

"*Sara*," A woman hissed from inside the tavern. "Get away from here, or I'll—"

Sara slipped between him and the wall, bumping into him as she moved back out onto the road to glare at them all as the woman who'd spoken stepped up to the door. An elderly woman, greying hair bunched up around her shoulders, glared back out onto the street for a moment before turning towards them with an affected smile.

"Come on in, please," The woman said, stepping back and giving them space to walk through. "You look like you've seen better days."

Chiyo took the opportunity to untangle herself from him, cheeks a bit red from the proximity, and she led Fubuki into the room at the woman's behest. Sora remained out on the front step, half turned towards Sara. The men at the docks seemed content to sit with the girl, but one of them had also called her a *wretch*—this woman seemed to dislike her outright, and it might have been mutual, given the look on Sara's face.

"What?" Sara said, watching him. "Got something to say?"

"Don't let her bother you," The woman said from just inside, "She's a troublemaker, through and through."

Sara scowled at the words, and while he would have much preferred to go inside, the fact that the girl had just stolen his coin pouch a few moments before left him in a rather awkward spot.

"I'd like to continue our conversation, I think; why don't you come inside?" Sora said, eyeing the girl. "I'll even buy you a meal if you agree."

Sara glanced down at where his left hand was, hidden from the woman's sight by the angle of his body—he deliberately tapped his hip once, the place she'd taken it from, and she hesitated, aware now that he had discovered the theft.

"She's trouble," The woman repeated, a bit hesitant.

"That doesn't bother me at all," Sora said, beckoning the girl to follow as he stepped up into the tavern. "Come along, Sara."

An enclosed room with walls, a roof, and *chairs*—it felt like a dream after spending every waking moment of the last week outside, fighting with the constant exposure.

"To be out of the elements and inside again," Sora said, putting voice to his relief. "I'm sorry—what did you say your name was?"

"Marlissa," Marlissa said, eyes on the door behind him. "Please, come find a seat."

Marlissa turned away as Sara stepped inside, and he closed his fingers around the coin pouch she pressed into his hand—it was definitely lighter than before, but he'd deal with that soon. Chiyo had already chosen a table in the corner of the room, a long cushioned bench that put Fubuki in the corner.

"Marlissa, we are in need of a room and perhaps three meals a day for—" Sora said, pausing to think about it as he reached the table. "Say, a week, for now; a double bed will do."

"Of course," Marlissa said, glancing down at the two already sitting. "You wouldn't like *two*, uh, rooms?"

"My wife and I are quite used to sharing a bed, I assure you," Sora said, waving his hand to dismiss the comment. "Her sister can't be left alone either—she isn't accommodating well to the loss of her sight, I'm afraid, so she'll be inside for most of that time."

"Oh, that's terrible," Marlissa said, glancing down at Fubuki. "I have a room with a double bed—If you like, I'll bring your meals up to the room?"

"That would be perfect, thank you," Sora said as he withdrew two dozen silver coins. "This should cover it, I believe?"

"That's very generous of you," Marlissa said, smiling. "I have some stew on already—should I prepare a bowl for each of you?"

"Please, and for our little friend here," Sora said, making it clear that the girl was to be included. "Something to drink, as well, if you would; ale will do."

"Of course," Marlissa said, eyes lingering on Sara for a moment. "I'll be back shortly."

Sora watched as the woman turned away, angling for the room behind the bar, and then he gestured to a nearby chair before sliding down onto the bench. Chiyo shifted around on the bench as she abruptly found herself trapped between him and Fubuki, thighs pressed against one another. Sara dragged the chair over to their table, uncaring about the noise she was making in the process.

"You're seriously buying me food after that?" Sara said, dropping down onto the seat. "Why aren't you mad?"

"Because it would take effort to forcibly retrieve the rest of my money from your pocket, and I really don't feel like chasing you around Judra," Sora said. "This way, you'll give it back willingly and save us both some time."

Sara scrunched her face up again, clearly annoyed that her second consecutive attempt to steal from him had been noticed. Chiyo leaned forward, somehow more distressed by the news than he was.

"She *stole* your money?" Chiyo said, startled. "What do you think—"

Chiyo jumped as he reached down, placing his hand on the top of her thigh, and without turning to look, he was certain that her face had gone red. He refreshed the spell through the contact and glanced over as Marlissa came back out of the back room. The old woman busied herself beside the bar, well within earshot.

"Nobody new ever comes to Judra," Sara said, carefully avoiding the topic of her theft while Marlissa was nearby. "Who are you, anyway?"

"My name is Shiro, this is my wife, Itsuka, and her younger sister, Fuka," Sora said, using the identities they'd agreed on. "We are—or were, I suppose, travelling entertainers."

"Were?" Sara frowned, glancing over at Fubuki. "Cause she's blind?"

Marlissa dropped a mug down on the bartop a little harder than was necessary, and Sara glanced over at her warily. Chiyo placed her hand down on top of his own, nails positioned for maximum pain against the skin of his hand.

"Indeed, I'm afraid she can't do much dancing at the moment, but

I assure you, she was *otherworldly*," Sora said before sighing. "We lost most of our belonging during the trip as well—nobody said anything about there being Ogres north of Karas."

Marlissa drew in a sharp breath at the idea before scooping up the four mugs, placing them onto a tray, and ferrying them across the room to their table.

"Near the lake?" Marlissa prompted, placing each mug onto the table in front of them. "Was anybody hurt?"

"A bit north of the lake," Chiyo said, speaking up. "We managed to run while it was busy stomping on our wagon, but we were lucky enough to escape unharmed."

Sara picked up the mug without waiting and then held it in her lap as if Marlissa might snatch it away if she left it on the table.

"Lucky indeed," Marlissa managed. "My, you're all in need of a good bath by the look of it—we have a bathing room; you can find it through that door and across the room. Should I prepare everything for after you've eaten?"

"A bath sounds perfect," Sora said, smiling. "Doesn't it, Fuka?"

"Yes," Fubuki murmured, voice whisper quiet. "Thank you."

"An actual bath?" Chiyo said, sounding genuinely relieved. "I can hardly wait."

"Oh, you poor dears," Marlissa said, shaking her head. "Don't fret; I'll take care of everything."

Marlissa strode away, placing the tray down on the bartop and vanishing into the back room again. Chiyo must have forgotten she was attempting to punish him because her fingers were now curled around his hand.

"She's only being nice to you because you're rich," Sara muttered, glaring at the empty doorway. "One time, I snuck in here, and she chased me out with a broom like I was some kind of rat."

"Because you stole from her?" Sora guessed.

"I've never stolen anything from *her*," Sara mumbled.

One of her customers, perhaps, or someone else in Judra—a place this small, everyone would find out pretty quickly if someone did something they shouldn't have.

"You shouldn't be taking things that don't belong to you at all," Chiyo said, her tone chastising. "Stealing is a crime for a reason."

"Whatever," Sara muttered.

Sora took his hand off Chiyo's thigh, shaking free of her grip in the process before leaning forward onto the table, elbows holding his weight. Chiyo turned to look at him, a bit startled at the sudden disengagement. Sara sat back in her own chair, visibly wary at the distance between them growing shorter. A girl at her age, underweight, dirty, dishevelled, who cursed more than he did and stole brazenly from those around her—he was more than familiar enough with the type of environment that created people like that.

"What?" Sara demanded.

"You were interested in healing magic," Sora asked, watching her. "Ask away—but know that each question is going to cost you one silver."

It went unsaid that she'd be paying for his time with the money she'd stolen from him only minutes before—that gave her about ten questions if he was judging what she'd taken correctly. Sara grimaced but pulled her hand out of her pocket and flipped one of the coins up onto the table.

"How much does it cost to fix someone?" Sara said, watching him.

"That depends on the ailment, the difficulty," Sora said, rocking his head from side to side. "The time it takes me to fix it and the conditions in which I'm working."

Sara frowned at the answer—detailed enough that it was worth a coin, but it didn't tell her an exact amount, which was clearly what she'd been looking for. Sora watched as she dropped another coin on the table.

"It's a sickness that makes somebody too weak to move around," Sara said, scrunching her face up. "Their skin is green, and you can see their veins in the light, dark green, almost black."

"Is there a question in there?" Sora wondered.

"What is it?" Sara said, annoyed. "That's the question."

"Not enough information to know for certain, there are a lot of things that can weaken a person, and translucent skin comes from a lack of melanin," Sora said, humming. "Greenish veins *could* be attributed to low oxygen in the blood."

"What does that *mean,* though?" Sara murmured.

Sora raised an eyebrow at the question, and belatedly, Sara placed the third coin on the table.

"There is probably something wrong with their heart, lungs or the veins themselves," Sora said, taking a guess. "Does the person have trouble breathing?"

"Yes," Sara said, placing the fourth coin down. "Is something like that fixable?"

"Maybe," Sora offered.

"That's not a real answer," Sara said, annoyed.

"I don't have the information to give you a definitive answer," Sora admitted, "How long has the person been sick? Are they deteriorating over time, or is the condition static? Is the cause magical or mundane? Is it something caused by what they're eating regularly, or was it something that was inflicted once, by chance?"

"Almost a year," Sara said, watching him. "It's been getting worse; she used to be able to move around—I don't know about the rest."

A sudden onset of a weak constitution that grew worse over the course of a year, interfered with the breathing, which was probably contributing to poor blood flow and a lack of melanin—if everything she'd said so far was correct. There were dozens of things that could cause something like that; diseases, poisons, infections, or organ failure.

"She?" Chiyo murmured, watching the exchange. "Is this person your mother?"

"It's my older sister," Sara said, frowning. "You still didn't answer my question."

"Stingy," Sora complained, "I think it's highly likely I could fix it, given what you've told me."

"How much would I have to pay you to fix it?" Sara asked, carefully sliding the fifth coin across the table. "Today."

At most, she had five stolen coins left—all silver—because he very much doubted she was brave enough to keep a gold after he'd caught her.

"Considering that I've spent a week sleeping on the ground, getting bitten by insects, bathing in the river, and eating burnt fish," Sora said, ticking them all off on the one hand. "I'd say the cost of pulling me away from a warm meal, a hot bath, and a steamy night with my cock buried between my wife's legs—is roughly about one gold coin."

"You *disgusting* beast," Chiyo squeaked, cheeks bright red. "Don't *say* something like that—"

Sara looked visibly upset, but he very much doubted it had anything to do with the crude words he'd used—but rather, the impossible cost he'd set to heal her sister.

"I don't have one gold," Sara muttered.

"Then I guess you'll have to wait until tomorrow, at which point, one silver should be enough to cover it," Sora said, ignoring the glare Chiyo was levelling at him. "That should leave you with about—*four* silvers? If my estimate was right."

Sara stared at him from across the table.

#

The bathing room was dominated by a single large tub, almost as tall as his chest, with a series of steps on one side, the planks sealed together through some clear type of resin that filled the gaps completely. Two rings of iron encircled the outside, counteracting the force of the water that had been poured inside. It was easily big enough for several people, but the level of the water was barely shin height at best. A large iron pot sat over the now-burning fire on the backside of the room filled with river water; a series of deep pots hung beside it for transferring the water into the tub—he was surprised Marlissa had managed to carry so much of it by herself.

"Are you sure?" Marlissa said, visibly sweating. "I'm happy to keep going."

"No, I'll handle it from here; you've done more than enough," Sora said, "Thank you, Marlissa—you won't mind if we lock the door?"

"Please go ahead; you're my only customers at the moment," Marlissa said, "Take as long as you like."

Marlissa vanished back outside, the sound of her footsteps taking her back towards the main room of the tavern and leaving the three of them standing inside the room. Sora shut the door and pulled the sliding lock shut on the inside.

"Shiro?" Chiyo asked.

Sora waved at her to wait before moving to check all of the walls, making sure there wasn't some crack or hole that would let someone peep on them and discover anything they shouldn't. But it was more or less solid, with undamaged planks and no real gaps worth noting; he nodded, considering it safe enough.

"No holes that I can see anywhere, so it should be safe," Sora said, stretching his arms above his head for a moment. "I'm dropping the spell—and Fubuki; you can take your disguise off now."

Chiyo pulled a lock of her hair forward, watching as it flushed bright red, the black fading away within seconds. Fubuki carefully reached up and pulled the blindfold free, revealing her eyes for the first time in hours. Sora moved over to the massive tub, building a pattern in each of his palms, before hanging both of his hands over the edge. He twisted the pattern of each, tuning them for increased temperature and rate of output.

"*Flow*," Sora murmured.

The water poured forth from his hand, more like a geyser now than the carefully restricted amount he'd used to fill the waterskins, and he closed his eyes against the sudden rising steam. Fubuki approached, coming to stand beside him, and tilted her head over the side of the tub, eyes on his hands.

"It's different than before," Fubuki murmured.

"This is about twice the standard output for *Flow*—and it's usually cool by default," Sora said, nodding. "You can affect the temperature, either way, hotter or cooler, but go too far in either way, and you'll end up injuring yourself from contact."

The water level was rising quickly, the twin streams working to fill it up much faster than ferrying two dozen pots of water over from the fire.

"Satu actually had these big concrete baths, some of them with a series of *Flow* spells etched into the pipes," Sora said, "Novice mages run around and fill up the *Permanence* spells with mana for a few silvers—it helps most of them afford the fee for the library."

"I had a bath like that at my home," Chiyo murmured, coming to stand beside the tub. "I've never actually seen anyone perform the maintenance, but we made sure to leave a silver out for whoever came by."

Sora cut the spells off when it reached about halfway full, not too sure how much water it could actually hold without breaking open.

"Must have had a lot of servants to miss some guy or girl coming in and out every week," Sora wondered. "Frilly skirts have it so rough."

Chiyo scrunched her face up at the comment, glaring at him from over the rim of the tub. Sora ignored her, ducking down in an attempt to unlatch his belt. His pants dropped to the floor, and he kicked his shoes off as best he could to get out of the tangled-up mess.

"I don't know about you two," Sora said, dragging his shirt up over his head. "But I'm getting in the tub."

When he broke free of the shirt, he found Fubuki staring down at his cock, and he tossed the dirty shirt at her in punishment. Fubuki caught it out of the air in the most casual display of reflex he'd ever seen, despite the fact that it had come from about a foot away without any sort of warning.

"I didn't think we would be bathing together," Chiyo managed. "You can't just—there's not much *space*."

Chiyo spun away from him as he stepped into view, and he started up the stairs, using the railing to steady himself. He stepped down into it, almost gleeful at the feeling of actual hot water—the week without it felt more like an entire year. Sora sunk down onto his knees and placed his back against the far end of the tub, the water level with his belly button.

"There's easily enough space for the three of us," Sora said, sinking down until the water was level with his sternum. "Oh my *god—it's* amazing."

"This isn't fair," Chiyo said, drawing in a sharp breath. "*Fine,* I'm getting in; just—close your eyes."

Fubuki's slitted eyes came into view above the stairs as she rose up, not bothering to use the railing. She stood at the top for a moment, staring down at where Chiyo was standing, hidden by the height of the tub.

"Sora," Fubuki murrmured. "Treasure."

Sora laughed out loud at the word, wondering if that wasn't the first time he'd heard her make a joke—or if she was even attempting to make one in the first place; she *might* have just been pointing it out for his benefit.

"*Fubuki,*" Chiyo said, "Stop watching me undress, get in the tub—*go.*"

Fubuki moved quickly, stepping down into the water, but her eyes remained locked on the wall of the tub where Chiyo's voice had come from. Sora relaxed back against the wall, letting it hold the rest of his weight.

"So far, everything seems to be going well," Sora murmured, "Marlissa and Sara will spread the word about a group of travelling entertainers from Karas to the rest of Judra; any of the flatboats that set out from here over the next few days will carry the news with them."

"Do we *want* that?" Chiyo said, carefully approaching the stairs. "We're still not sure if our story is going to hold up to scrutiny."

Chiyo stared down at the steaming water from over the rim and then spent a few moments looking between the occupants, hesitating.

"The earlier news of us arriving gets out, the faster that information will spread, become mundane and then fade away again; by the time we get there, the people in Maar will already be expecting us to show up," Sora said, "At that point, our existence as entertainers will be established in their minds as something entirely unrelated to the assassins that tried to murder Princess Eri."

Chiyo must have realised that neither of them was going to avert their gaze because she swallowed and quickly climbed up the stairs, attempting speed over concealment. Fubuki's too-long hair spread out around her, the water drawing it out to fill the surface of the tub; her mouth sat just above the waterline, only the top portion of her hair still dry, and her legs curled beneath her. Chiyo stepped down, sinking into the water, before crossing her hands across her chest—he felt her feet brush against his hip as she turned to place her back beside the stairs, directly across from him.

"You could have looked away," Chiyo murmured. "You're both so rude."

The embarrassment she'd been wearing seemed to be quickly melting into a heavy-lidded gaze as the brilliance of the hot water stole it all away.

"If I looked away, I wouldn't be able to see anything," Sora said, "That goes against everything I believe in."

Chiyo sunk another inch below the waterline and burbled something he couldn't decipher. Sora scooped up a handful of water and pressed it into his face, but it didn't feel like nearly enough. He stretched his foot out, hooking it under the bottom step, and drew himself down into the water. Chiyo drew her legs back towards her as their thighs made contact. Sora held himself underwater, scrubbing at his face as best he could, and once he thought he'd managed to make some progress, he pushed himself back up. He surfaced a moment later and raked his hands up through his hair in an attempt to comb through the knotted mess.

"Ugh," Sora said, "Is my face still dirty?"

"A little bit," Chiyo said, "Sora—why didn't you get upset with that girl? She stole your money."

"Because she's exactly like I used to be—if a bit older," Sora said, continuing to work his fingers through his hair. "Given the state of her clothes and the fact that she's resorted to stealing from people in a town *this* small, it's pretty clear that she's at rock bottom."

Fubuki turned to look at him as he spoke, the inky black mess of her hair pulled upwards with the movement, thick and laden with water.

"Do you think her parents are still around?" Chiyo asked, "I can't imagine they would let her get away with behaviour like this."

Sora frowned at the words before reaching over to pick a thin twig out of Fubuki's floating hair. The effort to clean it up made no real impact, given how many things had become stuck in it over the last week.

"Fubuki," Sora said, "Come here for a minute."

Fubuki eyed him for a moment before twisting onto her knees, her hands sinking into the water on either side of his thighs, catching her weight. She crawled towards him, lifting up out of the water in the process, trailing long strands of hair in every direction like some kind of anthropomorphic Riverblight. Sora pushed himself back against the wall, spreading his legs, and moving his right one into the space she had just opened up.

"Face the other way," Sora said. "I'm going to clean your hair."

Fubuki remained there for a long moment, inches away from his face, just holding his gaze—and then she finally twisted around to sit between his legs, facing Chiyo. Sora blew a long breath out of his nose in an attempt to fight down his natural reaction to the sight before giving up entirely. He scooped up a handful of her hair and pulled it back over her shoulder.

"*Get away with behaviour like this*—you say that as if people who are stealing to survive actually have another option," Sora said, finally moving to address Chiyo's comment. "What's the alternative for her? Whoring herself out to the old men of Judra? Or maybe she should just starve? Some life."

"I didn't mean it like that," Chiyo mumbled, "I just wonder why she would choose to do something like that, that's all."

Sora picked out another stick and tossed it up over the side of the tub.

"Did Fubuki *choose* to get bound in a coin? Did *you* choose to have Koshiro conspire against you? Do you think Princess Eri made a choice to get attacked? Do you think people like Sara woke up one day and just decided to have nothing?" Sora said rhetorically. "Sometimes the world is just shit or the people in it are—Chiyo, trust me, when you're shivering in an alleyway, wondering where you will find your next meal, you'll learn pretty quickly that you can't eat your morality, no matter how well you preserve it."

#

The spare set of clothes that Marlissa had given him to wear wasn't a perfect fit, but they were good enough. He hung the waistcoat up beside the door, still wet but no longer dripping as it had been when he'd first washed it. Chiyo and Fubuki's own clothing hung from two other hooks beside it, in much the same condition.

"It's so small," Chiyo frowned, looking around. "There's barely any room to stand up."

"That's a complaint," Sora said, leaning back against the door. "I'll have to start thinking about a punishment."

"That's not fair," Chiyo winced, "I forgot."

Sora snorted at the excuse; it wasn't like she was wrong, though; the room was tiny and completely dominated by the double bed, with only one side of it actually accessible, the other pressed flat against the wall. There was a chair and a single table to the left of it, taking up more of the precious space but allowing for something other than the edge of the bed to sit on. Fubuki stood in the middle of the room, locking Chiyo in between the table and the bed, staring straight at him.

"Not so bad, is it?" Sora asked. "Being in a human settlement again, I mean."

Chiyo turned around at the words before slipping down to sit on the sole chair, facing them.

"I don't know," Fubuki said.

"Nobody has run from you yet, at least," Sora said, "Which was what you were worried about, wasn't it?"

"Yes," Fubuki admitted before hesitating. "Maybe soon."

"Maybe never, if you keep on practising your spell," Sora said, amused. "Fubuki, I think we need to cut your hair."

Fubuki glanced down at where the two streams of hair were hanging over her shoulders and pooling in front of her hips.

"Why?" Fubuki said.

"Two reasons," Sora said, flashing two fingers to catch her attention. "The first is that it's hard to keep it clean, and the second is that people know you have exceptionally long hair, which means they will be looking for that."

"You cleaned it for me," Fubuki murmured.

"I did, but we aren't always going to have access to a bath or the time needed for me to pick out all of the stuff that gets tangled in it," Sora admitted, reaching out to about her chest level. "If we cut it down to even this long, it would be way more manageable."

Fubuki tangled her fingers in the hair at her hip, brushing her thumb over it.

"It's only getting messy because it's not contained, and she runs around a lot," Chiyo said, standing back up. "Her hair is pretty, and cutting all of this off seems like such a waste—we should just braid it instead."

Chiyo reached up over her shoulders, scooping the mass of hair from under her chin, before drawing it all back over her shoulders into a single thick cord.

"What if people recognize her by how long her hair is?" Sora frowned.

"A woman with long hair is a completely normal thing," Chiyo said, reaching forward to catch a few loose threads to add to the pile. "Nobody is going to find that suspicious, and we're supposed to be a group of successful entertainers—eccentricities should be expected; perhaps we should *all* braid our hair."

That wasn't such a bad idea, and it would give them a more cohesive group image as well, which would probably sell the whole thing. Fubuki seemed to be rallying under Chiyo's arguments, and once again, he found himself in a staring match with her—something he didn't have a chance of winning.

"You really don't want to cut your hair, Fubuki?" Sora sighed.

"No," Fubuki murrmured.

"Fine," Sora said, pushing off the door. "Chiyo, it just became your job to take care of it from now on."

"I don't have an issue with that," Chiyo said. "Fubuki, stand still, please."

He stepped forward, Fubuki tilting her head back to look up at him, and he turned sideways, placing a hand on her belly to steady himself as he slid between the two of them and the bed frame. Chiyo glanced up at him as he brushed past her, and then he made it through to the other side. Sora sat down on the bed and twisted, drawing his feet up onto the mattress, before moving to lay in the centre of the bed. It was nothing as comfortable as the one back in Satu, but it was a hundred times better than the cold, hard ground.

"That idea with the braids is a good one," Sora said, folding his arms behind his head. "I'm not sure my hair is long enough for that, though."

"Your bangs are; we could braid those," Chiyo said, "Fubuki, I can't do this while we're standing."

Fubuki was soon directed into sitting on the ground, and Chiyo sat directly behind her on the bed, the mass of hair streaming across her lap. Sora reached up with one hand and took hold of the clump of hair hanging on the right side of his face, wondering if she was right. He spent about a minute twisting it into a mess before giving up and leaving it to hang there.

"We will need to buy new clothing," Chiyo said, working at the back of Fubuki's head. "With spares, perhaps."

"The chance of finding anything of high quality, or high status here, is zero," Sora said, closing his eyes. "Akh isn't going to be much better."

"Maar is a relatively large city; the population was—thirty-eight thousand," Chiyo said, glancing up at the roof for a moment. "There is quite a bit of minor nobility living there along with a small population of high-end traders that skip between there and Bilaar."

"So they'll have better clothing?" Sora guessed.

"Most certainly," Chiyo said, tilting her head for a moment. "Maar is actually approaching its annual festival, if I'm not mistaken—a trio of entertainers arriving amidst that would be perfect."

"Festival?" Sora murrmured. "How long?"

"I doubt it's more than a few weeks away, but I'm not certain," Chiyo admitted, "We can ask Marlissa in the morning; she will be far more familiar with it than *I* am."

"If we haven't missed it, we should aim for the busiest part of the festival; arrive when there are lots of people coming and going," Sora said, closing his eyes. "If we get in contact with whoever's organising it, we might be able to earn some money doing a performance."

"Are you running out of money?" Chiyo asked.

"Not exactly, but it won't last forever either," Sora said, shaking his head. "Flatboat to Akh and then another one to Maar is going to cost us. Caravan from Maar to Bilaar is going to be enough to wipe me out entirely—although I suppose we could just walk."

"I would rather not," Chiyo managed.

"Didn't think so," Sora said, amused. "You better start practising those lute skills of yours then and get around to teaching Fubuki how to dance."

"How am I supposed to do that in here?" Chiyo said, turning to frown at him. "There's not room to do anything—"

"Two complaints in less than an hour?" Sora said, feigning empathy. "You want me to go get Marlissa to come powder your ass, sweety? Would that calm you down?"

"*I don't—*" Chiyo managed in complete anguish. "Stop *saying* that."

"Call me the nastiest word you know right now," Sora said, goading her. "Go on, do your worst."

"You're a—" Chiyo said and then frantically shook her head about, unable to bring herself to say the word. "*I don't want to.*"

"I've got two complaints to trade in for whatever embarrassing thing I want," Sora said, "This is one of them—have at it, you harlot."

"*Don't call me a—*" Chiyo squeaked. "You—you—you *cockhead.*"

Sora just laughed.

#

"Sora," Fubuki whispered. "Now?"

Sora cracked a tired eye open just enough to see her own, but they were still the same glowing yellow in the dark—her continued attempts to build the pattern weren't quite succeeding. Chiyo's quiet breathing told him that she'd long since given up on her own practice and was now sleeping with her back to him. Sora patted the small space between his left arm and the wall before pulling his hand up out of the way to tuck it behind his head. Fubuki glanced down at the space for a moment before slipping down to lay beside him with her back to the wall. He shifted onto his side, facing her. The pattern she'd been trying to hold onto was already fading, the movement stealing away her concentration entirely.

"Make the pattern again," Sora instructed.

It began to build up across her forehead, the mana streaming up her throat to pool there. The outer shell slowly hardening, the process happening over the course of a long minute. Eventually, she reached the limit of her current ability, the pattern a little over halfway finished. Sora reached up with his right hand and pressed his fingertips against her forehead. Fubuki shifted slightly at the touch—and then the pattern began to grow once more. The missing sections began to fill in as he traced the pattern across her skin, the sensation of his fingertips working to bolster her focus. Almost thirty seconds later, she managed to complete it, the entire pattern becoming a single unbroken stream of mana.

"That's good, Fubuki," Sora said. "Now start filling it up, you're still below the threshold."

Sora kept tracing the same pattern, his fingertips barely in contact, sharpening her focus. Fubuki's left hand lifted up from between them and moved to rest against the front of his shirt, fingers tangled in the material. The minutes passed by, mana slowly accumulating as she fought to stop it all from breaking apart.

"You just hit the threshold," Sora said. "You can cast whenever you're ready."

"*Colourant*," Fubuki said.

Sora felt the spell snap into place, the full cast working exactly as it should. Her brilliant eyes vanished in an instant, the new colour stripping them entirely of the glow he'd come to expect. Sora drew his fingers back from her skin, reaching up to his own face to rub at his eyes.

"Good job, Fubuki," Sora said, "That was perfect."

"Sora," Fubuki murrmured. "What does it look like?"

"I can't see in the dark, remember?" Sora said, stifling a yawn. "*Colourant* defaults to black, so if I were to guess, your entire iris is probably a solid black colour—which should work well to hide your unique pupils."

Fubuki let go of his shirt, carefully bringing her hand up to his face, and he squinted in the dark in an attempt to see what she was trying to do. The pads of her fingers pressed against his forehead. A moment later, she started drawing a familiar pattern on his skin, the faint contact sending a shiver down his spine—was this what it felt like when he'd done it to her?

"Careful," Sora murmured, closing his eyes. "Keep touching me like that, and I might just fall in love."

"Love?" Fubuki murmured. "I don't understand."

"Love is like—a shock across your skin when someone smiles at you or a shiver down your spine when they speak your name," Sora said, enjoying the touch. "You can't help but want to be near them, to touch them, and hold them. You want to thread your fingers through their hair. You spend a lot of time thinking about what's underneath their clothes. You *dream* about the face they might make when you—"

Fubuki shifted slightly against the bed, and then Chiyo spun around to face them.

"Just how thorough are you trying to be?" Chiyo accused. "Isn't that too much?"

"I knew it," Sora said, faintly amused. "Usually you snore, so it's pretty obvious when you're faking."

"I don't snore," Chiyo managed. "Besides, how could I possibly sleep when she's *touching* you?"

Sora pulled back from Fubuki, moving to lie on his back with a sigh.

"Touching me? She's drawing the *Colourant* pattern on my forehead."

Sora said, rolling his eyes in the dark. "What did you think she was doing—giving me a handjob?"

Chiyo drew the bedsheet up in front of her mouth, muffling her own protest to the explicit nature of his words.

"Sora," Fubuki murrmured. "You didn't finish."

"*Fubuki*," Chiyo squeaked.

"You *dream* about the face they might make if you leant in and kissed them," Sora said, folding his hands behind his head. "Happiness, attraction, affection, desire, safety—love is a combination of a bunch of complicated feelings, and everyone experiences it a little bit differently."

Fubuki was quiet in the face of his words—her eyes snapped back into existence as the *Colourant* spell faded away.

"You're getting close to being able to cast it on your own, Fubuki," Sora said, closing his eyes to escape her scrutiny. "Now, I don't know about you two, but I actually need my beauty sleep—goodnight."

#

"Dampish," Sora muttered, running his fingers along the legs of the suit, "Emphasis on the *ish*—looks like I'm wearing these then."

"How long are you going to be gone?" Chiyo said, sitting at the table.

"Could be an hour, could be several—no idea how sick this girl really is," Sora said, turning back around. "Marlissa shouldn't come knocking until lunch, but if you have to answer the door, I'd suggest hiding under the covers and sending *Fuka* to answer—maybe give her a prep talk on how that might go down."

Fubuki watched them from the back corner of the bed, her hair tightly braided in a long, thick cord that looped around her neck and shoulders.

"We could come with you," Chiyo said, "Maybe splitting up isn't such a good idea after all."

This was starting to sound suspiciously like the talk they'd had before he'd split off to find supplies in Alhat—and what had happened to her staying inside the room, no matter how long it took her to learn the spell?

"At which point I'll be forced to make an excuse every couple of minutes to refresh your *Colourant* while also trying to heal someone at the same time," Sora said, shaking his head. "That sounds annoying enough on its own—it's better for you two to sit this one out."

"Still, what if I need to leave the room?" Chiyo tried, "I won't be able to hide my hair if you aren't here."

"Fubuki, keep Chiyo from leaving the room, will you? It's for her own protection, really." Sora said, sighing. "If you give her too much time to wind herself up, all the maps will fall out of her head, and she won't be able to find anything at all—the delicate constitution of a frilly skirt."

"You're *not* funny," Chiyo insisted, crossing her arms. "We should *talk* about this."

"I will protect Chiyo," Fubuki murmured.

Chiyo seemed to be overcome by some mixture of flattered at the words and betrayed that they were teaming up against her. Sora gave the pair his best smile, swept his arm down into a bow, and then used *Blink* to place himself five feet backward in the hallway outside of the room. He heard Chiyo call something out that sounded suspiciously like Fubuki's name as he turned away from the door. There was light streaming in through the window at the end of the hall, illuminating everything, and it was only a matter of moments before he made it down to the tavern proper. Marlissa was sitting at the wall-length window bar, reading a battered old book whose title he couldn't quite make out, and she looked up as he crossed the room.

"Shiro," Marlissa said, "How was breakfast?"

"The best thing I've had in weeks—even Karas had nothing quite like it," Sora said, matching her energy. "After a bath, a proper night's sleep, and a wonderful meal, well, I feel like an entirely new man."

"I imagine so," Marlissa said, closing the book on her thumb. "How are the two dears? Are they awake yet?"

"They are both quite wiped out from our journey here," Sora said, affecting a sigh. "It's my belief that they both need some time to themselves—away from me, as well, I would hazard."

"So you've made yourself scarce for their sake," Marlissa said, covering her smile with her book. "That's very kind of you."

"The mantle of kindness is a comforting one, Marlissa," Sora admitted, "But I'm afraid my motives are far more in line with self-preservation—it was my idea to *walk* to Judra after all."

Marlissa laughed at the comment, just like he thought she would—self-deprecation and accountability both went a long way to endear people to you if used correctly.

"I've got some business to take care of today—threefold, really," Sora said, leaning against the bar beside her. "Perhaps you could offer some counsel."

"I'd be happy to," Marlissa said, raising an eyebrow. "You were looking for some clothing if I recall?"

"That's the first one," Sora said, nodding.

"We *had* a seamstress, but she left us late last year to set up shop in Maar. That's where most of our clothing comes from," Marlissa admitted, "We usually get together a list of items and send an order downriver with Kazu—he actually left yesterday, so he won't be back for three days if he keeps to his usual schedule."

Chiyo had already briefed him on the kind of small trade systems that went on in the river cities, but it was interesting to hear about it first-hand. The idea of giving his money to a man on a boat and then actually expecting them to come back—well, they must have developed quite a bit of trust for that to work. In a community built on something like that, Sara's actions would have driven most of them away from her almost immediately.

"Kazu?" Sora prompted.

"He owns one of the larger flatboats and spends most days moving goods, and people between Maar, Akh and here," Marlissa said, nodding. "Kazu stays the night here after his deliveries; he's got a permanent room at this point—I probably owe him more than the other way around, but I think we've both stopped keeping track."

"Sounds like a good man—dependable," Sora said, humming. "We'll end up heading to Maar eventually, could I trouble you to introduce us?"

"I'll make sure to knock on your door when he comes in next time," Marlissa agreed before her lip curled up. "Sure you don't want to walk up to Akh?"

"I don't think my wife would like that idea very much," Sora said, recalling how he'd said almost the exact same thing. "I was initially worried that Fuka would struggle to be on the water—but I think we're far beyond that now."

"Ah," Marlissa said, drawing her head back in a mute wince. "Yes, I can see how that might have been a problem."

Sora just nodded, leaving her to come to any further conclusions on her own.

"The second thing—we haven't managed to miss the Festival at Maar, have we?" Sora asked, furrowing his brow. "We heard it was happening soon, but nobody seemed to have an exact date for us, and then—well, the *forest* took far longer than we expected to get through."

"That's what drew you here, was it? I had a feeling it might have been," Marlissa said, nodding. "You're timing is rather fortunate, I'd say; it starts a week from now and runs for three days."

That put them on an even finer schedule than they already were if they wanted to make use of the festival to earn themselves some travel funds. A week *might* be enough time for Chiyo and Fubuki to get good enough to keep their disguises up, but it didn't give them much time to do that *and* design an act to perform. If Kazu was back in three days, they'd have to leave with him when he set out—a day to Akh and a day to Maar would put them there just before the festival started. That would give him some time to speak with the organisers and procure some proper clothing.

"Kazu arrives in—three days, you said?" Sora said, closing his eyes for a moment. "I suppose we'll need to leave ahead of schedule, then."

"If you're not going to be staying the full week," Marlissa started. "I'm happy to return—"

"Absolutely not," Sora said, holding up his hand. "Our transaction is complete; let's not worry ourselves with such things."

"If you're sure," Marlissa said, "There was a third thing?"

"I'd like some information about the girl from yesterday," Sora said, drumming his fingers on the bar. "She seemed quite skittish here—you don't get along with her, I presume?"

Marlissa seemed hesitant to pursue the topic, which was expected considering what he'd seen of their interactions and Sara's story about the broom. Still, he wanted to get some kind of idea of how she was perceived by the other people of Judra.

"It's not a nice story, I'm afraid," Marlissa said, "Tia was such a lovely girl, and it's an awful shame what's happened to her."

"Tia is the sister she told me about?" Sora prompted, "Bedridden and ill?"

"Yes, she was actually apprenticed to the Seamstress I mentioned earlier," Marlissa said, worrying at her lip. "She wasn't in any condition to travel anywhere, let alone to Maar, and it seems to have gotten worse since then—I haven't seen her outside in several months."

"No healers live here?" Sora asked.

"None here or in Akh," Marlissa said, shaking her head. "There's one in Maar that I know of, but he's expensive and only takes walk-in patients."

"Not one for a two-day journey?" Sora murmured, "Sara?"

"We all tried to help out at first, bringing them wood, food and clothes, but it's been over a year now," Marlissa said, sighing. "We've all got our own lives to live, and I certainly didn't sign up for taking care of two girls—one riddled with sickness and the other a thief as well."

Sora remained quiet as she spoke.

"Sara was always like *that*—maybe not as bad, when their parents were still around or when Tia was still capable of keeping her in line," Marlissa murmured. "She's stolen from just about everyone at one point or another; food, small items, and silvers if they were left unattended. Far as I know, she never nabbed anything of mine, but I had to fire her after she stole from a guest."

"No one's offered her a job?" Sora asked.

"She's worked for me, for the fishermen, the lumberers, and just about everyone else, but she always ends up taking advantage," Marlissa sighed, "Maro, the Mayor of Judra, has locked her up a dozen times—never more than a few days—he's been remarkably patient, but she's almost an adult now, and that patience will eventually reach an end."

"What'll be her punishment when that time comes?" Sora asked.

"She'll be chased out of town or sent down the river to Maar in shackles," Marlissa said, drawing in a steadying breath. "I'm not sure Tia will—the situation is headed for a bad end."

Sora eyed the short tuft of blonde hair that was peeking out behind the outer wall of the tavern, just out of Marlissa's line of sight. He wondered how long she'd been waiting out in the alley for him to come downstairs.

"Whereabouts could I find her if I were to look?" Sora asked. "I'm only an Adept, but I studied a bit of healing way back when—perhaps I can remedy the situation."

"Truly?" Marlissa said, a bit surprised. "They have a little home across the river, near the edge of the village."

"Then that is where I'll search," Sora said, nodding. "Thank you for your time, Marlissa—you've been very helpful."

Sora pushed off the bar, and Marlissa turned a bit to watch him.

"That's a kind thing you're doing, Shiro," Marlissa said.

"A little bit of kindness to the unfortunate goes a long way," Sora said, managing a smile. "I'll return in a few hours, I suppose—until then."

Sora stepped out of the tavern, eyes on the space where Sara had been standing. It was now empty, but it was obvious enough where she was. The stack of crates at the end of the alley was easily tall enough to hide her from view. He stopped at the mouth of it for a moment and curled a finger towards himself before continuing on.

"How'd you know?" Sara said after she'd caught up to him.

"Your big head was sticking out from behind the wall," Sora said, "How long were you down there waiting?"

"Fuck off," Sara said, almost on reflex before wincing. "Not long, I guess."

"Hours?" Sora pressed.

Sara just huffed—but if it had been him, he'd have been in that alley for the entire night if he could have managed it. The bridge loomed ahead of them, and the sound of water quickly reached his ears.

"Was anything she said to me a lie?" Sora asked.

"All of it," Sara declared.

"Impressively deceptive, that woman," Sora said, rolling his eyes. "Tell me, why would you resort to stealing if they were nice enough to give you a job?"

Sara frowned but said nothing in response; instead, she stuffed her hand into her pocket—the faint sound of several coins rattling against one another rang out, muted by the cloth. They reached the middle of the bridge, and Sora caught sight of the same fisherman sitting on the docks as the day before, and they looked up at the movement.

"I probably shouldn't have sicked her on you." The old man said, "She's not bothering you, is she?"

"Fuck off, Tallen," Sara squawked. "I'm not a dog that you can sick on anyone—I only did it cause I *wanted* to."

Tallen shook his fist at the girl in warning, but his eyes weren't angry in the slightest—they were just eyes, bland and without any real care behind them.

"Not at all," Sora said, "How's fishing?"

"Shit," Tallen admitted, thumbing his nose. "Might want to check your coin pouch and see if it's still hanging on your belt—that girl has a tendency to collect them."

Sara glared at the man, but Sora just smiled at the warning.

"All accounted for," Sora said, starting forward again. "Good luck down there."

Tallen called something back, but Sora didn't pay any more attention to the man. Judra was a small place, and the two clearly knew each other well—years of interaction at least and were likely aware of her situation. Content to sit by her in the daylight and fish, but more than willing to sell her out to a complete stranger who might well have killed her for the offence. Friendly enough on the outside but callous and entirely indifferent to those around him—the kind of person he hated most.

"Why do you sound different when you talk to them?" Sara said, frowning. "Are you messing with me?"

"Stealing is a good skill to have when you're in a bad spot, but it's far from the best one," Sora said, still looking ahead. "Acting is better—it leads to more opportunity, and it can actually be used to get *out* of trouble instead of into it."

"So you're pretending to be nice to them?" Sara said, eyeing him. "Why bother? You're not going to be here long enough for it to matter."

She'd definitely heard the entire conversation with Marlissa then.

"What makes you think I'm pretending to be nice to them rather than mimicking *you* in order to make you drop your guard?" Sora wondered. "You did steal from me, after all—and now I know where you live."

Sara came to a stop in the middle of the road, but he didn't stop walking, eyes searching the buildings, looking towards the ends of the side streets at the edge of the village—a particularly rough building came into view, small, rundown and with two piles of firewood sitting next to the front step, untouched and left out where it might rain. Sara ran past him, slipping in front of his path, and then held her arms out to stop him from moving forward.

"Stop," Sara said, glaring now. "I gave you back your money."

"I sold you some questions, and you paid me one silver to heal your sister," Sora said, eyeing her. "We're not quite square yet, *girl*."

Sara ripped the rest of the stolen coins out of her pocket and tossed them at his feet.

"Take it then," Sara snapped, "If you even think about doing any-thing—"

Sora covered his mouth in an attempt to stop his laughter, but he only managed to muffle it.

"That's why acting is better than stealing," Sora said, stepping past the coins on the ground. "I didn't even have to do anything, and you're already throwing money at me."

"Fuck you," Sara said, visibly unsure about the situation. "Stop."

"You better pick those up," Sora said, glancing down at her for a moment. "I'd like to heal your sister *sometime* in the next century, you know?"

Sora stepped past her, hands in his pockets—he tracked the sound of her feet sliding across the dirt as she snatched up the coins and then took off back towards him. He came to a stop in front of the door, waiting for her to catch up.

"Don't fucking do that, man." Sara breathed, "I thought you were serious."

"Maybe I was, and this was just to get you to lower your guard again?" Sora said, wriggling his eyebrows. "Hopefully you'll be better prepared for double-cross two and three—those are coming up soon."

"*Ugh*," Sara managed. "I don't think I want to let you inside anymore."

"I could get inside without your help," Sora said, studying his nails for a moment. "Sara—you should bring your firewood inside; if it rains, you're going to fill the entire house with smoke when you use it."

"I *know* that," Sara said, scrunching her face up. "I just haven't gotten around to it yet."

"No shit, genius," Sora said, voice dry. "That's why it's out here instead of inside the house."

"Fuck *off*, you're such an asshole," Sara said, wrenching the door open. "Tia? I'm home."

Sora caught hold of the door before it could crash into him, amused at the attempted hit and stepped inside after her. It wasn't a large building, and it certainly looked like it had seen better days. Nobody had replaced any of the water-damaged boards—anybody with the skill to do so was either unwilling to work without pay or adverse to the people to who it belonged.

"Tia?" Sara called again, opening a door a the back of the house. "Are you awake yet?"

"Sara?" Tia mumbled, voice faint. "I thought you were going to fish today."

Sora could see a bedframe, low the ground, and without space beneath it, a thick brown blanket sat on top of it, rising up in the shape of a body. The torso was out of view, but the outline of a pair of feet was visible through the space beside Sara's knees.

"That was yesterday, and I already went," Sara said, dropping down beside the bed. "I found a healer guy, and he's going to fix you up—or murder us both; I'm not sure yet."

"What?" Tia said, sounding startled.

"I'd never dream of hurting anyone; it's simply not in my nature," Sora said, stepping forward into the doorway. "Good morning to you, miss; I've heard you're not too well at the moment."

"Stop pretending," Sara groaned. "You fucker—"

"Sara," Tia snapped and then struggled to cover her mouth as a burst of coughs took her. "Don't—*speak* like that."

"You don't have to yell," Sara managed, taken aback. "I was just—he's totally lying, is all."

Tia shook her head as best as she could manage, unable to form the words to argue—she actually looked a great deal worse than Sara had managed to convey. Her skin was translucent, but it also carried a green stain that was far too strong for it to be a trick of light and blood. Without even touching her or casting a spell, he could tell it was magical in nature—because it was something he'd seen before.

"Sara, this is going to take a while," Sora said, reaching up to rub at his neck. "Most of the day, at a guess—how unfortunate."

"But you'll still fix it, right?" Sara said, twisting around to look up at him. "If it's not enough, I'll give you the rest of your—uh, I'll pay you more."

Tia reached out in an attempt to catch hold of Sara's hand, but she managed to pull herself back out of range in time.

"You already paid me," Sora said, shaking his head. "I'm going to need you to do something else for me, though—"

"Gross," Sara said, "Don't you have a wife for that?"

"*Sara*," Tia managed.

"My *wife* is expecting me back around midday at the latest, and I'd rather she didn't worry," Sora said, rolling his eyes. "I'd like you to go knock on the door of my room at the tavern—it's the last room, upstairs and on the left—tell them this is going to take longer than I expected."

"Marlissa won't let me go inside," Sara said, frowning.

"Is something like that enough to stop you?" Sora said, tilting his head. "Maybe I was giving you too much credit after all."

Sara narrowed her eyes at the challenge before glancing back at Tia as she started coughing again.

"I'll be back," Sara said, patting her leg once. "If he tries anything—you better not try anything."

Sara slipped past him, and he slapped her hand away from his coin pouch as she took a grab at it—a moment later, the door slammed closed, and she was gone. Sora stepped into the little bedroom and closed the door behind him before sitting down beside the bed.

"How much did she take from you?" Tia mumbled.

"My entire coin pouch at first," Sora admitted, "But in her defence, she gave it back when I caught her."

Tia let out a sort of tortured groan at the words, the actions of her sister apparently more painful than even her current condition. Sora reached up and hooked a finger into the blanket, carefully pulling it down and folding it up around her feet—she was wearing a shirt that must have fit her once upon a time, but she'd clearly lost a lot of weight since then.

"It's been a while since I've been outside, but I think I would have remembered a mage taking residence in Judra," Tia murmured, "How long have you been here—I'm sorry, I don't think I heard your name."

"You can call me Shiro. We arrived here yesterday, but we're only passing through," Sora admitted, "Rather fortunate that I met Sara, I suppose; I might well have left without knowing you needed help."

"I'm sorry if I sound ungrateful, but I feel like I should ask," Tia murmured, "How is Sara paying for this?"

"With the coins that she forgot to give back to me after she returned my pouch, of course," Sora said, "I have to give her points for audacity."

"I'm so sorry," Tia said, giving another tortured groan. "Sara isn't a bad person. It's just—I suppose it's my fault that she's done all of this."

Rather than make her sit up, he pulled his knife from his belt and cut her shirt open at the front, carefully working it up to her neckline. Tia shivered but made no attempt to chastise him or stop him as he opened it and started work on the sleeves.

"I don't think she's a bad person at all, nor do I find you at fault—you may well be the *cause*, however," Sora admitted, "Her actions are definitely consistent with someone who is desperate to help a loved one."

Sora removed the remnants of her shirt, tugging the ruined cloth out from under her and dropped it down beside the bed.

"I'm sorry," Tia repeated, "Shiro, what did she mean that you might murder us?"

Sora gave a short laugh in an attempt to wipe away any unease she might have felt about the comment.

"I believe she might have seen my agreement to take a look at you as suspicious, given that she'd just stolen from me," Sora said, muddying the waters a bit. "I can't say I blame her; I would have expressed the same amount of scrutiny in her place."

The green tint of her skin wasn't uniform; instead, it was patchy, darker around her sternum, belly, and throat, and lighter everywhere else—almost like a large, faint bruise. The veins were much darker, showing through the skin, inky green spreading out from her chest, down her shoulders, to her fingertips.

"I'm going to slip your pants off as well," Sora said in warning. "Don't bother lifting your hips; I've got it handled."

Sora pulled them down, working both of her feet out of the mess, one after another and dropping the clothing in a pile with the shirt. The inky green stretched down her legs all the way to her toes, the pale green tint present but nowhere near as noticeable.

"Sara said it took a year for it to get this bad," Sora said, reaching out and placing his hand against her belly. "You didn't try and catch a ride up to Maar for someone to look at it at the start?"

"I was hoping it would go away on its own," Tia mumbled, "Jalin told me how much it costs, and I just couldn't imagine spending that much."

"The dreaded wait-and-see approach," Sora said, nodding, "Where were you when you got stung?"

"Stung? I—was in the forest, in a clearing west of here," Tia managed, a bit avoidant. "All of this was from that wasp? I'd wondered."

"That wasn't a wasp, it was a Skirai, and the stinger is still buried in your skin," Sora said, shaking his head. "The real question here is why were you in a forest clearing with your shirt off?"

"I'm not saying," Tia mumbled.

"Then I'll have to count on my imagination to fill in the blanks," Sora said, accepting her answer. "The normal process for this is to just remove the stinger and then let your body flush the venom out on its own, but you're too far gone for your body to fight this off on its own."

Sora placed his hand between her breasts, twisting his mana into an all too familiar pattern—after using it to drag out all of the contaminates in Fubuki's body, this felt almost like overkill.

"Long-term exposure to the venom will cause very slight damage to everything it touches, but it all accumulates over time—your skin, flesh, veins, and organs are being slowly deprived," Sora said, murmuring the command for *Scour* under his breath. "What I'm going to do, is remove the stinger, drain the mess that it's been pushing out into your body and then mend the damage manually."

The stinger slipped out of her chest, a sheer angle that left it hidden deep within her skin, barely five centimetres long and razor thin. It came out covered in a film of thick, brackish-green liquid, the black sliver filled with a tiny spark of Tia's mana, causing the reaction on contact with her flesh. The real insidious nature of the creature was that it had no mana source of its own; instead, the reaction was fueled by the mana of the victim—outside of her body, the spark vanished within seconds.

"A Skirai embeds the stinger deep enough that you can't reach it, and the venom kills feeling in the immediate area, stopping you from realising there's anything there," Sora said, breaking the stinger between his thumb and forefinger. "The venom is very slow acting, and it's weak enough that the first sign of trouble is actually the pale green colour spreading through the body and the numbness that it brings with it."

Sora pressed his hand back down over the area where the stinger had been and built up a pattern he rarely got to use.

"*Transude*," Sora murmured, "You shouldn't regain feeling until we get to the third step, but the areas that are least affected by the venom may still be painful—tell me if anything is unbearable, and I'll take care of it first."

Sora focused on what was happening inside of her—a needle of mana slipped through her skin, intersecting with the largest mass of green veins. He carefully added more mana to the section of the pattern responsible for the shape and teased out two extra points, splitting it into a trio of needles. Once all three were situated in the largest mass, he let it activate—inky green began to slide up into the points, reaching the centre and rising more quickly. It reached the top of the needle and pooled there, a sheath of white light holding the growing mass above the needle.

"Is that my blood?" Tia managed.

"No, this is the venom that has been slowly seeping into you," Sora said, eyes sharp as he forced the three points to maintain their shape. "There is a tiny mesh of mana at the tip of the needle, and blood is unable to pass through the filter—Tia, I know you want to see what's happening, but please don't move."

"I'm sorry," Tia said, letting her head rest back down against the pillow. "I—think I'm excited."

#

The inky green mess that had lined her body was gone, replaced by a duller blue colour, the translucency of her skin leaving it almost as visible as before. That wouldn't be changing any time soon and was something she would need to take care of herself.

"You're severely underweight," Sora asked, checking along the side of her calf. "Have you been struggling to keep things down?"

"Yes," Tia mumbled, "My appetite has been gone for a long time, as well."

"Your sister isn't in much better condition," Sora added, "Were the two of you having trouble with getting food as well?"

Sora shifted her leg, checked the inside of her thigh for any signs of green, and then nodded—he could move on to repairing the damage. He rolled his shoulders back in an attempt to stave off the ache from sitting on the floor for so long. Sora moved down to sit crosslegged beside her feet, deciding to start in the areas where she still had some feeling and get a headstart on mitigating the pain.

"Yes, when my fingers started going numb, I stopped being able to work at all," Tia said, taking a steadying breath. "Sara would fish some days, but eventually, we had to use my savings to keep us fed. It didn't last long."

"*Meldflesh*." Sora said, "The villagers?"

Tia shifted against the mattress, her toes twitching slightly as his mana seeped into her skin.

"They've helped us much more than I could have ever asked for," Tia said, closing her eyes for a moment. "But I've become such a burden to everyone—I should have done this differently."

Unlike singular cuts, punctures, tears, or most of the common types of injuries he'd sealed up, this kind of damage was odd—entire areas of her body had been starved of proper blood flow for long amounts of time. Every vein was surrounded by a localised pocket of starved flesh, and in the areas where the venom had leaked throughout her actual skin, there were large tendrils of affliction that followed no real structure, simply spreading where it could.

"Easy to say when you're looking back, not so easy to predict ahead of time," Sora offered, "It does make me wonder; if you had some savings, why didn't you use it to get help?"

Tia's fingers twisted against the bedsheets, and she opened her eyes again.

"It took me so long to save even that much, and I couldn't just—it was supposed to be for our future," Tia said, turning her gaze to the ceiling above. "There's nothing for us in Judra, nothing that Sara could do, and now that's become more true than ever."

"A bad reputation does have a habit of following you," Sora said with quiet irony. "Marlissa mentioned you were working as an apprentice before all of this?"

Tia reached up with her hand, carefully touching it against her chest, finger pressed against the place she'd been stung.

"A seamstress," Tia murmured, "Jalin taught me everything I know; if I hadn't become sick, I would have completed my training by now, and we might have even been living in Maar."

"A lot more opportunity than a place like this," Sora asked, "You and you're sister might well be the only people under thirty I've seen since arriving."

"Judra—the village of the wise," Tia said, the words spoken like a well-worn phrase. "There were a few others our age, but they may have moved on already."

The sound of boots sliding across loose gravel caught his ear—the floor shook a moment later as the door crashed into the front of the house and bounced off again. The sound of heavy breathing and footsteps on creaking floorboards followed a pattern leading to the door directly behind him.

"Tia?" Sara said, pulling the door open a crack. "He didn't kill you, did he?"

"Sara," Tia sighed.

"Whoa," Sara said, opening the door further. "You're not green anymore—that means it's working, right?"

"It's working," Sora said, not bothering to open his eyes. "It's been over an hour, did you run into some trouble?"

"Marlissa was reading on the fu—uh—fricking stairs," Sara said, cutting herself off for a second, "I had to wait for her to move before I could get inside; it took forever."

The fact that she'd actually stuck around for that long spoke of a surprising amount of patience—which made twice now, first the alley-way, and now this. It made him wonder if she was more reliable than she first looked or if this whole situation held a sort of singular motivation for her. Sara slid into the small room and crouched down beside the head of the bed, furrowing her brow.

"How are you feeling?" Sara asked.

"I still can't feel much of anything except the tip of my toes," Tia mumbled, "I think I might be breathing a bit easier, though; it's not quite as hard to talk as it usually is."

"Yeah," Sara said, hesitating. "Are you still coughing?"

"A little," Tia said, turning her head to frown at her. "Sara—I can't believe you stole from him."

"I gave it back, so it's not a big deal," Sara defended, shifting around a bit. "Besides, he wouldn't be fixing you if I hadn't."

"Which was complete *luck* and not by design," Tia said, "He could have turned you into Maro, and you'd be sitting in a cell right now, *again*."

Sara dropped from her crouch down to sit against the wall but didn't say anything in response. Tia reached out to grab at her sister's hand, and Sara caught it before her arm started to sag to the floor.

"You can't *do* things like this anymore," Tia managed, "Okay? You have to promise me."

"I won't have to," Sara muttered. "Can't we talk about something else?"

"I'm assuming you actually spoke to Itsuka," Sora said, bailing her out. "Anything to report?"

Sara grabbed onto the topic with both hands.

"Yeah, but she wouldn't open the door, which was *total* bullshit because Marlissa could have come upstairs at any point," Sara said, annoyed, "I told her you would be busy for the rest of the day, and she asked me a bunch of questions—your wife is kind of a weirdo."

"Sara," Tia chastised.

"The three of us have been having something of a terrible week, so you'll have to forgive her—she's usually much more personable," Sora said, fighting down a smile. "Did she want to tell me anything?"

"Not really, only to send me back with another message if anything changed," Sara said, twisting her lips into a frown on one side of her mouth. "It sounded like they were playing some kind of game when I first got there."

"What sort of game?" Sora wondered.

"Your wife was making up puzzles for the blind girl to solve," Sara said, digging her toes into the bedframe in an attempt to entertain herself. "Something about a fisherman trying to decide who the best person to sell his fishing rod to—which is pretty stupid; how's he going to catch anything?"

Sora just nodded—the puzzles had become a pretty common point of discussion between the three of them, although it was almost always Fubuki who brought them up. It felt a bit strange to be away from them after he'd spent so much time with them since leaving Satu—he hadn't expected to grow so attached.

#

By the time he'd made it all the way up to her throat, his hands were stinging from the amount of channelling he'd put them through. He'd learned some interesting things about the interaction between Meld-flesh and the esoteric kind of damage he was clearing away—namely that he could actually bring in healthy flesh from an undamaged area and then kind of mix it in with the damaged parts, which brought the overall condition of the area up *far* more quickly than working inch by painstaking inch. It did mean that he had to do a bunch of cleanup afterwards, but it had cut at least a few hours out of the total time. Even with that, it had still taken him long into the afternoon to get as far as he had, and his empty stomach was getting harder to ignore.

"It feels so strange to be able to feel my fingers again," Tia said, voice a bit shaky. "I'd begun to think that I might never feel anything again."

Sora slid his hand further up, cradling the back of her head—she'd been lucky to have so little damage above the chest. If it had made it into her brain and started shutting things down up there, she wouldn't have lasted half the time she'd managed.

"Let that be a lesson to you about doing strange things in fields without clothes on," Sora said, arching his back a bit in an attempt to deal with the ache. "Being a rebel must run in your family, huh?"

"Not anymore," Tia said, sounding a bit cagey about it, "I'm a changed woman, honest."

"I bet," Sora said, amused. "Tia—despite everything I've done here, you're not going to be at a hundred percent for a while."

"This *isn't* a hundred percent?" Tia wondered. "I feel so much better."

"Your energy levels are going to be way down from what you used to be at before all of this, and that's probably going to last for a few months," Sora said, moving up to the top of her scalp. "You can shorten that time by eating regularly—the more food you get inside of you, the better."

"I'll make sure to eat as much as I can manage," Tia said, "Is there anything I should look for in particular?"

"Red meat would be the best thing for you right now, but given where we are, fish might work," Sora admitted. "You'll also need to start moving around as soon as possible, short walks at the start, and work your way up to longer ones, giving your body a nice easy transition back to where it was."

Sora shifted his hand down onto her forehead and started doing a final check to make sure he'd done as much as he could for her. Tia closed her eyes as he pulled his hand down over them and then opened them again when he continued on past.

"That's pretty much it for health advice," Sora said, "But I've got some more general stuff for you if you're interested."

"Please," Tia said.

"Get out of Judra as soon as you can manage it," Sora advised, "You might be on the road to recovery, but you and your sister are going to waste away here if you stay."

"While there may be no future for us here, we still have a home, as poorly kept as it is," Tia murmured, glancing away. "We would have nothing if we left; it takes time to prepare for something like that."

"What sort of preparations?" Sora wondered.

"A flatboat to Akh costs five silver per person, and from there to Maar is the same," Tia murmured, "We would need to stay in a tavern while we looked for work, and if we can't find something, we would quickly end up on the streets."

"What about Jalin?" Sora said, speaking up. "She wouldn't help you out?"

"I—I am sure that she would take us in if I were to ask," Tia murmured. "But even then, there's still so much to consider."

Sora shook his head at the words, running his hand down her shin.

"I decided I was going to leave my hometown when I was fifteen years old," Sora said, speaking up. "I had a goal, a destination, the resources, and I'd planned everything out in intricate detail—do you know how long it took me to work up the courage to actually leave?"

"A year?" Tia said, "Two?"

Sora switched legs as he spoke, sliding his hand down to her toes and then nodding at the result—it was as good as it would ever be. He leaned back on his hands for a moment, letting the satisfaction roll over him, and then did his best to crack his back.

"I left a week ago," Sora said, working his way to his feet. "Trust me when I say that you'll never be ready to leave—there will *always* be another excuse to stay, something new to consider, another angle to cover, more preparations to make."

Sora looked down for a moment, considering her, before reaching down into his coin pouch and pulling out a pair of gold coins. He placed them on the mattress beside her leg before straightening up again.

"I can't take that," Tia said, startled. "Shiro—"

"Judra isn't *the village of the wise*; it's *the village that stung you*," Sora said, "Tia, you can either waste away here, hoping that things will get better on their own, or you can get off your ass and take your sister to Maar."

#

Six

"It doesn't have to be anything too complicated," Sora said, thinking about it. "I'm sure whatever you decide on will work."

"That's the least helpful thing I've ever heard," Chiyo said, cradling the lute in her lap. "What type of story is it?"

"It's a story about an undefeatable hero who sets out to slay all the monsters in the world. He's eventually defeated through trickery rather than power," Sora said, "It starts off pretty positive, gets a bit darker near the end before his sudden tragic fall."

"Okay, that's way more useful," Chiyo said, biting her lip. "How long is it—the entire act, I mean."

"Probably about two or three minutes?" Sora guessed, "I could probably embellish it a bit, stretch it out to five."

Chiyo ran her fingers across the strings, the sound muted by the palm of her hand.

"Sora," Fubuki murmured. "Will you use magic?"

"Yes, because the only way we're going to be able to get a last-minute spot at a festival like this is if we show something special," Sora admitted, closing his eyes for a moment. "It will probably be a combination of illusionary magic; *Gleam, Construct, Fade*—maybe some elemental magic to make it more ambient; *Mist, Flow, Gust.*"

"That won't give away your identity?" Chiyo hedged.

"The only magic I really used in public were healing spells, but even then, the clients had no idea what I was using on them," Sora said, shaking his head. "The guard I attacked will know I can use *Shockwreath* and

Sleep. We were spotted using *Haste* to run, and they saw us *Blink* outside the walls—but other than that, my capabilities aren't well known."

"Fine. I'll start with a progression that's bright and quick, then transition to something slower and more sombre near the end." Chiyo said, "What is Fubuki going to do—I've been teaching her to dance, but I don't think we'll have anything ready by the time we get to Maar."

Fubuki looked up from her place on the floor, half hidden beneath the table beside Chiyo.

"There's a character right at the start of the story that gives the hero a magical sword and then acts as a kind of observer throughout his life, watching him from the shadows," Sora said, planting his cheek on his palm. "We could dress her up, and she can stalk around the stage, interacting with the illusions—you feel like doing that, Fubuki?"

"People will be watching," Fubuki said.

"They will," Sora admitted. "Are you still worried about someone discovering your secret?"

"Yes," Fubuki said.

"You'll be wearing dark clothes with a hood, and your pale skin will fit the character from the story," Sora said, "I'll be able to help you maintain you're *Colourant* while we're performing as well—nobody is going to think you're out of place."

Chiyo leant forward to look under the table, clearly trying to get a read on how she was feeling about it. Fubuki looked up as the noble girl's hair swept into view and then glanced away from the attention.

"Fubuki?" Chiyo asked. "Do you want to?"

"I don't know," Fubuki murmured.

"That makes me really, really sad, Fubuki," Sora said, unashamedly attempting to tug on her feelings. "I don't even want to do it if you're not up there with us—"

"Don't *guilt* her into it," Chiyo accused, "If she doesn't want to—"

"I think I feel a big cry coming on," Sora said, sniffling. "Huge wet tears, filled with all of my hurt feelings, rolling down my cheeks—"

"*Sora,*" Chiyo said, outraged. "That's terrible."

Fubuki eyed him from under the table, no doubt taking note of his extraordinarily dry face—he was half a second away from using magic to rectify the situation when there came a knock on the door. Sora sat up, clearing his throat, and Fubuki slipped out from under the table. Sora tapped Chiyo on the head as he passed by, murmuring the command for *Colourant* as he went.

"One moment," Sora said, making a lot of noise on his way to the door. "*Ouch*, right in the shin—"

Sora made a big show of getting to the door, giving Fubuki enough time to get her blindfold and floppy hat back into position before finally cracking it open—he reached down and rubbed at his shin, over-selling it all.

"Marlissa," Sora said, straightening back up. "Sorry about that, did you need something?"

"Kazu arrived a little while ago; he's sitting downstairs if you'd like to meet him," Marlissa said, glancing down at his leg for a moment bemused. "I explained some of the situation to him, so he knows you'll be travelling to Maar."

"That's fantastic; thank you for coming to get me," Sora said, shaking out his leg. "Itsuka, Fuka—are the two of you feeling up to coming down?"

"Absolutely, I need some fresh air," Chiyo said. "Come on, Fuka."

"I'm just about to put some dinner on if you're all hungry?" Marlissa asked.

"Please," Sora said.

Sora stepped out into the hall, giving Chiyo room to lead Fubuki out by her arm. Marlissa gave them both a smile and then set off down the hall. The three of them followed after her, slowing at the stairs to let Fubuki take her time with them, and Sora caught sight of a man sitting at the window bar. He was tall, with wide shoulders and a thick neck. The man turned at the noise of their descent, and Sora placed him somewhere in his forties, the scraggly beard making it hard to narrow it down.

"Kazu, these are the ones I told you about," Marlissa said before gesturing to the back room. "Are you hungry?"

"Even if I wasn't," Kazu said, "I'd never turn down a chance to eat your cooking, Marlissa."

"Uhuh," Marlissa said, amused. "Shiro, don't let him intimidate you, he may be big, but he's really a softie."

Marlissa turned away without another word and set off to complete her self-assigned task, leaving the group of four to speak on their own. Sora stepped up to the bar and stuck his hand out to the man—the appendage was twice as big as his own and rough with callouses, but the man's grip was careful. Chiyo directed Fubuki to sit down at the table behind the two of them and then chose the seat beside her.

"It's a pleasure to finally meet you, Kazu," Sora said, "Marlissa has been singing you praises since the topic of our destination was first broached."

In the aftermath of the shake, Kazu glanced down at his hand before plastering a smile on his face.

"She's a lovely girl," Kazu agreed, "I nosed around for a bit before I ended up here, and I heard you took care of Jalin's old apprentice— you're a mage, are you?"

"An Adept," Sora said, nodding. "Healing is not exactly my wheelhouse, but it's not too difficult to pull a stinger out of someone's chest— so long as you know it's there to begin with."

"What would your wheelhouse be?" Kazu said, leaning his elbow against the bar. "Fighting? I heard something about an Ogre."

"Entertainment, actually," Sora admitted, holding his hand out, palm facing up. "I've got something of a talent for light shows—*Gleam*."

A cascade of sparks swept up onto the bartop, twisting into a strange scene—a wagon being pulled along an embankment by a horse. A second figure charged into view, twice as tall as the wagon and just as wide, crashing into the side of it shoulder first. The wagon was toppled over, and the Ogre stepped down onto the side of it, crushing it beneath his weight. Three indistinct figures fled from the scene, the entire thing vanishing as they stepped off the edge of the bar.

"A talent, huh? Never seen anything like it," Kazu said, whistling.

"Marlissa said you were headed to Maar for the festival—you're going to put on a show?"

"That was our hope, but we're quite a bit behind schedule," Sora said, nodding. "I was hoping to have a week to work something out with whoever's organising the events—but things don't always go to plan."

"You'll need to speak to a man called Levin; he's the one who handles that—assistant to the mayor," Kazu said, scratching at his beard. "That little light show you just did, is that the kind of thing you'd do on a stage?"

"The very same, only scaled up—essentially a story with magic and music accompaniment," Sora said in answer. "You wouldn't happen to know if they're still looking for talent?"

"I'm not in the know about the details, but I doubt Levin would turn down something like that," Kazu said, "I'll introduce you to him when we arrive."

"Thank you," Sora said, "If I may, what do you charge?"

"It's about six hours from here to Akh and seven from there to Maar; each step will cost you five silvers per head," Kazu said, gesturing with his hand. "If you haven't got that on you, I'm happy to wait until Levin pays you—you seem like the trustworthy sort."

The man seemed pretty certain that Levin would be hiring them—without a meeting having ever taken place—which seemed like a pretty good sign overall.

"That's very kind of you," Sora said, fishing out his coin pouch. "But fear not, I can pay upfront."

Sora counted out the thirty coins as he spoke and then slid them across the bar towards the man. Kazu scooped them into a loose pile with a word of thanks and then left them there on the bar.

"What time will we be heading out?" Sora asked.

#

"Once a pattern is built up, and the spell is cast, it goes through something of an automated process," Sora said, sitting with his back to the headboard. "That process is informed by the distribution of mana throughout the pattern, and trying to tune a spell after it's been cast is an advanced technique that neither of you will be ready for any time soon."

Chiyo's eyes were closed, the pattern she was building at the top of her scalp slowly coming together. Fubuki acted as the third point in their triangle, her own pattern already in place behind her forehead.

"For *Colourant*, the distribution of the pattern will affect hue, vibrancy, brightness, opacity, and duration," Sora said, listing them all off. "You *can* add details to it with a fine application of mana, but that's beyond you for now as well."

"I think I have it," Chiyo murmured.

"Once the spell is active, the mana that is inside will start to slowly be consumed at a rate determined by the duration you set initially," Sora said, watching them. "Maintaining a spell requires keeping track of how much mana is inside the pattern and then injecting more when it begins to run low."

Chiyo started to relax a bit as the strain of building the pattern began to lessen, maintaining it much less taxing for her. Fubuki had even managed to open her eyes a fraction, a pair of glowing yellow streaks of light peeking out through her eyelashes.

"If you exceed the maximum amount of mana you set when you first cast the spell, it will shatter instantly, but if you fail to inject anything or you do it too slowly, the spell will consume everything and fade away on its own," Sora said, keeping his voice level. "This can make for a frustrating experience if you're forced to maintain a spell with a very short duration because you'll constantly be concentrating on refreshing it—so we're going to give you each some more breathing room."

Sora leaned forward a bit and lowered his voice; he reached forward and pressed a finger against the middle of Fubuki's forehead before moving his hand over and tapping Chiyo on the top of her scalp—both locations were carefully chosen.

"The point that determines the duration for *Colourant* is directly in the centre point of the pattern—but that is rarely the case with spells," Sora said, sitting back. "I want you to very carefully move more mana into the pattern and shift it towards the centre."

Chiyo made a quiet noise of effort in the back of her throat, her hand clenched around the bedsheets beneath her as she attempted to complete the task. Fubuki closed her eyes completely before somehow growing even more still than before. It took a while, but both of them slowly managed it, the centre of the respective patterns growing brighter as they shifted more mana inside.

"There is a threshold for every spell when it comes to twisting the structure of a pattern, and while it's possible to go above that limit, the difficulty and strain of holding it together will grow exponentially the further you push it," Sora said, "The base duration for *Colourant* is about two minutes, but with practice, the average mage can easily reach five, after that it starts to become a lot more difficult—both of you can stop reinforcing the duration now."

Chiyo sagged at the words, visibly relieved of a burden that only she could feel. Fubuki's eyes cracked open again, and she made eye contact with him.

"At a guess, you're both at about three minutes right now," Sora said, "Which is the exact amount of time you'll have to figure out how to inject mana into it without disturbing the shell—cast your spells."

The two of them murmured the command phrase and then shifted, suddenly free from the massive mental weight of holding it all together as the automated process took on the burden. Chiyo started to panic almost immediately, closing her eyes, already trying to push mana back up to her scalp. The difference in difficulty had resulted in something of a skewered result, and more than once over the last two days, Chiyo had made a muttered comment about falling behind. It didn't seem quite as much of a rivalry as he'd expected, though, because they'd turned *to* each other rather than fallen into a competition. Using the touch method and tracing the pattern on each other's skin worked just as well without him being part of the equation.

"Sora," Fubuki murrmured.

He could feel her channelling her own stream of mana, stretching up her throat, jaw and cheekbones before settling around the pattern in a loose, formless cloud. It pressed inwards, inching close before pulling away again—she was hesitant about how to proceed.

"Pick a single point of entry, and push inwards," Sora said, "Start with a trickle and work your way up."

Chiyo hijacked his advice for her own attempt, but her stream of mana was wider and less focused than what was optimal. It pressed against the shell of the pattern, shattering the outer edge and causing a bleed which would shorten the overall duration.

"Chiyo, you need to rebuild the edge of the pattern, or it's going to vanish in about thirty seconds," Sora spoke, "Once you've fixed it, work on thinning out your stream of mana, there's too much surface area."

Chiyo abandoned the injection and focused entirely on fixing the hole she'd made. The repair was far easier with her focus already directly on the area, and with the mana still pooling there, she had a close source to use for the task. Fubuki punctured her own pattern, but she was being overly cautious, the slow trickle he'd suggested nowhere near enough to counteract the cost.

"Fubuki, double your input and then slowly increase from there," Sora advised. "Chiyo, ten seconds left, make a new injection."

Fubuki's stream increased, but it went over the suggested amount and shattered part of the pattern—she pulled back on the stream, attempting to rebuild it before the mana could bleed away entirely.

"*This is*—" Chiyo strangled out, face flushed with frustration as the spell came apart. "*Ugh.*"

"I hope I didn't give you the impression that you were going to get this on your first try," Sora said, amused. "It's easy for *me*, but your not me; you're a *Himura*."

"Shut up," Chiyo managed, blowing her hair out of her face. "I'm starting again—don't talk to me unless it's to give me advice."

Sora laughed at the words but accepted them without complaint. After fifteen seconds of frantic switching between upping the output, shattering the pattern and then attempting to rebuild the holes, Fubuki's spell collapsed.

"Uh oh, that was kind of embarrassing, Fubuki," Sora said, grinning.

"You've got this look on your face right now—I don't think I've seen you mad before; it's cute."

"Sora," Fubuki said, glaring.

"Okay, *okay*," Sora said, holding his hands up in defence. "I'll just sit here, tortured by boredom, while you two flail around—go on, don't mind me."

#

Sora held the door open, eyeing the room they'd spent the last three days in one last time and wondering once again if they shouldn't just hide out in Judra until they were old and grey. The immediate panicked and dangerous nature of their status as fugitives had managed to fade in the little village where people went to grow wise. Maar would have their bounties posted, and while Kazu hadn't made any connection between the three of them and the people depicted, they would be exposing themselves to thousands of people. As tight as their disguises, cover story, and motivation for being there were, it was still a risk. While they'd made a great deal of progress on learning how to maintain their respective *Colourant* spells, they were one lapse in attention away from it all coming crashing down—and six hours on a boat with nowhere to hide from the owner left a lot of opportunity for something to go wrong. Sora simply couldn't risk letting Chiyo's hair give them away.

"I'm going to handle your spell today, Chiyo," Sora said, stopping them from leaving the room entirely. "You're one mistake off blowing our cover, and it's visibly obvious that you're straining—sorry."

"No, it's fine," Chiyo said, sighing. "I'll practice more when we get to Akh."

"Sora?" Fubuki murrmured.

"So long as your blindfold stays on, nobody will notice any mistakes, so you'll be handling that, Fubuki," Sora said, reaching out to plant his hand on Chiyo's head. "*Colourant*—you two didn't forget anything, did you? My book? Chiyo's smelly panties?"

Chiyo pressed her hand against his chest and shoved him back out into the hallway, glaring. Fubuki carefully lifted up the edge of her cloak, revealing the book cradled in her arms, and he patted her on the shoulder.

"Time to go," Sora said.

They descended the stairs in relative silence, but this time there was nobody down there waiting for them—but that was okay, he'd already said farewell to Marlissa, and Kazu had told them he still had some crates to shuffle onto his boat, so he was probably working on that already. They left the tavern behind, moving as a group towards the bridge. Just as the docks came into view, he caught sight of a familiar pair sitting on a crate and talking with Kazu.

"Good morning," Sora said as they followed the little walkway down to the docks. "I'm terribly sorry if we're late."

Sara twisted around at the sound of his voice, opened her mouth, paused and then grimaced. Tia's hand, wrapped around her wrist, seemed to work as a kind of ambient restraining force for her to choose her words with more care than normal.

"You're all good; I'm almost done loading up," Kazu said before turning back to the two girls. "I'll be back here about three days after the festival ends; I'll lock down a spot on the boat for you both then, alright?"

"That would be perfect," Tia said, carefully withdrawing an envelope from her pocket. "If I could trouble you for one more thing? I was hoping you could deliver this to Jalin for me—if she's still in Maar."

"Jalin's put her roots down; I don't think she'll be going anywhere for a long time," Kazu said, taking the letter. "I'll make sure she gets it—it's a *letter*; I'm not going to charge you for a bit of paper, girl; put that away."

"Thank you very much," Tia said, smiling. "Sara."

"Thanks," Sara said, rolling her eyes. "What? I *said* it didn't I? Why are you looking at me like that?"

"She's alright, " Kazu said, waving it off. "Try not to come down with anything else before I get back, would you? Shiro, you're good to board whenever you're ready."

"Thank you," Sora said, nodding. "Itsuka? If you would go ahead for a moment."

Chiyo led Fubuki across the docks towards the boat, careful to make sure she stepped over the small gap without an issue. Kazu stood beside them during the transition, making sure they were fine, and then turned his attention towards the crates sitting on the edge of the dock. Sora waited for the man to move out of earshot and then spoke up.

"You're looking a bit more energetic today," Sora said before glancing down at Sara. "You, on the other hand, still look like shit—ever heard of a bath?"

Tia looked startled at the words, but Sara looked entirely vindicated.

"I *told* you," Sara said, eyes lighting up. "He's a total prick."

"Keep that one between the two of you, please," Sora said, dragging his mask back into place. "It would cause me a lot of trouble if someone were to look at us too closely."

"Fine," Sara said, frowning. "Will you be in Maar when we get there?"

"I'm sorry to say that we won't," Sora admitted. "This might be the last time you see me."

"Whatever," Sara mumbled.

"Shiro," Tia said, squeezing her sister's hand. "Thank you for everything you've done for us."

"You're welcome, Tia," Sora said before catching the younger girl's eye. "Sara, you better not cause too much trouble for your sister when you get there—while she might have a startling amount of luck on her side, second chances are rarer for people like you and me."

#

The flatboat moved silently across the water, pushed along by the force of the long pole Kazu wielded—ten feet long at least and presumedly used to fight off all the Nymphs that might catch sight of the man's bulging muscles. The speed wasn't anything extraordinary, but between Kazu's efforts and the current of the river carrying them along, it easily outpaced travelling by foot several times over.

"Marlissa mentioned it was recent, but that was about it," Kazu admitted, voice untouched by the effort. "Something magical related?"

"A month ago, I attempted to teach her something she wasn't ready for, and the backlash stole her sight," Sora said, "Fortunately, it's not permanent, and my efforts to fix it are finally starting to bare fruit—if we're lucky, I might manage to restore it before the festival."

Or rather, Fubuki might reach a level of skill with maintaining *Colourant* that would allow her to do away with the blindfold entirely.

"You sure this isn't your wheelhouse?" Kazu said, bemused.

"An Adept with an education in healing would probably have fixed this up in a few hours," Sora said, shaking his head. "A month of trying, and I've *stumbled* onto the solution—at least, I hope I have."

"Best of luck with that," Kazu said in agreement.

"Kazu," Sora said, "I've heard that there's a shrine in Akh; you wouldn't happen to know how to get there, would you?"

Chiyo glanced over at him, her brow furrowed at the topic he'd never spoken up about before.

"You might be the first outsider I've ever heard mention it," Kazu wondered, "You're interested in that kind of thing, I gather?"

"I'm interested in anything that might be worthy of a good story," Sora offered, "It's kind of my job, after all."

"It's really not much, just a small statue of a monk sitting on a pedestal; it's been restored a few times, apparently," Kazu said, eyes on the treeline. "I asked around once, but nobody seemed to know who it was—probably an old river god, if I had to guess, there's half a dozen of those at least."

Chiyo and Fubuki both turned to look at him, finally making the connection between a statue of an unknown monk and *The Dragon's Marble*. Considering they were on the Third Talon, one of the three rivers that led to the Dragon's Claw, he'd expected they would pick up on it eventually.

"How interesting," Sora said, smiling. "Is it something we could reach before nightfall?"

"Easily," Kazu said, nodding to the left-hand side of the river. "It's about fifteen minutes East of the village; there's a long set of stairs, so you can't really miss it."

Sora beckoned Chiyo with his finger, her decision to sit on the other bench making it more of an issue to refresh her spell.

"Shiro?" Chiyo said, standing up. "Will we be going to look at it?"

Chiyo stepped over towards him, reaching down to touch his shoulder for a moment, and he caught her wrist, pulling her down onto his lap—she glared at him, cheeks red as he wrapped his arms around her waist to keep her there.

"An interesting tale is something I can't exactly turn down, even if nobody knows what it's about," Sora said. "I think we should—Fuka, would you like to go?"

"Yes," Fubuki said without pause. "Kazu, how long?"

"You're an impatient one, huh?" Kazu said, laughing. "We're a little over halfway there, so I'd say two and a half hours to go."

Fubuki shifted around on the bench at the words—a flicker of something pale green amongst the trees behind her caught his eye, a short, stubby form with shining black eyes watching them from the forest. It wasn't the first goblin he'd seen since they'd set out, either. With such sparse numbers, they wouldn't be bold enough to approach even a village of Judra's size—a single man with a weapon could kill a dozen of the things on his own. The forests north of Bilaar, however, were going to be filled with them and in much more dangerous numbers. The city worked to keep them from coming south, but that was all they'd managed. The population had grown too large to deal with easily, and they'd entrenched themselves in just about everywhere between Bilaar and the ocean. Numbering in the tens of thousands, they'd have needed a significant fighting force to clear them out, but Goblins weren't the kinds of creatures to meet you on an open field in the first place. Stretching across the border of both Fabah and Malnia, neither country wanted to front the cost associated with the monumental task of clearing them out, and neither was willing to work together to manage it. Instead, it was simpler for Bilaar and the surrounding cities to set a small price for goblin ears on the town boards and let the aspiring adventurers work to keep the immediate surroundings clear. An unfortunate danger that he would need to confront in the distant future—Chiyo shifted in his lap, and he glanced up at her for a moment.

"Is something wrong?" Chiyo said under her breath. "You have a strange look on your face."

"Just thinking about the future," Sora said, slipping his hand around to her back and pushing her back to her feet. "Go on."

#

Akh was definitely bigger, but it had enough in common with Judra that he'd have expected some kind of shared system of city planning— or one had simply copied the other. Another bridge crossed the river, wider and a bit higher up off the water. The docks were longer, two-tiered, and on both sides of the bridge, rather than just one like in Judra. The east side of the village was much, much larger than the west, and he couldn't actually see the edge of it; the houses just kept on going—interspersed with some trees that hadn't been cleared out entirely. The east side was actually cleared off forest for a few hundred meters, far enough that he could make out what was definitely some kind of farm. The road kept on going, twisting away and vanishing into the distant forest, presumedly leading off towards the grassy plains far south of Bilaar. Kazu left them at the bridge with a brief rundown of the city, the location of the tavern he'd be staying at, and a promise to meet them at the docks early the next morning.

"We can go book a room now, or we can investigate the shrine," Sora said, conferring with the two of them. "Either of you has a preference?"

"I don't want to come back out again once we get a room," Chiyo said, shaking her head. "We should finish whatever we're going to do now and then head in for the night—Fubuki?"

"I want to see the nameless monk," Fubuki murmured.

"So do I," Sora admitted, taking Fubuki's arm to lead her east. "Come on then, let's go see if I was right about this."

Fubuki curled her fingers around his wrist, the grip deceptively soft; Chiyo came to stand on his free side, within touching distance for when the spell needed recharging. As they got closer to the farm, it became clear that there was much more of the forest cleared away than had been visible from the bridge. There was a large stable set up near the front of it, a trio of men sitting down at a table out the front of the building—three Pangolems and six horses were tucked away inside the building, their heads hanging over the railing, their respective saddle and harness hanging from a series of hooks in front of each. Fubuki's grip tightened around his wrist as one of the Pangolems let out a rattling groan, and her head turned to face the direction it had come from.

"Sora," Fubuki murrmured.

"It's a stable with three Pangolems inside," Sora said, voice quiet. "Use your spell and have a peek, but be quick; there are people ahead of us."

Fubuki's mana surged up her throat, her desire to see what was going on gifting her a sort of hyperfocus, and the pattern twisted itself into existence far faster than she had managed up until this point. Sora stopped for a moment, turning until his back was between the three men and Fubuki, reaching up under her hat under the guise of fixing the clothing. The spell snapped into existence as she murmured the word, and he pulled the blindfold down an inch before reaching back behind her head to unknot the tie.

"They're looking at us," Chiyo said, keeping her smile up. "Be quick."

Fubuki stared over his shoulder at the creatures, solid black irises flicking about at a speed that he couldn't quite track. He drew the blindfold back towards him, straightened it out in his hand, and then leaned back in, covering her eyes with it. Sora tied it closed behind her head, tugged it once to make sure it would stay there, and then turned back to face the way he had.

"That's better," Sora said, raising his voice a bit. "Come on, Fuka."

Fubuki took his arm again and let him lead her on, leaving the stable, the creatures, and the three men behind. A minute of silence passed as they kept on moving, the sounds of the village fading behind them as they followed the twist in the road and left direct sight.

"Are you okay, Fubuki?" Chiyo asked.

"Yes," Fubuki murmured. "I—just wanted to see it."

Sora took note of a break in the trees, far ahead of them, a single stone step visible from their position. Chiyo touched his sleeve for a moment, and he nodded, slipping back a bit to allow her to take his place beside Fubuki.

"Those ones were pretty young; they actually grow up to twice that size," Chiyo said, leaning down to her ear. "Their scales also come in three different colours; a dull silver, a murky brown, and a rust red."

"Silver," Fubuki murrmured.

"The one you encountered before? I'm afraid I didn't see the colour of the scale; it was too dark." Chiyo said, "They are actually quite friendly —I've seen stablehands scrub them clean with these wire brushes, and they end up really shiny for a few days afterwards."

Sora was content to listen to their quiet conversation, Chiyo's attempt to fulfil Fubuki's clear interest in the creature. Considering that her only apparent encounter with them before now was a negative one, it might have been her attempt to wash some of that away. The stairs that Kazu had mentioned were not quite as many as he'd been expecting, but there were easily a hundred at his best guess, winding upwards to the top of a hill buried amongst the untouched side of the forest. Sora led the way, setting off upwards in front of the others, keeping his senses on high alert—but there was nothing magical about the area, no sign of mana anywhere nearby, other than the three of them. He crested the last step and found himself atop a small plateau, ringed by a railing that looked like it had seen better days. In the middle of it sat a large squat foundation, six inches raised up off the floor, and above it was the statue of a thin man sitting cross-legged. A length of beads was strung about his neck, a simple cloth robe wrought in stone, unadorned by any kind of symbolism. The man's hands were cupped together in front of his belly, a few inches above his lap, and in the middle was a single large bead, not unlike the ones he wore across his body—Sora smiled, suddenly certain that there was something more to *The Tale of the Dragon's Marble* then just embellishments and rumour.

"Chiyo," Fubuki murrmured.

"There's no one nearby; you should be able to take it off," Chiyo said, helping her untie the blindfold. "Just keep it ready, okay?"

"Okay," Fubuki agreed.

Sora reached down and pressed a single finger against the bead in the monk's hand, a spark of mana flowing into it—which remained entirely unreactive because it was nothing more than a simple stone.

"You knew about the shrine," Chiyo said, watching him. "That's why you wanted to pass through here."

"Correct, as far as I can tell, it's the only one around here that still exists—and the only reason for that is they went to the effort of maintaining it," Sora agreed, "There used to be one in Maar, but they knocked it down about a decade ago."

"If the only reason they survived this long is that people are maintaining them, then there's no reason to believe that anything will be at Dragon's Claw, is there?" Chiyo said, speaking slowly. "What if we go all that way, and there's just *nothing* there."

"There might be nothing," Sora admitted, eyeing the nameless monk. "There's no real way to know."

"We do know it's dangerous, though," Chiyo said, "There's a *reason* the place is restricted, and people don't just go walking in there; the entire place is overrun by goblins."

"That's true as well," Sora said, nodding.

"Then we're risking our lives for something that might not even exist," Chiyo said, voice quiet. "Sora, wouldn't it be better if we joined a caravan from Bilaar to Lyston and forgot about all of this?"

Sora reached down and placed his hand flat against the floor, a complicated pattern twisting into existence within his palm. It took a moment for it to reach the threshold, and then once it had, he spoke.

"*Resonance*," Sora said.

A pulse of mana flashed outwards in every direction, rising up into the air, pushing through the trees around them and sinking into the stone platform, looking for anything that might react to it—but there really was nothing here.

"You're right about everything; it is dangerous, there might be nothing there, and your idea is much smarter overall—but there's a reason I'm called Sora the Seeker," Sora said, "I believe there is *something* at

Dragon's Claw, and while it may be nothing more than pieces of a shattered statue lying at the bottom of the river, I'm going to find out, no matter what."

Sora pushed himself up to his feet and turned to face them.

"By the time we get to Bilaar, you'll both be more than capable of getting along without me; I'll make sure of that," Sora said, smiling. "I'm not going to force either of you to go into danger that you want no part of, so you should start thinking about what you're going to do—because you'll have an important decision to make when we get there."

#

The room was a bit bigger than the one they'd had in Judra, but that might simply have been a result of it lacking the table and chair entirely. The extra space felt pretty unnecessary when all three of them had staked out a spot on the bed. Fubuki had used most of the day's travel time to figure it out for herself, and as far as he could tell, she'd managed to maintain the most recent attempt for almost half an hour without any mistakes. Chiyo, on the other hand, was playing catch up, with her lute lying across her lap, untouched for the moment. Her attempts were slower, given the difficulty of her spell placement, but they were steady improvements nonetheless, and without any sort of distraction, she'd almost managed ten whole minutes of frantic juggling. Sora had used the time to pick up a new set of travelling cloaks for the three of them and then cannibalised Fubuki's old one to start work on a costume for her to wear during their act—it was still up in the air whether or not she wanted to participate, but he was hoping to convince her to change her mind before the night in question.

"*Ugh*," Chiyo muttered as her spell came apart. "One more time."

He'd bled the cloak entirely black through the use of *Stain* and then used *Shapecloth* to fuse the front of the cloak shut near the top. Fubuki's short stature allowed him to cut the length of it down by two feet, and he added a serrated pattern along the bottom of it for some extra flare. He used the extra mass he'd stolen to add a series of rigid and curved spines along the top of the hood, sweeping back up into the air in a dark mass that almost looked like locks of black hair, inside of which her horns would be easily hidden. He added a second serrated edge around the shoulders of the cloak, like a mantled layer, to give it some extra depth and detail. The whole thing was hanging up beside the door, strategically placed so that Fubuki could see it from her place on the bed. Every now and then, he'd catch her looking at it, her now spell-black eyes studying it. He'd used some of the leftover material on his own costume, thickening the thinner parts and fixing up the issues he'd noticed after wearing it for several days. Chiyo's own costume was still in the works, a smaller, tighter version of the same waistcoat suit he would be wearing to give them an extra boost of uniformity to match the braids they all wore. Three travelling entertainers with a clear theme, a practised act, and a solid history behind them—if anyone could see through it all, then they had probably earned the right to catch them. Fubuki slipped off the bed, rising to her feet, before stepping over to the cloak, then she turned to look over her shoulder at him.

"Sora," Fubuki murmured, finally giving in to her curiosity. "Who is the observer?"

"The character from the story?" Sora said, feigning distraction with the coat in his hands. "I didn't think you were interested."

"Don't tease her—" Chiyo managed, the effort of speaking up almost causing a critical destabilisation within the pattern. "*Ugh.*"

"Sora," Fubuki mumbled.

"The observer is an ancient faery, one who finds herself indebted to the hero," Sora said, amused. "They have only one interaction throughout the story, but she spends the following decades watching him grow into a man and then witnessing his final moments—but despite her fascination with him and the kindness he once showed her, she doesn't act to help him."

"Why not?" Fubuki asked.

"Faery in old tales are humanoids, who look, speak and act like humans, but only on the surface," Sora said, "Their behaviour is constrained by rules that cannot be enforced on us."

Fubuki reached out to touch the clothing, running her fingertips down the front of it.

"Their mythos may well have been informed—in part—by some of the ways your own species function," Sora said, "The most notable similarity being that they cannot lie, and they are bound by the deals they swear to."

"They are like me?" Fubuki murmured.

"Only by those two factors, Fubuki; they may look like you and me, but a Faery is an alien being who is driven by motivations beyond our comprehension," Sora said, shaking his head. "They are terrifyingly intelligent and are compelled ubiquitously towards deceit, dominance, and trickery—when they make deals with mortals, it's not for personal gain or desire; it's simply a result of their nature."

"Are they real?" Fubuki asked.

"I can't point to a single thing that would prove they ever existed," Sora admitted, "But with all things like this, I can't discount it either."

"There is always an element of truth in stories like this," Fubuki murmured.

It was an odd experience to hear his own words repeated back to him—outside of magical instruction, the fact that she had apparently internalised something he'd said well enough to locate and then identify a situation in which it applied was strangely flattering.

"It's such a shame that I'll never get to see you wear it," Sora said, raising his voice in feigned distress. "I suppose I'll just have to find some other girl who will appreciate it—maybe I can find someone in Maar?"

"Sora—" Fubuki said.

"I suppose I could just throw it away?" Sora said, flapping his hand at her. "In a muddy alleyway or behind some smelly crates—perhaps someone will find it before it gets *too* dirty."

Chiyo's spell suffered a sudden irreparable breakdown as a lapse in her attention tore a hole through the side of the pattern and carved away the too many critical components to keep it in place—a noise that could almost be described as a growl dragged itself up out of her throat.

"Sora," Fubuki said, staring at him now. "I want to wear it."

"*You're both so distracting,*" Chiyo strangled out. "Can you just—"

#

"There's usually not that many people travelling between the river cities, honestly," Kazu said, sinking the long pole into the river and pressing the boat forward across the water. "Most of the traffic is from Akh to Maar, rarely does anybody actually head down to Judra."

"Then your job is more focused on transporting goods?" Chiyo said.

"For the most part," Kazu confirmed. "Wood and woodwork are the usual export from Judra—plenty of trees down that far. Maar and Akh have both cleared a lot of the forestry out over the last hundred years, so it's a pretty stable source of coin for Judra."

"We saw some of that at Akh; the east side of the river was starting to appear pretty thinned out," Sora said, "Looks like they were trying to make a road straight through to the plains—are they trying to open up a land route to Bilaar?"

"That's the plan, or so I've heard," Kazu nodded.

"They're currently entirely reliant on Maar for supplies and population growth; opening up a land route would give them the ability to grow independently," Chiyo said, humming. "It's a smart decision, but it's an awful lot of forest to clear, even if they do make it a straight shot east—how far off completion are they?"

"They're about halfway there, but they've been having trouble with the local goblin population," Kazu said, "Further from the city they get, the larger the numbers; it seems like a few groups have managed to dig in long enough to start breeding—makes me miss the days where we only had to worry about Redcaps."

"Bilaar is doing a terrible job of keeping them from coming south," Chiyo said, frowning, "I hadn't heard anything to indicate it was this bad."

"If they're only encountering them after striking out that far, the news probably hasn't had time to spread yet," Sora said, "They'll have to start doing what everywhere else does and post rewards for ears."

"They've got it up on the board in Maar already," Kazu admitted, "Doubt it'll be too long before Akh gets sick of dealing with them."

"There's regular trade between Bilaar and Maar, or so I've heard,"

Chiyo said, catching Kazu's eye. "Do you know when the next caravan is setting out?"

"I don't get much to do with that lot, so I couldn't tell your their schedules—there are enough middlemen between us that I couldn't really give you a name either," Kazu said, thinking about it. "Levin handles a lot of the logistic and trader stuff on behalf of the Mayor; he'll be able to point you in the right direction when you speak to him—at a guess, I'd say there would be *someone* setting out within a few days of the festival's end."

"Something for us to look into," Sora said, nodding. "Fuka—how are your eyes feeling? Can you see more than shadows now?"

A prepared point of discussion to complete the transition from blindfolded to being able to see again in front of the only person who knew about it and would be in Maar. Fubuki reached up and untied her blindfold, carefully pulling it down to sit around her neck, and then opened her eyes. Kazu looked back towards them, interested in seeing her uncovered face for the first time.

"It is better than this morning," Fubuki murmured, black eyes staring across the bench at him. "I'm starting to see details now as well."

"That's good," Sora said, sighing. "Why don't you leave the blindfold off for a little while and see if that doesn't help speed it along—if you start to feel any pain from the light, however, please make sure you cover it once more."

"Okay," Fubuki murrmured.

The pattern was holding strong, a small trickle of mana passing up her throat and pooling behind her forehead, ready to be used to recharge the spell. At least for Fubuki, she could close her eyes if it did fail and keep them that way until she'd recovered. Chiyo, on the other hand, had no safe way to hide her hair. She'd managed to hold it in place for almost fifteen minutes before she'd finally turned in the night before, but that had been under controlled conditions—her time would come, likely within a few days, but for now, the responsibility fell to him.

"We're getting close now," Kazu said, speaking up. "I'd say an hour left until we start seeing the trees thinning out, and then you'll catch sight of Maar ahead—it's a pretty sight from up here."

"Is that right?" Sora said, wriggling his eyebrows. "I guess you could call it a sight for sore eyes."

Fubuki stared at him with a furrowed brow, apparently not understanding the joke.

"We're getting divorced in Maar," Chiyo decided. "I can't handle this a single day longer."

Kazu just laughed.

#

Seven

Maar was nothing like the other river cities in size, shape or construction. It looked more like Satu than anything else, with its all-encompassing wall striking out from each side of the river and continuing long past his line of sight. The buildings were taller and built with far more trimmings than the more pragmatic style he'd grown used to seeing. They'd even gone as far as to paint parts of the buildings—whites, creams, beiges—to offset the dark, stained wood. There were farms outside of the walls, and enough of the forest had been cleared out for them to see straight through to the plains. Sora knew it would be the same to the north of the city, right up until the main trading route between Satu and Bilaar. There were two tiers to the city, with the highest points being on the east and west side and flattening out towards the centre. From a distance, the entire thing gave off the impression of a massive crustacean having seated itself right on top of the river, with its claws cradling the water.

"Kazu," Sora said, staring at it. "It's a crab."

"That's not the first time I've heard that," Kazu said, amused. "Levin thinks it started off completely accidental, figures that the city planners noticed it about halfway through, and decided to try and lean into it."

"A happy mistake, huh?" Sora said. "Most of mine end with my options getting fewer and my coin pouch getting lighter."

Chiyo shifted a bit at the words, but she said nothing in response; she'd grown progressively quieter the closer they'd gotten to Maar. This was going to be the first real test of their disguises and would either confirm the strength of them or end with them getting attacked, beaten and dragged back to Satu—or outright killed if their hunters weren't feeling like putting up with the struggle. He couldn't exactly blame her for feeling worried either, considering what had happened the last time she'd been caught. Fubuki was as quiet as she always was, but there was something in the way she began to grow ever-stiller that made it clear to him that she was just as worried about the upcoming leg of their journey. The walls rose up as they approached, the city growing to loom over them, showering them with the cool shade, and then all of a sudden, Maar had swallowed them. Almost immediately, the noise reached his ears, people calling out to each other, foots scuffing the wood of the docks ahead of them, and the sound of a hammer striking something metal—the sound of a city, with people spilling out into its streets. It reminded him far too much of Satu, and a new curl of home-sickness sunk its hooks into his chest.

"Kazu, you've only gone and done it," Sora said, fighting to maintain his smile. "Those arms of yours are worthy of a tale on their own—one a piece even."

Kazu's own mood had a rhythm to it that ran in the opposite direc-tion to their group, slowly growing more bright the closer they got to Maar—the man wasn't immune to the desire for home either.

"Is that right?" Kazu laughed, "Can't say I've heard many myths starring a boatman."

"There's more of them than you'd think," Sora said, eyes on the buildings framing the river. "Crossing bodies of water are usually a pretty common facet of stories, although those ones usually end with someone getting eaten."

"A fate I'm more than happy to avoid," Kazu said, amused. "It's been an interesting trip, a lot less boring than most of them—docks coming up on our left here."

The group did a quick check to make sure they had all of their belongings as Kazu brought them to a stop beside a pair of almost iden-tical boats, one of which had a blonde man lying on his side between the benches. Kazu tied it off to one of the posts, and they followed him off onto the solid ground.

"I've gotta run these guys in to see Levin," Kazu said, waving to the blonde man. "Keep an eye on my load, will you?"

The blonde man gave him a lazy wave but said nothing in response. It must have been a confirmation, though, because Kazu tossed a thank you back to him before starting up towards the stone staircase. A pair of men in armour stood at the end of the bridge bisecting the river, swords at their hips, simply leaning against each side—guards to keep the peace. Sora nodded to one of them as the man looked over, feeling Chiyo attach herself to his arm. He put it down to a combination of fear, and pragmatism, to ensure he could keep the spell in place. Fubuki followed beside her, not quite touching. Sora started noting down the general structure of the buildings, alleyways, and streets and how they all intersected. If they did get found out, they'd need to escape the walls, and that meant being able to find their way back to the docks—with only two guards in the vicinity, it would be far less protected than any of the other gates. They passed the two guards without issue, moving north down the street that bordered the river.

"This here is the main stretch, as you can see," Kazu said, kind of gesturing to both sides of the river with his arm. "There are a few little shops along the waterfront."

The windows on the buildings were actually made of glass instead of just open frames with drop-down slats. Most of them were opaque, murky, or bubbled, but a few of the more upscale buildings had the clear stuff.

"Mayor's building is to the east, up topside; I wouldn't bother him if you can help it, guys a bit of a prick—excuse my language," Kazu said, gesturing to the massive mansion peeking out over the rooftops to their left. "Town centre is up ahead of us; that's where most everything is. Levin has his own building down here, easier for people to get in and talk to him, rather than head up to the Mansion every time they need something."

There were certainly more people moving around the further they walked, adults sitting at tables outside of houses, kids sitting on the railing watching the river and even a dog that seemed to be chasing after a bird that couldn't quite seem to shake it.

"Levin's in charge of interfacing with traders?" Sora said, speaking up. "Assistant to the mayor—what was his name?"

"Mayor Karia," Kazu nodded, "Levin handles all the day-to-day stuff; Karia stays up in his mansion, meeting with nobles and making the big deals."

"Delegating is a skill all of its own," Chiyo murmured, speaking up for the first time. "Some people are just better at certain jobs or have a particular talent for it."

"Sure," Kazu said, entirely unconvinced.

The town centre seemed to be built with the river as a centrepiece; another bridge, much wider than the little one near the docks, sat on top of the river. Around it was a massive stone circle of empty space, framed by a zigzag of buildings that encircled the entire thing. Benches, tables, trees, and fountains dotted the area, the entire thing almost like a park except for its stone floor. Popup stalls, large tents, buskers, entertainers and a singular large wooden stage that dominated the centre were set up in the area, the preparations for the festival already mostly in place. Kazu led them through the mess, then to one of the larger buildings on the edges; a group of six women whose clothing declared them as shrine maidens were lined up outside of the door. In front of them were a man and a woman, their ankles, shins, wrists and forearms all bandaged up with a rough cloth.

"Looks like there's going to be a bit of a wait," Kazu said, scratching at his chin. "Tell you what—you three line up, and I'll have a quick word to Levin."

"Of course," Sora said, "Thank you for all your help, Kazu."

Kazu waved him off, already walking past the line and letting himself into the building. Sora edged the three of them over to the line and settled in to wait. Chiyo detached herself from him for a moment, moving to whisper into Fubuki's ear—almost certainly explaining the odd clothing of the group in front of them. Sora spotted a town board nearby, a hundred pieces of parchment pinned to it in a rather haphazard manner. Some of them were letters, the writing too far away for him to read, while others were sketches of furniture, pieces that were for sale. A reward posting for goblin ears dominated the far right side of the board, a rough sketch of the creature's face clearly visible— one silver each. A trio of pictures near the centre of the board drew his eye; the faces were different than the last time he'd seen them, with new names and information attached. The door opened, and a woman stalked out, glaring at everyone around her. The man and the woman at the front of the line were let in a moment later, a nervous woman wearing eyeglasses waving them to enter. The shrine maidens shifted forward into the gap, a huddle occurring in which they began discussing strategy for convincing the man inside to let them perform on such short notice. Sora couldn't quite feel any of the frantic energy they'd managed to build up. The door opened up again, and the pair came out, flashing a smile of success at the rest of them. The nervous girl spoke with the two shrine maidens at the front of the group and allowed only them inside before shutting the door. The rest of the shrine maidens moved away, removing themselves from the line proper, and Sora stepped forward to lean against the wall beside the door. The door opened a few minutes later, emitting the two Shrine Maidens, the happy energy trailing after them enough to tell him that they'd succeeded in getting their own slot.

"Good afternoon," The nervous woman said, leaning out of the open doorway. "Levin will see you now, but we've got a limit of two people per group—I hope you understand."

"Thank you," Sora said, "I'll handle this on my own—Itsuka, Fuka, stay here."

Sora let his arm linger on Chiyo's shoulder, tuning the spell for the maximum duration he could manage before he moved to follow the woman inside. They crossed the front room towards a door in the back, and she knocked once before opening it. Kazu leaned against the wall opposite the door, a few feet behind a strikingly thin man, who, even sitting down, was almost as tall as the woman. He wore a maroon yukata, draping down his thin shoulders and billowing around his too-long arms.

"Thank you, Mela," Levin said, looking up over his eyeglasses. "This was the last?"

"For the moment," Mela admitted, glancing between Sora and the man. "I suspect there will be more eventually."

"Most likely," Levin agreed, "Good afternoon, Shiro, was it?"

"Yes, and it's a pleasure to meet you, Levin," Sora said, "I'll have to keep my pitch short, given my wife appears to be growing closer to divorcing me the longer this day drags on."

"More bad jokes?" Kazu wondered.

"Something like that," Sora agreed, "I'm a storyteller who uses illusionary magic as an accompaniment. My wife provides music, and her younger sister often performs the roles of specific characters—she dances too, but I'm afraid she's entirely unpracticed for our current performance due to a recent injury."

"Interesting," Levin said, folding his arms across the desk in front of him. "Kazu mentioned that you recreated a scene involving an Ogre and a wagon?"

"Our unfortunate trip to Judra," Sora said, affecting a sigh. "Yes, would you like a demonstration of what I'm capable of?"

"Please," Levin said.

Sora took a step away from the door, turning to face the entirety of the room with his back to the corner. Mela looked like she was half a second from attempting to escape the room, unsure where to stand or how to hold herself now that she was in view. Sora eyed the room for a moment, checking for space and props and working out the distances involved before nodding. A dozen patterns built up inside of him, and he slowly lifted his arm up, murmuring the command phrases—*Gleam, Construct, Gust*. A breeze spun through the room, avoiding the papers on Levin's desk entirely, but sending his ponytail swishing about. A translucent *Construct*, shaped like a massive serpent, coiled into existence in the middle of the room, as thick around as Kazu's body. It circled the room in a blur before rising up before the desk, a dusting of sparks emerging from its now open mouth. A twist of the *Gust* pattern sent a wash of cool air outwards, the creature's breath ruffling their clothes as it opened its sparkling *Gleam* enhanced eyes.

"That's even crazier than the Ogre," Kazu said, stunned.

"This is one of the characters in the story we intend to perform," Sora said, spinning his hand. "The entire tale will take about five minutes to complete, and I'll likely add in some magic for ambience—wind like you've just felt."

The massive snake began to crumble, flakes of mana rising into the air and vanishing, leaving the office empty once more.

"That is amazing," Levin said, glasses hanging too low on his face. "How are you able to create so much detail?"

"Are you a mage?" Sora asked, "It will inform how I answer, is all."

"No, no, I've not the skill for something like that," Levin said, fixing his glasses. "We've had a few illusionists appear for previous festivals, but I've never seen ones with such complexity."

"Then my answer is that I'm singularly talented at illusionary magic," Sora offered.

"What would you have said if I *had* been a mage?" Levin asked, visibly curious.

"I'm quite good at tuning patterns and layering them to evoke certain effects," Sora said, "Once you're comfortable with holding a few dozen patterns at once, it becomes much easier to split that attention in other ways, such as building more complex shapes with a single spell."

"I see, a far more technical answer I'm in no position to critique," Levin said, nodding. "How many times can you perform this story in a single night—I'm assuming night here for obvious reasons."

"Night is best for something like this, I agree. We could perform it three times, with an hour break in between each to recover," Sora said, estimating it. "After that, I'd start getting pretty low on mana, and my accompaniment would have their own issues."

"It's common for people to tip the performances they enjoy, and there is a box attached to the stage for just that reason," Levin said, "The standard deal for something like this is a flat rate per performance depending on its perceived popularity, and a thirty-seventy split of the tip, with seventy going towards Maar."

Sora nodded at the information, thinking about it.

"Given the spectacle involved, you're certain to receive a large number of tips," Levin said, "Three performances, each night, at six, seven and eight—twenty silver per performance as a flat rate, and thirty per cent of the tips."

"Thirty silver per performance," Sora said, "After the first performance, the word is going to spread—because it *always* does, I assure you —which will draw in more and more people to come to watch. You'll more than make that up in your share of the tips."

"Twenty-two silver and forty percent of the tips," Levin said, "If you're so confident about your power to draw people in."

"I've often been told I'm too confident for my own good," Sora said, stepping forward. "So, of course, I'll have to take a deal like that."

Kazu laughed at the comment, still content to lean against the wall. Sora stuck his hand out over the desk, and Levin took it, shaking on the agreed amount.

"Perfect, Mela will be at the stage to let you on at the start of each hour, so please make sure you find her when it's time," Levin said, "The day after the festival ends, please return here, and I'll settle our agreement in full."

"Thank you very much; I'll do that," Sora said before pausing for a moment. "Levin, who would I speak to about joining a caravan to Bilaar after the festival is over?"

"Ah, yes, Kazu mentioned that as well," Levin said, clicking his fingers. "I've got someone in mind for that, but I've yet to speak with them—I'll make sure to introduce you to her when you return here for your payment."

#

Sora stepped into the room, swung his travel pack off his back, and dropped it beside the bed on the left side of the room. The sound of the door shutting reached his ears, and he spent a moment stretching in an attempt to crack his back before dropping down onto the bed. He folded his hands behind his head and closed his eyes, mind focused on the performance they'd be handling in twenty-four hours' time. He'd spent plenty of time in the last few days going over it all already, but the fact that they'd be doing it in front of a crowd brought a bit of extra urgency to it all.

"Three performances each night of the festival, twenty-two silvers per performance," Chiyo said, seating herself on the edge of the opposite bed. "That's just under two gold—how much did he say the tips usually were?"

"He didn't, but we get forty percent of whatever comes in," Sora admitted, keeping his eyes closed. "His original offer was only thirty percent, so I imagine they make a fair bit off tips alone."

"How much do *we* get?" Chiyo said, voice a bit quieter. "What kind of split did you have in mind?"

"One-third to each of us," Sora said, "If we pull in another hundred silver through tips, then that might be one gold each—more than enough to get you from Bilaar to Lyston."

"A caravan from Bilaar would cost us fifty silvers each," Chiyo said, the slight pull to her voice telling him that she was biting at her lip again. "Thirty silvers each from here to Bilaar in the first place—we'd be stranded in Lyston with barely any money."

"Lyston is pretty far away, so unless you're going to walk it, that's about as good as travel costs are going to get," Sora said, kicking his shoes off without getting up. "Either way, I already said I'd pay for you both to get to Bilaar, so you can stop worrying about that part."

"Why even pay our way to Bilaar if you're just going to break off on your own?" Chiyo said with a frustrated breath. "You don't make any sense—are you seriously going to Dragon's Claw?"

"I told you I was the last time you asked," Sora sighed, "Asking me the same question over and over again isn't going to get you a different answer, Chiyo."

"I'm hoping it will eventually break through whatever delusion you're stuck inside," Chiyo said, a bit heated. "There are *tens of thousands* of goblins in those forests."

"Bilaar is a city filled with tens of thousands of guards, adventurers, bounty hunters and worst of all, mages—it only takes one of those with an ability to sense nearby active spells to realise what you are doing with *Colourant*," Sora said, shrugging. "People or goblins, both of those groups want us dead, so neither option is particularly safer than the other if things were to go wrong."

"Which is why we should stick together; our disguises are *working*," Chiyo said, face in her hands. "But they aren't going to do anything to stop a goblin."

"If you're that worried about going any further on your own, you could always wait for me to come back to Bilaar," Sora offered, "Not sure how long it's going to take for me to investigate Dragon's Claw— two weeks, I suppose, if there's really nothing there."

"A week, there and back?" Chiyo said before shaking her head. "No— it's not going to take that long because if you go into that forest, *you're going to die*."

"Agree to disagree," Sora said, unconvinced.

"Sora." Fubuki murrmured.

Sora cracked an eye open to glance over at the other end of the bed, where she was sitting, watching him with coal-black eyes—she was getting better and better at holding the spell together and recharging it. The duration was growing longer every time she took it down completely and recast it, seconds at a time perhaps, but it was a clear improvement.

"Fubuki?" Sora said, voice dry. "Did you want to try your hand at convincing me not to go as well?"

"No," Fubuki said, "I want to go to Dragon's Claw with you."

"*Fubuki*," Chiyo strangled out. "Don't you understand—goblins *eat* people."

"I don't want Sora to be eaten," Fubuki murmured. "Chiyo, I will protect you both."

"I—I can't," Chiyo managed. "It's too *dangerous*."

Chiyo let herself flop back onto the bed with her face buried in her hands and flailed her legs about in what was starting to look like some kind of tantrum—she settled down after a moment, feet pulling up onto the bed as she turned over to face the wall, away from them both.

"You can come with me if you want, but I don't need protection, Fubuki," Sora said, "You should be looking out for *yourself*, not me."

"This is so stupid," Chiyo muttered, face half buried in the bedsheet. "Something bad is going to happen to you; I know it."

\#

"You look nervous, Fubuki," Chiyo said, leaning in to see her face. "Are you okay?"

"There are lots of humans outside; I can hear them," Fubuki murmured, "What if they know?"

Sora adjusted the mantle of the costume around her shoulders, making sure it sat evenly, and then took hold of her braid, carefully feeding the end of it down the back of her top.

"They won't, okay?" Chiyo said, "The three of us are nothing like what they're expecting."

Sora slipped his hands down her shoulders, hooking his fingers into the neck of the costume, and used the offshoot of string he'd left there to tie it closed. Once he was done, he drew his fingers back along the inside of the neck and drew the spiked hood up to cover the back of her head, settling her horns inside the two hollow spikes.

"Fubuki?" Sora said, placing his hands on her shoulders and giving them a squeeze. "Do you remember your lines?"

"Yes," Fubuki mumbled. "I remember."

"Good girl," Sora said, nodding. "Chiyo, you ready for this?"

"I am," Chiyo said, breathing out. "You better not laugh at me if I make a mistake—I've never played for an audience before."

"You played for Fubuki and me," Sora said, raising an eyebrow. "Don't we count?"

"Fubuki thinks every song sounds nice, and I question your taste in *everything*," Chiyo said, "So no, you don't count."

"Ouch," Sora said, rolling his eyes. "You can pay for your *own* trip to Bilaar if you're going to malign me, frilly skirt."

Chiyo just stuck her nose up into the air, but he could see her peeking at him from behind her lashes, a tiny slit of white giving her away. Sora gave Fubuki one last check-over and then nodded before directing them to the door. They left the inn, crossed the two streets to get back to the waterfront, and then angled south towards the town centre. Fubuki hadn't been wrong; there were people *everywhere*, men and women standing by the railings, groups striding across the walk-bridges that crisscrossed the river, and residents lingering in doorways watching all the people move about.

"What are those?" Fubuki murmured, watching the river.

The river was filled with paper lanterns, short stubby candles illuminating the inside of them; tiny platforms, they floated downstream, a reflection of the stars above. He'd seen them before, although only a few solitary ones that people sometimes set in Satu's twin rivers.

"Lanterns—they're supposed to symbolise the departure of the souls," Sora said, "It's an old custom, a final goodbye to those who have died recently, and perhaps a way to guide them to somewhere beyond here."

"Beyond here?" Fubuki murmured.

"The afterlife, if such a thing even exists," Sora said, "Fuka, Itsuka—there's our stage."

His use of their aliases seemed to jolt them out of the comfortable silence they'd fallen into, and he offered them both a smile in an attempt to offset it. The town centre was packed; the popup stalls had multiplied tenfold, a haphazard maze of tents and tables filled with merchandise. The stage sat in the centre of it all, half a dozen lanterns posted up on top of the railing, illuminating it well. The man and the woman he'd seen in the line from the day before were already up there, doing battle with one another in a choreographed, acrobatic fight—hands, feet, elbows and knees striking out, clashing in an intricate dance of almost blurring movements. The skill alone put them above most of the fighters he'd seen in his life, although how much of it was effective in combat, as opposed to being built for the spectacle, was anybody's guess. Sora brought them to the gate that led to the stage, where Mela was sitting at a small table that had been set up. A large lockbox sat on top of the table, and she seemed to be counting through what must have been the tips of the previous act, marking it all down on a thick pad of bound parchment—she looked up as they came to stand beside the gate.

"Oh, you're here," Mela said, "It shouldn't be long; I believe they are just finishing up."

"Thank you," Sora said, smiling. "How are you handling things, Mela? You're looking a bit frazzled."

"I—I suppose I must be, but I'm doing quite well, thank you," Mela managed, adjusting her glasses. "I've been looking forward to seeing your performance; what I saw in Levin's office was quite striking."

"Then I only hope we can meet your expectations," Sora said, glancing up at the stage. "It looks as if you were correct; our turn approaches."

The gate opened from the inside, the sweating pair grinning at the applause that followed them as they left. The man carried a lockbox in his hand, not unlike the one on the table. He placed it down when he arrived; a quiet exchange between him and Mela occurred before he stepped away into the crowd alongside his partner.

"Shiro, if you could please take this up with you—and place it on the slot in the railing at the front?" Mela said, sliding the first box towards him. "When you finish, please bring it back, and I'll count up the tips for you—you're more than welcome to watch that process if you'd like."

Sora scooped the box up off the table and held it under his arm as Chiyo slid open the gate.

"Something to worry about afterwards, I think," Sora said, nodding. "Wish us luck."

"Good luck," Mela called after them.

Fubuki stuck to Chiyo's side as they climbed the stairs onto the stage, and Sora snagged one of the stools from beside the gate, bringing it with him as he went. The vantage of the stage allowed him to see a fair deal further than before, over the tops of the people and stalls, all the way to the bridge, although he didn't have the elevation to see the river itself. He slotted the lockbox into the railing at the front before moving to place the stool down beside Chiyo, who gave a startled thank you as he directed her towards it. Fubuki remained completely still beside her, black eyes shadowed by the hood, and he stepped in front of her for a moment to lean down.

"Everything is going to be fine," Sora murmured, "I won't let anything happen to you, so try and relax, alright?"

"I can't," Fubuki murmured.

"You can," Sora said, whisper quiet. "Focus on us, okay? Forget about everyone else; it's just the three of us here."

He heard her draw in a shaky breath, the twin streams of mana collecting behind her forehead solidifying as she recharged the waning spell. Sora smiled at her for a moment longer and then turned around—he took two steps forward into the centre of the stage and spread his arms out around him as if to encompass the crowd, a dozen patterns twisting into existence beneath his skin. Chiyo began to play, plucking at the strings in a wavering, bouncy tune.

"Once upon a time, there was a young boy named Arte," Sora said, projecting his voice out. "The son of a farmer, who dreamt of quests, of monsters, and of lands far beyond his own."

He cast *Gust* without the command phrase, a precise stream of air circling the railing and taking with it each lantern's flame. *Shade* came next, lowering the ambient light of the stage to a curl of shadow. A dozen voices cried out at the darkness, taken off guard by the suddenness of it all, and then *Construct* took effect. Arte stood up from a crouch at the front of the stage, rendered in a translucent blue light—a boy no older than twelve.

"From youth till adulthood, he toiled, he mucked, and never did he find himself closer to his dream—for farmboys farmed, and heroes were the ones who set out on quests," Sora said, twisting the pattern as he spoke. "Until one day, when he woke, he found himself in the presence of something entirely outside of the mundanity."

Chiyo played a single discordant note before transitioning into something tighter but still light. The magically evoked shadow receded as he twisted the pattern, revealing Fubuki sitting near the front of the stage, legs curled up beside her and one hand pressed against her stomach. The young man spun around to face her, startled at the sight of the pale woman wreathed in black cloth.

"Anette, an ancient and once powerful faery, struck down by her own kind, injured, weak and alone," Sora said, lowering his voice a few shades. "Arte, too, found himself struck by the beauty of the creature before him—and so he acted; he ferried her away to his home."

The young man swept downwards towards Fubuki, cradling her for a moment before the *Shade* spell took everything from sight once more. He followed the mana in Fubuki's forehead as she moved to lay down on the stage and then twisted the *Construct* into existence beside her, once again revealing it to the crowd. Chiyo's song became slower, more searching, and far less airy.

"Six months it took for her health to return, and through it all, she slept, unaware of the young man who spoke to her every night," Sora said, "Anette awoke then to find him by her side, as he always was—and this time when he spoke with her, she replied."

"You have chained me," Fubuki said, "Tell me of your dreams, hero, so that I may dispel this twisted bind."

"Dreams?" Sora said voice pitched high. "But I have so many, I don't know where to start."

Shade took the stage again, and Fubuki slipped back up to her feet, moving to sit on top of the railing, one knee peaking high, where her chin soon sat. Arte twisted into existence again beside her, gesturing to the array of sparks, *Gleam* had wrought in the air above them. Goblins, Ogres, and Dragons—a depiction of the boy's dreams of adventure.

"You wish to slay monsters?" Fubuki asked.

"I do," Sora said as the sparks rained down on them. "But I have not the courage to leave my farm nor the skill to fight—my dream is impossible, I suppose."

"You will wait here, and I will return," Fubuki said, watching the *Construct*. "Then I will be free."

Shade stole away the light, and Fubuki slipped down off the railing, moving to stand in the centre of the stage once more. This time, when Arte reappeared, it was with a large, sparkling blade held in his hand. *Gleam* took the boy's eyes, dozens of shifting sparks appearing, brightening the dull colour to a brilliant ocean blue.

"A Faery blade of great power, whose magic would embolden the wielder and let them find victory in any conflict they sought out," Sora said, "Arte took the blade, still not certain of the ways of the Faery or the deal that he'd unknowingly discharged—only that this was the last time that he would wake with Anette beside him."

Fubuki stepped back into the darkness, only her pale chin visible amongst the spell-wrought dark, watching the *Construct* from a distance. Arte turned forward again, the speed of the movement concealing the changes that took him, his cheeks growing more defined, his shoulders broader, a beard of bright lines growing on his face, and all the while, his eyes sparkled that same ocean blue.

"Arte set out from his farm, his lack of training no obstacle, and his fear erased beneath the might of the blade," Sora said, "He cut down a dozen monsters in his travels, a hundred after that, and a thousand more, his name falling from the lips of men in reverence, and drawing the voracious gaze of women."

Arte strode forward on the spot, creatures, monsters and bandits sparking into existence and being left in pieces as he went, nothing more than a single stroke of his blade required for each. His hair grew longer, and his eyes sparkled—but all the while, the pale shade watched him from the darkness, a silent observer. Chiyo's song turned more sombre, moved slower, and she spent more time on each string, letting them ring out across the stage.

"News came to Arte of an unstoppable beast, whose reputation was almost as fearsome as his own, and so he set out, confident in his victory," Sora said, "Verge, a great serpent who arose from the depths of the ocean, said to have coiled around mountains, and once threatened to strangle the sky."

Sora breathed out and lifted his arms, the patterns shifting as Verge's immense *Construct* lifted up out of the stage, towering above the crowd, a sickly green hue. The monster's eyes burned orange, *Gleam* working to match Arte's own ocean-blue fire. He could hear more cries from the audience as Verge coiled around the stage and swung its head over the crowd before it turned back to face Arte.

"Verge was powerful, but the Faery blade brought victory to its wielder, just as it always had, toppling the great serpent in a single strike and leaving it fatally injured," Sora said, "But defeated as it was, it wasn't yet dead, and so Verge offered Arte a deal."

Verge fell down onto the stage, a glowing blue wound arcing through the middle of its body, and Arte stood beside the fallen monster's head, their eyes meeting. The serpent's mouth opened, and *Gust* washed outwards over the crowd. Fubuki stalked beside Arte on the edge of the visible area, her cloak passing into the light, and she leaned down to the serpent's head, her pale skin visible for just a moment.

"A single wish granted in exchange for my life—*tell me your dreams, hero*," Sora said, affecting a voice like gravel. "Anything at all."

Arte tilted his head at the words, sensing something familiar in them, and then the *Construct* sheathed his sparkling blade.

"A single wish?" Sora said, affecting the voice of Arte. "I desire the power to grant wishes, monster, so that I may make real *all* of my dreams."

The *Shade* spell crawled inwards, wrapping everything in a cloak of darkness, and then only Fubuki remained on the stage, in the sliver of light that was left. Chiyo's slow, deep plucking stopped entirely as Fubuki began to vanish.

"So be it," Fubuki murrmured.

When the veil finally pulled back, only Verge remained, lying on the floor of its lair, injured and asleep. The great monster shifted, lifting its head, and then its eyes peeled open, sparkling ocean blue—Sora let go of the patterns all at once, and the *Construct* shattered, crumbling away into sparkling dust. Within moments he couldn't hear anything except for the clapping, cheers and calls of the crowd nestled around the stage. He watched as they pushed forward, dropping silvers into the slot on the top of the lockbox. Sora beckoned for Chiyo and Fubuki to join him for a moment at the front of the stage.

"We'll be here again in an hour," Sora said, offering a smile. "We'll also be performing again tomorrow and the next night after—thank you."

#

"I can't believe how *well* that went," Chiyo said, practically vibrating. "Fubuki, you did so well—you got all of the lines right, and everything was *perfect.*"

Sora closed the door to the room, a bit bemused to see her so excited; the only thing that had come close was the news of the bath back in Judra, but even that hadn't held the same potency as right now. The light caught in her eyes, the brilliant red hue sparkling almost as if she was using *Gleam* on herself. Fubuki remained frozen inside of Chiyo's grasp, the taller girl's arms wrapped tightly around her back as she squeezed her.

"Chiyo," Fubuki managed, sounding a bit overwhelmed. "I liked the song too."

Sora leaned back against the door for a moment, watching them from his place, and wondered if this was what Chiyo had been like back before Koshiro had ruined her—bright and happy and vibrant and beautiful.

"You were both amazing," Sora said, pushing off the door.

He shifted sideways to shimmy past them before dropping down onto the bed he'd chosen earlier, content to call the night a success and, finally, get something more substantial than a nap—he'd used up a lot of his mana after all that, the scale of the illusions more costly then he'd estimated.

"Sora—*gosh,*" Chiyo breathed.

"You are *really* pretty when you're happy," Sora said, eyeing her from the bed. "Did you know that?"

Chiyo flushed at the words, but her giddiness didn't recede, too powerful to be stripped away by something as weak as embarrassment.

"Thank you," Chiyo said before burying her face back into Fubuki's neck. "*It went so well—*"

Fubuki stared at him from over Chiyo's shoulder, seeking some kind of guidance on what she was supposed to be doing. Sora mimed, curling his hands around in front of him, and after a moment, Fubuki followed his direction, hugging her back—Chiyo made a wordless sound that seemed to be caught somewhere between awe and laughter.

#

The two sets of spare clothes sat folded at the bottom of the bag, compacted to take up as little amount of space as possible; his book sat on top of them, safely tucked away out of sight beneath his cloak. The new metal canteen hung from the side of the pack, replacing the water-skin entirely, holding more water, and now without a chance of leaking. A rolled-up sleeping bag made from cotton and thread was strapped to the top flap of the bag, not quite as tightly wound as before he'd first opened it up, but close enough. An array of small tools joined them, a whetstone to sharpen his knife, a sharp hook for puncturing leather and some thick thread to make repairs to their shoes, should anything get damaged that he couldn't fix with magic—and a half dozen other things for those just in case scenarios. Now that Fubuki and Chiyo both had a similar travel pack of their own, he found himself able to shuffle out all of the things he'd been holding on to for both of them, which seemed to leave him with so much more space than before. He'd taken another closer look at the town board barely an hour before, and it was official; the bounties had been updated with all the information he'd expected—although there were still a few oddities within the posters. For one thing, his name had changed to reflect his title—*Sora the Seeker*. A clear indication that they'd been inside his house and discovered his master documentation. The artist for his picture had changed entirely, and while the sketch was significantly detailed, it looked almost noth-ing like him—the sheer sharpness of the features made him look like some kind of bird with a chin that could rend flesh. No extra details had been added to describe him, but his bounty had jumped upwards to match the others, resting at a cool five hundred gold alive, three-hundred dead. Fubuki's picture had changed artists as well, no longer the scratchy mess of scribbled black lines, but once again, it wasn't quite right—the slitted pupils were a dangerous detail to be included, and he was glad that Fubuki had taken to the *Colourant* spell as well as she had.

While her name still wasn't included, three words had been added, a title and a descriptor both—*Oni, yellow eyes*. Chiyo's picture remained the same as before, but there were a few written descriptors added beneath her face; red hair and red eyes. The hair they had covered, but the fact that her eyes were still red, a rather uncommon colour, left him a bit uneasy. While she had enough of a handle on recharging her *Colourant* spell, she was nowhere near the skill level of being able to hold two patterns at once—that wasn't something either of them would be ready for any time soon. They'd also been seen quite a bit during their three days in Maar, enough for her red eyes to have been observed, and if he were to suddenly correct that oversight with a *Colourant* of his own, it might well be noticed. Without knowing who else would be travelling alongside them to Maar, they couldn't risk making a change during transit either—and once they reached Bilaar, Chiyo would be splitting off from them entirely, in which case he wouldn't be able to maintain the second spell for her in his absence. A tricky situation, but the disguise had held up well to the scrutiny of several thousand people already; only under direct investigation would he expect it to fail.

"It feels nice to actually have a little bit of money again," Chiyo said, hand buried in her coin pouch. "I do wonder If they gave us the full forty percent, though—perhaps we should have stayed and watched her count it."

"Two gold is a *little* bit of money, is it?" Sora said, amused. "You've got a pretty warped perspective, *Himura*."

"Don't say my name like that," Chiyo said, scrunching her face up. "The amount of money that was trading hands last night taken in its totality was far more than something like *this*."

"Interesting," Sora said, strapping the pack shut. "It occurs to me that I didn't tell you, but I gave Tia and Sara two gold before we left."

"*What*?" Chiyo said, startled. "That was almost *half* of your money, at least."

"How would you know that, exactly?" Sora said, raising an eyebrow. "I would have thought a frilly skirt would have more manners than to go digging through a man's coin pouch."

"That's—nothing to do with the topic of discussion," Chiyo said, retreating from the accusation with haste. "When did this happen? You didn't say anything."

"After I healed her," Sora said, doing a final check over the bag. "We had a discussion about the lack of opportunity for the two of them in Judra, and I figured I could help them make the jump."

"That's why they were talking to Kazu at the docks," Chiyo said, staring at him. "I thought it was just us, but you really have no sense of financial responsibility, do you?"

"Financial?" Fubuki murrmured.

"Money and how it's used, Fubuki," Chiyo said before turning her gaze back to him. "Well?"

"I think I'm far more aware of the worth of two gold than you are," Sora said, hefting the pack up to his shoulder. "You think it's a *little* bit of money. *I* think it's something that, when placed appropriately, can change the course of a person's life."

Chiyo looked a bit taken aback by the verbal jab and seemed to bite back a response of her own. He was content to let the subject drop rather than get stuck arguing about something he didn't much care for in the first place.

"According to Levin, we've got about two hours before the Caravan actually sets out, which is more than long enough to handle payment," Sora said, rolling his shoulders back. "I'm ready to go whenever you two are—got everything?"

Fubuki's pack looked large on her short frame, but she held the small weight of it without any kind of issue. Chiyo lifted her own pack off the bed, sliding it onto her shoulders, looking not quite as outweighed due to her taller height, but the burden was far more visible in the set of her shoulders.

"I am ready," Fubuki murmured.

"So am I," Chiyo said, not quite looking at him. "Where are we meeting them—the north gate?"

"That's the one," Sora confirmed, stepping past them and taking hold of the door handle. "Any last-minute adjustments you want to make before we're outside?"

"Hold on," Chiyo said, closing her eyes for a moment. "I want to redo it."

The pattern spread across her scalp vanished as she pulled it apart, and her red hair returned, overtaking the black in a wash of vibrant colour. Then she began to rebuild it in the same location, using the already local mana to bring it back into existence in half the time it usually took her to manage it. Sora closed his eyes to focus on her progress, the distance and lack of contact making it difficult to discern entirely—she funnelled mana into the central point, pumping up the duration beyond what the minimum required, the strain visible on her face. It snapped into place as she murmured the command phrase, and the red was drowned in black once more.

"How was that?" Chiyo said, relieved of the strain. "I think I got a lot in that time."

"Six minutes, at a guess," Sora said, nodding. "You know, it's funny—most people learn *Colourant* and then never use it again, but you've constantly been using it since Judra. I'd say you both have more practice with it than the majority of masters."

Chiyo's smile returned at the words, the prior disagreement falling away beneath the praise. He opened the door a moment later, leading the two of them out of the room, the inn, and into the streets of Maar. There were still a few people moving around, but now, in the wake of the festival, it was nothing like it had been before. Sora took them in the direction of the north wall, not quite sure where the gate was located, but knowing that it was somewhere on the left side of the river. Within minutes they'd come close enough to see the gate, a dozen meters away from the water, a large open area preceding it and filled with wagons, carriages, pangolems and horses. The largest grouping was easily identified by the matching blue-dyed canvas—six horse-drawn carriages already prepared for carrying people. In the front were a dozen unmanned carriages filled with crates, boxes, barrels and long rolls of cloth and drawn by the much larger pangolems—a woman with dark skin and dark hair stood a few meters away, directing the people who were ferrying more crates into the wagons.

"Chiyo," Fubuki murrmured. "Can you see them?"

"I see them, Fubuki," Chiyo said, hooking an arm around the shorter girl's elbow. "It'll be okay—just stick with me."

Sora led them towards the dark-skinned woman, scuffing his feet on his approach to give her notice that someone was approaching from a blind angle. The woman turned her head at the noise, then the rest of her body as Sora moved to stand near her.

"Good morning," Sora said, "I hope I'm not mistaken, but would you happen to be May? Levin advised me to speak with you about securing travel to Bilaar."

"Yeah, he told me about you; but even if he hadn't, I would have recognized you from the stage last night," May said, rubbing the knuckle of her index finger across her jaw. "Three people, a week's worth of food and water included—that sound about right?"

"That sounds *remarkably* right," Sora said, smiling. "Shall we discuss compensation?"

#

Eight

The interior of the carriage wasn't quite as large as their room back in Judra, and it lacked even something as simple as a bed. Two bench seats ran the length of both sides, leaving the occupants facing one another. It was easily enough to seat eight people, but there were simply not enough people ready to leave Maar, and so the three of them were left with a carriage all to themselves. Twenty extra silvers were the cost to make that official because May had seemed intent on compacting all the travellers to a single car and filling the others with more goods—although they hadn't been the only ones to make that request, it would seem because there was another carriage with only a singular mana source sitting within. He'd caught a glimpse of the occupant only once while peering out of the curtain-covered window before they'd left the city—a Marmaros woman travelling by herself. It was rare to see them outside of Cornalria, and impossible for him to identify the age by sight alone—for they stopped aging around that of an adult human, and so long as they weren't killed by outside influence, they would continue to live on indefinitely, far outstripping the lifespan of most. The rough nature of her mana told him that she was barely more than a novice, which pointed towards her not being quite as old as he might have guessed. Almost all of their people learned magic eventually, their long lives leading to an eclectic gathering of skills, and magic had a significant draw to it for those who could access the resources needed to learn. It was lucky, perhaps, that she wasn't more skilled because a master would have sensed the patterns beneath Chiyo and Fubuki's skin. The Marmaros, much like Fubuki, would have possessed enhanced hearing, which posed a far greater risk.

"There is a Marmaros travelling in one of the other carriages, two behind us at present," Sora said because it was better to curb any kind of mistake, even if that meant alerting their potential eavesdropper. "I do believe their kind are capable of hearing words spoken from great distances, so speak nothing you do not wish to be overheard."

"Marmaros?" Fubuki murmured.

Fubuki turned to look towards the back of the carriage as if she might see through the thick wood and out the other side.

"I suppose you've never encountered one before, have you, Fuka?" Chiyo said, attempting to navigate the new circumstance as best she could. "They are like us in shape and feature, but their bodies are quite unique—I suppose you could liken them to moving statues of polished marble."

"I think the oldest one on record right now is around six hundred years old? Left alone, they would live forever, I imagine," Sora said, leaning back on his bench for a moment. "As far as interaction goes, they are isolationists for the most part and tend to remain within the borders of Cornalria; they've had something of a tumultuous past with humans—Hondan is quite hostile to their kind, which is a shame considering they have a shared border."

Fubuki stared at him as if she might be able to silently pull all of the thoughts from his head; her interest clearly peaked.

"Did you see her clothing?" Chiyo asked.

"No," Sora admitted, "I only saw a short glimpse of her before she entered a carriage—she was *almost* as beautiful as you, my sweet wife."

Chiyo flushed at the sneaky comment, completely unprepared for it—catching her off guard had become something of a pastime for him now, to see just how red he could turn her. Eventually, she would probably catch on, but until then, he was enjoying himself.

"I wonder what she's doing all the way out here?" Chiyo said, avoiding his gaze now. "I think I've seen only two of them in my entire life and only in passing."

Sora found himself in something of an odd place; he couldn't reveal that the Marmaros woman was a novice mage without also revealing his ability to sense mana from a rather significant distance, which in turn, would reveal his status to her as a master. That meant that any instruction he gave them during the week to Bilaar would have to be done under the knowledge that she would be listening. Sora hummed to himself for a moment, working out the rules of the situation in full. It was likely that the Marmaros had seen their performance, so there was no point in trying to hide his status as a magically inclined. Adepts were capable of teaching and tutorship—Wartol had made good use of that fact—so it wouldn't be entirely unexpected for him to provide some instruction to the two travelling with him.

"Neither of you has had much time to practice magic for a few days now," Sora said, widening the pool of subjects for them to speak about. "We have a week to ourselves—in relative privacy—so I'd like to suggest you use that time to experiment with *Gleam*."

Sora reached up and tapped Chiyo on the head, disrupting her spell entirely, and leaving her hair to turn red once more. Chiyo sat straight up, startled at being without her disguise for the first time in several hours, and pressed the curtain flat against the window as if to prevent someone from peering through the thick material. Between the curtains being on the inside of the carriage, and the fact that he would sense anyone approaching the door, it was as safe an environment for them as he could get.

"We've got until nightfall to mess about without bothering anyone with flashing lights or dancing sparks," Sora said in explanation. "Fuka —why don't you show me your progress?"

Fubuki held onto her *Colourant* spell for a moment longer before the pattern vanished, and her glowing yellow eyes bled back into existence, the slitted pupils locked onto his face with a burning intensity that had been masked, but not lost. She seemed far more accepting of the sudden practice session than Chiyo, either her own senses telling her she was out of sight or a simple show of trust in his ability to navigate the situation. A stream of mana moved from her chest, rolling down the inside of her arm and pooling in her fingertips, moving with a speed that only someone channelling into their hands could accomplish.

"It feels different," Fubuki said.

Chiyo turned to look down at her own hand, wide-eyed as her own stream of mana sparked to life in an instant, all of the carefully honed focus she'd been mustering to direct mana into her scalp, bringing its full force towards the now simple task. The pattern wrenched itself into existence quickly enough that she jumped—she looked up at him in shock, startled by the ease of the process.

"Shiro?" Chiyo managed.

"The hands *are* the easiest place to channel, and with your focus unburdened by distractions, it only makes sense for it to be so simple," Sora said, smiling. "Perhaps you should spend some time practising using it in different parts of your body to see if you can't grow accustomed to it—I suggest starting with the feet and working your way up."

#

"There's a travel bed set up for each of you under that canvas over there, so feel free to use it after you've finished eating," May said, nodding. "You *can* sleep in the carriage if you want; the benches aren't too bad for it, but keep in mind that there are only two of them."

Sora scratched at his chin for a moment and wondered exactly when his beard had grown long enough to cover his face—had it been that long in Maar? He couldn't recall.

"I've never liked sleeping out in the open," Sora said, "I think we'll stick to the carriage; Fuka can have one of the benches—my wife and I can share a bedroll."

Chiyo lifted her head, the thin wooden spoon trapped between her teeth, her eyes flickered between each of their faces—then she swallowed as May turned to look down at her.

"Try not to make a mess of my carriage, will you?" May said, voice dry. "If it starts to smell, I'm going to charge you a maintenance fee."

Fubuki tilted her head at the words, her own bowl of stew sitting untouched on her lap, the spoon sticking straight up in her fist like a tiny wooden flag.

"We'll behave ourselves," Chiyo managed, glaring at him from behind her hair. "Won't we, *husband?*"

"Absolutely no promises," Sora offered, "May, I noticed that one of our fellow travellers was a Marmaros—I'm curious, do you get many of those in Maar?"

"First one I've ever seen in Maar," May admitted, "About a dozen of them have come through Bilaar over the last couple of years, though—most of them seem to be headed to Satu or leaving Satu and heading for Lyston."

"Treated as nothing more than a stopover point, is it? Poor Bilaar," Sora said, feigning sadness, "I suppose the majority are seeking education at the Library if I were to hazard a guess—still, it's a long trip to make unless they took a stroll through Hondan."

Chiyo scoffed at the comment, clearly at odds with him after he'd gone ahead and poked her with his bedroll comment.

"I'm sure that would go over well," Chiyo said, eyeing him. "What's next, delving into the Dread Forest of *Sagia?* How reckless."

Sora let the jab roll off him; it wasn't the first comment she'd made one the same manner. Chiyo's stated goal of talking some sense into him hadn't been a lie, and while she hadn't made any outright attempt to argue with him about Dragon's Claw again, she was clearly looking for gaps in his delusional armour.

"Not my idea of a fun time," May said, waving her spoon at them. "Skirted round the edges of it once, on the way from Satu to Zala—whole place is just fog, trees, and voices, the source of which I'd rather not think about."

"Sprites, supposedly, trying to lure people in by mimicking human speech," Sora said after he'd swallowed the mouthful of stew. "There was an attempt to send an expedition in there—three years ago? I think—the edges of the forests are a breeding ground for the things, and after a few hundred meters in, they gave up; the fog just became too thick to see anything at all, and people started to go missing."

"*Sprites* get them?" May asked, tilting her spoon at him.

"I very much doubt it; even in high numbers, they aren't too much of a threat," Sora said, shaking his head. "They'll shock you if you get close, but it's not really enough to keep an adult from running away—given the size of the place and how long it's been off limits, there might be *anything* in there."

"Well, I'll be happy if I never have to go near the place again—not worth the sleepless nights, honestly," May said, dropping her spoon into her now empty bowl. "Leave your bowls out when you're finished, and someone will come by to grab them."

"Thank you, May," Chiyo said as the woman stood up. "What time will we be setting out again?"

"First light, I'll knock on your door before we set out to make sure your inside, but feel free to sleep in," May said, stepping back. "Makes no difference to the horses or me if you're awake or not—night."

"Goodnight," Sora said.

He glanced over at Fubuki, who still hadn't touched her food, and she murmured out a goodbye of her own, picking up the silent signal he'd been trying to send. May tossed a wave back over her shoulder and then set off towards the larger camp, leaving them to sit beside the carriage.

"You haven't touched your food," Chiyo said, finally speaking up. "Is something wrong with it?"

"Nothing," Fubuki murmured.

"It's good, you know," Chiyo said, reaching over and directing her towards lifting the bowl up off her lap. "You need to eat something—come on, do you *want* me to feed you?"

Maybe that *was* what she'd wanted, but Fubuki never had the chance to explain because Chiyo had already pressed the spoon against her lips and then bullied the shorter girl into eating it. Sora laughed at the odd look Fubuki gave her not-quite assailant, clearly a bit uncertain of the situation. His own bowl of stew vanished within two minutes, and he spent the time tracking the mana signature of the Marmaros as she rose from her spot inside the main canvas and he got a proper visual on her for the first time as she brushed the cloth door out of her way—a liquid, shining stone, with impossible motion. If she'd been a statue, it would be one with the most detail he had ever seen, the curve of her lips, eyes, and cheeks, the million individual strands of hair wrought by some kind of inhuman patience. The Marmaros paused outside of the canvas for a moment, seeing them, and then Fubuki lifted her head—the two of them seemed to share a moment of impossible stillness—then the marble woman's lips curled up into a smile. Fubuki seemed almost enthralled by the woman as she turned and stepped up into her own carriage.

"It's like your *Golem*?" Fubuki murmured.

Sora winced.

"I'm willing to take that as an *obscene* compliment to my skill with that spell, but there's no way I could ever create something so perfect with *Golem*," Sora said, keeping his voice gentle. "I know you didn't mean anything by it, but something like what you just said is *probably* considered quite rude to her."

Fubuki turned to stare at him, clearly unable to bridge the gap.

"I don't understand," Fubuki murmured.

"I know you don't, and it's okay," Sora said, nodding. "Consider for a moment if I used *Golem* to create a statue that looks exactly like—your sister."

He caught himself at the last moment; not the first time he'd almost called them by their real names. Fubuki glanced over at the subject of their discussion for a moment and then back again, most likely thinking of the *Golem* they'd sent off upstream wearing Chiyo's panties.

"Would it be *her* or just a lifeless copy?" Sora prompted.

"*Golem* has no soul; it would not be her," Fubuki murmured, repeating what he'd told her back then. "Does that woman have a soul?"

That was something of a timeless question and one which had led to a lot of violence, wars and death—something which Fubuki clearly had no context for.

"If you asked that question in Fabah, the answer would be 'we do not know,' if you asked it in Hondan, the answer would be 'most assuredly not,' if you asked it in Cornalria, the Marmaros would ask you, 'what *is* a soul?'" Sora said, painting the wider picture for her. "The question is unanswerable in its totality, and the ones who suggest they know the answer have no real foundation for it—just ideologically driven rhetoric that will justify the wrongs of the past and present."

"What do *you* think?" Chiyo asked, watching them.

"I think they are living, breathing creatures, with a consciousness that mirrors, exists adjacent to or even surpasses our own," Sora said, "If we are going to assume that Humans, Meld and other intelligent species have souls, then we should absolutely extend that same courtesy to them on principle alone."

Sora placed his bowl down on the ground and pushed himself to his feet; he stepped up onto their own carriage, ducking to get inside. He had to squint a bit to see in the darkness of the carriage, but he managed to locate his pack and unfurl the bedroll with a bit of fumbling around. He spread it out on the floor of the carriage, deciding to take that space for himself, not entirely willing to risk rolling off the bench in the middle of the night. He dragged his shirt up over his head and dropped it down beside the bedroll, intending to use it as a makeshift pillow. The others followed him in just as he was attempting to lay down, and when Fubuki closed the door, he was forced to fumble around in the dark to open up his bedroll.

"I can't see anything," Chiyo complained, moving to sit on the bench. "Where's my bag? I need my bedroll."

Fubuki crawled up onto the bench above him, or at least he assumed that was what she was doing because he couldn't really see her.

"Are you certain you don't want to spend the night in *my* bedroll?" Sora said, still trying to get comfortable. "Think of all the cuddling we could get done, sweet wife."

Chiyo said nothing to his comment, and though he braced himself for some kind of kick, it never came. He waited a moment longer, just in case she was biding her time, and then rolled over to face away from her—maybe she was getting sick of the back and forth after all.

#

"I can hear water," Fubuki murmured.

Sora shifted inside his bedroll, feeling like a great big slug, and one that was currently assailed by Chiyo's knee pressed into his spine. Her own bedroll was now wedged between his and the bench, leaving roughly zero unoccupied space on the floor—her singular attempt to sleep on the bench the first night had ended with her rolling off amidst a dream and just about killing him in the process. The second night had been fine for the most part until she'd turned over in her sleep and then he'd been forced to deal with her unfortunately placed knee ever since.

"Are we crossing a bridge?" Sora yawned.

"There is one ahead of us," Fubuki said, peeking through the curtain at the world ahead of them. "Another river?"

"It's one of the smaller rivers that lead into the Third Talon," Chiyo mumbled, apparently awake. "There's about a dozen of them along the entire length of it; I think only two of them actually have names—this one doesn't."

"That puts us right before the border of Fabah and Malnia," Sora said, covering his eyes with his wrist. "At a guess, we'll probably end up crossing through a Malnia border gatehouse around midday; they'll probably want to talk to everyone to make sure we aren't carrying any illegal contraband."

Chiyo rolled over, finally removing her knee from his back, and propped herself up on one shoulder. He twisted to lay on his back, amazed at the sudden space he'd been gifted, and lifted his arm for a moment, just enough to get a peek at her face—she didn't look surprised by the knowledge, but she did seem a bit concerned.

"I doubt it will be much more than a quick check of the carriage and a few questions," Sora said, catching her gaze. "I'll do the talking, so neither of you will have to worry about anything—okay?"

"Okay," Fubuki agreed, still looking through the gap in the window. "We're on the bridge."

Chiyo shifted a bit further, laying down on her shoulder to face him completely, the bedroll open enough that he could see the uncovered skin of her collarbone and a wealth of flesh beneath it. She caught him looking down her shirt once she'd settled, but she said nothing in complaint nor made any motion to cover herself; she simply glanced away, unable to hold his gaze.

"By tomorrow, we'll be halfway to Bilaar," Chiyo said, voice quiet. "Have you—changed your mind about anything?"

Even without her saying the words, it was clear enough to him what she was talking about. There were only four days between now and the moment in which they would go their own way.

"I'm sorry," Sora murmured. "But I think you know the answer to that."

Chiyo said nothing in response; instead, she turned her gaze down to her hand, barely emerging from the side of the bedroll. He felt the pattern for *Gleam* twist into being as she withdrew, clearly intending on burying herself in practice rather than continue the interaction. While he had no intention of changing his goals, he did feel completely uneasy about leaving her behind. Other than her ability to maintain the *Colourant* spell, she had no real defence against anyone that would come after her, and all it would take was for one person to sense the spell or for her to make a single mistake in public. At least if he was nearby, he could try and mask the signatures. Chiyo owned no weapons, and she couldn't fight with one even if she did. He hadn't taught either of them anything with an offensive use simply because they weren't skilled enough to manage something like that without injuring themselves in the process. If she was revealed at any point, she would either be murdered or be dragged back to Satu in chains—at which point she would be tortured and killed. Not an outcome he wanted for her, but he wasn't willing to sacrifice his own desires like that, not after he'd *finally* managed to find a way out of Satu, where he'd been eternally trapped by his own complacency and fear. Chiyo was an adult—someone who was older than him, even if it was only a year—she could make her own choices about her future, and that was all there was to it.

#

The things he'd said to Sara back in Judra had been the truth; of all the skills he'd managed to accrue in his short life, the one that had brought him the most success had always been acting—the ability to lie to a persons face and the confidence to do it with a smile, it was a weapon that could be used in every part of his life, and this was just another excuse to unsheath it. Sora eyed the door of the carriage and then stood as the trio of signatures approached the outside. Chiyo looked up, a faint strain visible on her face as the stress of the situation fought for externalisation against her tight control. Sora took hold of the doorhandle and then pressed the door open a few seconds before they reached it, taking a single step down onto the rough dirt of the road. He paused, half out of the carriage, hand still on the door, as May and two unfamiliar men came to a stop beside him, fully armoured, with their hands on their sheathed weapons.

"Morning—afternoon, now," Sora corrected, stepping completely down onto the road and turning back to offer his arm to Chiyo. "I suppose it's our turn? Come on, Itsuka, Fuka, let's get out of their way."

Chiyo took his offered hand, using it to step down from the carriage, and once she'd managed it, he took hold of Fubuki's hand and led her down as well. The floppy brim of the hat bobbed with each step, and he smiled.

"Makim, you check inside; I'll talk to them," The taller man said, nodding to the carriage. "Good morning to you as well, and welcome to Malnia—or the border, at least. Itsuka, Fuka, and what did you say your name was?"

"Shiro, I'm an Adept, originally from Satu, although it's been a few years since I've actually called it my home," Sora said, brushing the thick braid bang back over his ear. "Itsuka here is my wife, and Fuka is her younger sister. I'd hesitate to call either of them a *novice*, considering they've got no real formal training, but it's probably the correct term— what was your name again?"

Chiyo turned to stare at him as he deliberately went out of his way to draw the interaction out for as long as possible. A fugitive wouldn't want to keep this discussion going; they'd want it to be over quickly—which is why he'd suddenly become the most talkative man in the world.

"Latre," Latre said, shaking his hand. "You're coming from Maar and heading to Bilaar—or so May here has told me; what's your purpose in Bilaar?"

"Coin, of course—we're entertainers; performing in the festival was quite lucrative, and we're hoping to build upon that in Maar," Sora said, looking hopeful. "I've had nothing but time to practice with all this sitting about we've been doing—I've never been good with that; I'm a people person, you see? Say, would you like a demonstration?"

"That won't be necessary," Latre said, holding up a hand. "A few more questions; do you or your family own property in Malnia?"

"Property? We do not own anything—we had a wagon at one point, but I'm afraid we parted ways with that a while ago," Sora said, shaking his head. "We'll only be passing through Bilaar as well, although we haven't quite figured out our next destination. My wife has her eyes set on Lyston, although I think we might head back towards Satu—"

"Sure," Latre interjected, "Have any of you committed any crimes we should know about?"

Makim stepped back out of the carriage, shaking his head, and rejoined the other man.

"Not that I can think of," Sora said, tapping a finger against his chin. "Although I don't know every law by rote, it's possible we've tread over some strange, esoteric ruling—did you know that in Hondan, failure to consummate your marriage within two weeks is punishable by up to one month in jail? For both parties."

There was an odd pause that rolled over the group at his answer, and then Makim spoke up.

"Wait, is that true?" Makim said, a bit taken aback. "Wouldn't that just *prevent* them from consummating the marriage?"

"Makim," Latre said, sighing.

"That's *exactly* what I said when I first heard it," Sora said, snapping his fingers at the man. "It's a ludicrous law—"

Chiyo reached out and grabbed hold of his wrist, causing him to glance over at her, her jaw was tight now, and her stare had become strained again.

"We have one more question, and you can be on your way," Latre said, "Are you carrying anything illegal?"

"I can't imagine so," Sora said, "If you'd like, I could grab our packs for you to look through?"

"That won't be necessary," Latre repeated, glancing at Makim for a moment and receiving a shake of the head from the man. "Please make sure you adhere to all the laws of Malnia while you're here—you may return to your carriage now; thank you for your cooperation."

"Of course," Sora said, offering a handshake to both of them. "Thank you for such professionalism—come on, let's get you two back inside."

Sora repeated the process of helping them both back up into the carriage and then paused on the step for a moment, watching the three of them move onto the next carriage behind them. The Marmaros woman, drawn outside by a knock on her door, stepped down onto the road to meet them.

"Makim," Latre said, directing the man to check the carriage again. "Good morning. Can I have your name?"

"My name is Valcoatl," Valcoatl said, smiling. "It's nice to meet you, Latre."

The woman's voice seemed to come from deep in her throat, the tone low, with an audible grain to it; each word hung in the air, deliberately stretched out for a shade longer than needed. Latre seemed a bit caught off guard by her, either the alluring voice or the way she'd known his name before he'd told it to her. Sora stepped up into the carriage and shut the door behind him. He sat down beside Fubuki without a word, and the three of them remained like that, completely silent for almost ten minutes, at which point the carriage started moving again—Chiyo sunk down onto the bench, her previously rigid posture melting under the relief.

"If you'd asked me a month ago, I would have never even considered that we'd be leaving Fabah behind," Sora said, leaning his head back against the window. "Even a week ago, I wouldn't have been so certain —how quickly things can change."

#

The roof of the carriage was black, but he thought he could almost see moving shapes in the darkness, his eyes inventing interpretations in the low light. Sora listened to the quiet breathing of his two companions and wondered just how long their luck was going to keep on holding out. They'd come a long way from Satu already—leaving the country even, if only just—but the King's arm was long, and his fortune extended that reach far into the surrounding countries. They weren't safe from reprisal, and they wouldn't be for a long time, certainly not in Bilaar and probably not even in a place as far as Lyston—if any of them ended up making it that far in the first place. He wondered about the man who'd kicked all of this off and what he might be doing at this very moment—Koshiro Konishi, advisor to the king and the one who had actually conspired to kill the princess. Sora wondered about the guard he'd spoken to and if anything had come from his attempt to reveal the treachery. Somehow he doubted it; the words of a fugitive wouldn't be worth the air they were spoken through, let alone someone like him. Nobles like Koshiro had a sort of inborn advantage when it came to slipping through these situations entirely unharmed and, more often than not, unobstructed by the struggles that everyone else had to deal with. The man had status, wealth, and the ear of the king to whisper all sorts of things into, it simply wasn't the kind of situation that would unravel without a concerted effort from outside forces, and something like that was impossible, at least not from their current position—Chiyo shifted, ever so slightly, but her breathing remained perfectly even, and he realised that she was pretending to be asleep again. He left her alone, her thoughts were probably just as muddled as his own, and he very much doubted that she would want his help to untangle them. He closed his eyes and then immediately opened them again as Chiyo shifted a second time. He felt her sit up, the movement almost completely silent, as she peeled the flap of her bedroll open. His assumption that she was going to go outside to take a piss was disrupted as she reached down to touch his own bedroll, carefully lifting the flap up. Chiyo slipped inside his own bedding, and he felt her press flush against his side, her hand trembling against the skin of his chest. Her breath rolled across his neck, warm and a bit uneven as she moved closer. If he'd been struggling to sleep before, any chance of that happening had just vanished entirely.

"*Are you awake?*" Chiyo mumbled, the words barely audible.

The feeling of her mouth moving against his neck as she spoke the words and the feeling of her body pressed against him was more than enough to set him off. It had been weeks since he'd touched anyone, or even himself; there simply hadn't been a good time for either. He brought his hand out from under his head, slipped it into the bedroll, and curled it around her back, pulling her further against him.

"*You're playing with fire here,*" Sora said, speaking at the same volume. "*Are you sure you know what you're doing?*"

He drew his hand up her back, slipping it up over her hip before his fingertips slipped under the hem of her pants, dragging against the soft skin beneath.

"*Do you?*" Chiyo managed.

Despite the brave words, he could *feel* her swallowing—it made him wonder why she was coming on so strongly, considering just how nervous she seemed to be about it. Sora took hold of her wrist and moved her hand downwards. Chiyo pressed her face against his neck, attempting to hide from him, even as he curled her fingers around him The feeling of her hand on him was like liquid fire in his veins, and he brought his now free hand up to take hold of her chin, lifting her face away from his neck. Chiyo's hand remained exactly where he'd left it, wrapped tightly around the base of his cock, unmoving.

"*Kiss me,*" Sora murmured.

Chiyo leaned forward at the words, pressing her lips against his own, and he pulled her into him again. His hand slipped down from her cheek to her neck, over her arm, and caught her hip right against the hem of her pants. He slipped his hand under the cloth and down between her thighs, fingers lingering over the patch of hair before sinking further down—he smiled into the kiss as Chiyo pressed forward into his hand, her grip on him becoming tight. It was pretty clear to him that she'd never done anything like this before, and he also knew that he could probably take things as far as he wanted—it felt like far too much power to have over someone. Chiyo made a small noise in his mouth as he settled his fingers firmly between her legs, rolling them against her sensitive skin. Her participation in the kiss began to falter, her free arm wrapping around his neck like it might help her weather it all. Sora took control of the now entirely one-sided kiss, taking what he wanted from her mouth as she tried to muffle her reaction to his touch as best she could. He decided to bring some of the fire he'd spoken of, sub-vocalizing a command for *Meldflesh* and sinking his mana between her legs—and then Chiyo was shuddering against him as she came, unable to last under the unfair assault on her senses. He buried his tongue in her mouth, making sure she understood that she was entirely at his mercy, and once he thought she had received the message, he leaned forward, pressing his mouth against her ear.

"This is the part where you return the favour," Sora murmured. *"Do you need me to tell you how?"*

Chiyo buried her face against his neck and whispered something that sounded a lot like a yes.

#

Chiyo could hardly look at him the next morning, which was both amusing and a little bit sad to think about. She also seemed to be unnaturally interested in the pattern on the wood of the ceiling and entirely unable to look anywhere near the floor of the carriage. For all the intrinsic advantages he knew the noble-born to have, he hadn't expected her to know literally *nothing* about sex. Although the more he thought about it, the more he realized it may have been something more cut along the lines of gender than simply a class distinction—he'd seen plenty of nobles at brothels before, but it was exclusively men. He couldn't remember a single time he'd seen a noblewoman in a place like that—except for once, when a lady had come storming into the place, calling for her husband to reveal himself. By custom, a noblewoman was supposed to remain a virgin until marriage, although before now, he'd always thought of that as something of a societal delusion that everybody said they adhered to but never actually did. Women had to worry about things like getting pregnant, so it made sense to him—in a pragmatic sort of way—for them to avoid actually *fucking*, but there were so many other ways to get off, and Chiyo seemed to be living proof that they avoided *everything*—even as risk-free as a god damned handjob. The idea of *never* having had any kind of sexual encounter until he was eighteen was a fate he wouldn't have wished on anyone—Koshiro Konishi, perhaps—but everyone else deserved better than that.

"This is driving me crazy," Sora said, sighing. "We're doing another impromptu lesson, everyone, front and centre."

Fubuki rose from her place at the front of the carriage and moved to sit on the floor, almost between the two of them. Chiyo looked down at her, apparently caught a glance of the floor, and then buried her face in her hands.

"The command phrase is an intrinsic part of every spell, not because the words carry any real magic on their own, but because of the emotions, feelings, and experiences we learn to associate with them," Sora said, "Those associations are a structure by which your attention and willpower are focused, and by which mana is then given direction."

All things he'd already taught them both, but he wanted to make sure they understood it properly, and that meant breaking it down into the component pieces. Chiyo must have managed to find some willpower of her own because she was now looking in his general direction, albeit at a spot somewhere below his chin.

"You speak a word, the word evokes an internal response, and mana moves," Sora said, holding his palm out. "Every spell has a command phrase, but speaking the word out loud isn't a requirement; it's an externalized heuristic—a shortcut to evoking the associations."

Sora built half a dozen patterns in the palm of his hand and then cast *Gleam* without speaking; a bright red figure made of a shifting mass of sparks twirled to life on the palm of his hand—Chiyo shifted on the bench for a moment; the figures bright, braided hair making it clear who it was supposed to be representing.

"You didn't say the command phrase," Fubuki observed.

"Precisely; subvocalize the words and trace the letters in your mind to evoke it," Sora said, nodding. "It's not a difficult thing to do once you understand how it works—familiarity is your god here, and repetition is how you practice your faith."

"Subvocalise?" Fubuki mumured.

"Mouthing the words but not making any noise," Chiyo said, finally finding her voice, "Is this difficult to do?"

Chiyo met his gaze for the first time in what must have been hours, and he smiled at her.

"It's something that might take you a couple of hours to figure out for *Gleam*, but it's also something that you will be coming back to many times in the future," Sora said, nodding. "Each spell you learn, you'll need to retread the same ground until you can consciously evoke the correct associations."

Chiyo nodded at the answer, some of her visible avoidance stolen away by the complicated nature of the conversation and her interest in the subject.

"Now, the first step here is for you both to start recognizing exactly what associations you've built up already," Sora said, leaning forward. "Go ahead and create the pattern for *Gleam* in the centre of your palm."

The two of them closed their eyes and lifted their palms up, something they'd apparently taken as some kind of odd requirement for the process—he'd caught them both doing it even outside of the lessons. It was something he'd address eventually, but for now, it seemed to act as a sort of gesture to trick their bodies into a deeper state of focus.

"Good, now think about the effect of the spell and what you expect to happen when you cast it," Sora said, "You expect the pattern to lock into place, you expect it to begin burning mana to fuel the effect, you expect the transformation from mana to illusionary light, you expect a shower of sparks emerging from your palm, you expect there to be light, but no heat, colour but no substance."

Fubuki seemed to be not-quite-nodding along with each one as he spoke, like some internal checklist she was attempting to fulfil. Chiyo had pulled the corner of her lip between her teeth, and he couldn't help but remember how her lips had felt, pressed against his own in the dark.

"I'll let you speak out loud this time, but I want you to focus on the feeling of the spell taking hold," Sora said, "Cast your spell."

They both spoke the word out loud, and the carriage was filled with sparks of light. He waited for the spells to run their course, and once they'd burned away, he nodded.

"Good, now think about the effects of *Gleam* and the expectations you just had when you cast the spell," Sora said, linking his hands together in front of him. "Try to rebuild that feeling in your mind—no mana, please; you're not building the pattern yet, just thinking."

Fubuki's brows furrowed together, her hand still raised in front of her, and the mana receded from her palm.

"There is a general feeling that *all* spells hold, and you will have noticed it already; it's like a static shock. Individual spells also hold a *specific* feeling of their own." Sora said, "The static feeling isn't useful because it applies to everything, so any associations you build with that are going to get entangled with other spells; what you need to focus on is the signature that *Gleam* holds—rebuild the pattern now, please, and cast when you're ready."

He hadn't expected teaching to be so interesting or that he'd end up having as much success with it. The instruction he'd received from Salas was the only thing he could compare it to, and while neither Chiyo nor Fubuki seemed to possess the inherent advantage he had been born with, they seemed more than capable of understanding the material. They were also far more willing to take instruction than he'd been when he was younger; the countless arguments, heated exchanges and his stubborn attempts to do things his own way were completely absent. Both of them followed all of his instructions without any sort of desire to stray from the path he was illuminating for them. He wondered if that was a result of them both being significantly older and more mature than he'd been when he'd learned. Outside of instruction, Chiyo seemed to maintain her autonomy entirely, ready to argue with him on just about any subject that she thought he wasn't taking seriously or looking at in the correct way. In Fubuki's case, she seemed to have ceded almost all control over to both him and Chiyo; even as far back as Satu, she'd followed his every direction with little or zero pushback—something which concerned him a little bit. Ceded may have been the wrong word for it because she might not have possessed that sense of direction in the first place—a lifetime trapped in servitude had bound her mind in ways that restricted her way of thinking. He'd hoped that presenting her with choices where she had to make the decision herself would help her build that back up, and the word puzzles that he and Chiyo had been creating for her to solve were a part of that. He'd seen some progress there, in a few stand-out moments where Fubuki had actually stepped up and made a decision on her own—her initial desire to avoid performing because of her fear of humans and her more recent decision to follow him to Dragon's Claw being the most prevalent.

"Take hold of that feeling, entangle it into the rest of the expectations," Sora said after they'd both cast the spell. "Those are all the individual components to casting without a command phrase, so now it's up to you to practice—build the pattern and alternate between casting it normally and attempting to sub-vocalise it. If you need any more help, or you have a question, just ask—okay?"

#

"We'll be there by tomorrow afternoon, I think," Chiyo said, studying the map in his book. "Just after midday, so long as we keep good time."

"Is there a mayor in Bilaar?" Fubuki murmured.

"Malnia is a principality; the cities are governed by ministers who are appointed by the prince," Chiyo said, explaining it. "The minister of Bilaar is called Alarok, although I've heard that he was currently preparing for retirement and for a new minister to be chosen."

"Why?" Fubuki murmured.

"He is turning eighty-seven, I believe, so he is quite old, but I think the reason is more politically inclined," Chiyo admitted, "The prince has been slowly replacing his father's chosen ministers since his death; Bilaar is just one of the later cities to undergo that change."

"Where is the prince?" Fubuki asked, watching her.

"The prince lives in Lyston, the capital city of Malnia," Chiyo said, tilting her head. "You're so talkative today—are you okay?"

Chiyo seemed to have finally noticed the increased attention she'd been getting over the last couple of days, which seemed to correlate quite strongly with their proximity to Bilaar.

"No," Fubuki said.

Sora cracked an eye open at the word—Fubuki never lied; she *couldn't* lie. However, whenever she found herself pressed, she usually shielded herself by resorting to revealing that she wasn't sure about how she felt; 'I don't understand' or 'I don't know' seemed to be her go-to method of avoidance—but the fact that she was actually staking a flag into the ground here meant that she'd reached some kind of threshold in which she could no longer let things continue.

"You're *not* okay?" Chiyo said, concerned. "Would you like to talk about it?"

Fubuki slowly turned her gaze over to him, making it clear to everyone in the carriage just what the subject was. She held his gaze for a long moment, silently asking for some kind of assistance with handling the situation. Sora was pretty sure what she wanted, but he had no intention of influencing Chiyo's decision, not when it was something that held such a high risk.

"Sorry," Sora said, closing his eyes. "I'm not going to try and convince her to do something she doesn't want to do."

Chiyo looked down for a moment as the situation revealed itself to her.

"Why?" Fubuki asked.

"Because it's her decision to make," Sora said, "If she wants to continue on to Lyston and find her own way, then she's allowed to make that decision, just like you got to make the same decision."

"No," Fubuki said, leaning forward. "It's not safe in Lyston."

"How do you know that?" Chiyo said.

"Because we won't be there," Fubuki said, frowning now. "You should come with us."

"That's not safe either," Chiyo said, swallowing. "You know it's not."

Fubuki slipped forward on the bench to sit directly beside her, carefully reaching down to take hold of her hand, cradling it between her own, almost like a mirror of one of their lessons.

"I will protect you," Fubuki insisted.

"Fu—*Fuka*," Chiyo tried, catching herself.

"I don't want you to leave," Fubuki said, glancing over at him for a moment. "He doesn't want you to leave."

"Please don't bring me into this," Sora said, "I told you already that—"

"*You don't want her to leave*," Fubuki managed, raising her voice for the first time he could remember. "Why won't you say it?"

There was a terrible silence in the carriage after the words, and for a moment, he was taken aback by just how upset she seemed to be. Chiyo reached out and touched the smaller girl's cheek, already looking like she was about to cry.

"I won't say it because there's a chance that anyone who comes with me is going to die," Sora said, voice quiet. "If I *convince* her to come, and she gets hurt, then I'll have to carry that with me for the rest of my life."

"She will get hurt if you aren't there," Fubuki said, staring at him. "Tell her to come with us."

Chiyo pulled her into a hug, arms wrapped tightly around her neck. Fubuki's view of the situation was of a single note, but in that simplicity, there *was* a sense of security. If he convinced her to come with them, he would be putting her in direct danger, but he'd be present to effectively shield her from it. If he stayed true to his previous decision and let her slip away, then he was removing his ability to protect her entirely, essentially trading her life for the ability to say, 'it's not my fault; she made the decision on her own.' Of the two perspectives, his one left him blameless but would end with Chiyo dead. While hers, simple as it was, put him in a good position to stop anything from happening to her.

"Tell her," Fubuki said.

"You're kind of pissing me off right now," Sora said through gritted teeth. "It's not fair to either of us for *me* to make the decision for her."

"You say that like you *could* convince me," Chiyo mumbled.

Sora ignored Chiyo's protest entirely because the process of convincing her wouldn't even be *difficult*. Fubuki's burning gaze continued to stare at him from over Chiyo's shoulder, and he sat rigidly on the bench, trying to get a hold of his building frustration.

"She will listen if you say it," Fubuki insisted. "Tell her."

"Why are you trying to force me into this?" Sora snapped, "You're putting me in a very difficult position—"

"*Tell* her," Fubuki swallowed, faltering a bit at his anger. "*Please.*"

His carefully constructed distance shattered at the word, and his breath came out in something approaching a hiss, boiling from his frustrations. Sora reached out and took hold of Chiyo's shoulder, pulling her back until she was forced to meet his gaze.

"I don't want you to go someplace where I can't see you, so now you *will* be coming with me," Sora said, a furious edge to his voice. "Do you understand?"

"Yes," Chiyo managed, caving immediately. "I understand."

"I'm going to sleep," Sora snarled, letting go. "If either of you—just don't talk to me—*fuck.*"

Sora turned to look at Fubuki for a moment, and she wilted under the expression, turning her face to hide from him. He waited just long enough to make sure neither of them was going to speak and then lay back down, rolling over to face the bench.

"Thank you," Chiyo mumbled, barely audible. "I—I don't want to go away on my own; I'm just scared."

"I know," Fubuki managed. "We will protect you."

#

Nine

The walls of Bilaar swallowed the caravan as it passed through the gates; a dozen fully armoured guards stood by, a few of them waving them on into the city proper. The city was easily three or four times as large as Maar had been and perhaps half as large as Satu—something of a significant achievement. Considering just how much traffic came through, it was no surprise that the place had grown so large. If the atmosphere in the carriage had been awkward on the third day, it was far worse now, on the seventh—he'd kept to himself almost entirely throughout the last night and day, making no attempt to engage either of them in conversation or lessons. He was simply too mixed up emotionally, frustrated at his failure to keep himself morally isolated from the situation, ashamed of his own angry outburst, and sickly ecstatic that Chiyo had agreed so readily to do what he told her—it was a mess he was having far to much trouble working through, but he felt almost compelled to separate himself from them. He held far too much power in the dynamic the three of them now shared—even after he'd solved the issue with him being the only one in the group with money—his status as the Master and they the apprentice was carrying too much weight *outside* of their lessons. That was why he'd wanted Chiyo to make the decision for *herself* because he'd been recognizing just how one-sided the entire dynamic was becoming, and while he *was* happy that Fubuki had finally found the ability to ask for something she wanted, she'd chosen the absolute worst subject to use it on. Now he'd gone and used his leverage to—not even *convince*—he'd outright told Chiyo what she was going to do, and she'd fallen in line. Whether she had rationalised her own agreement or decision to change her mind as a good thing after the fact, he'd still trampled over her agency in a way that ground against his senses. The carriage came to a stop minutes later, and not a single word had been exchanged between the three of them in that time. Sora pulled his pack up off the floor, shouldering it, and moved towards the door. He stepped down from the carriage with a feeling of relief brimming in his chest after a week of being stuck in confinement and the last twenty-four hours of stilted silence; the open space felt *good*. He silently offered a hand to both of them in service of maintaining their cover, helping each down onto the road.

"May," Sora said, stepping away from the carriage. "Thank you for taking such good care of us."

"That's what you paid me for, isn't it?" May offered with a nod. "The three of you are heading off?"

"We are indeed, but before we do," Sora said, "Say we're heading out from here in the future, who might we speak to about organising another trip like this one—to Lyston, perhaps."

"Not me; we're headed to Satu after this in about a week's time. Not sure you'd find a Caravan straight to Lyston either; there would be at least two stopovers first." May said, reaching up to brush some hair behind her ear. "The most common route is from here to Anar, to Strolt and then to Lyston, say about three weeks total? If you head to the town centre, there's a building with a wooden compass nailed above the door—they'll set you up with a travel plan."

"Fantastic," Sora said, stepping back. "We better get going."

"Best of luck with your next trip," Chiyo said, speaking up. "Fuka?"

"Goodbye, May," Fubuki said before pausing. "Your stew was nice."

"Thanks," May said, amused. "You three look after yourselves."

Sora led them away, the affected smile falling from his face once he'd turned. He started making a mental map of the area, noting the roads, alleyways, balconies, rooftops, and fenced-off areas as they walked. Bilaar was a city of angles, and elevation changes, like someone, had described to the architects the idea of an inverse ziggurat in the vaguest of terms and then set them loose on the city. Everywhere he stepped was a stair, and everywhere he looked was a tall, thin, austere building looming over him, never on quite the same level as he was. The city centre was visible from afar, set below the rest of the city, and by the time they made it there, he was already sweating. He noted the building with the compass that May had spoken about but made no attempt to investigate further. Instead, he sought out an inn, an artistic depiction of a sun nailed above the door followed by the words—*The Sundog Tavern*—they wouldn't be in Bilaar for more than a night, but setting out in the late afternoon was just asking for trouble.

#

The soft mattress beneath him felt like a dream compared to the bedroll he'd spent the last week inside of. It was better than the one at Judra, Maar, and somehow even his old bed, which was strange to think about—he wondered if his memory of it had become distorted after so long being without it. Thinking about his bed turned to thinking about the building it had been contained within, which in turn led him to wonder if they'd already ripped away everything he'd owned and sold the building off or if they had left it untouched to use as a trap, to see if he might try to sneak back in.

"Sora," Fubuki murrmured. "Are you still mad?"

"Yes," Sora said, hands folded beneath his head. "I am."

The sound of the bed that the two women were sharing filled the silence, shifting beneath their combined weight. He waited for a moment to see if she would press on, but her confidence seemed to have fled her in the wake of his admittance. Rather than let his thoughts linger on the unresolved nature of their conflict, he turned his mind forward to the structure of the next day. He'd already stocked up on some long-lasting foodstuffs, but they had about enough for a week each in total; after that, they would be relying on hunting and gathering once more. They'd be able to stride straight out the gates without issue, he knew, because they were only really worried about who they were letting inside. The real problem they were going to face was bypassing the gatehouse, about two hours north of Bilaar. The only thing past that point were forests, goblins and the Dragon's Claw—and they'd long since stopped allowing people to head that way without a good reason. If they wanted to get past, they had three options to make it happen. The first was to get an exemption from the Minister—something that he absolutely had no intention of pursuing because the man would be surrounded by guards, mages, and an army of nobles. The second was to acquire an adventuring license under the guise of seeking goblin ears to bring back for coins, something they could purchase at an adventurers guild. The third option was to attempt to use stealth to bypass the gatehouse entirely and hope that they didn't get spotted—as unlikely as it was for them to send people after them if they were noticed, they would generate a large amount of attention on their eventual return to Bilaar.

"I don't care if you're mad," Chiyo said, taking a deep breath. "It's been hours, and I want to know what's going on—when are we leaving?"

"We're leaving at six in the morning," Sora said, scrunching his face up in annoyance. "Our first stop is going to be the adventurers guild—we're going to need to buy a license to pass the gatehouse to the north."

"How much is it?" Chiyo asked.

"Ten silvers each, every month," Sora said, "I had one back in Satu, but I never ended up needing it, and it's probably out of date—showing the guards my old one would have only ended up with us getting stabbed anyway."

"Do we need to pass a test?" Chiyo asked, concerned. "I don't know how to fight—"

"Why would we need to pass a test?" Sora said, baffled.

"What if we don't know what we're doing, and they just send us out with an unearned license," Chiyo said, taken aback. "We could die out there—wouldn't they want to avoid something like that?"

Sometimes he forgot that she lived on an entirely different planet than he did. Chiyo had no idea about it because she'd never even considered the idea of going outside of the city to fight monsters for money—namely because she'd been born filthy rich.

"You're paying for permission to enter a restricted area, not taking fighting lessons," Sora said, shaking his head. "The entire system is run by frilly skirts; I doubt they give a single shit about people dying, so long as we keep on paying the fee every month."

"That's *absurd*," Chiyo said. "They did it like this in *Satu*?"

"Of course they did; how do you not know about this?" Sora said, frowning. "Have you never seen a restricted zone, map-for-brains?"

"I know all about the restricted zones *and* licenses," Chiyo said, flushing. "I just didn't know how little barrier for entry there really was—I always assumed it was *difficult* to earn a license."

"*Earn* a license," Sora snorted. "Listen to yourself."

"Don't *laugh* at me," Chiyo said, flinging her pillow across the room. "It's not funny."

Sora picked up the pillow after it bounced off his face and then rolled over on top of it, intending to keep it for himself.

"What is a restricted zone?" Fubuki murmured.

"It's an area that's too dangerous for normal people to go; as that *buffoon* said, you must own a license to gain entry," Chiyo said, blowing a breath out of her nose. "The Dread Forest of Sagia is one, and the Dragon's Claw is another."

"Sunken Spire as well, because of how dangerous it is to travel by ship," Sora said, lifting his head just enough that it wasn't muffled by the pillow. "Evanescent Atoll is also a restricted zone, but that's because of how many people have disappeared after going there—no one knows what's going on with that; it appears and vanishes, seemingly at random."

"There are hundreds of them all over the world," Chiyo said, "A few of them *have* been cleared out already, but those seem to be exceptional cases—the fact that it's restricted was one of the reasons I didn't want to go."

There was something of a silence after that, and he found his thoughts drifting straight back to the spiral he'd been fighting to drag himself out of since the argument in the carriage.

"Can I have my pillow back?" Chiyo said.

Sora ignored her entirely, having absolutely no intention of handing it over—besides, it kind of smelled like her. He grunted in annoyance as she yanked his own pillow out from under his head and returned to her bed with the prize.

"Sora," Fubuki murmured, "Are you still mad?"

Sora grunted.

#

"I can't believe she just *gave* it to us without even checking if we knew *anything*," Chiyo said in muted outrage. "How many people have gone in and died because they were unprepared?"

Sora said nothing as the walls of Bilaar fell away behind them, the green of the forest far ahead of them already visible. The gatehouse was a tiny speck of grey sitting before it, a short but immensely long wall of stone stretching away on both sides. It wasn't even the first time she'd expressed the sentiment since they'd left the building—although the fact that she was repeating it pointed towards her wanting some type of engagement on the topic.

"I told you already, it's structured that way to bring in money, not to ensure the safety of the people seeking a license," Sora said, "If you want to look at it in terms of safety, keep in mind that the vast majority of commoners are not going to even have ten silvers spare a month to waste on a license they probably won't even use."

"In Satu, they might not use it, given the distances involved," Chiyo said, a bit of the wind taken out of her sails. "Here, though, with the incentive of making money from killing goblins, they might take the risk."

"Incentive?" Fubuki murrmured.

"Something that would make a dull task more attractive," Sora said, speaking up. "If I asked you to dig a hole, it sounds pretty boring, right?"

"Yes," Fubuki said.

"What if I offered to teach you a spell if you dug the hole?" Sora asked, "Does that sound more interesting?"

"Do you want me to dig a hole?" Fubuki asked.

"No, he doesn't; it was just an example," Chiyo said, taking hold of her arm. "Teaching you the spell would be the incentive—do you understand?"

"I understand," Fubuki said before hesitating. "Will you teach us a spell?"

They'd spent a lot of time since the argument in the carriage ignoring each other, or rather, he'd spent it ignoring them. Last night had worked to repair the bridge to some degree, but he hadn't been in the state of mind to offer them any kind of guidance, and so they'd been left to practice on their own. They'd had the *Colourant* spells in place before he'd even woken up, so he wasn't sure if they'd managed that wordlessly or not.

"Have you figured out how to cast without vocalising the command phrase yet?" Sora asked, glancing over at her.

"Yes," Fubuki said, watching him. "For *Gleam*."

"Neither of us has managed it with *Colourant* yet," Chiyo frowned, "It's harder."

"If you can figure out how to cast *Colourant* without the command phrase," Sora said, turning his eyes forward. "I'll teach you a new spell."

"What type of spell are we talking about here?" Chiyo asked.

"I'll let you each choose one of the spells you've seen me use already," Sora said, "The exceptions to that are all the attack spells, along with *Blink* and *Haste*—you're not ready to throw around offensive magic, and the last two are master-level spells."

"Incentive," Fubuki murmured.

Sora nodded at the correct usage of the word—she seemed to pick up on those types of things pretty quickly once they'd been explained to her.

"*Any* of them?" Chiyo said, biting her lip.

"Any of them," Sora agreed. "Better hurry up, though, because I'm putting a time limit on it—you've got until we reach the gatehouse."

Fubuki was already channelling mana into her palm, the *Colourant* spell keeping her eyes black vanishing as she pulled it apart.

"That's not fair—" Chiyo said, outraged.

"Are you sure you've got enough time to stand around powdering your ass?" Sora wondered. "I mean, I can *see* the gatehouse from here."

Chiyo made a strangled noise in her throat and then flipped the hood of her cloak up to cover her hair.

#

Neither of them managed it before they reached the gatehouse, and they were both forced to abandon their continued efforts in order to pull their disguises back into place. There were almost twenty-five men lounging around by the gate, and he could see a dozen more spread out before the wall, one every hundred meters to act as a lookout for anything that might come creeping out of the forest in an attempt to approach Bilaar. Sora angled his approach for the man who'd stood up to greet them and met him almost directly beneath the gate.

"First ones of the day," The man said, yawning. "Going hunting?"

"We're in need of some pocket change," Sora said, smirking. "Figured this was the best way to make some quick coin—we'll probably stay inside for a week or so."

"That long?" The man whistled. "You sure? You can see the little bastards at the treeline during the night; figure they're keeping an eye on us as well—you might be better off coming back on this side of the wall to sleep."

"Got it covered, boss," Sora said. "I'm not coming out until we've got a hundred ears—you want my license?"

"Protocol," The man said, "You're a braver lot than me, I'll tell you that."

Sora dragged it up out of his pocket and handed it over, waving the other two to hand there's over as well. The man barely gave them more than a cursory look over before handing them back.

"You've only got knives?" The man asked. "You sure you don't want something more substantial?"

"The three of us are Adepts," Sora said, "Bigger weapons would only slow us down—a knife each is fine."

"Listen, I've seen a lot of people go in there over the years," The man said, "I've only seen about half of them come out—make sure you're not one of those, yeah?"

"You got it, boss," Sora said, winking. "We'll come have a chat when we're finished working—keep up the good work out here."

"Sure thing," The man said, shaking his head. "Good luck."

Sora clapped the man on the shoulder on his way past, striding through the gate without another word. Chiyo and Fubuki fell into step beside him, speeding up a bit to reach his position.

"You sounded like that back with the girl who sold us the licenses," Chiyo mumbled. "Why do you change the way you talk to everyone?"

"Alhat thinks an old man visited to buy some replacement clothing, Judra, Akh, and Maar think a group of well-off travelling entertainers came through from Karas, and now the people of Bilaar will think of us as adventurers seeking coin," Sora said, without care. "If anyone can figure out the three of us are the exact same group that left Satu as fugitives, then we deserve to get caught—if you could look less like a trembling frilly skirt during every discussion, it would be a great help."

Chiyo flushed at the taunt, but before she could toss something back, Fubuki spoke.

"Sora," Fubuki murrmured. "Is this an act as well?"

"The way I am with you two?" Sora asked for clarification. "I think *some* of it might be—I'm a lot quieter when I'm on my own; maybe you guys bring out the best of me."

"The *worst* of you, maybe," Chiyo said, finding a place to stab at. "You're *incredibly* rude."

"Says the girl who climbed into my bedroll in the middle of the night and stuffed her hand down my pants," Sora said, lip pulling up at one side. "I don't think you've got much room to talk, *Hi-mu-ra.*"

"*Sora,*" Chiyo squeaked. "*Fubuki, don't listen to anything he's saying—*"

#

"Goblins are small, weak, and they aren't even intelligent enough to communicate through language," Sora said, eyes on the trees. "They primarily live in caves or dug-out tunnels they create by hand."

"What else?" Chiyo said, closely attached to Fubuki's side.

"They use rudimentary tools, like branches and rocks, to attack—they've also been known to steal the equipment of humans, so if you see one with a sword or something, that's where they got it from," Sora said, "They tend to live in groups that range from a dozen to about forty. Too many of them in one place will inevitably cause infighting, and the group will fracture."

Sora continued his search of the trees, looking for signs of movement.

"They are omnivores in that they'll eat just about anything—plants, insects, fish, wolves, birds, humans, horses, and even each other when they get hungry enough." Sora continued, "They won't fight anything bigger than them in the open, so the main thing we need to be on the lookout for is ambushes."

"That guard said we should go back over the wall to sleep," Chiyo said, "What if they find us while we sleeping?"

"I'll be taking care of that with exclusionary spells—offensive ones, this time," Sora said, "But you're both going to have to pay close attention because they target things indiscriminately, which means once they're up, you won't be leaving the area until I take them down."

"Will they hurt us if we try to leave?" Chiyo said, concerned.

"No, but you won't be able to get back *in* without them targeting *you*, and you really don't want that," Sora said, glancing over at the two of them. "You both understand, right?"

"Yes," Fubuki said before pausing. "I see a goblin."

"*What?*" Chiyo hissed. "Where is it?"

Sora followed her gaze to a distant tree ahead of them; the thing's large, shining eyes peered at them from behind the trunk, barely three feet off the ground. He frowned, checking the surrounding trees, but it was the only one in sight. He lifted his hand up in its direction, drawing his knife from his belt.

"Chiyo, you might want to look away," Sora offered, building the pattern. "*Wrest.*"

The spell snapped into existence, mana striking forward and winding through the trees, directed by his willpower. It curled around the monster's neck, clamping down, and then pulled taut, ripping it up off the ground. The creature's body collided with the trunk and then bounced across the ground, drawn inextricably towards them. Chiyo gave a terrified cry and dragged Fubuki in front of her as the little monster crashed to a stop before them. Sora stomped down on its body before it could gather its bearings and pushed his knife through its eye.

"If you see any more of them, please speak up," Sora said, straightening. "If we leave them alone, they will return with a larger group."

Sora wiped the knife clean on the thick bolt of cloth he'd tucked into his belt and then returned it to the sheath. Chiyo stared down at the unmoving creature with wide eyes, holding tight onto the back of Fubuki's cloak. Sora stepped past the body without bothering to take its ear, and he heard them move to follow him once more.

"You just killed it like it was nothing," Chiyo managed. "It almost looks like a child."

"If that's a sentiment born out of empathy, you should get rid of it because goblins aren't like the three of us," Sora advised, "They're like wasps, belligerent and without care for anything other than their immediate wants—it's all instincts, and the present, with no thought for places where they aren't."

Sora glanced over to find her looking at him.

"People have tried to domesticate them dozens of times, but it never goes anywhere, and no conditioning seems to hold," Sora said, shaking his head. "Trust me—they'll eat you alive, from the feet upwards, not because it keeps the meat fresh for longer, but because they like the noises."

"Stop," Chiyo managed, "I get it—I don't want to know anymore."

"I'm not trying to scare you, Chiyo," Sora said, reaching over to pat her on the shoulder. "I just don't want you to hesitate when one of them eventually comes at you, okay? Don't hold back if you're in danger— you've got your own knife now; use it."

"Okay," Chiyo swallowed.

Fubuki turned to look to the side, the motion catching their attention, and then she turned back to look at him.

"Sora," Fubuki said.

"I'll stay with Chiyo," Sora offered. "Go ahead."

Fubuki vanished in a blur of shocking movement that he hadn't seen since before they'd made it to Judra, and a wave of detritus washed upwards at her passing—there was a muted crack a moment later as she slid into view beside a distant tree, yellow eyes glowing in the low light, and a goblin hanging limp from her hand.

#

Sora watched the *Flamestay* spell, an odd impatience at the idea of having to stop moving in order to wait out the night. The tracery of mana encompassing them touched his mind. *Sanctum*, to hide their presence, and *Phlogiston*, to set alight anything that might stumble inside by accident—more than enough to alert them to something crossing into their camp. Chiyo remained enshrined within her bedroll, less than two feet away from the fire, her covered legs almost touching his thigh.

"Can you move your bedroll closer, Fubuki?" Chiyo murmured. "I don't want you sleeping so far away."

Fubuki abandoned her most recent attempt at sub-vocalising the *Colourant* spell. She crawled past the fire without a word, taking hold of her bedroll and dragging it right up to lay flush against the other one. Fubuki curled her legs up beside the other girl's head before reaching down and carefully brushing her fingers through her hair. Another distant cackle rang out in the forest, sharp, high and without any real humour in the noise.

"Why do they keep laughing?" Chiyo managed, shifting closer to Fubuki.

"I figure that's kind of like asking, 'why does a wolf howl?' or 'why does a bird whistle?'" Sora said, leaning back on his hands. "They don't have a *language*, but it's a way for them to report their location to the rest of the group."

"It's an awful noise," Chiyo mumbled. "Like they're laughing at *us*."

"We cleared out all the ones that were nearby already, which means these are ones that came into the area later—*hours* after we had the spells set up," Sora said, glancing down at her. "They have no idea we're even here, Chiyo."

"I know, but that doesn't help," Chiyo hedged, "I'm never going to be able to sleep like this."

Sora eyed her for a moment longer before leaning over and placing a hand against her blanket-covered foot, a pattern building up in an instant. Chiyo glanced up at him for a moment, perhaps thinking he was attempting to comfort her—

"*Sleep*," Sora said.

The spell took effect slowly, and he watched as she seemed to struggle to find her response.

"If it was that easy," Chiyo mumbled, trailing off a bit. "I would—have—*wait*."

Fubuki stared down at her for a long moment, carefully brushing the now sleeping woman's hair out of her face, but she didn't stir. Sora leant back on his hands again as she turned to look at him.

"You used a spell," Fubuki said.

"I did," Sora admitted, "I'd rather her be mad at me in the morning than so tired that she can't walk straight."

He sighed at his own word choice because he caught the shift in Fubuki's shoulders as he said it and knew exactly where the conversation was headed.

"Sora," Fubuki said, voice quiet. "Are you still mad at me?"

"Fubuki," Sora sighed, turning to gaze at the fire. "I—think I'm actually mad at myself now."

It had been a very long time since he'd been as invested in someone other than himself as he was right now. The last person he'd found himself actually caring about had been Salas, but now he had two more. Not exactly a long list, but it was what he had.

"I'm feeling kind of stuck right now, I guess," Sora admitted, closing his eyes. "I really wanted both of you to make your own choices—untainted by my own desire—because that's what I'd have wanted if the situation was reversed."

Fubuki lifted her head slightly as he spoke.

"On the other hand, I *didn't* want Chiyo to go off somewhere where you and I couldn't protect her if something went wrong," Sora said, cracking one eye open to look at her. "The ideal situation here was for Chiyo to realise—*on her own*—that she would be safer with both of us, and we still had several days before that decision had to be made."

"Sora," Fubuki murmured.

"You already got to make the *exact* same decision that you and I were both hoping Chiyo would make; only *you* got to do it without outside influence," Sora said, still watching her. "You took that choice out of her hands when you forced the issue back in the carriage, and I ended up bending to my own desires, telling her that she was coming with us because it was what *I* wanted."

"I didn't want her to go," Fubuki said, running her fingers through Chiyo's hair.

"I know, Fubuki; I didn't want her to go either," Sora said before sighing. "I think deep down I was just being selfish anyway, wanting her to make the choice *I* wanted while also avoiding being the one to convince her because of the burden of being responsible."

Sora shook his head at his own confession.

"Fubuki, I'm sorry I got mad and that I didn't talk to you after it happened," Sora said, "I think you might have had the better answer in the end, or at least the braver one. If you hadn't spoken up, I might have let her go without saying a damn thing—I'm kind of shitty for a Master, huh?"

"No," Fubuki murrmured. "You're not."

#

"*Finally*," Chiyo breathed. "I did it."

Sora glanced back over his shoulder to where she was walking beside Fubuki; Chiyo had a lock of her own hair pulled up in front of her eyes, entirely black—and he hadn't heard her speak the words.

"That makes two of you," Sora said, nodding. "Shame the gatehouse was, I don't know, three whole days behind us?"

"Shut up," Chiyo said, her smile untouched. "I still did it."

"Can you repeat it?" Sora asked. "It wasn't a fluke?"

He felt the spell vanish as she pulled it apart and then felt it build back up again, the pattern returning to the exact same place, recycling the unused mana. It reached the threshold, the central point growing brighter as she added to its duration—and then it snapped into place, a single, almost seamless, completely silent, full cast.

"Well done, Chiyo," Sora said, smiling. "That was perfect."

Fubuki looked startled as Chiyo swept her up off the ground, arms wrapped around her back in a hug. The bright happiness on her face caused him to blow an amused breath out of his nose, and he wondered when the last time *he'd* felt something like that. It had been weeks since he'd learnt anything new; without access to the library or the books he'd tucked away in his home, he was forced to simply experiment with the spells he already knew—and while he wasn't exactly pressed for choice, it wasn't the same kind of bright feeling as overcoming a wall like she just had.

"How long until I'm no longer a novice?" Chiyo demanded. "I'm practically there already, huh?"

"You've got a *long* way before that happens," Sora said, snorting. "You two could barely be called beginners. The old bastards in the Great Satu Library only consider you a novice when you can cast five spells."

"We know two spells, though," Chiyo said, pulling back from Fubuki. "That means we're pretty close?"

"I'm afraid you're further away than you think. The spells you need to know aren't random, they are carefully chosen, and neither *Gleam* nor *Colourant* is on that list," Sora admitted, starting forward again. "You two are in a really weird spot right now compared to most people training to pass the novice exam."

"Really?" Chiyo said, frowning.

"For a start, you are both highly specialised, with only two illusionary spells under your belt—one of which is, ironically enough, far more complicated than all five of the novice spells—but you also have a deeper understanding of how mana actually works and how to control it than anyone who's been trained conventionally," Sora admitted, holding up three fingers. "You've learned to focus mana in non-standard areas, you've learned to maintain spells through mana injection, and you've also learned the process for sub-vocalisation—the first two of those things are skills taught to novices who've actually *passed* the test, and the third is something that usually isn't covered until after you've completed the exam to become an Adept."

"An Adept skill?" Chiyo said, startled.

"Sora," Fubuki said, speaking up. "What are the five spells?"

"*North, Dispel, Illuminate, Gust, Screen*," Sora said, "Take a guess at what each of them does—Fubuki."

"I don't know," Fubuki said almost immediately. "Chiyo?"

He stopped to look back over his shoulder again, and Chiyo glanced away from the attention, scratching her cheek.

"*Fubuki*," Sora repeated.

"*Gust* makes wind," Fubuki said after her ploy had failed. "You used it to blow out the lanterns."

"Any more guesses?" Sora asked, and when Fubuki shook her head, he moved on. "Chiyo."

"*North* probably acts like a compass, and *Dispel* must stop spells from working?" Chiyo said, faltering a bit as he remained without expression. "*Illuminate* is most likely an illusionary spell that creates light, and *Screen*—I don't know, either it creates a wall, or it tells you if someone is lying."

Sora reached out and patted them both on the head like they were dogs before mussing their hair up. Chiyo squawked at the attack and attempted to batter his hand away, but Fubuki just stared at him, nonplussed.

"Well done, four out of five correct," Sora said, amused. "The last one is a combat spell; it creates a wall of force in front of your hand that blocks a single attack."

"Will you *stop* that?" Chiyo huffed, attempting to protect Fubuki. "You're messing it up—I'm going to have to redo her braid now, idiot."

"Now, since you both failed to meet the deadline I set, I suppose I should teach you one of those," Sora said, retrieving his hand. "You already know how to destroy your own internal spells, so we could probably do *Dispel* first to let you break down external ones—oh, you look like you've got something to say, apprentice mine?"

"I want to learn *Screen*," Chiyo asked, crossing her arms. "*Dispel* sounds far less useful right now."

"Oh?" Sora said, "Fubuki, which one did you want to learn?"

"*Gust*," Fubuki murrmured.

"I see, I see; in that case, you are both—denied," Sora said, scratching his beard. "Chiyo will be learning *Gust*, and Fubuki will be learning *Screen*."

"That's totally unfair," Chiyo said in protest. "Fubuki, it's not my fault—don't look at me like *that*."

"Come here, Fubuki," Sora said, beckoning her closer. "Give me your hand."

Fubuki stepped forward, placing her hand in his palm without another word, and he watched as Chiyo moved closer to them both, unwilling to stand on her own amidst the forest. Sora cradled her hand between his own, slowly pressing his mana into her palm, building up the pattern for *Screen*. Fubuki stared at her hand for a moment before closing her eyes, and he could feel her own mana moving, surrounding the foreign energy he'd injected into her.

"That's the pattern," Sora said, still holding her hand. "Take your time, and tell me when you think you've memorised it."

Sora smiled at the glare Chiyo was aiming at him from over Fubuki's head—as much fun as it was to wind her up, there was a method to his decision other than just that alone. Learning patterns wasn't a particularly difficult task, but it was time-consuming. For a lot of people, motivation played a big role in the process, and being able to keep working on the same thing for hours at a time wasn't easy, especially when the progress you were making was sometimes undetectable. The problem for most mages—because this was something that hit novices, adepts and masters alike—was that the motivation wasn't always there. You couldn't count on it to appear when you needed it to, and something like that would inevitably affect both your progress and the spells you learned. If you only found enjoyment in learning flashy spells, you'd never have the motivation to learn ones that were more subtle. If you only wanted to learn magic that healed people, you'd end up being almost incapable of defending yourself. If you only learned the spells you found the most motivation to go after, you would train yourself to only succeed when the motivation was there—and when it wasn't, you'd find yourself stagnating.

"I've got it," Fubuki murmured, eyes still closed.

Sora let her go as she stepped backwards, and Chiyo caught hold of her shoulders before the two of them could collide. Once Fubuki had regained her bearings, he beckoned Chiyo towards him.

"Why can't we learn the spell we wanted?" Chiyo asked, "Are you just trying to annoy us?"

Chiyo stared at him in defiance, clearly worked up over the entire thing. Sora reached down and took hold of her hand, pulling it up between them. He brushed his thumb over her fingers and into the centre of her palm. Chiyo's defiance faltered as he carefully turned her hand over, suddenly having much more difficulty meeting his gaze.

"Stop smirking," Chiyo managed, ducking his gaze entirely. "It's not funny."

"The reason I'm teaching you the opposite spell is that I want the two of you to work together on this," Sora said, "There is a lot that can be learned through the act of teaching another person, so once you've both managed to learn the spell I've assigned, you're going to teach it to each other."

Chiyo closed her eyes a moment after his mana passed through her skin, the pattern for *Gust* coming into existence.

"It makes you look at things in a different way and shines a light on details you might have known subconsciously but never actually had to think about consciously," Sora added, tracing the pattern with his thumb. "I suppose I could have you try and teach *me* the spell, but as amusing as I would find that, this is simply a better method."

It also meant that each of them would be paying far closer attention to what the other one was trying to convey because it was the spell they'd wanted to learn in the first place. It also acted as an incentive for them to put in a lot of work learning the spell he'd assigned because they now knew they would need to teach it to someone else in the future—something that would be embarrassing if they couldn't do it.

"I think I have it now," Chiyo said, slowly opening her eyes. "Thank you."

"Sure thing," Sora said, squeezing her hand once before letting her go. "Are the two of you ready to keep moving?"

#

"Given the place we started and our direction, we should be coming up right between the Second and Third Talons," Chiyo said, with his book spread out on her lap. "If we get up early again, we should reach it by tomorrow, just after midday."

"See how energetic she gets with a map in her hands?" Sora said, stage whispering to Fubuki. "She must be getting ready to eat it."

"Chiyo," Fubuki said, "Don't eat the map."

Chiyo scrunched her face up at the comments but didn't dignify either with a response. Instead, she started flipping through the pages —he eyed her for a moment, wondering if her request to look at the map had been a ruse to get another look at the other things contained within.

"In the story, they were at Dragon's Claw, where all three Talons meet," Chiyo said, running her finger down the page. "The big statue of the nameless monk was already at the bottom of the river, and the dragon's body was sinking, I suppose?"

"That was an embellishment on my part," Sora admitted, "There's actually no mention of what happened to the dragon after she cut out the marble; it's never referred to again."

"Okay fine. The butcher's daughter tosses the marble into the river to be watched over by the statue—what makes you think that it's still going to be there?" Chiyo said, biting her lip. "It's supposed to have been thousands of years old, right? The current of the river could have taken it away at any point."

"You're still kind of hung up on the literal interpretation of the story," Sora said, shifting down to lie in his bedroll. "Say this happened two thousand years ago before any of the current countries were the way they are now—different leaders, different borders, different languages."

Sora folded his hands behind his head and closed his eyes.

"There's a marble with some kind of power—maybe it lets you enter and exit hell, maybe it transforms you into a dragon, maybe it allows you to cast *Fireball* without knowing the pattern," Sora said, wriggling his toes against the inside of his bedroll. "Where do you think an object like that *comes* from?"

"Magic?" Chiyo guessed.

"Correct, and the only kind of person who would be able to make a magic marble is a mage," Sora said, "So we've got a magical artifact that was, most rationally, created by an ancient mage—likely a Master, given the difficulty of making any kind of lasting artifact."

"A Sora," Fubuki murrmured.

"I'll take that as a compliment, but making permanent magical artifacts is something I'll probably never bother attempting," Sora said, amused. "I could learn a thousand new spells in the time it would take to design, craft and then charge the weakest magical artifact, and the former is much more fun than the latter."

"Okay, so somebody made the marble in the past," Chiyo said, trying to pull them back on track. "What does that mean for the story?"

"It means that when you look at the component pieces of the story, you have several things—One, the nameless monk, who, according to the story, was a *master mage* who went around the world helping people. Two, there is a *magical artifact* in the story that only a *master mage* is capable of creating. Three, there are statues of the man *holding* the marble, which, when considering the timeline of the story, he should have never possessed while he was still human." Sora said, tilting his head to the side with each one. "Inputting each of those components into a new story, what do you think could have happened?"

Fubuki turned to look at Chiyo, clearly waiting for an answer, and the noblewoman flushed at the sheer expectant nature of it.

"Um," Chiyo managed, "Okay, give me a second."

Sora closed his eyes again, content to wait for her to put together an updated interpretation based on the new information.

"There was a master mage who was well-liked enough that people built statues of him," Chiyo said, and he could tell by the sound of her voice that she was biting her lip. "At some point, he created a magical artifact—that let him do one of those things that you mentioned—and then somebody killed him for it."

Sora cracked an eye open at the conclusion.

"What makes you think someone killed him for it?" Sora wondered.

"The butcher's daughter with the knife was part of the story, and she killed the dragon before getting the marble," Chiyo said, "There's also the hooded man who cursed him to hell—that's not in here; it just says that he woke up in hell without knowing why—which means *your* interpretation of it was that there was a bad actor involved."

"You're missing some context that would help reshape the narrative," Sora said, "But you're on the right track."

"Context?" Fubuki murrmured.

"Information about a subject that would explain why it happened a certain way," Chiyo said, explaining it to her. "What am I missing?"

"I gave you a hint about it before, actually," Sora admitted, "The time it takes to create a magical artifact."

"A thousand spells," Chiyo said. "No, wait—you said that was for the weakest one. How long does it take to make a magical artifact like this one?"

"A magical artifact like that takes hundreds of years to make," Sora said, "But it depends on the spell you're working with."

"*Hundreds?*" Chiyo said, startled.

"Hundreds, which is why there are so few of them," Sora offered, "That fountain we were talking about—the one in Satu we used for the visualisation exercise—that thing technically counts as a magical artifact."

"It does?" Chiyo asked.

"It's got an old—and super outdated—water-purifying spell etched into it, along with a bunch of other spells." Sora explained, "It also has a mana siphoning system set up that takes a tiny sip of mana from everyone that comes within five meters of it."

"It's a magical artifact because it keeps on refuelling itself?" Chiyo guessed.

"That is the *process*—a magical artifact is an object that has a written spell embedded in it, one that is connected to a *Permanence* spell and a *Siphon* spell that has been fed an unbroken stream of mana over such a long period of time that the pattern crystallizes to the point where it will never degrade," Sora said, turning onto his side so he could see her better. "The internal reaction that occurs in every spell—the consumption of mana formally referred to as mana-burn—cannot consume the crystalline mana, but the *effect* of the spell still occurs."

"So a magical artifact can cast a spell without consuming the mana inside of it," Chiyo frowned, "That means you don't *need* to fill the pattern with mana to cast with it?"

"Correct—so with the added context that the nameless monk couldn't have created a magical artifact within his lifetime, we are left with one of two options," Sora said, "Option one is that the marble depicted in the statues is actually an existing magical artifact made by someone else hundreds of years before it came into his possession—"

"Or he was in the process of making one when he died," Chiyo said, staring at him. "You think there will be some kind of *Siphon* at Dragon's Claw that's feeding mana to the marble, like the one in the well in Satu."

"You really are smart, Chiyo," Sora said, watching her. "You're entirely wasted as a map-for-brains."

"Um—thank you?" Chiyo managed, a bit flustered. "I think."

"Sora," Fubuki murrmured. "What spell is in the marble?"

"That's one of the questions I'd like to find out," Sora admitted, "Along with whether or not it ever existed, to begin with."

#

Ten

"*Wrest*," Sora said, bringing his knife into the path of the creature. "Fubuki, on our left."

Fubuki spun low, rising behind Chiyo in a blur that left her braid swinging outwards from the motion. Sora felt the moment her foot hit the ground, a sharp vibration washing over them as she burst forward, crossing the distance before the goblin had even crashed into his knife. He stepped, right hand rising to face the trees.

"Chiyo, cover your ears now," Sora said, watching the shining black eyes flicker in the shadows of the trees. "*Scream.*"

The air distorted in front of his hand, the leaves kicking up into the air as a cascade of noise washed forward. The bark on the trees shattered, and the overlapping cackles cut off, drowned out by the overpowering sound. A dozen pairs of shining eyes vanished, exploding as the wave of sound reached them, their bodies erupting on contact. Chiyo cried out, hands covering her ears, the unsullied knife in her hand sticking out over her shoulder. Sora took another step to the right, hand still raised in front of him, the cone tearing through the trees as it passed over them, killing everything within fifteen meters and sending the rest of the goblins scattering away from the terrifying noise. Fubuki pulled back as he continued his slow lap, rotating in turn, keeping Chiyo between them, and once he'd ruined everything around them, he let his hand drop down—the pattern shattered, and the noise cut out, leaving a ringing silence in the air.

"Fubuki, we're moving; bring Chiyo," Sora said, placing his hand on her shoulder as he passed. "*Haste.*"

He cast it on himself a second later and then took off running to the northwest. His eyes flickered around the trees, looking for movement; he curved wide around a tree, stooping low and stabbing three goblins on his way past before circling back onto his previous path. Fubuki appeared beside him, Chiyo nestled in her arms and her face tucked into the oni's neck. They were too far east; that had become clear when they ran into the Third Talon again. Moving along the river had been a mistake; the area was far too populated by goblins, and their slow progress forward had ended up pulling several different groups of the things out of hiding. While they wouldn't work together long term, the short term was a different story when there was food to be had—intergroup fighting would occur after they'd brought their prey down. Sora angled further west, reaching down and killing another goblin in passing, not bothering to stop and watch as the rest of its group scrambled to their feet. He repeated the process three more times, killing one to three goblins from each group before continuing on, drawing as many of them into the hunt as he could manage. They were starting to run out of forest now, the dark blue of the Second Talon reflecting the sunlight through the trees ahead of them. Sora pointed towards the embankment, and Fubuki flashed forward, jaunting through the trees in a dance he couldn't hope to match. He continued on staying slow enough to keep the groups that were following him interested in the chase. Sora started to turn again, angling away from the water and back into the forest, leaving the flood of shining black eyes scrambling to try and cut him off. He cut his speed again, slowing down to allow them to keep up, now almost a singular column of black eyes trying to scramble past one another to reach him first. He started building up the pattern for *Etch* in his right hand, waiting until the last minute before bursting forward again—he tagged the tree ahead of him, burning a complicated pattern into the tree in an instant. He cut left around the group and hit another two trees before cutting back towards the water. He slid to a stop next to his last target, slapping his palm against the final tree.

"*Phlogiston*," Sora said, working to keep his breathing even. "Good luck, assholes."

He cut the *Haste* spell to help conserve his mana and then angled back towards where he'd directed Fubuki to go. The cackling turned to screams as the goblins attempted to cross the inverted and invisible barrier of the spell. The rest of them scattered away from the now-burning front runners, but they were entirely boxed in. In the panic that followed, they scattered in all directions, but without being able to see the lines or understand what was happening, they just ended up exactly like the others. By the time he'd made it to the embankment, the sound of their screams had vanished entirely. The Second Talon looked exactly like the Third, for all intents and purposes, a large mass of blue-black water stretching what had to be fifty meters to the opposite bank. He turned his gaze right and spotted Fubuki twice that distance ahead of him standing on the shore. He jogged along the bank until he reached them, keeping his eyes on the treeline.

"*Where did you go?*" Chiyo strangled out, still trapped in Fubuki's grip. "*I thought you—*"

"I got most of them," Sora said, interjecting. "The noise from that spell should have scared some of them off as well—they aren't going to go after something that could make a noise like that."

He passed the two of them by, waving them to follow him all the way to where the Second and Third Talons met, a peak of open land that was soon swallowed by the water. The First Talon was hidden by the opposite embankment, stretching out a bit further than the one they were on. The Dragon's Claw was twice as wide as any of the Talons on their own, almost a hundred meters across at his best guess, and stretching away to the horizon. Even without obstructions, he couldn't see the ocean, it was too far away, and the light was starting to fade, robbing them of even more clarity.

"That bank over there would have been a better spot to camp, but it would cost too much mana to *Blink* us over there, and we'd need to clear out the goblins again," Sora said, frowning. "We'll set up camp here, Fubuki; you can put her down."

He started checking the area for the best placements; with no trees on the shore, he'd have to use rocks. Sora kicked around on the ground for a bit, finding a couple of large stones and dropping them into a pile.

"What are we doing?" Chiyo said, keeping her back to the river. "Sora?"

"Try to calm down; I'll need your help in a moment," Sora said, patting her on the shoulder. "Fubuki, sorry to ask you this without a good incentive, but can you dig me four holes, about a foot deep? There, there, there, and there?"

Fubuki stepped forward without any kind of complaint and slammed her hand into the ground in the first spot he'd pointed to. Her arm sank in up to the elbow, and when she pulled it back out, she brought out a mess of roots, dirt and rocks. Sora turned his own attention towards the rocks, using *Etch* to carve both *Phlogiston* and *Sanctum*. He added a *Permanence* component to a fifth rock and linked it to the system but left it uncharged.

"Chiyo," Sora said, handing the first of the rocks off to her. "Put that in the hole, and cover it over. Stake a little stick above it when you're done, so we know where the boundary line is."

He completed each of the stones in turn, passing them off to Chiyo each time. Fubuki returned once her own task was done, her arms completely covered in muck. He handed one of the stones off to her, and she took it over without asking for instruction, following Chiyo's example. Once he had everything finished, he dropped the charging stone in the middle of the area, leaving it there.

"It's probably not going to rain tonight, but just in case, we should try and make some kind of basic shelter," Sora said, rubbing his neck. "Fubuki—see that branch? Can you break it off and then find me three more at the same length?"

#

The shelter was up—four thick branches buried in the ground and a single sheet of thick canvas tied to the top of each, and three of the sides, leaving them with a small covered-in cube. He finished tying the last sheet up, giving them something of a hanging flap of a door and then nodded. He stepped outside the shelter and scooped the charging stone up off the ground. Fubuki and Chiyo remained where he'd asked them to keep watch on the treeline, but so far, nothing had attempted to come after them.

"Fubuki, Chiyo," Sora said, holding up the stone. "Come here—impromptu lesson time."

"Is this really the time?" Chiyo managed, hand curled around Fubuki's wrist. "Can't we do this after the barrier is up?"

"This is about the barrier," Sora admitted, "I don't want to use all of my mana up now, in case something requires me to use it later—so you two are going to be charging the barrier for me."

"Okay, fine," Chiyo said, a bit relieved. "Just tell me what to do."

He moved to a place where he could watch the treeline and then held the rock up for each of them to hold onto.

"Have either of you attempted to direct your mana outside of your body yet?" Sora asked, "Close your eyes—Chiyo, I'm watching the trees, just do it—thank you. Take a deep breath. Direct your mana down to your hand—into your fingers now. Perfect."

He could feel their fingers growing bright, more and more mana condensing there.

"You can't feel the stone because it's not a part of you, so you're going to lose control of the mana almost immediately after it leaves your body," Sora said, voice quiet. "That's okay, keep your fingers on the pattern—now push the mana further *through* your fingertips."

The barrier snapped into existence almost immediately, Chiyo's mana surging out of her hand at a startling rate. Her desire to complete the task and lock herself away behind the barrier gifted her an intensity of focus beyond what she could normally do. The rate of depletion was enough that by the time Fubuki had figured it out, he had to drag Chiyo's hand away from the stone before she bled herself dry.

"Chiyo, stop," Sora said, fingers pressed against the inside of her wrist. "You pretty much dumped your entire mana pool—you need to calm down, okay? The barrier is up, and nothing is going to get through."

"How am I supposed to be calm after *that*?" Chiyo said, voice shaking. "We almost died—just like I said we would."

"Chiyo, I know you're scared," Sora said, voice quiet. "But everything's fine; neither of us would—"

"Don't *talk* to me like I'm—*like I'm*—" Chiyo managed, tears building at the corner of her eyes. "*I'm not some child—you—*"

Chiyo turned away from him with a sob and fled inside the shelter without another word. He swallowed at the sound of her crying, not at all muffled by the canvas. Fubuki's stream of mana wavered at the noise, and he carefully pulled the stone back out of her grip.

"Thank you, that's more than enough, Fubuki," Sora said, touching her on the arm. "The barrier is up now, so please don't go past the markers, okay? Maybe you could go inside and tell Chiyo for me?"

"Sora," Fubuki murrmured.

"I'll be fine out here," Sora said, offering her a smile. "Go on."

Fubuki hesitated a moment longer before slipping around to the door and into the shelter. Sora turned his back on the treeline, content with the fact that nothing was getting through the barrier, at least for the next forty-eight hours. He took in the sight for a long moment and wondered if there was a single person alive who'd seen it other than the three of them.

#

Sora watched the water until the sun had vanished, and then for an hour more after that, trying to give Chiyo as much space as he could manage under the circumstances, but eventually, the cold was starting to get to him. The proximity to the water lowered the temperature to something he couldn't bring himself to brave for much longer. He rubbed at his cold fingers before slipping back into the shelter—he found two slitted yellow eyes watching him, low to the ground.

"Sora?" Chiyo mumbled. "That's you, right?"

The voice was coming from where Fubuki was, the two of them sharing a bedroll at his best guess.

"It's me," Sora said, "Do you want a fire, or are you happy without one?"

"I want one," Chiyo mumbled. "Please."

Sora searched the ground with his foot to figure out the best place to put it and then cast a *Flamestay* spell—he winced at the sudden light, far too used to the dark now that even the soothing orange glow felt like staring straight at the sun. Fubuki watched him from the shared bedroll, trapped in Chiyo's grasp, clearly uncertain about her current predicament. Sora detached his own one from the pack and unrolled it, placing it at an angle that would leave space for the fire.

"I'm sorry," Chiyo said, voice now muffled by Fubuki's chest. "I shouldn't have yelled at you."

He pulled out a spare shirt to use as a pillow, not quite willing to sleep without one, and then slipped into his bedroll—between the covers and the *Flamestay* spell, he was even starting to get feeling back in his fingers.

"I'm not going to hold it against you; it was a stressful situation," Sora said before breathing a sigh of relief. "God, it feels so good to lie down."

"Sora?" Fubuki murmured. "Did you find anything?"

"I wasn't really looking," Sora admitted, "I was just watching the water and using the time to go over my strategy."

"What is your strategy?" Fubuki asked.

"I'm going to have to do a search of the area, including the water, for any traces of magic," Sora said, "That could take a few hours or a few days, given how much area I need to cover."

"How do you search the water?" Fubuki pressed. "Will we swim?"

"That's probably going to be something we can't avoid, but it's also not something we should do right away either," Sora said, "After I check the immediate area for magic, we can move on to searching the water."

"I don't want to swim," Chiyo mumbled, "There might be monsters in the water."

"There absolutely are monsters in the water," Sora admitted, "I'm almost certain there are crocodiles here as well, so be very careful about getting too close to the shoreline, and make sure you stay on this side of the barrier at all times."

"*Sora,*" Chiyo managed. "You didn't say anything about crocodiles—"

"Fubuki," Sora said, rolling over and pulling the cover up to his chin in an attempt to get as comfortable as possible. "Your job is to distract Chiyo from thinking about all of the monsters."

"How do I do that?" Fubuki murmured.

"You could always try kissing her," Sora said, yawning. "That seems to work wonders."

"*Kissing?*" Chiyo said, startled. "*Fubuki—wait—we're not supposed to—*"

Sora closed his eyes and found the image of the Dragon's Claw waiting for him, the immense amount of water roiling in his mind, deep, dark and stretching on forever. All those years wasted, too scared to leave the city, and now here he was—it felt even better than he'd imagined.

"*He can—see us—and—*" Chiyo managed before squeaking. "*Fubuki—that's my—*"

#

Waiting for the sun to rise was the hardest thing he'd ever done, and Sora found himself wondering exactly when he'd become so impatient. It was just as cold in the morning as it had been the night before, although he was starting to wonder if it wasn't actually getting colder, even as the first light appeared. He'd refined the strategy a bit, his mind having nothing else to focus on in the dark. The first thing he was going to do was check to make sure the water around them wasn't hiding any kind of ancient spell because it was possible that a properly designed *Siphon* system could keep something running, even for that long. If there were any reactive defences waiting for him to trigger, then he'd have to destroy them outright. He waited for as long as he could tolerate, but the moment he could spot the opposite bank of the river, he decided he'd done his best. Sora placed his hand down on the ground closest to the river, on the inside of the barrier surrounding the camp. He brought the pattern into existence, carefully making sure everything was perfect and then started feeding an additional stream of mana into the points that dictated the radius and the speed of the spell. He took his time with it, shoring up every part of the spell until it was perfectly balanced, and when he was stressing the edge of the two points, he readjusted a final time.

"*Resonance*," Sora murmured.

Mana washed outwards in an invisible wave, pinging all five of the barrier stones, his book tucked away in his pack, Chiyo and Fubuki still nestled together inside the bedroll, thirteen goblins investigating the line of carnage they'd left behind in the treeline, three Riverblights less than ten meters into the water, an array of fish carefully avoiding the monsters, a massive crocodile, twenty-three meters out, an oblong shaped mass of highly condensed mana buried inside the trunk of a tree, twenty-seven meters into the forest behind them, four more similar shapes inside other trees, empty of mana, but pressing oddly against the ping in a way that told him they were mana reactive, thirty-eight meters out into the water was another one, shining even brighter than the one in the tree. The *Resonance* spell vanished, reaching the maximum range and fading away—he felt a thrill run down his spine at everything he'd just discovered.

"I knew it," Sora managed.

Sora eyed the water where the signal had come from and then reached down, using *Etch* to scribble on the ground in black ink. He drew a circle, then drew a line from the circle to each of the signals inside of the trees and the one in the water, listing their distances down beside each one. The five signals in the forest were arrayed in a long curve, seeking to cover a large swath of the forest. The one in the water, on the edge of the spell's range, was almost a continuation of the pattern, only spaced further apart because of the lack of trees. Without going to investigate the signals, he was already fairly certain of what they were, *Permanence* spells set up to feed a *Siphon* system. If he had to guess, there would be similar spells set up in an arc that cut through the mouth of each Talon and the forest between. That left him with a thrill of excitement racing through his body because there was *something* here after all—even if it only ended up being the ancient remnant of a failed attempt at magical artifact creation. Part of the *Siphon* system was still active, and considering the mana inside of the *Permanence* wasn't crystallised—which would turn the thing into a fancy paperweight considering there was no effect embedded in that spell for an artifact to make use of and no external source could use that hardened mana to power another spell—it meant that the system had been set up to rotate through each of the spells. It used up the accumulated mana before shutting them down, one after another or in assigned groups. That explained why some of them were currently inert while some were still running. Unfortunately, that opened up the possibility of there being some kind of inert spell waiting to activate, and considering the still active *Permanence* spells, it would have plenty of mana to call on.

"I need more information," Sora said, eyeing the opposite bank. "Tricky, tricky."

#

Sora dragged himself up out of the water and onto the bank, tired, wet, and below half of his mana remaining. He approached the barrier burning at his senses, paused well outside of it and then closed his eyes. The pattern for the *Blink* spell twisted into existence, his experience with it making the process a simple one, even with his exhaustion. He murmured the command phrase and appeared on the opposite side, two meters behind, where he could feel Chiyo and Fubuki standing.

"—can't hear me," Chiyo said before drawing in a surprised breath. "Where did he—"

Sora dragged his shirt up over his head, struggling with the wet, clinging material. He grunted when he finally managed it before dumping it on the ground with a sigh. He started work on his belt a moment later, wondering why everything had to be so difficult.

"Why didn't you wake us up or tell us you were going?" Chiyo said, "You should have—don't just start undressing whenever you feel like—*Sora*."

"You both slept in, and I don't know about you, but staying in a goblin-infested forest for days on end isn't fun—I'd like to get this done sometime this century," Sora said, letting his pants drop down to his ankles before stepping out of them. "I've got good news and bad news—which one do you want first?"

Sora turned around to face them, brushing his hair back up and out of his eyes, attempting to wring the water out as best he could. Chiyo, red-faced, seemed to be trying her best not to look at anything—Fubuki was staring straight at little Sora like it was about to teach her a spell.

"The bad news," Chiyo managed.

Sora dragged his wet clothes up off the ground and then moved to the shelter, hooking both of them over the front left upright before stepping through the door. He rifled around in his pack until he found something to dry himself with and then dragged a spare set of clothing out.

"The bad news is that there are a *lot* of crocodiles in the river, big ones, hungry ones," Sora said, hoping for a second wind. "The good news is that I'm going into the river again tomorrow."

"*How is that good news?*" Chiyo demanded.

"It's good news because there *is* a *Siphon* system here, which means we didn't come all this way for nothing," Sora said, dragging his new shirt on. "Unless someone has beaten us to the prize, something *should* be down there."

The door flap opened up as Fubuki stepped forward, lifting it with her hand—Chiyo drew in another breath.

"*Fubuki,*" Chiyo chastised, "Let him get dressed in peace."

"There are twenty *Permanence* spells set up in an arc and grouped in sets of four, stretching from the First Talon all the way to the Third," Sora said, trying not to shiver from the cold. "Each of them is aligned in a way to absorb ambient mana gathered from the trees, animals, creatures and the river itself before feeding it into the central spell— which, judging by the placement of everything, is directly in the middle of Dragon's Claw."

Sora stepped into his new pants, dragging them up onto his hips, and attempted to thread the belt through the loops with his shaking fingers.

"It's real?" Fubuki murmured.

"It's starting to look like it," Sora admitted, "Although there's a chance that I get down there and it's already been taken by someone who beat us here or that it failed entirely—or that someone set up a bunch of *Permanence* spells to trick people into getting eaten by crocodiles."

"Stop saying that," Chiyo said, glancing back at the water. "Did you actually see one?"

"Three of them. I killed one, and they left me alone after that," Sora said, locking his belt in place. "I think I scared them off—or they were distracted eating their friend, I'm not sure; I didn't want to stick around and find out."

"Sora," Fubuki said, "I want to swim."

"Fubuki," Chiyo said, clearly attempting to find some kind of in-human patience. "Why do you want to go swimming *when there are crocodiles in the water?*"

"Swimming is nice," Fubuki said before hesitating. "I want to see the crocodiles."

Chiyo made an odd noise, not unlike someone being strangled with a rope.

"I haven't finished checking the water for spells, but as long as you stay within twenty-five meters of the shoreline, you can swim," Sora said, catching her eye. "Let me eat something first, and I'll come watch you—and bring you back inside the barrier when you're finished, I suppose."

#

Surprisingly, he wasn't the first person awake when morning came again. Instead, Chiyo sat in the corner of the shelter, watching them both. He pushed himself up in his bedroll, wondering if she'd been overcome by the same impatience that had taken him.

"Couldn't sleep?" Sora murmured, rubbing at his face.

"I slept," Chiyo said, watching him. "I just wanted to make sure you didn't leave without telling me again."

"Sorry," Sora offered.

"No, you're not," Chiyo said, "You would have done it again if I'd still been asleep."

"Probably," Sora admitted without shame. "You worry too much when your awake; it seemed kinder to try and get everything done before you had the chance."

"I *worry* the appropriate amount that any situation requires," Chiyo said, "This one just happens to warrant a lot."

Sora huffed out a laugh at the words.

"If you'd told me a month ago that I'd have a frilly skirt worrying about me at all, I'd have called you crazy," Sora said, studying her face. "If you're going to confess, you should probably do it *before* I go into the crocodile-infested waters and get eaten."

"Idiot," Chiyo accused, looking away. "Don't say things like that."

"Your cheeks are red," Sora teased.

The early morning chill *had* turned Chiyo's cheeks red, and without the covers pressed against his own face, he was sure it wouldn't be long before the same happened to him—still, it had the desired effect.

"It's cold," Chiyo mumbled, covering her face. "That's all."

"If you say so," Sora said, cracking his neck. "We've got sunlight, a plan, and my mana is back to full—I'd say it's about time we got this show on the road."

"You never said anything about your plan; you just said you were going swimming," Chiyo said, frowning. "How do you plan on searching the water? If there's anything down there, it will be impossible to see anything."

"I know roughly where everything is feeding the mana to, but I'll need to get close enough to set off a full cast of *Resonance*," Sora said, glancing over at where the two yellow orbs were peeking out from inside Chiyo's bedroll. "That will tell me what's down there and if there are any defences we need to worry about."

Sora slipped his legs out of the bedroll, catching himself in the process of pulling on his shoes before realising there was no point considering his destination.

"Fubuki, I'm going to need your help for a couple of minutes, just to keep an eye out for anything in the water while I'm charging up the spell—it's something that takes a lot of concentration, even for me," Sora admitted, "After I get a sense of what the situation is down at the bottom, I'll either go down there straight away if it's clear or retreat and figure out a way to bypass whatever defences are there."

"You're going to leave me on my own?" Chiyo said, hesitating.

"You'll be safely behind the barrier, and it's only for about three minutes at the most," Sora promised, "Fubuki will be coming right back here after I'm done to make sure you're safe; she'll just have to wait on the shoreline until I can ferry her back inside the barrier—yes?"

"Yes," Fubuki murrmured.

"Sora," Chiyo said, swallowing. "You'll be careful?"

"It's me we're talking about," Sora said, smiling. "When am I not?"

Sora pushed himself to his feet, tucking his braided bang behind his ear as he rose up. The two of them followed him up, and he stepped outside of the shelter, taking in the immensity of the water once more.

"Fubuki—" Chiyo said just as he crossed the barrier.

He glanced back over his shoulder at the empty air in front of him, wondering what she'd been about to say. Fubuki appeared out of thin air a few seconds later, moving to stand beside him. Sora took a moment to remove his shirt, not willing to leave another one soaking wet; it would be easier to swim without it anyway. Fubuki followed his example, only she didn't bother keeping her pants on—he wasn't quite so willing to risk it, not when a crocodile might bite his willy off.

"Did she want to say something?" Sora wondered. "Good luck? A confession of love?"

"Chiyo told me not to leave you in the water by yourself," Fubuki murmured. "Even if you tell me to go."

"Of course she did; come on, let's not keep her waiting," Sora said, offering her a smile. "Fubuki, sorry to make you do all the work, but I'm going to need to conserve mana in case we need it—you're on defence, okay?"

"I understand," Fubuki murmured.

Sora took a deep breath and then stepped into the shallows, the burning chill of the water striking up his body to settle in his neck. He began building the pattern for *Sense* as he went and cast it a moment later—he turned his head to the side as a large white signature crawled towards them, hidden just beneath the water. The creature sprung forward, sending water everywhere as it attempted to catch hold of his leg. Fubuki stepped around him, moving impossibly quickly, and reached out, her hands catching hold of both sets of jaws. The massive thing thrashed in the water, trying to dislodge her unbreakable grip, but she dragged it up out of the water and turned it away from both of them before letting it go again. The crocodile surged back under the water, moving away from them twice as quickly as it had come. Sora kept on moving, sinking into the water until it reached his chest and then switching entirely to swimming. Fubuki dove under the water, the white outline of her body passing under his legs until she was in front of him. Sora checked over his shoulder, judging the distance from the shore, and readjusting his course. Once he'd reached where he thought the limit of his last spell had gutted out, he slowed down. Fubuki surfaced beside him, and he held an arm out towards her to keep her from moving forward.

"Stay behind or underneath me for now," Sora said. "We're moving into an area I haven't checked."

Sora carefully moved forward, mind reaching for any incoming spell effects. He kept his eyes on the water below him, making sure nothing was going to take the opportunity to attack. He came to a stop at about the sixty-meter mark, and in that time, not a single spell effect had been triggered.

"Fubuki," Sora asked before closing his eyes. "I'm going to be distracted for a minute."

"I will protect you," Fubuki murmured.

Sora closed his eyes, building up the pattern for *Resonance*. It was more difficult while also having to concentrate on staying afloat, but he worked at it until he'd reached the same level as yesterday and then pushed it forward beyond that, better balancing the points with what he'd learned from multiple consecutive casts around the mouth of each river.

"This is it," Sora murmured, diving beneath the surface of the water. "*Resonance*."

The command phrase came out as bubbles, and the pulse of mana washed outwards in every direction. Thirteen crocodiles were within the radius, only three of which were close enough to worry about, and one of which was in the process of being attacked by a Riverblight. Six more *Permanence* spells registered below him, twenty meters north, only one of which was currently active, which made it the fourth one in the group that he hadn't been able to find yesterday. They were set in a wide ring around a large hollow shell of oddly moving mana, and in the middle of the active spell effect was a tiny orb of brilliant, crystalline mana.

"*Breath*," Sora murmured.

The spell snapped into place, his lungs filling up with mana-infused air, and he reorientated himself in the water, aiming for where the signature had been. There wasn't a single defence in place, or if there had been, it had met some unknown end. It was possible that the man who'd created it had been relying more on the impassable nature of the terrain to keep it safe. Without being able to translate the tablet, nobody would have known it even existed. Without the ability to fight through the mass of goblins that called the area home, they wouldn't have been able to get here. Without training as a mage, nobody would have been able to recognize that anything was even here. Anyone who actually knew about its existence when the tale had been spread around wouldn't have had a reason to go after it either—attempting theft on an artifact that wouldn't be complete for several hundred years was completely pointless. All of that had cumulated in an untouched, permanent magical artifact whose worth was, at a rough estimate—*priceless*. His hand caught painfully against the rocky bottom of the river, and he started building the pattern for *Illuminate*. Fubuki surged forward through the water, passing by his arm and crashing into another crocodile before it could reach him. The light of the spell passed over her, and for a moment, he watched her wrestle the thing, the absurd sight of the slight woman manhandling the massive creature just as strange as the first time he'd seen it. He reached out and touched her on the back, hitting her with the *Breath* spell before she got out of range. Fubuki chased the creature away before turning to face him, hair spreading out through the water, slowly breaking free of the braid. He panned his hand across the river-bed until he caught sight of a greyish-green lump ahead of him. Sora felt it appear within his range a moment later, glowing like a sun to his senses. The two of them approached it—it was a familiar statue, only a dozen times the size as the one at Akh, settled flat against the floor of the river. In its hands sat a large bead about the size of his head, and buried in the middle of all that stone was a tiny glowing presence. When he touched it, the muck that had accumulated on its surface was wiped away, revealing the perfect untouched stone beneath. It wasn't damaged in the slightest, despite what must have been millennia of water wearing away at the surface. The spell effect he'd felt was still there, a layer of mana held tight against the outside of the stone, and while it felt vaguely familiar to a few of the spells he knew, it wasn't an exact match for any of them. The magical artifact in the centre of the bead was inaccessible from the outside, and when he pulled his knife free of his belt to strike the stone, it came to a complete stop with-out doing any kind of damage. Sora waved to get Fubuki's attention, miming a strike at the stone. Fubuki hooked her foot under the statue's finger and then struck forward, the crack audible, even underwater, but her hand glanced off to the side without effect—the artifact's spell was some kind of physical barrier, a predecessor to *Invulnerability*, perhaps. There was no way they were getting through it from the outside, not if it could withstand the force of Fubuki's attacks, but using brute force was rarely a good answer to problems like this—if he couldn't break it, then he'd just have to move it. The real issue was the size of the statue, and the amount of mana needed to displace something that big was outside of his ability. Sora turned in the water, kicking off the statue and swimming forward towards the other glowing source of mana in the vicinity. He directed the light of the Illuminate spell over the floor and found the long, smooth lump of metal that had been used as an anchor for the *Permanence* spell. He snatched it up, surprised at how heavy it was, even under the water, before pulling it back towards the statue. Fubuki swam past him, intercepting another crocodile that had been drawn towards them by the light. Sora built up the pattern for *Etch* and sub-vocalised it. He encircled the older, primitive spell with the standard version that was taught today, cutting the entire thing off from the *Siphon*. Then he used *Dispel* on the older one, letting all the accumulated mana drain into the brand-new *Permanence*. Pressing his thumb flat against the temporarily etched pattern, he placed his other hand against the statue's massive foot. He started creating the pattern for *Blink*, manipulating the stolen mana from the *Permanence* and fed it into the two points that dictated the size and weight of the spell— within seconds, he reached a mana cost that was far beyond anything he'd used before. He added a second pattern, layering it beneath the first and using it to create a rough outline of the area he wanted to target. A third pattern joined it, tightening the shape until it targeted everything except for the tiny glowing marble. He kept going, reinforcing the opposing points in the spell to keep everything in balance until he'd reached an amount that was sufficient for something as large as the statue. Once he was sure it was perfect, he opened his eyes.

"*Blink*," Sora murmured, a spread of bubbles washing upwards past his face.

The mass of stone vanished from in front of him, leaving a vast statue-shaped hole that was entirely empty of water; a glowing red orb sat above him, visible in the darkness before it began to fall through the air—and then the water crashed inwards to fill the gap, dragging him forward with it. He managed to cover his face before he was dashed against the riverbed, but the force of it had his arms crashing into his head. Pain flashed out across his senses, and he was jerked backwards as the force of the water shifted again—for a moment, he spun in the darkness, listless and disorientated. A small red orb settled amongst the rocky riverbed directly below him, and after a moment of groping mindlessly, he managed to catch hold of it. He remained there for a long moment, trying to figure out what had just happened, and then something crashed into him from the side. A pair of glowing yellow-slitted eyes appeared in the dark, inches away from his head, and for a moment, he was certain it was a crocodile attempting to tear him in half. He reached down, placed his hand against its collarbone, a pattern wrenching its way into existence—and then he paused.

"*Fubuki*," Sora managed, the word coming out as bubbles. "*Fuck*."

#

Sora staggered out of the river, not entirely under his own power and only really standing because Fubuki was holding him up. His face was on fire, and his thoughts were distant scattered things. He lost his balance and crashed down onto his knees, Fubuki catching him before he could entirely hit the ground. Sora pulled back on his arm until he could lay on his back and stayed there, trying to get his mind in order.

"Sora," Fubuki managed. "You need to fix your face."

His face? He managed to open his eyes again, blinking past the burning pain—he'd never seen Fubuki look quite as terrified as she did right now. He reached up and pressed his hand against his face—he flinched at the bright pain and the wet flap of something that was hanging off his face. He was bleeding because he'd hit his head—what was the spell for fixing bleeding heads?

"What's the—fuck," Sora managed, "My head isn't working."

"Fubuki," Another voice spoke, approaching from somewhere behind him. "*Oh god*."

What was it called? The thing that pulled everything together. The old bastards always hated it. They wanted a specialty list to standardize the pricing, and the spell broke their system—It was warmth and a soft glow—it was falling from his mind like the water running down his body. A black-furred *Himura* appeared above him, her mouth stretched open in a tortured expression of horror.

"I can't remember the word," Sora said, pressing his hand against the source of his pain. "Himura, what's the word for bleeding heads?"

"*Scour?*" Chiyo tried, voice shaky. "*Meldflesh*—"

The word sparked to life in his mind, a pattern wrenching its way into existence in his palm, warmth, revitalisation. It blurred the edges, mixing them together, sealing wounds. It masked the pain, and through a delicious, precision twist, you could inverse it, stimulate the nerves, excite them directly, *revitalise* the flesh—the spell snapped into existence as it always did, imagery of a thousand casts, a thousand different faces.

"Fuck," Sora said. "*Meldflesh*."

The pain fled, masked beneath the soft glow of the spell, and in there, he found a foothold against the dizziness. He could feel the damage now, the extent of it injected directly into his mind. Half of his face had been torn open from the collision between his face and the rocks covering the riverbed. A strip of thick flesh hung loosely from his left cheek to above the bridge of his nose. Sora used the focus while he still had it, unwilling to take the time to learn anything from the mess. He rebuilt the connections between the strip and the rest of his face, sealing it back down and working his way up. He moved onto the swelling in his head, his thoughts starting to clear as he wiped it back into nonexistence. The side of his face came next, the massive contusion that was currently taking over his head faltering against the force of his mana. Without the overwhelming pain dominating his mind, he noticed the torn-up flesh of his forearm for the first time. The limb that had taken most of the damage and likely prevented him from killing himself outright.

"Sora?" Fubuki whispered. "Are you okay?"

"I'm okay," Sora managed. "Thank you for getting me out of the water."

"*What happened?*" Chiyo said, trying to stifle her crying. "Did one of them bite you?"

Sora moved to seal the series of gouges closed, his arm almost entirely red from the mess of blood. It was a simple matter to address now that his head was working again, but his mana was starting to get dangerously low, and it was taking the last of his stamina with it. The dizziness remained, probably a direct result of the blood loss.

"There was a massive statue down there, and I had to displace it," Sora said, letting the spell end once he'd fixed the majority of the damage. "I didn't consider that the water would rush into the space it left behind—I ended up getting smashed face-first against the rocks."

"I *told* you to be careful," Chiyo cried.

"Up until that point, I was," Sora said, attempting to stand up. "I think I need to lie down—and eat something; probably, I've lost a lot of blood."

Sora managed to get to his feet before either of them could assist him, and he built up two *Blink* spells—the mana cost like a drop of water in the ocean compared to what he'd just used—but still, more than enough to leave him hovering just a sliver above depletion, and the wave of tiredness grew worse. He cast the spells, sending Chiyo and Fubuki to the inside of the barrier, and then unable to muster the mana to *Blink* himself, he simply stepped through it. Fire washed upwards, taking over his entire body in an instant, licking at the outside of the *Invulnerability* spell and failing to find purchase.

"Are you insane?" Chiyo cried. *"You're on fire—"*

The fire lasted all of three seconds, and without anything to fuel it, it vanished, leaving him and everything he was carrying entirely untouched.

"If you need to go outside of the barrier, you can get back in by carrying this," Sora said, throwing the marble towards them. "Hold onto it for me, will you? I'm going to sleep."

The moment it left his hand, the *Invulnerability* spell that had been encasing him vanished. Fubuki snatched it out of the air with her inhuman reflexes, and he stepped between the two of them. He slipped in through the door and barely made it to the bedroll before he fell. Sora lay there for a long moment, half on the bedroll, with his soaking wet pants still on, and considered doing something to remedy the situation—and then he just gave up entirely; he could deal with it when he woke up.

#

"Sora?" Chiyo said, voice quiet. "How are you feeling?"

Sora cracked an eye open, taking note of his situation, now secured within the bedroll he'd failed to reach. A quick internal check of his body told him that he was still dangerously low on mana, and he still felt pretty off, his arms heavier than what he was used to—the blood loss.

"I've felt better," Sora admitted, "It's dark already? You need a fire?"

"Please," Chiyo said, "Fubuki killed a crocodile earlier, so I was going to cook that—if you can cast anything."

Sora rolled over and stretched his hand past her hip into the open space behind her, his chest resting against his knees for a moment as he built up the pattern for the *Flamestay* spell. Orange light washed over the canvas surrounding them and left Chiyo's outline glowing.

"I remember when you were scared to eat a rabbit," Sora said, letting himself fall back onto the bedroll. "Now you're eating crocodiles—you've become so powerful, my sweet wife."

Chiyo reached down and pulled the dislodged blanket back up before pressing it flat against his chest.

"You're *not* funny," Chiyo accused, voice quiet. "You might be the most *unfunny* person in the world."

"That's a lie," Sora complained.

The door flap peeled back a few inches, revealing Fubuki standing there watching them, still not wearing anything at all.

"Sora," Fubuki said, waiting at the door. "Are you okay?"

"I'm not okay," Sora decided. "Chiyo is bullying me—*you* think I'm funny, don't you, Fubuki?"

"Sometimes," Fubuki said.

Chiyo snorted at the clear uncertainty held within the answer.

"I can't believe this," Sora said, "You two are the meanest apprentices I've ever had."

"We're the *only* apprentices you've ever had," Chiyo said before hesitating. "Sora—what do we do now?"

"Are you taking requests?" Sora wondered, "Because it's been a long time since I've seen you with your shirt off."

"Gosh—can you just—*ugh*," Chiyo said, breathing out of her nose. "You found the magical artifact. Are you going to sell it?"

"There are roughly eighty magical artefacts in the world right now— discovered ones, I mean," Sora said, thinking about it. "The one we just found is more or less completely unknown, and it's possible that there are more of them that nobody's spoken up about finding."

Fubuki watched him as he spoke while Chiyo remained facing away, working on cooking the meat skewers she'd prepared.

"Most of those are weapons—swords, specifically, make up about thirty of them—that are passed down family lines," Sora said, "The owners will most likely never sell them because of how powerful they are, but if they had the inclination, each one would be worth enough coin to buy a country."

Sora lifted up the flap on his bedroll and spread his arms out, uncaring of the fact that he wasn't wearing anything. Fubuki eyed him for a moment before carefully crawling behind Chiyo and into the bedroll beside him. He dropped the cover down over her and curled his hand around her waist—her skin was freezing to the touch. Sora slipped his other arm past her shoulder, pulled her flush against his chest and then tucked her head beneath his chin, trapping her there—as much as anyone could trap someone as strong as Fubuki.

"That much?" Chiyo said, glancing back at the two of them. "Um—why is—what about this one? It protects against fire—is it good?"

"It doesn't protect against fire," Sora said, "It's actually some kind of predecessor for the *Invulnerability* spell—it protects against all direct attacks."

"There's a spell for that?" Chiyo said, turning to keep both of them in her sight. "Do you know it?"

"Yes, there is, and yes, I do—but the spell is absolutely useless," Sora admitted, "Because of how broad it is—impact, heat, shock, and everything else under the sun—it costs an obscene amount of mana. On my best day, I can hold it for roughly five seconds before It depletes me."

"But this is a magical artifact," Chiyo said, "So it doesn't cost any mana to use, right?"

"Correct. It's pretty powerful, and it would be easily worth as much as the rest." Sora said, playing with Fubuki's fingers under the blanket. "That doesn't mean there are actual buyers, though, and the kinds of people who have that kind of money are far more likely to hire a few dozen bounty hunters and send them after us to retrieve it."

"So we can't even sell it without putting ourselves in danger?" Chiyo said.

"Unless there is a very trustworthy buyer, then it's safer to keep it hidden," Sora said, "That's just the nature of these things, I suppose."

Fubuki shifted back against him, and he pressed his hand flat against her belly, attempting to hold her in place.

"What do you plan to do now?" Chiyo asked. "There were more myths in that book—are you going after them, now?"

"That is exactly what I'm going to do," Sora admitted, "The question is, are you two coming with me, or have you had enough?"

"We're obviously going with you, just—it's not going to be as bad as this was, is it?" Chiyo said, hesitating. "You mentioned the ones you were most interested in—the second one was *The Bone Needle*. Where does that take place?"

Fubuki shifted again, and his hold on her shattered as she turned over to face him. He did his best to ignore the fact that his cock was now pressed against her thigh, embarrassingly hard.

"The Island of Bone, which is directly between Berzaria and Pyeon," Sora said, "Think you can guess the route I planned?"

Fubuki continued to stare at his face, but he kept his own gaze safely locked on Chiyo.

"You already said you wanted to go to Lyston next, so that means you intend to take an airship from there to—Larta?" Chiyo said, "You can only get to The Island of Bone by boat, and that's the closest port city in Berzaria."

"You really are a map-for-brains," Sora said, "I'll make sure to feed you lots of maps when we get back to Bilaar—we've got to keep you running at full power."

"You're clearly delirious from the blood loss," Chiyo said, flushing from the taunt. "Maybe you should just stop talking."

"No more talking, huh? Fine." Sora said, "Fubuki—I'm going to kiss you now."

"Okay," Fubuki murrmured.

"*Fubuki*," Chiyo squeaked. "*Don't just let him do whatever he wants.*"

\#

Afterword

This was one of the first books I ever wrote, I've learned a lot since then, and now it's been rewritten at a much higher level of quality. Please consider leaving a review; I'd love to know what you think.
Kind regards,
Clinton Campbell.

Cast

<u>Main</u>

Sora the Seeker/Shiro – Mage
Chiyo Himura/Itsuka – Noblewoman
Fubuki/Fuka – Oni

<u>Satu</u>

Elric Manus – King
Unnamed Prince – Prince
Eri Manus – Princess
Mashirao Himura – Master of Commerce
Koshiro Konishi – Advisor
Wartol – Mage
Malko – Bounty Hunter
Salas the Scholar – Mage

<u>Judra</u>

Sara – Thief
Tia – Seamstress Apprentice
Marlissa – Tavern Owner
Tallen – Fisherman
Maro – Mayor
Tine – Guard

<u>Maar</u>

Kazu – Boatman
Karia – Mayor
Levin – Mayor Assistant
Mela – Assistant

May – Caravan Trader
Jalin – Seamstress